HOUSE
OF
ECHOES

D0038642

a novel

BRENDAN DUFFY

author of THE STORM KING

Praise for

HOUSE *of* ECHOES

"Shades of *The Shining* are spattered through Brendan Duffy's debut novel—a large isolated house, a young family, nutty and somewhat supernatural goings-on—but *House of Echoes* grounds itself in different ways for an enjoyable read." —*USA Today*

"An exquisite novel . . . expertly plotted, beautifully written . . . It's complex, deft and, once you dive in, you want to stay in this often-scary world. . . . This is a book that deserves to be savored." —*The Star-Ledger*

"Duffy's debut is a riveting blend of horror and family drama. The remote location, creepy townspeople and the village's savage history produce a harrowing tale that keeps readers quickly turning the pages. As this complex family struggles with mental illness and their child's isolation, their redemption comes in the revelation that they can survive anything together." —*RT Book Reviews* (4½ stars)

"Duffy expertly builds suspense, leaving readers eager to know what happens while simultaneously dreading the outcome. This creepy page-turner will appeal to fans of Stephen King and anyone who loves a good ghost story." —*Library Journal*

"*House of Echoes* is one of those stories where you know something bad is going to happen, but you hope it won't. It's one you'll remember long after reading the last page." —*New York Journal of Books*

"Duffy walks a fine line between crime and horror, skillfully manipulating the threats of a punishing winter, creepy historic setting, and strange villagers. . . . This unsettling, atmospheric tale is right up the alley of those who enjoyed Jennifer McMahon's *Winter People*." —*Booklist* (starred review)

"A fluid, suspenseful yet subtle thriller, with touches of humor, evocative writing, and characters that are both familiar and uniquely fascinating. A wonderfully tense and heart-wrenching debut."

—*Kirkus Reviews* (starred review)

"*House of Echoes* is that rare debut that grabs the reader by the lapels with both hands and never lets go. It's compelling, brooding, atmospheric, and propulsive—and it accomplishes something frightening and unique: a portrayal of the great outdoors as beautiful, amoral, and claustrophobic at the same time. It will stay with you long after you read the last page, and it may very well haunt your dreams."

—C. J. Box, *New York Times* bestselling author of *Endangered*

"*House of Echoes* is the captivating tale of a bruised family's escape to their dream house in a bucolic small town, only to find themselves trapped by its dark legends. In this relentlessly chilling story, Brendan Duffy breathes new life into the gothic tradition. Uncanny and hypnotic, it will freeze your heart."

—Keith Donohue, *New York Times* bestselling author of *The Boy Who Drew Monsters*

"*House of Echoes* is dark, emotionally affecting, and truly creepy. Brendan Duffy dives straight into the ugly core of small-town America and doesn't flinch a bit—a fantastic story and a great book."

—Kelly Braffet, author of *Save Yourself*

"Brendan Duffy's *House of Echoes* is one of those wonderful stories that come along only once in a while, a beautifully nuanced and riveting family drama set within a terrifying landscape that has you turning pages long past bedtime. But keep the light burning and read to the end. That's when you realize you've been in the hands of a very clever storyteller, and that what you thought you'd been reading was all along something else."

—Carla Buckley, author of *The Deepest Secret*

HOUSE *of* ECHOES

HOUSE *of* ECHOES

A NOVEL

BRENDAN DUFFY

BALLANTINE BOOKS

NEW YORK

2018 Ballantine Trade Paperback Edition

Copyright © 2015 by Brendan Duffy
Excerpt from *The Storm King* by Brendan Duffy
copyright © 2018 by Brendan Duffy

Published in the United States by Ballantine Books,
an imprint of Random House, a division of
Penguin Random House LLC, New York.

BALLANTINE and the HOUSE colophon are registered
trademarks of Penguin Random House LLC.

Originally published in hardcover in the United States by
Ballantine Books, an imprint of Random House,
a division of Penguin Random House LLC, in 2015.

This book contains an excerpt from the forthcoming book *The Storm King*
by Brendan Duffy. This excerpt has been set for this edition only and
may not reflect the final content of the forthcoming edition.

LIBRARY OF CONGRESS CATALOGING-IN-PUBLICATION DATA
Duffy, Brendan.
House of echoes: a novel/Brendan Duffy.
pages cm
ISBN 978-08041-7813-6
Ebook ISBN 978-0-8041-7812-9
1. Families—Fiction. 2. Life change events—Fiction. 3. Moving,
Household—Fiction. 4. Upstate New York (N.Y.)—Fiction. I. Title.
PS3604.U376S25 2015
813'.6—dc23   2014024343

Printed in the United States of America on acid-free paper

randomhousebooks.com

4 6 8 9 7 5 3

Book design by Dana Leigh Blanchette
Title-page and part-title photograph: © iStockphoto.com

HOUSE *of* ECHOES

THE SWANNS *of* SWANNHAVEN

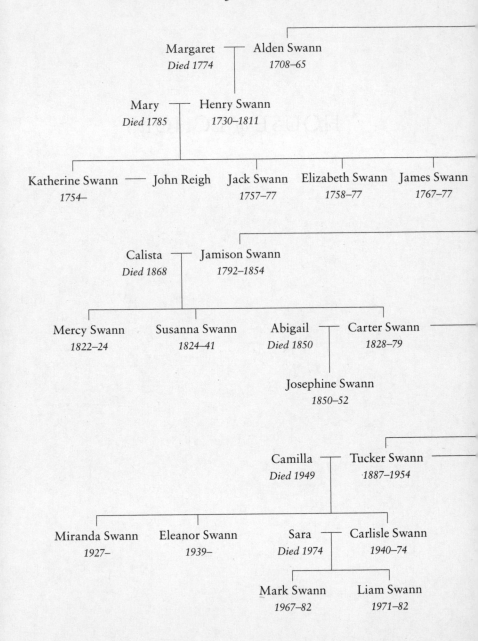

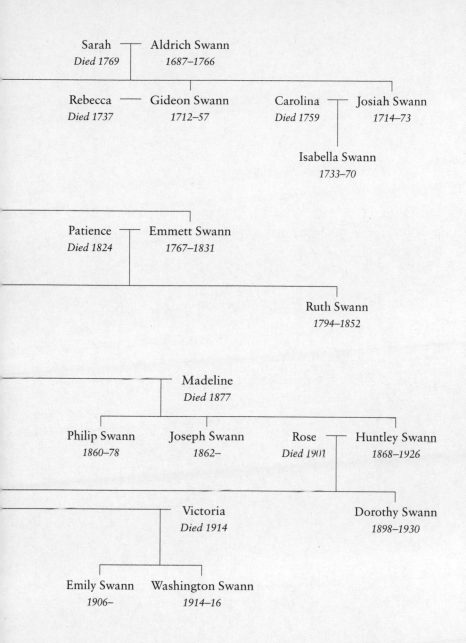

I

BETWEEN *the* MOUNTAINS

JUNE

December 23, 1777

Dearest Kathy,

 It is over now, sister, but for how long?

 From our window I still see the Drop. I see the fields and forest where we once played. I can still see our brothers tumble in the grass and hear the elder tree whistle as the wind tears through its branches. However, I know in my heart that it is all gone. It is gone and it shall not return in this life.

 I am cold, Kathy. I see my breath and I cannot feel my feet, but I do not care. Not even fear is left in my heart. Fear has departed with hate and anger, and hope has been a stranger for longer still. Now there is nothing left but me, and I cannot face my reflection.

 There are demons in us, Kathy. I see that now. Our blood is cursed, and doom haunts us always. It is too late for us, but I pray it is not too late for you.

 Should this letter find its way to you, sister, you will think me mad. You may not understand now, but you must stay far from this place. Forget that you ever called it home. Do not even whisper its name to the children I pray you will one day have. I wish you many children, Kathy. If there is any goodness left in this land, I pray it will find its way to you.

Remember me as I was, dear sister, when we slept in peace and our every dream seemed possible. I cannot sleep anymore.

Forgive me.

Your Bess

1

There were times in each day when Ben believed a happier life waited only for them to claim it. He was a dreamer by trade, and it didn't seem far-fetched to hope their troubles would depart as quickly as they had surfaced. Such optimism was purest in the clear mornings when he took Hudson on the day's first walk.

Spring had come late but suddenly. The last of the snow had melted only weeks ago; now the grass was nearly to Ben's waist. He monitored Hudson's progress through the fields by reading the furrow carved by the beagle's passage.

The dew had evaporated but its chill lingered, and the breeze carried its own bite. The wind was strong and invigorating on this part of the Drop—the plateau that sat in the lap of two mountains, hulking cousins of the Adirondack Range. The updraft from the valley sent the acreage undulating as if it were a single breathing thing.

He put his hand to his eyes to shield them against a gust and did his best to keep track of the dog. Hudson had picked up the scent of something and filled the air with his ecstatic baying. No one was happier about the Tierneys' new life in the mountains than the beagle. His previous circumstances having amounted to little more than a Manhattan apartment, Hudson hardly knew what to do with a thousand acres of field, forest, and lake. If he missed his dog-walk runs and leashed jaunts down the avenues, he hid it well.

Ben smiled and dropped his hand to his pocket, searching for his phone before remembering that he'd left it back at the Crofts, their home on the Drop. He hardly carried it around anymore, but like a phantom limb he sometimes imagined its presence.

He watched the dog dart from the field and across the gravel drive that connected the Crofts with the county road nearly a mile away. The husk of a shattered outbuilding was just a hundred yards off the drive, on the near side of another copse of trees, and the beagle made straight for it.

Ben cupped his hands around his mouth and called Hudson's name. Ruined structures of uncertain purpose were scattered across the Drop, but Ben had picked his way through this particular one not long after he and Caroline had closed on the property. The place was a mess. The roof had caved in, and the rotting floor was on the brink of collapse under the weight of rusting farming equipment and other scrap. Anyone could see it was a death trap.

He called Hudson again, but he was too far away; Ben could feel his shout whipped back to him by the steady wind from the valley.

Clearing these outbuildings was something Ben had wanted taken care of before they moved in, but that was a battle he'd lost. Caroline thought that they contributed to the ambience. She imagined the guests at their inn roaming the grounds, delighting in the discovery of some ancient building from a forgotten time. She said this would give their guests a sense of ownership over their stays at the Crofts, so that the Tierneys' inn would become a place they'd return to year after year.

Their son, Charlie, was forbidden from venturing anywhere near the ruined buildings, but even an eight-year-old was easier to control than a beagle that had just plucked a tantalizing smell from the air.

Ben broke into a run when he cleared the tall grass. He'd lost sight of Hudson, but a mournful howl told him the dog was close by.

The wind backed off as Ben ran across the gravel drive, and he didn't need to be a dog to pick out the scent that had captured Hudson's attention. It was a musky smell with metallic notes, the tang of an animal, a tease of death that hadn't yet turned sweet.

Ben reached the building and was greeted by Hudson, eyes big and beseeching, tongue wagging.

"In trouble again," Ben said.

He crouched to give Hudson a rough rub around his neck, and the beagle's panting slowed.

"You stink, too." His hands came away from the dog, smeared red. He resisted the impulse to wipe them on his jeans.

Hudson gave a short bark and executed a small circle in front of Ben.

"All right, show me," Ben told him, and followed the dog around the shattered building.

He wasn't surprised by the death; he had guessed as much from the smell. It was the blood that caught him short.

The animal looked as if it had burst. The creature's entrails were spread over several yards in two perpendicular streaks of intersecting gore.

"No, Hudson," Ben said, as the dog started sniffing the mess.

The smell was stronger here, but not as bad as Ben had expected. The pools of blood were liquid, rippling in the breeze. The absence of birds and other scavengers made Ben think this hadn't been here long. A fresh kill.

His eyes scanned the ruined canvas of the animal and settled on a pair of prim gray hooves. A deer, Ben thought with some relief. The anonymous quality of the shredded viscera had made his imagination spin.

The beagle walked through the carnage and began nosing around the edge of the woods.

"Might have been a bear," Ben told Hudson.

He'd heard coyotes at night, but the men in town told him there were black bears in the woods. They'd also told him that there were wolves and mountain lions up here on the Drop, but he'd actually seen the bear tracks for himself along the edge of the lake.

"Come on," he said.

Hudson started to bark at the trees.

"We'll have to hose you down before you go inside."

Ben headed back toward the gravel drive, hoping the dog would follow. But Hudson wouldn't stop growling at the forest. Ben squinted to see what might have caught the beagle's attention. He was a good dog and rarely fussed without a reason.

"Let's go, Hud." Ben turned away from the woods and took some of yesterday's bacon out of a plastic bag he kept in his pocket. "Look what I've got for you."

Hudson veered around and licked the bacon fragments from Ben's hand.

"Come on, you smelly dog," he said, rubbing Hudson on the side of one ear. He took off in a jog back to the Crofts, and the beagle trotted after him.

A great elm stood a solitary watch on the lip of the Drop, and when Ben reached its shadow he glanced back at the woods by the ruined building. All he saw were trees rocking gently in the updraft from the valley.

2

The Crofts was a monster.

The lawyer who'd handled the sale told Ben it had been the original home of the Swann family, the first colonists to settle the Drop. It had begun as a simple residence, but he said they'd added to it over the years. Then again, that had been obvious.

Rising to four floors, the house had sixty-five rooms, five entryways, and four staircases. Though sections of the building had been constructed centuries apart, its exterior was wrapped in uniform walls of gray granite. It sat like a castle on the lip of the Drop, overlooking the village of Swannhaven and the rest of the valley.

It had been a farming estate and was ancient by the metric of the New World, built back when agriculture was the only game in the rambling North Country. It hadn't been a fully operational farm since the 1940s, but the outlines of the old fields remained, as did the bones of stone walls and survivor strains of wheat, rye, and barley grown wild.

Ben had seen castles a third its size. And while the scale of the place was imposing, its opulence was tempered by its condition.

Parts of the residence hadn't been inhabited in decades, its last owners spinster sisters who'd lived their entire lives within these walls. Ben didn't know what two old women were doing so far from the village in such a huge house, but he could see it hadn't involved much in the way of home maintenance. Water stains marked the ceilings, warped planks buckled the floors, and windows rattled in their frames.

Sometimes he looked at the Crofts and saw a sprawling monument to impetuous decision-making. But in moments of hope, Ben saw an ember waiting to be rekindled. They were ready to put their sweat into the place; he hoped only that the Crofts would accept it.

"Windy out there," he told Charlie when he opened the side door and stepped into the kitchen. He made right for the sink, giving the soap dispenser a double pump before nudging the handle to hot.

From their first tour of the place, Caroline had been convinced they could renovate the entire estate by themselves. Ben had his doubts. He had insisted that contractors add air-conditioning, install bathrooms in the guest rooms, and upgrade the plumbing and electrical. He could take his chances sanding floors and painting walls, but he thought anything involving pipes, wires, or gas lines was worth paying for. It had taken a team of live-in workers some months to get the house into shape before the Tierneys moved in.

Though budget-conscious, Caroline had taken up cooking again and spared no expense in updating the kitchen in a modern French country style. Two walls of custom-made cabinets flanked a professional Wolf range with two large ovens. The original floor had been ripped up in favor of wide-plank antique walnut. Gray granite counters gleamed under inset lighting.

When they weren't working to renovate the rest of the house, they spent most of their waking hours here. At first it had been only for meals, then Charlie had begun reading in one of the corners instead of in his own room, then Ben and Caroline had moved their laptops to a side table. Ben told Caroline it might have been withdrawal from their close city living that led them to cluster together in this small room, but the truth was that he felt like an intruder any-where else in the vast place.

"Where's Hudson?" Charlie asked through a full mouth. He and Bub were seated at the table, which held four plates of pancakes, each stacked six inches high.

"He made a mess of himself out there," Ben told him. "I'll clean him off after I eat." He watched the last of the blood-tinged water swirl out of sight.

"Mom made pancakes," Charlie said.

"I can see that." Ben dried his hands and kissed Bub on the head. The baby gurgled and showed him the pancake he was playing with.

"What are in these things?" he asked, examining Bub's breakfast.

"I made two batches," Caroline said. The pantry door slammed and a moment later she was halfway to the counter. She'd always been beautiful in jeans and killer in the right dress, but untucked flannel and blurry with flour was a relatively new look for her. "One with cherries and one with raspberries. I thought they might be good with chocolate, so I'm going to melt some down, add cream and maybe a dash of vanilla." She emptied a bag of chocolate pieces into a saucepan fitted over a water bath.

"Are we expecting company?" Ben asked, pointing to the plates of pancakes.

"I'm trying out a recipe for the guests, Ben. I wasn't sure about quantities."

She clicked the burner until a burst of blue fire blossomed under the water bath. As she churned the chocolate, her foot beat a rhythm against the floor. Ben had wondered, as he did on all of his morning walks, what kind of day they would have together. The towering stacks of pancakes were a bad omen, and the note that had crept into Caroline's voice when she spoke his name was more troubling still. But it was only eight-thirty, and Ben was not ready to count the day as a loss.

Ben kissed Charlie on the forehead as he sat down next to him. "Do you recommend the cherry or raspberry?" he asked him.

"I like them both," Charlie said.

Ben leaned into Charlie. "I'm going to need your feedback on this one. I mean, how many pancakes would you say you've eaten in your time?"

"A lot." He had a smear of syrup on his cheek, and Ben rubbed it away with a napkin.

"I'll say. And not just ones made by Mom or me, right? You've eaten these things in restaurants across the tristate area. And what about when we went to California? You had some there, didn't you?"

"They were good."

"So you're speaking from the position of having some pretty formidable experience under your belt in the arena of pancake eating." Ben was talking to Charlie, but he was watching Caroline stir the saucepan at the stove. "Now, you should stop me if I'm overselling your credentials."

"I will," Charlie said.

"So how do these *stack* up?" A stupid pun, but some days he'd try anything. He was grateful to see the side of Caroline's mouth twitch. Charlie was spare with his smiles, but not nearly as spare as his mother. Her face was as delicate and perfect as a doll's, and these days almost as inexpressive.

"They're good," Charlie said after a moment. "Sweet."

"Follow-up question: Do you think that the quart of maple syrup you've poured on them has anything to do with that?"

A smile, small but undeniable, opened across Caroline's face.

"Maybe," Charlie said.

Ben speared three pancakes of both varieties off plates in front of him. "These are excellent," he said after he'd eaten one of each.

Caroline brought her tea over and sat at the table. The ghost of a smile lingered on her face, and that made some of the tension ebb from Ben's shoulders. "Your phone buzzed while you were out."

Ben reached back to pick it off the counter. There was a missed call and voice mail from the lawyer who'd been handling his grandmother's estate. More bad news, Ben expected; the man never had any of the good variety.

"Any luck on those butterflies, Charlie?" Ben asked. He slipped the phone into his pocket.

Charlie had become very attached to a book that Ben had given him before they'd moved up here. It was about Hickory Heck, a boy who'd left his city life to live in the wild. Heck made his own clothes, gathered his own food, and he'd even hollowed out his own home under a massive tree. One of Heck's many fantastic nature-themed adventures involved filling mason jars with butterflies of every color and training them to dance in the candlelight that illuminated his cozy burrow. Charlie had found some caterpillars a few days ago and put them in a jar filled with leaves. He hoped to teach them to dance when they turned into butterflies.

"I think they just need to eat some more. I gave them leaves, but they don't like the dandelions," Charlie said. "I don't know why. You'd think they would."

"I called someone about getting a truck up here to take away that mess in the basement," Caroline said.

The Crofts had been filled with the detritus of the house's previous inhabitants. Furniture had been left to molder, along with stacks of newspapers and magazines, piles of warped boxes, and dozens of broken appliances from past decades. One of the first things Caroline had Ben do was to move it all into the basement.

"If I were a caterpillar, I'd eat dandelions," Charlie said.

"Me too," Ben said. "And you *know* Bub would eat them, too, if we gave him a chance."

"But the man I talked to won't carry it out of the basement himself," Caroline said.

"Did you offer to pay him extra?"

"Of course, but he said he had a bad back and no insurance. Besides, I don't really want anyone from the village inside until we've finished fixing up the place."

"When's he coming?"

"Tomorrow, sometime in the morning. He wasn't specific."

"Okay." Ben tried to keep his face expressionless, but Caroline still heard something in his voice.

"What was I supposed to do, Ben? We need that crap out of here."

He could see the cords of her neck tense, and he didn't need to look under the table to know that her well-muscled runner's legs were jackhammering away at the antique walnut.

"It's just that it'll take a long time to get all of that outside," Ben said.

"What else were you going to do today?"

"I was going to sand the floor in one of the second-floor bedrooms," Ben said. "And the bookstore in Exton called. My order's ready. I was hoping to pick it up."

"Maybe it won't take as long as you think," Caroline said.

But the garbage in the basement took up rooms and rooms of space. Much of it had been there before Ben had added to it with the junk from the rest of the house. He was sure that Caroline had no idea how much was down there.

"You're probably right."

"I can help you, Dad," Charlie told him.

"Thank you, buddy," he said. It was rare for Charlie to volunteer for indoor work on a sunny day when the forests and fields waited just beyond the door. Ben saw that today could still be a good day, and that was enough to buoy him. He pulled the boy out of his chair and onto his lap. Charlie was too big for this, but this morning he let Ben get away with it. His hair was dark and thick like Ben's.

Caroline picked Bub out of his chair and wet a napkin with her tongue to scrub the cherry juice from his face. Bub's hair was blond and fine like his mother's.

"What books did you order?" Caroline asked.

"A couple that people have been talking about, and a few more that sounded interesting."

"Do you have an idea?"

She was asking about his next book. Ben enjoyed how mysterious his process seemed to Caroline. To her analytical mind, this whole part of his life was opaque.

"An idea," he said. He drew his fork through the syrup to see the glistening script it left behind. "But not much more than that."

The truth was that he'd written a good hundred fifty pages of what he'd thought would be his third book, but the novel had soured on him since he'd moved up here. It was a problem he couldn't account for. His last literary thriller had been a success, and he'd begun this next project with an abundance of confidence, but it had somehow fallen apart. It was as if the gravity had dissipated at the core of the thing, and the pieces had drifted apart. He was just beginning to admit to himself that it had all been a terrific waste.

He looked up to smile at her. "If it turns into anything, I'll let you know." Charlie stirred restlessly on his lap. "This one's had too much sugar to sit still," Ben said.

"Best thing to do with energy is to put it to work," Caroline said.

Ben moved Charlie back to his chair and stood up. "Help Mom clean up here, okay, buddy?"

"Where are you going?" Caroline asked.

"Hudson found a dead raccoon," Ben said. "Made a mess of himself. I have to wash him off and I want to bury the thing so he doesn't get into it again."

"Can I see?" Charlie asked.

"It's really stinky, Charlie." He ruffled the boy's hair. "Help Mom with the dishes, and I'll be back soon."

"Don't come back stinky," Caroline said.

Ben was halfway out the door when he turned around. "And I saw more bear tracks by the lake, so if you guys go outside, make sure to bring a whistle." He'd read on the Internet that bears were afraid of loud noises. He'd bought a set of whistles for that purpose.

"It would be cool to see one, wouldn't it, Dad?"

Ben thought about the eviscerated deer, about the long red streaks that had been drawn over the ground with its insides.

"No, buddy. I don't think so."

He hosed Hudson off in the shed. As the beagle shook himself dry, Ben stood out of range to listen to the lawyer's voice mail. The saga of his grandmother's estate had gone on for months longer than he'd expected. The meager price they'd gotten for her tiny house in New Jersey, a few thousand dollars in savings, and a tract of virtually worthless land attached to a derelict farmhouse here in Swannhaven were the extent of the estate's assets. Neither Ben nor his brother, Ted, had known that Grams owned land up here—land inherited from her own parents, Ben assumed. But it was on a trip to see this old farmstead that he'd learned the vast house between the mountains was for sale. It was then that the notion of an escape from the city had been born.

Caroline handled their finances, but at the time of Grams's death, Ben hadn't wanted to put any further stress on her. Such matters were beyond his expertise, but his grandmother's legacy barely amounted to six digits, and Ben had expected it would be a simple matter to deal with the estate. In this, he'd been wrong. There were times when he thought that the lawyer was taking him for a ride, eking out every possible penny, one billable hour at a time. Other times Ben thought this was just another example of how their luck had suddenly soured.

According to the voice mail, Ben's mother was the newest problem. While Grams had bequeathed her daughter a few thousand dollars, she'd split the majority of her assets between her two grandsons. All Ben's mother had to do was sign a few documents to receive the behest, but these signatures had proved elusive. Which could only mean she wanted something more.

Over the last decade, Ben had made it a personal mission to indulge the woman as little as possible. As with all addicts, her needs were an abyss that only deepened with each shovelful of good intentions you tossed in. But every phone call and certified letter the lawyer wasted in prodding her cost money. As Ben deleted the voice mail, he knew he would have to call her himself, despite the fact that this was surely exactly what she wanted.

"Clean again, but how long will it last, Hud?" he said once the dog finished shaking himself dry. Ben stooped to rub the beagle's head and got a lick to his face.

After he dropped Hudson just inside the kitchen door, Ben returned to the shed for a shovel. With it hoisted over his shoulder, he made his way to the ruined building off the drive.

Birds were all over the deer when Ben got there. The nasty black things moved only when he menaced them with the shovel. When they hopped away, they scattered blood from the ends of their glossy wings. Either ravens or crows—he'd have to look up the difference. Whatever they were, an entire ugly flock of them.

Ben dug a shallow hole a few feet from the tree line, then heaped the guts into it. He was again struck by the damage the animal had taken. Other than the hooves and the odd intestine, he couldn't identify many of the body parts. He guessed that the bear had taken the rest of it, but he didn't see how it could have eaten the head or so much of the hide. It occurred to him that he didn't even know if bear ate deer or would be able to catch one in the first place. Perhaps there were wolves after all, he thought. Ben had believed that the howls they heard at night were coyotes, but he could only guess at what lived in the dark of the old forest.

Once he'd scraped up as much of the animal as he could, he did his best to cover the hole. By the time he was finished, he knew that it wouldn't fool any of the scavengers in the forest. Wouldn't even fool the crows. A dozen of them were perched on what remained of the fallen building's roof, utterly motionless as they watched with their obsidian eyes.

Ben trudged back up to the shed to rinse the shovel. He'd have to walk Hudson on the upper fields by the lake until nature disposed of the animal's remains. The trees by the lake were older than the rest. Standing in their shadow made Ben feel like a child. The first time Hudson had seen the lake's mirror surface, he couldn't resist throwing himself into it, and it had taken Ben ten minutes to coax him out. Ben smiled at the memory, then the sound of wings shook him from his thoughts.

He turned around to see the group of startled crows aloft, cawing as they filled the air with their dancing shadow bodies. A murder, he remembered. That's what a flock of crows is called.

3

Ben didn't like the cellar.

A single stained bulb lit its front room, casting the space in a murky orange; the light wavered as if it might desert its station at any moment. The air was musty with the rot of ancient upholstery and the moldering that takes grip when moisture meets neglect. Chairs, tables, old mattresses, piles of ragged clothes, broken clocks, boxes of photos, and bundles of newspapers were arranged around the room. Ben grimaced—a claustrophobe's nightmare.

The cellar had many rooms; even Ben wasn't sure how many. Only one set of stairs reached this floor, and the space was too packed to traverse. At first he'd thought that if he spent an extended amount of time working down here, he'd get used to the noises from the pipes and the heavy presence of the rooms just beyond his sight. Instead, he shuttled back and forth, carrying things outside, and every time he came back down the stairs, he had to reassure himself that nothing had occupied the space while he'd been gone.

Considering what Charlie had gone through back at his old school, Ben wouldn't have blamed him for giving the cellar a wide berth. But the boy often surprised him, and Ben was happy for his company. When they'd finally cleared a path through the junk he'd put in the cellar a few weeks ago, they began on the junk that had been there before. More of the same: clumps of ancient periodicals fossilized into solid blocks, fragments of broken furniture, and pieces of rusted sewing machines. He was glad when they reached an empty light socket. He held his breath as he screwed in a new bulb. Ben vanquished more of the dark but paid for the privilege with the sight of another century's worth of mess in the rooms within the light's range.

"Not that, Charlie," Ben told him, and Charlie put down the rocking chair he was trying to lift. "How about the newspapers?"

Charlie looked suspiciously at the towers of newspapers. "They smell."

"Everything down here smells, buddy."

"Do you think Hickory Heck's burrow is like this?" Charlie asked.

Ben smiled; he remembered when he'd been young and could get so caught up in the world of a book.

"It's probably dark like this, but I bet it smells a lot better," Ben said. "It probably smells like earth and rain where Heck lives. That's a nicer smell, isn't it?"

"A lot nicer," Charlie said.

"Everyone working hard down here?" Caroline asked as she came down the stairs. Her hair was pulled back, and a smear of blue paint stretched from her nose to her cheekbone. She was flushed and grimy from painting one of the second-floor rooms. Ben thought she looked beautiful like this. "God, there's a lot."

"We're making a dent. Aren't we, Charlie?" Ben said. He put down the box he'd been unburying from a pile of ancient couch cushions and reached around to the small of Caroline's back, pulling her toward him.

"I'm filthy," she said, pushing him away.

"So am I." He kissed her neck.

"Those old ladies must have been crazy to keep all this junk."

"I'm going up," Charlie said, as he headed to the stairs. His skinny arms strained under the weight of a packet of bundled newspapers.

"Is he going to hurt his back?" Caroline asked Ben.

"Kids can't hurt their backs," he said, stooping down to the storage box to test its weight. "Thirty-four-year-old men with old track injuries, however . . ."

"Poor baby." She laid both hands on his shoulders. "A morning around this house is better than a session at Equinox," she said, prodding his muscles with the tips of her fingers. She hardly ever touched him like this anymore.

"Are you hitting on me? Tell me again how filthy you are."

"What's in this thing?" she asked. She bent down to get a better look at the box he'd uncovered.

"Just clothes, but they're packed in there pretty tight. I might need your help carrying it up."

"I wish they'd cleaned out the place," she said, referring to the bank from which they'd bought the Crofts. "You'd think it would be standard to do something like that."

Few things about their purchase of the Crofts had been standard. After the death of the spinster sisters, a local bank had taken possession of the property on account of unresolved debts. When that bank collapsed last summer, it was bought by a larger bank, which had to sell itself for pennies on the dollar a few months later to an even larger bank. This last bank, headquartered almost a thousand miles away and saddled with the same toxic assets that had sunk the previous two, was happy to rush the sale of the Crofts to the Tierneys. A year ago the local bank might have laughed at their offer on the property, but times had changed. With the local staffs of the two previous banks terminated, a lawyer from the city had rushed north to manage the sale, and many a corner was cut in the name of expediency.

Caroline opened the box and pulled out a pair of matching floral-print sundresses. Yellow tulips against red cotton, the flowers arranged as if they had rained from heaven. The house had stood for over two centuries, and the little sundresses made Ben wonder how many children had been born and raised within its walls. It was hard to imagine the people who had lived here before them when all he could do was guess from the ruined things they'd left behind.

The baby monitor clipped to Caroline's waist emitted a short blast of noise. Ben and Caroline listened until they were sure that Bub hadn't woken up.

"Baby dream," Ben said.

"There's a big pile up there, Mom," Charlie said on his way back down the stairs.

"How big is this truck that's coming tomorrow, anyway?" Ben asked her.

"Don't tell me you're giving up already."

"It's just that there's a big difference between filling up a van and filling up an eighteen-wheeler. If he doesn't have enough room for it tomorrow, I'm not sure we want all this rotting on the lawn."

"I hate the idea of all this stuff down here," Caroline said.

"Actually, some of it isn't too bad. This is a nice little piece, isn't it?" He turned his flashlight on a small dark-wood captain's desk with inlaid leather. "What do you think?"

"No, Ben. It's all got to go." Her voice got hard-edged as she shook her head, her blond locks coming loose to whip at the air. "That's not the style we're going with. The last thing I want is for this to look like a patchwork of different styles. I *hate* that."

"I'm sorry, you're right." Ben nodded quickly. He hadn't meant to wind her up, but these days almost anything could do it. "A clean slate. Don't worry, I remember."

"I mean, that's why we're killing ourselves to get this right, isn't it?"

"Yes, of course," he said. "I'll bring some more of this outside; then if you could give me the guy's number, I'll find out how big his truck is. If it's on the small side, I'll schedule him again for his next available slot. Okay? We want all this out as soon as possible."

"Otherwise it's just festering down here."

"Yep." Ben found himself nodding again, and soon Caroline was nodding as well.

Bub's gurgles came out of the baby monitor as digitized spurts laced with static. The sound sent Caroline for the stairs.

"If you could put the guy's number on the kitchen island?" he called after her. When he turned back, he saw Charlie trying to pick up the captain's desk. "Leave the big stuff for me, okay? How about you get some of those couch cushions?" Charlie picked one off the floor. "No, not that one, Charlie. Get one of the really disgusting ones. Yes, that one. Thank you. That's a huge help." He watched Charlie lumber up the stairs with a cushion as large as himself.

Ben stooped to pick up the captain's desk. He thought it was better to get rid of it now, in case Caroline saw it down here again and thought he'd forgotten. It had been a stupid thing to say to her. He knew better, but more than that he knew in his guts that he didn't want to keep any of these old things. No matter how much the Tierneys made the Crofts their own, the presence of the house's former inhabitants would linger if given the chance. He felt this in the way that every empty room seemed to recoil at his presence when he walked the halls on sleepless nights. Better to throw it all away and be done with it. Better not to give the ghosts any furniture of their own to sit on.

But it was still a shame. The desk was made of good wood, which could be worked to a glossy depth with a little polish. He tested its weight and was surprised by its heft. He checked the drawers to see if anything heavy had been stashed there, but they were wedged full with nothing more than old paper that disintegrated in his hands. Peering through a large keyhole, he saw that there was a compartment under the writing surface, but it was locked. He tried to force it, but it wouldn't budge. The lock had been built to last.

Bending from his knees, he hoisted the desk to his chest, wincing at the strain. As he lifted it, he felt something shift inside. Something heavy enough that he had to adjust his balance to compensate.

Threading his way between mounds of junk, he crossed the room and started up the stairs.

His sweaty hands grappled the desk's worn contours, but just as he found a better grip, his trailing leg went through the planks of a stair. Ben fell backward, shoving the desk to the side as he lost his balance. Ribbons of pain bolted up from his shin as his center of gravity shifted with the fall. He caught the banister. One of the spokes broke, but the next one held. The desk picked up momentum as it descended. Ben didn't watch, but he heard the old thing scream as it splintered against the wall at the foot of the stairs.

"Dad?"

He heard Charlie padding back down the hallway. The boy poked his head through the doorway.

Ben swiveled so he could see the foot of the stairs.

The weight of the desk had worked against it at impact. Its final gasp was a haze of ancient paper remnants, exhaled like the release of an earthbound spirit.

"Help me out here, buddy?"

Charlie walked down to Ben. He peered into the hole Ben's leg was wedged in. When he looked up, a rare smile filled his little face.

"I think you liked Mom's pancakes too much," he said.

Ben braced himself against Charlie's shoulder and the banister to lift his calf out of the hole. He sat down heavily on the stairs. Charlie sat next to him as Ben hoisted the leg of his jeans.

"Does it hurt?" Charlie asked.

Skin along his calf had bunched up, and the flesh below was already turning purple.

"Not really. Going to be sore tomorrow, though."

"Do you still need help carrying stuff?"

"I think we earned ourselves a break, don't you?"

Charlie scampered back up the stairs, but Ben walked down them. He pulled the desk away from the wall to examine the damage. The lock on the lid of the desk had loosened but not enough for him to pry it open. But the side panel had splintered, and he forced his weight against it until it broke away with a satisfying crunch.

He pulled the flashlight out of his pocket and positioned the desk so that he could shine the light into the hole in its side. Upstairs, Charlie was calling Caroline to come look at Ben's leg.

The hollow space was filled with scrolls of thick paper. Ben slid one through the hole and unraveled it to find a schematic of the Crofts and a small map of the grounds. He removed another to find a similar document dated a few years after the first. While interesting, these architectural plans didn't explain the shifting weight within the desk. Once Ben had removed all of the blueprints from the compartment, he finally saw what looked like a thick black box. He used the back end of the flashlight to break away more of the cracked wood to make space for the object. When he pulled it out, he saw that it wasn't a box; it was a book. A black book with a metal cross embedded in its front cover. A Bible. Ben again tested its heft, but it didn't seem large enough to justify its weight. The cover was thorny and ridged, as if it had been bound with dragon skin.

"Are you okay?" Caroline called from the top of the stairs.

On impulse, Ben slid the Bible into a pile of yellowed linens, out of sight.

"Foot went right through the stair. Didn't draw blood, but it'll leave a nasty bruise." He walked back up the steps, pausing at the one with the hole in it. "Rotted through."

"Makes you wonder about the rest of the place," she sighed.

Before signing on the dotted line, Ben had warned Caroline about the thousand things that could go wrong in an old house like this. Rotting wood, vermin infestations, toxic mold, leaky roofs, rusty water, noisy pipes, warped floors, lousy insulation. But none of that had mattered to her at the time. She'd wanted her clean slate.

"Better that it happened to me than to you or Charlie," he said, resuming his climb up the stairs. "I'm hungry."

"Already?" she asked. "It's barely noon."

"I want to ice this. May as well eat while I do."

The hall was wide, white, and cold. More than a dozen other rooms had doors that opened onto this hall. Huge rooms with wooden floors with inlaid ebony borders, and tall windows with once-proud moldings that stretched to the soaring ceilings. Each one, imperious, alien, and staggeringly empty.

"I had something planned for lunch. But it'll be a little while before it's ready."

"Need help?"

"What, you don't trust me in the kitchen?" she asked.

Ben looked at her and was grateful to see a playful twist to her lips. Caroline was an excellent cook, but during their busy years she'd rarely flexed those talents. The exceptions had been special occasions, when she might spend days on a perfect meal. The first birthday Ben had spent with her, she'd baked him a staggering chocolate cake filled with hazelnut pastry cream, wrapped in seamless fondant, topped with blown-sugar flowers. He still remembered the awe of the moment when that extraordinary cake had been set in front of him, back when it seemed that Caroline could do anything.

"It's mostly the fact that you're making food in the first place. No Thai takeout, no hermetically sealed packages from FreshDirect."

"I was thinking cucumber, yogurt, lemon, and dill sandwiches on whole-wheat bread. And I was going to boil down some of that tomato soup from two nights ago, add some cream, and toast some croutons." She slid her toned arm inside his as they walked down the hallway to the kitchen. Even with a few bumps along the way, today was going better than Ben could have hoped.

"Very civilized. Maybe too civilized for a humble laborer like me," Ben said. They didn't banter like this much anymore, and he had missed it.

Caroline's pregnancy with Bub, coupled with the stress of her bank going under, had awakened something inside her. Ben thought of it as the Wolf. One night, after a bad day, he'd written on the back of a Con Ed bill, *He skirted the forest as close as he dared. Though he could not see it or hear it, he knew the Wolf was there.*

Even with medication, Caroline had been lost to him for weeks, broken and raging in a way that Ben hadn't thought possible. Trying to care for her, Charlie, and a newborn all on his own had almost undone him. After Charlie's problem at school, Caroline thought that a change in geography would be good for all of them. She thought that the million tasks necessary for turning the Crofts into an inn would keep the Wolf at bay and help bring all of them close again. From the outside, it was a crazy idea—moving hundreds of miles to restore a decaying house with a second-grader and a baby. But their old life no longer fit them. Something had to change.

"You'll like it."

He let himself believe her. She knew him as well as anyone. And he knew her. That's why there was always a flame of fear in the back of his mind. The Crofts was the perfect distraction for Caroline. There were so many things to do. But Ben didn't know what would happen to them after all the walls were painted and the floors sanded. Caroline wanted to believe that this was a whole new life, but it wasn't. Not really. Ben knew that no matter how far you run, you're still yourself when you get there.

4

Ben had a city person's bias against cars in general and big cars in particular. But he loved his big black Ford Escape: the way its shocks absorbed the irregularities of country roads, the way it hummed when he accelerated on steep inclines. A sedan wasn't practical up here—and, besides, the Escape was a hybrid. Caroline had one in silver.

He had the windows open, and his iPod blared the exuberant yet wistful sound of an album his brother had gifted him through iTunes. An A&R man for a record label, Ted was more likely to send Ben the music of the moment than to call. Which was fine with Ben. He liked the songs Ted sent, and the exchange reminded him of when they'd shared a room as teenagers. They'd do their homework on opposite ends of a folding table while listening to the radio, sometimes springing up in unison to press record when the opening chords of an admired song sounded through the speakers of their plastic Casio.

Their grandmother had died almost nine months ago, but Ted still had not seen the ruined farmhouse she'd left them. He'd promised to visit, but Ted's promises were generously bestowed and unevenly honored. Ben knew his brother would show up eventually, and he'd be glad to see him. But sometimes a little of Ted went a long way.

After lunch, Ben had confirmed that the vehicle the man was using to pick up the junk was just a bit larger than the one Ben was currently driving and that he'd have to reschedule tomorrow's pickup, anyway. Caroline wasn't happy to hear this, but she cleared Ben to drive to the bookstore in Exton, as long as he picked up a few things from the general store in Swannhaven while he was out.

Over the last few weeks he'd learned that the locals kept fluid business hours, so Ben decided to get the groceries first. He turned onto the village's primary thoroughfare. If it had a name, he didn't know it. It flanked an overgrown village square that Ben had once walked through. He'd been surprised by the buckling cobblestone plaza, the scattered remnants of broken stone benches, the rusted iron fountain at its center. It had once been a handsome place, but the good years were long gone.

Only a dozen ramshackle structures bordered the square. Harp's General Store was sandwiched between a building that served as the village's police station/municipal building/post office and the Lancelight, a little diner where Caroline and Ben had once eaten. Other than a mechanic's shop and a small church, the rest of the buildings on the street were residences. Their condition made it hard to tell how many were occupied.

There was no sign of life in the village this afternoon. From what Ben had seen, it was like this most of the time. Sunday mornings were the exception. After attending service at the church down the street, many of the villagers gathered at the Lancelight for coffee and breakfast. The Tierneys had discovered this firsthand a few weeks ago when they'd eaten brunch at the diner.

Though they'd first been mistaken for motorists searching for the interstate, they were soon seated, their orders taken. Their waitress had been polite, but Ben noticed the surreptitious glances and whispers of patrons. As the diner grew more crowded, it seemed to Ben that he and his family became more and more the center of its attention. The villagers had reacted to them as if they were not just new to town but new to the planet. In the weeks since, that had yet to change.

Ben parked on a patch of barren ground outside Harp's. He could have gotten his groceries from one of the supermarkets in Exton or North Hampstead, but he made it a point to buy from the village when he could.

"In and out," Ben told Hudson as he cracked the windows and put the Escape into park.

Hudson whimpered.

"You go in there and you'll get sliced up and labeled as beef. I'll only be a minute."

A bell tinkled when he walked in. It was the kind of place Ben imagined might have greeted frontiersmen a hundred fifty years ago. The floors were dusty wood planks, and what little fresh produce the store had was displayed in shallow barrels along the front windows. The proprietor also fit the bill. Walter Harp wore a wreck of a face and lips blistered by chewing tobacco. Deputy Simms, who seemed to spend more time here than at the police station next door, was working on the same look, though Harp had a forty-year head start.

"Afternoon, Mr. Tierney." Walter Harp offered a toothy smile that didn't quite reach his eyes.

"Hello, Mr. Harp, Deputy," Ben said with as much enthusiasm as he could muster. Addressing everyone with an honorific was something he was still getting used to. He had to work to make it sound right.

"Anything I can help you with?"

"Just have to pick up a couple things." Ben made for the refrigerated closet, the store's single concession to the past century.

"We got some rain on the way if you can believe the radio," the deputy said. Some of his nasal drawl got lost in the mug of coffee that covered his mouth.

"Yeah?" Ben pulled out two dozen eggs and two jugs of milk.

They sold a local label of milk, and their eggs were so fresh that their shells were dotted with mud and hay.

"Heard that Henry Bishop is heading out to the Crofts tomorrow to help you with some of the Swanns' old things."

"We had to reschedule, but, yeah. Lot of old stuff up there," Ben said. He piled the eggs and milk on the counter.

"Shame it has to go," Deputy Simms said.

Harp nodded. "Bound to be some nice things."

"The Swanns were nice people, a fine family," the deputy said. "Took in all kinds of kids. Filled that house with them."

"Yeah? Foster kids? That kind of thing?" Ben grabbed a can of the peaches that Charlie liked. He guessed they were no more healthy than a cup of sugar, but they sometimes bought him a smile.

"Real saints they were," Harp replied, adding up the groceries.

"Oh, and four of those apples, if you don't mind."

"How's that pretty wife of yours?" the deputy asked.

"She's well, thanks." Ben made eye contact with the deputy for the first time. He guessed the man was in his late twenties—about thirty years too young to say something like that without it sounding like a threat. "Happy to be out of the city."

The deputy nodded and smiled, displaying the black coin of dip wedged in his gums.

"You make sure that roof's fixed up right, Mr. Tierney," Harp told him. He took the twenty Ben handed him. "Easiest way to take down a house is to pull off a couple a shingles and wait a season. Hard winters here, too. Rain and snow's a bother, but the wind's the real curse. Especially up on the Drop."

"Thanks. I think we're in good shape," Ben said. This wasn't true, but he didn't see what business it was of theirs.

Harp frowned and handed him his change.

"The heat, too," the deputy said. "Gonna need that as much as a roof. Even with that good-lookin' lady to warm you." He stretched his arms behind his back casually, letting his muscles tense against his uniform.

"Well, so far so good," Ben said. He gathered the bags up into his arms.

"I can come up and look at it, if you like," the deputy said. Ben caught the man send a wink and a smirk Harp's way. "Be my pleasure."

"I'll let you know if it gives me any trouble." Ben backed into the store's door. "Have a good day, guys."

"Nope, that fella don't need help from the likes of us," he heard the deputy mutter before the door slammed shut behind him.

Ben put the groceries in the cooler he kept in the back of the Escape and closed the trunk. It wasn't until he was back on the county road, music blaring again, that he let himself feel anger. He indulged himself by revising the scene in the store. He edited his dialogue, adding an edge that his character otherwise lacked. With this tweak, the confrontation escalated. Instead of leaving with a friendly nod, Ben ended the encounter by throwing the deputy out the store's window. He closed the chapter by leaving the man's body lying on the pavement, a stripe of blood stretching from his split lip. A satisfying conclusion, one any reader would cheer for.

He was almost out of the valley, a good ten miles from the Crofts, and he had yet to see another car on the county road. There was no reason for anyone but locals to take this route. He'd heard that Swannhaven had only forty households. Most were scattered across the floor of the valley on tired dairy farms, like the one his grandmother was born on.

When Ben reached the highway, the Escape roared its approval.

The battery of signage confirmed that he'd left the remote and insular world that the Crofts and Swannhaven comprised. There was Montreal up ahead and Boston to the east. The signs told him that he could go anywhere on this road. There was strong Canadian beer, or seafood that had been swimming freely an hour before landing on his plate. Turn around and in only three thousand miles he could watch the sun set over the ocean.

The young man on his iPod sang about crashing a party thrown

by the friend of a friend in a sweltering studio off the Bowery. He
crooned about vodka and getting high and a girl with green eyes and
arms covered with tattoos. The singer didn't pretend to have it all
figured out, but he knew enough that life was good and every moment was a gift.

Ben liked songs like this, but today he skipped to the next track.

April 4, 1776

Dearest Kathy,

    I am well and back safely at the Crofts. Thank you again, my dearest, for such a lovely visit.

    Jack and the twins were there to greet me in Albany. James has grown nearly to my waist now, and Emmett's health is much improved since I last saw him. They were both so pleased to be out of the valley and on a real adventure with their elder brother and sister. Of course, Jack wanted to hear everything about the war. And I think the lot of them are in awe of me now, as the three days' ride gave me much time for embellishment. They had already heard that the redcoats had fled Boston, which is a pity, as I wished to tell them myself so that I might watch their faces. It is true that good news has swift wings.

    Mother was proud when I told her of John's commission with Colonel Phinney, and I believe Father to be pleased, too, in his own way. News of the militia's battles against the king's armies had made Mother afraid for us, but finally seeing me in person has again set her mind to rest.

    And I know I ought not to say it, but it was an adventure, was it not? You mustn't think me wicked for saying so. But it was so good to be free of this place, if for only a while. You know as well as I the menace of the woods and the contagious gloom of the ancient oaks.

You must think me foolish to revert to our childhood fears. But what am I to complain about without regiments of British Regulars at my door? You have only yourself to blame, my dear Kathy. You spoil me with bright frocks, bustling cobblestone streets, and nothing less than revolution itself, so this is what you must expect of this provincial relation from now on.

We had a wonderful time, did we not, dear sister? I already miss you terribly. Think fondly of me, and I shall pray daily that God will keep you and your dearest John safe and happy.

Your Bess

5

The Crofts was Charlie's house, but the forest was his home.

He ran through the trees and he imagined himself as Hickory Heck running from his old life in the city. The trees here were shorter than the buildings Charlie was used to, but they made him feel smaller than any skyscraper ever had. They made him imagine a world beyond the one he knew.

At first, Charlie had been afraid of the emptiness. The land here was as wide and spare as the city had been tall and crowded. But that was before he had learned what to look for.

After running away from his family, Heck had wandered through the mountains for three days until he came to the tree where he dug out the burrow that would become his home. Before then, he'd slept between roots and alongside boulders, and some of the trees he passed along the way had been taller and older and thicker than the tree he eventually chose. But when he found the right one, he knew it. This was just how Charlie had felt when he first laid eyes on the clearing in the woods to the east of the lake.

He liked to sit on the stump in the center of the clearing. The breeze there carried a collection of scents: the faint rot of wood from the stump he sat on, moss from the green carpet that covered it. There was a hint of stale water from the nearby lake and of blooming grass from fields to the north.

Dad once saw a picture Charlie had drawn of this place, and he had called it a faerie circle, but Charlie didn't know why. He had never seen faeries there.

Even on a day as nice as today, there were no faeries. There was the angel, but the angel lived on the other side of the lake. Here there was only the forest and the air and the earth. The sound of branches playing on the wind and roots stretching in the ground was a conversation he listened to through long afternoons. This was where he had learned to be still.

Mom and Dad believed that he spent hours here playing alone, but they were only half right. It was a game of a sort, though not one they would have recognized or approved of. And while he was by himself, he wasn't always alone.

When he reached the clearing, he sat on his stump and waited, as he did each day. It was not long until he felt the gaze of something just out of sight burning into the back of his head. He had not yet been fast enough to see the one who watched him, but Charlie was patient. In time, he was sure, he would catch sight of the stranger in the trees.

Charlie often tried to imagine the eyes that followed him from the forest. It could be anything, Charlie told himself, and his heart thrilled to the thought of it. The world here was as alive as it was in the pages of *Hickory Heck*. There were beavers up at the lake and groundhogs in the fields. There were snakes under the rocks and frogs by the shore. There were deer in the grasslands and mountain lions in the caves.

But Charlie felt certain that his watcher in the woods was something else entirely.

6

Exton, with its brightly painted Victorians and handsome shops, was two valleys but an entire world away from Swannhaven.

Embroidered banners strung along lampposts announced an annual dance festival, and the outdoor seating areas for the town's restaurants bubbled with the conversations of patrons. When Ben picked up his books from the bookstore on its main street, tourists and locals alike basked in the warm summer light.

Ben would have enjoyed his time in town, if not for the ugly task ahead. He chose a pay phone across from the bank to call his mother. His dread grew with each coin he thumbed through the slot.

"Hello?" She'd had a nice voice once, but years of liquor and smoke had left their scars.

"It's Ben, Mom."

"Ben?" It was early evening, but Ben got the impression he'd woken her.

"Yes. How are you?"

"I'm fine. I got a little place not too far from the beach. Can walk to work, and they let me pick all my shifts. And I—oh, you were just being polite, weren't you? Asking me how I was."

"I'm glad you're okay." She rarely slurred her words, but there was a thickness to her voice that he recognized well. "The lawyer says you haven't signed the papers from Grams's estate."

"Oh, Benj. It's just too hard. I look at the papers, all ready to sign, but then I think that if I sent them off, then your sweet Grams would really be gone."

A lie, and not a convincing one. Mom and Grams had rarely spoken over the last decade, and Ben doubted that any conversation they might've shared would have left either of them eager for another.

"Well, there would still be the money."

"It is a nice sum, that's true," she said.

Ben grimaced as she coughed wetly into the receiver.

"But then I think of that house she had and all the nice things she had in it, and I wonder what happened to that. Still had that land upstate, too, I imagine."

He was surprised she knew about the farmstead.

"She had expenses at the end," he told her. "The assisted-living facility, hospice, the medications, the aides, the funeral. If she'd ever run into trouble, Ted or I would have helped, but you know how she was. She'd never want to burden us." He couldn't resist adding a note of insinuation to his voice.

"It still hurts to think I couldn't afford the airfare to get to the funeral," she sighed into the receiver, her turn to make an oblique recrimination. There was something else in her voice, too. Her tongue seemed slowed by age as much as by alcohol. She was getting old, Ben thought to himself. A pang sounded in a dormant part of his heart. *My mother is getting old.* "And it would have been a chance to meet my grandchildren, too. How many do you have now?"

"By the time the house sold, the market had already collapsed," Ben said. He knew it was important to stay on topic. "And no one is ever going to buy that land upstate." In her will, Grams had made clear that she wanted her grandsons to sell the old homestead. *She'd* never been one to saddle others with her problems. "The farmhouse there is just a ruin. She'd didn't leave us much."

"You went up there, then? Way the hell upstate? I always wondered about that cursed place. The stories she'd tell about it would frighten the sleep out of me for days at a time when I was a girl. Demons in the wood and devils at the door."

Ben hesitated, but just for a moment. He knew she'd said such a thing only to get him to ask her about it. He would give her neither the satisfaction nor the leverage.

"Plus the hospital fees. And the lawyer's fees keep piling up, all charged against the estate."

"Oh, yes? Some lawyer fattening his bank accounts with fees. They add up, don't they? Guess they'll keep right on adding up until I finally fix my John Hancock to these papers." The age had fallen from her tone, and the thick-tongued singsong of her voice formed into something with more bite. Suddenly she was again the fearsome woman who'd raised him. Ben could almost feel her bourbon-scented breath on his cheek. "But it's curious that Grams didn't leave more to me, isn't it? Instead, she left it to her grandsons, who so fiercely kept me, her only child, from her in her last days. And she was so vulnerable at the end. So suggestible. I wonder what a court might make of that if I decided to contest the will. It would be interesting to find out, wouldn't it? And all the while, the lawyer's bills keep piling up." Ben could practically hear her smile through the receiver. "A scandal, isn't it? People think life is expensive, but draw it out long enough and the cost of death could bury anyone."

In his time Ben had thought of his mother as a drunk, a liar, a grifter, an addict, and on occasion a plague cultivated in the deepest pit of hell. She was so many terrible things, but stupid wasn't one of them. For just a second he'd forgotten that, and now he had a feeling of sick certainty that it was going to cost him.

The sky's glow had dimmed by the time Ben returned to Swannhaven. When he reached the village's valley, the woods along the sides of the broken county road were thick with shadow. Just as well, because the twilight matched his mood.

The negotiations had begun high, but in the end Ben could live with the amount they'd settled upon to put the issue to rest. Though his and Caroline's accounts were not so flush as they'd once been, it seemed a small price to pay to conclude the matter and to be rid of his parasitic mother a while longer. A net win, he told himself. Not that this rationalization made him feel any less manipulated.

The few village buildings he could see from the road looked deserted, except for the Lancelight, with its modestly lit sign. While the single meal that the Tierneys had eaten there had not been pleasant, the food itself had been surprisingly good. The waitresses' old-fashioned uniforms had lent the place an appealing retro feel, and the swollen pies under the counter glass had been perfectly browned.

Ben's lunch had been early and light, and the memory of those pies made his mouth water. Caroline preferred that they prepare their own food, but she also talked a lot about building relationships with the villagers. And as a rule Ben preferred not to return home in a mood as bleak as the one he now found himself in. Their delicate domestic equilibrium demanded a certain level of affability on his part. A detour before heading home might put some space between him and that phone call.

The Lancelight's parking lot was empty except for two tired-looking Toyotas. When he went inside, there was no one but an old man at the counter.

He stood just inside the doorway for a moment, waiting for someone else to materialize. The old man turned to him and then looked away, more interested in the coffee at the bottom of his mug. Ben coughed into his hand.

As he was about to leave, a woman burst out of the kitchen, tying her apron behind her as she walked.

"Knew that wasn't Old Billy coughing," she said. "He's got that nasty old smoker's hack."

Ben guessed she was in her sixties. She wore a loose blouse that billowed behind her as she walked.

Old Billy muttered something into his drink that Ben couldn't catch.

"If I'm a nag, you're the sorriest ass I ever laid eyes on," the woman replied. She turned to Ben. "Look at you, all proper. We don't stand on ceremony here, sugar. Sit it down wherever you like."

He stole a glance at the name tag she wore on her blouse.

"Lisbeth," she said, noticing his interest. A smile deepened well-exercised lines around her mouth. "I'm the owner. Make the girls wear the tags, so I figure I should, too." She leaned back, appraising. "I feel like I know you, honey; now, why is that?"

"I was in here once, with my family."

Lisbeth hummed and slid her mouth to one side. "Mostly local folk around here; don't see many blow-ins."

"Actually—"

"You're the one they talk about." She slapped the top of her ample thigh. "Tierney. You're up at the Crofts."

"That's right," Ben said.

"My, you're a young fella. Didn't expect that. Was just asking myself the other day when you'd come down and visit. What took you so long?"

"We came in once," Ben said again. "A couple weeks ago."

"I'd remember," she said, shaking her head. "Coulda been the week I got laid up with some bug. You get that fever that's been going around?"

Ben shook his head.

"You're not missing anything there. Now, you find a seat and I'll get you some water. You want some coffee, too?"

"Actually, I was wondering if I could buy a pie to take out."

"Just a pie? Baked some fresh last night. I think we have a cherry and an apple that haven't been nibbled at yet. Let me get you a little slice of each so you can make an educated decision."

"Oh, no, that's not necessary."

"Be my pleasure," she said, heading back to the kitchen. "And if you like both of them, that'll be a good excuse to visit again, won't it?"

She was back a minute later with a full plate and a can of whipped cream. The cherries' crimson juice slid toward him when she placed the plate on the table.

"Can't eat whip myself," Lisbeth told him. "I'm a bit of a health fiend, as you can see." She clutched her bulging stomach and laughed.

Lisbeth slid into the bench across from Ben and asked how he'd decided to move to Swannhaven. Between mouthfuls, Ben performed the sanitized version of the story. In this fiction, Ben explained how he and his family been visiting the farmhouse that he'd inherited from his grandmother when they first learned that the Crofts was for sale. The thought of buying the place had occurred to him and his supremely dependable and entirely well-balanced wife at once. They'd set it aside at first, thinking it sheer lunacy, but it hadn't gone away. It hadn't gone away, and now here they were.

Without all the mental illness, bullying, and economic Armageddon, the whole thing sounded rather romantic.

"Now, why are you on your own?" she asked him. "Where's your beautiful family? And I already know they're beautiful, because you're a handsome man, and in my experience, pretty people tend to stick together."

"Oh." Ben felt his face warm. "They're back at the house. I've just been running some errands."

"You lot must be busy up there, with that big house to whip into shape. They say you're turning the Crofts into an inn?"

"That's the plan."

"Be nice to see it fixed up, that's for sure. Some around here aren't too happy about it. But houses are meant to be lived in, aren't they? And in its day, that was one fine house. Who better than you to restore it?"

"Well, I wouldn't say that."

"You're the Lowells' kin, aren't you?"

"My grandmother was a Lowell."

"Then so are you," she said. "Names are nice, but people around here know better than most that it's the blood that matters. Lowells were one of the first to settle here, with my kin right alongside them. You know that?"

Ben shook his head.

"Then you've got some catching up to do. The Lowells were one of the Winter Families. And the Winter Families have done their living and dying together for the better part of three hundred years."

"Winter Families?"

"Your grandmother never told you anything at all?"

"Not that I remember."

"Well, it's a long story. Probably better for another time."

"You can't tease me like that," Ben said. Both pies had been good. Nothing remained on his plate but a trough of livid juice that thickened along the rim.

"Hard to know just how to tell it right. It's the kinda thing that if you look at it straight on you may miss something. But once a month, me and a bunch of the other old biddies from the village meet at the church to talk about the village history and keep the flame of it bright and burning. We call it the Preservation Society. Truth is, half the time we spend chatting about whose cows are with calf and which teenage lovebirds have most lately been caught tumbling in a barn. If you're there, maybe we'll have an easier time keeping to the matter at hand. Your family has long been an important part of Swannhaven, and now you're back. Lost and now returned."

"I'd love to learn more about the village," Ben said. And it was true. At the very least, he wanted to learn more about the history of the Crofts.

"Well, sure you would," Lisbeth said. "This is where your people are from." She stood and smiled at him. "And, God willing, this is where your people will be from again."

7

Ben had bought a book for everyone.

"Is this the one where she goes to India?" Caroline asked. She squinted at the back-cover copy.

"Look, there are boats, too," Charlie said. He hefted his copy of *The Book of Secrets* over his head to show Ben the schematics of small floating platforms made from sticks and bark.

"We can play with them in one of the streams near the lake," Ben said.

"For meditation and yoga or something?"

"I know where we can find bark like this, too," Charlie said. "It's like paper; Heck uses it to write his journal."

"Everyone else seemed to like it, Cee," Ben said. Bub was in his exersaucer, sucking on the corner of a board book about caterpillars. "I think Bub likes his."

"What did you get for yourself?" Caroline asked Ben.

"Couple of things," Ben said. "Picked up a copy of Connor's new book."

"For the uneven nightstand in Charlie's room?" she asked.

The kettle clicked, and Ben seized the opportunity to turn away

from her. She'd always had a problem with his friends. She thought
they were snobs, and the feeling had been reciprocated. Most of
them dated people in media or the arts, and at their dinner parties
Caroline inevitably had been the only finance person in attendance.
Everyone talked about the *Observer* and the *Times;* she read the
Journal. Their coffee tables held copies of *New York* and *Vanity Fair*
instead of *The Economist.* At first they'd treated Caroline politely
and then like a curiosity, but things had gone south at about the
same time as the economy.

"I read the most entertaining review of his new one on Amazon.
I almost forwarded it to you," she said.

"I appreciate the restraint. Did you get much done while I was
out?"

"I finished a coat of paint in one of the rooms. How do you think
we should keep the rooms straight? Numbering them seems a little
sterile, don't you think?"

"We could name them after plants or flowers—no, that's lame,"
Ben said. "We should try to bring in something local. Nearby mountain peaks?"

"Or name them after something special about the house—like
the Gable Room or the Tower Room?" Caroline asked.

"That's a good idea." Ben nodded. "Yes, sir, the Ceiling May
Cave in on You as You Sleep Room is available next weekend. Oh, of
course we can accommodate your children nearby. The Absolutely
No Insulation Anywhere Room is just across the hall."

"Thank you, Ben. That's really constructive." She shook her
head, but Ben saw that one side of her mouth had curved into a
smile.

"Or maybe we could name them after some of our favorite slack-
jawed yokels. Post their pretty profiles on each door. We can furnish
the Deputy Simms Room with empty Milwaukee's Best cans and
Skoal containers."

"Did things not go well at the general store?"

"Oh, no, it went great. We're actually getting together later to-night. Going to knock back a few and watch the game."

"Can you please try to make more of an effort?" she said.

"I met the owner of the Lancelight, actually," Ben said. He'd chosen the cherry pie. "She was friendly and told me a little about Grams's family. She also invited me to a meeting of the town's Preservation Society."

"Well, that's good. Showing an interest in the town would be a good way to integrate with the locals. We're going to need their support if the inn's going to work. There could be a real synergic benefit in pitching the restoration of the Crofts as a manifestation of their civic pride."

"Sounds good to me," Ben said. He'd learned long ago that it was best to simply smile and agree when Caroline drifted into industry jargon.

"Speaking of community integration, one of the Catholic schools returned your call. Did you ever get back to the prep school in Northbridge?"

Ben sighed. "They're still holding his spot."

They had been all set to send Charlie to Northbridge Day until their last visit, when Charlie sat in on a class while Ben and Caroline spoke to the headmistress. The headmistress had had a lot of questions for them: about the problems in the last school, about why they had moved up here, and then about Ben's books. Their meeting had gone on longer than they'd expected, and when they went to the class to get Charlie, they found that the teacher had left and the room was empty except for three boys who'd blocked Charlie into a corner, pushing him and pulling at the collar of his shirt. Charlie had stood there, letting the boys shove him, wearing an uncomprehending look that had made Ben want to reach across the room and shake him.

"Was St. Michael's the name of the Catholic school?" Ben asked. There were more options for private schooling up here than he'd expected, but because he was a stranger to the region, it'd been hard for Ben to keep them straight. From what he'd been able to find out, St. Michael's had a good reputation.

"I wrote it down." She found the notepad. "The Priory of St. Michael's." The oven dinged and Caroline scurried over to scrutinize its contents. A wave of succulence wafted through the open door. Ben was about to ask her what she was cooking when an explosive noise came from the hall.

Caroline shut the oven and stood up. Charlie put down his book and cocked his ear. Hudson sprang up from where he had been lying, his nose probing the air. Bub paused his bouncing in his exersaucer. They stayed poised like that for a few seconds.

"Must have left a door open," Ben said. He turned away from where he'd been watching the door to the hallway. "The wind probably slammed it shut." He rubbed Hudson on the head. "That a pork roast, Cee?"

The sound came again, louder than the first time, loud enough to make them all flinch. It was a deep sound that reverberated throughout the house, like the bolting of a huge lock at the building's heart. Hudson trotted across the room and began to pace in front of the door, a growl gathering in his throat.

"Ben?" Caroline asked.

"It's just a door getting blown by the wind," Ben said. "The dead-latch must have jammed." He opened the utensil drawer and pulled out a knife. "It's only to pry it loose, if I need to," he told her.

He kissed Caroline lightly on the neck on his way past her. "Relax, Hud." He grabbed the beagle by his collar and pulled him over to Caroline. "Smells good," he told her before closing the hall door behind him.

The lights were out in the hall. The sun had fallen behind the mountains at the west end of the valley, and the day's last light littered the rooms in the geometry cast by the immense windows.

The hall seemed even more cavernous in the dark. It had been designed to be wide enough for two women in hoop skirts to pass each other with ease, but now it could have been twice as broad.

The sound came again, sending him back a step. It was a slamming door, he was sure, but the impact against the house's wooden bones was such that it seemed almost to have a physical presence.

Ben picked up the pace, his footsteps keeping time between the crashing sounds. He counted the number of rooms he passed, but he couldn't remember how many there were supposed to be.

The hall was a straight shot except for the last leg, which took a hard right turn. There was a cold draft in the air when he turned the corner, and he was just in time to see the door slam into its frame again.

He grabbed the handle to prevent the door from swinging open and saw that the deadlatch had indeed become jammed. The wind must have been knocking the door open, then a draft from another room would slam it shut.

He heard Caroline's distant call.

"Just a door," he yelled.

Ben realized he was shaking. The lock would need to be looked at, but not now. He used the knife to pry the latch loose so the wind wouldn't push it open again. It was caked with a sticky residue, which surprised him, because all the locks were new. On his fingers it had the pine tang of tree resin. The door's dead bolt worked fine, and he slid it closed. He ran his fingers along the door's glass paneling, surprised that it hadn't cracked in the repeated assaults.

He turned on the exterior lights and looked out the glass. Placed in the center of the stoop like the morning's newspaper was a severed deer's head, staring at him with black, blood-flecked eyes.

II

THE EYES *of the* FOREST

JULY

November 9, 1777

My Dearest Kathy,

The road is closed and I do not know when I will be able to post this letter. The snows fell early and heavily, but even if they had not, the Iroquois are certain to kill any horseman. It has been some four weeks since we have had contact from beyond the valley.

We heard rumors of the Iroquois alliance with the British, but before Father gave any credence to the idea, a raiding party burned Swannhaven. The church, Porter's Store, the Hall, the Coplins' Farm where we used to play—all of it up in flames. I cannot do justice to how it looked from the porch of the Crofts, the gleam of flames and tiny figures fleeing like motes of shadow against the frosted fields. I watched as they lost ground to the marauders and fell still against the cold of the earth. I was not certain it was real until I smelled the smoke for myself.

The Porters, Van Epps, Stevensons, Cartwrights, all of the Coplins dead, except for Raymond Coplin. There are more, but what good would it do to tell you? Thirty souls found their way here, and the rest made for the northern gap. We and the tenant families here on the Drop took in those who fled up the mountain, but for the others, I dare not guess what became of them.

The Indians have long feared the mountains, and Father believes they will not venture here. He has established a rotating watch. His sermon this Sunday was of David and Goliath, and all of us left in elevated spirits. He has ordered the forest to the east chopped down. The widened visibility gives us some comfort. And with all the firewood, we will not freeze this winter. But for food, there is concern. The thirty extra mouths will push us beyond our limit. But we've already reduced our daily portions, and the men still hunt in the northern fields with some success.

These hunters saw smoke from the south this afternoon past, and we fear that the trading post on the Albany Trail has also been destroyed.

I am not permitted outside unaccompanied, but I went with Jack to review the men on watch. They do not see the Iroquois, but they hear noises in the wood.

It is so empty here. Do you remember what it was like on winter mornings when we were children? How from the porch we could peer into the face of the wild with nothing but the smoke from Swannhaven's hearths to remind us of civilization? Now Swannhaven is gone, and it is as if we were the last people in all the world.

Pray for us, dear sister.

Your Bess

8

Ben swirled the remnants of his coffee. It was cold, and had been for a while.

He watched Bub in his exersaucer, where the baby played with his unspillable cup. Bub held the cup out by one handle and Ben clinked his mug against it, sending the boy into a series of delighted noises.

The kitchen was bright: a relief after the week they'd had.

The storms had been a sight. The dark cumulus clouds had billowed from the west, turning the sky a trembling green before unleashing torrents of rain.

Ben now understood the warnings about the wind on the Drop. It had a way of finding weaknesses under the eaves, generating drafts throughout the house. He'd wake in the night to its screams when it collided with the rough angles of the roof; it sometimes electrified entire rooms with a tremendous, unwavering hum. And it shook the forest into a frenzy, filling the house with a riot of branches rapping against one another.

After the deluge came gray days of drizzle. Ben had found himself with the animal need to escape the Crofts, coupled with an agoraphobic revulsion of leaving it. He wondered if this was just a

preview of what the winters would be like: endless months of clois-
tered suspense.

He hadn't told Caroline about the deer's head he'd found on the
stoop. The mutilated body had been easy enough to dismiss as an
animal attack, but the dismembered head was not the work of forest
creatures. Ben threw the head into the forest and wrote the episode
off as a prank, some sort of initiation by the village's men. The animal had probably been hit by a car or killed by a hunter who figured
he'd try to get a rise out of the new guy, the city guy with the pretty
wife and the big house. He didn't see the point of worrying Caroline
and Charlie about it. The most they could do was file a police report,
and, in a village as small as Swannhaven, that was certain to cause
more harm than good.

"Wah?" Bub asked him, again holding out his cup.

Ben accepted the cup and filled it with filtered water from the
fridge. He could hear Mick Jagger upstairs. Caroline was on the
third floor, sanding the hallway. Ben was supposed to be working on
his novel; Bub was supposed to be napping.

After the incident with the deer, Ben told Charlie he could no
longer play outside by himself. Hearing this, the boy looked as
though he'd been run through. His gray-blue eyes had widened as his
lips had thinned. Tears didn't seem far off, but then Charlie's face
had settled and he'd left the room without a word. He'd hardly said
a thing in the week that had passed.

Ben also hadn't been thrilled with the situation. Back in the city,
the idea of Charlie going outside by himself had been unthinkable.
Whenever they'd left the apartment, Caroline and Ben would be all
over him with instructions and cautions. Stay on this side of the sidewalk; watch the curb; stand behind the yellow line; don't touch that;
don't stare. It had been easy to find danger in every step. It had been
exhausting. And in the end, none of it had ended up keeping him
safe, anyway. But things were different up here. This morning, Ben
told Charlie he was allowed outside as long as he kept the Crofts
within sight. He was out there right now.

Bub took a few pulls from his cup, then started trying to knock it over again.

"We should get you to your nap," Ben said as he lifted him out of his saucer. He fit the boy over his shoulder and let him pretend to whisper into his ear for as long as he could stand it.

"You're tickling me." He tickled his son back, and soon Bub was laughing, too.

They took the kitchen stairs to the second floor. The Stones were louder up here, but music never seemed to bother Bub. He was an easy baby. Charlie had been good, too, if not exactly easy. He'd been fussy in the same ways he still was: utterly intractable on some issues. But Ben couldn't complain about either of them. His mother always said that he and Ted had been little nightmares. Crying constantly, hungry when they were supposed to sleep, tired and surly when they were supposed to eat. But raising his own children, Ben thought that perhaps his difficult childhood had more to do with her qualities as a mother than his shortcomings as a son.

"Now, if Mom asks, you've been here for an hour already, okay?"

"Ma," Bub said.

"You got it." Ben switched on the baby monitor and clipped the portable unit to his belt. He leaned over to kiss his son on the forehead. "Now sleep, and dream happy dreams."

He walked down the hall to his and Caroline's room. They'd ordered a couch to put by the fireplace, but the room still seemed indecently large. Three windows stretched to the fourteen-foot ceilings, offering a triptych of the valley and the hazy blue distance. Caroline had the contractors install a new bathroom and huge walk-in closets, which now struck Ben as ridiculous. It had been months since he'd worn anything fancier than jeans and sneakers. He walked to the one with his old things: dry-cleaned shirts and pressed suits that now seemed more like costumes than clothing. He reached for a Thomas Pink box he'd placed on the top shelf alongside boxes of shiny wing tips and handcrafted oxfords, but the sound of a slamming car door stopped him.

Their room looked west, and Ben craned his neck south to see who had pulled up to the Crofts. All he could make out was the back half of a blue pickup. He ran downstairs to the kitchen, and midway down the flight he heard a tentative rapping against the kitchen door. He opened the door, startling the young man on the stoop.

"Didn't know which door to try," the kid said. He couldn't have been much older than eighteen. He wore torn jeans and a white T-shirt. A few wayward curls of his brown hair showed from under a faded Patriots hat. "I'm here to haul out some of your things. I think my dad spoke to your missus last week?" He tilted his head slightly to peer around Ben and into the house. "Maybe it's the stuff in the pile outside?"

"Oh, right. I forgot you were coming today. That pile's been there since last week," Ben said.

"Yeah, sorry about that." He smiled lopsidedly. "Dad's back was hurting. I would've come earlier, but our truck crapped out. Got this one as a loaner from Joe Mills." He pointed to the blue pickup. "You know him?"

Ben shook his head.

"Real nice guy. *Your* rides look pretty new." He pointed to the twin SUVs parked beside the shed. "They don't give you any trouble?"

"So far so good," Ben said. "I'm Ben." He stuck his hand out as he stepped outside.

"Jake Bishop."

"So, yes, it's mostly this stuff on the lawn," Ben said. They walked across the wild grass to the pile of refuse that he and Charlie had assembled the week before. The mound of trash had been soaked by the rains. Upholstery and piles of newspapers had melted into one another, a congealed mass.

"Some old crap here," Jake said thoughtfully, prodding the edge of a waterlogged cardboard box. "This the Swanns' stuff?"

"I assume so, or whoever else lived here. There must be a hundred years' worth of junk down there."

"No one but Swanns ever lived here," Jake said. He glanced back at the Crofts, then turned to the pile. "You just want this outta here, right? You don't care what I do with it?"

"I just want it gone."

"'Cause some folks could use this stuff." Jake opened up the cardboard box at his feet and revealed a heap of yellowing children's clothes. "Tough times and all."

"It's yours if you want it."

Jake nodded. "Might take a couple trips."

"It's only the tip of the iceberg, I'm afraid," Ben said.

"More of this in there?"

"Acres of it. Your dad said he didn't do stairs, but if that doesn't bother you, I'd love your help."

"Can't say no to paying work."

"How long are you home for?" Ben asked.

"Home?"

"Before you head back to school?"

"Done with school." Jake shrugged. "School's done with me."

"Oh." Ben nodded. He turned away and squinted at the sun. "Well, if you want to take care of this pile, we can figure out the rest later. Okay?"

"Sure, boss. You in any rush today?"

"I guess that depends on whether or not we're paying you by the hour."

Jake laughed. "Your missus got a daily rate. Dad says she's a tough one."

"That's why I let her do the talking. I'm heading back in. Yell if you need anything."

"You got it, boss."

Once inside, Ben drained what was left of his coffee and returned to his bedroom. The Stones were still doing their thing at the other end of the hall, which meant Caroline was still sanding.

He returned to his closet and took the Thomas Pink box off the top shelf.

He sat on the floor and took the ancient Bible out of the box. He'd shown Caroline the old architectural drawings he'd found in the battered captain's desk, but he'd hidden the Bible from her, afraid she might throw it out. Since then he'd taken it out a few times just to look at it. It was a beautiful book: stark and dramatic, with its metal cross fastened onto the thick black leather. It was certainly old. He wondered if he'd ever held a book so old. The type was a tight Gothic of some kind. Some of the passages had been marked with the spidery handwriting of the past age.

Ben ran his fingers over the dragon-skin binding and began to hatch the bones of a story. He imagined colonists risking dangerous passage across the ocean to the New World, the family Bible clutched dearly in hand while the small ship is caught by the whims of a tempest. He tried to visualize those pilgrim believers trekking as deep into the northern wilderness as any settlers dared go. Building a town from nothing, clearing a mountainside for a grand house.

"Ben? You in here?" Caroline asked.

"Yeah," he said. He put the Bible into its box and lifted it back to its place on the top shelf. He found Caroline in their bathroom, washing her hands and face. "Taking a break? I can make you some tea." Low barometric pressure gave Caroline headaches, and the last week had been tough on her. But her mood had subsided under the clear skies. Ben hoped it would last for a while this time.

"The sander heats everything up. Is there any lemonade left?"

"I'll check," Ben said. As he headed for the door, his thoughts wandered back to the Swanns. He wondered what kind of strength, audacity, and mad faith could have driven them. Not just to settle this place but also to dwell here for centuries, until their bloodline was utterly spent.

"Do you hear that?" Caroline asked, heading to the closest window. "I think someone's out there."

"It's the trash guy—his son, actually."

"Almost gave up on them."

"Yeah. Let me check on that lemonade." He thought about how

the first people on the Drop must have felt, laying the foundations for the Crofts. How they'd imagined it into being before even the first stone had been set.

"You get any work done?" Caroline called after him.

"A little," he called back.

This time it felt like the truth.

9

The week inside had been terrible for Charlie. As he ran to the woods, he felt like someone allowed to finally stop holding his breath after seven days.

During the storm he'd watched the forest through the windows, hoping the rough weather might shake some of its secrets loose from the trees. But all he saw were squirrels, rabbits, and deer.

Heck had found a cave of albino lizards and a nest of scarlet-plumed birds in his adventures, but Charlie felt sure that something even better lived on the Drop. This feeling had begun as a vague sense of being watched, but sometimes he was sure that he caught sight of something out of the corner of his eye—something that shouldn't have been there. It was frustrating not to be able to fully see a thing he knew was there. He was sure Heck would have found a way around this problem.

Heck was older than Charlie, and Charlie thought that was one reason why Heck always knew what to do. He knew how to build a fire that wouldn't smoke, knew how to cure leather and read tomorrow's weather in the clouds. But sometimes even Heck needed help. His friend, Shoeless Tom, had taught Heck which roots had to be boiled before they were safe to eat. He showed Heck how to run through the underbrush without a sound and how to talk to every bird that lived in the trees.

Charlie wanted to know the forest as well as Heck and Shoeless Tom did. That was why he'd been so happy to get *The Book of Secrets*. The book explained a lot that Heck already knew and other things that Charlie thought he should learn.

Digging his burrow had been the first thing Heck had done, and Charlie also wanted a safe place for himself. *The Book of Secrets* had a chapter that showed how to make a hunter's blind. From there, Charlie thought, he could watch even the shyest of woodland creatures. He wanted to see the way they moved, the way they ate and drank and smelled the air. He knew just where to build it, too. The faerie circle among the big oaks east of the lake was the perfect spot.

When he reached the lake, Charlie saw that it was full from the rains. The Drop was quiet today, but he could feel the eyes from the forest. Sensing the Watcher's gaze made him feel less alone.

There was a good tree on the west side of the faerie circle. It had long and level branches where he could build his perch. He was studying the arc and angle of its limbs when he heard a branch snap behind him. He thought he saw a blur of black when he spun to meet the sound. He caught it at the farthest edge of his vision. The forest grew quiet.

When he turned back, he heard another noise from the same direction.

Charlie walked to the edge of the faerie circle and searched the trees for movement. A noise came from deeper in the wood—a sound of urgent tapping, as if a tree's branch were trying to remind its trunk of something.

He began to pick his way through the trees toward the sound. He tried not to hope that the stranger in the forest had finally decided to show himself, but it was hard not to.

The sounds ahead moved and changed. They were hard noises, like the clack of wood banging against wood, but over time they rang like the notes and rhythm of an unknown song. Charlie followed with a focus that made the rest of the world fall away.

He did not know how long he tracked the sound as it wandered toward the slope of the mountain, but when the noise finally faded and did not return, Charlie saw how high he had climbed. Blue sky shone through the trees when he looked downslope, which meant that he now stood higher than the mountains on the far side of the valley.

Charlie thought about this as he felt the eyes from the forest on him again. The strange gaze had been fleeting before, but now it burned his back. Charlie waited for the creature's attention to move on, but it did not.

As the silence grew and thickened, Charlie gathered his breath. He knew Heck would not be so afraid. He clenched his fists and forced himself to face the one who watched from the trees.

10

St. Michael's stood at the head of a long gravel road that switch-backed up the slope of a wooded peak. An imposing wall built from the same brown rock that formed the mountain greeted Ben at the path's end.

Ben was early for his meeting with Father Caleb, the school's headmaster. "Let's look around, Hud," he said once he'd parked. After their experience at the last school, he wanted to learn as much about St. Michael's as he could before enrolling Charlie.

Hudson hopped out of the Escape. They struck out on a small trail etched along the perimeter of the wall. Ben admired the slender trees, the fractals of blue sky that gleamed through their foliage. The wall gave way to an English garden, then a grassy field, and beyond that a drop to the valley floor.

Ben followed Hudson among the blooms of bergamot and star-tling thatches of blue cornflowers. The air smelled of thyme and lavender.

At the far end of the garden, Hudson stopped at a fountain, and Ben saw that a freestanding wall had been erected near it. The wall was the kind against which kids might play handball or some such game. But once Ben circled to its other side, he doubted this wall had ever been used that way. A large mosaic had been crafted from small, vividly colored enamel pieces. Set against a flaming sunset was the silhouette of a giant winged beast, its body wrapped in shadow except for the underside of its wings and a portion of its head and neck. The black pit of its single visible eye bore upon the lone figure in front of it: a man in white, standing on a rise that overlooked a landscape charred save for a single tree. His sword, barely the size of one of the creature's claws, was raised above his head.

It was a stark scene, especially in contrast to the surrounding peaceful garden.

"St. Michael and the dragon," said a voice from behind him. "A dramatic rendering, but the boys like it."

Ben hadn't heard him approach. The man was dressed in the black capuche of the Dominican Order, which looked otherworldly in the July sun.

"I'm not surprised," Ben said. "Doesn't seem like a fair fight, does it?"

"Some days it doesn't," the priest admitted. "But look at Michael there, brandishing the sword over his head like that, almost daring the beast to lunge at him. Some days it seems as if all Michael needs to do is stand there, on the edge of that dark valley, to defeat the enemy. As if the grandest evil is just a schoolyard bully whose weakness is exposed by a single act of defiance." He glanced up at the sky. "On a day like today, it feels as if it's the dragon who doesn't have a chance."

"It's beautiful up here. A really nice garden."

"Thank you; it's our chief indulgence. And a daily exercise in faith—if the rabbits don't get into the blooms, then it's the groundhogs or the deer or the voles. And you have your own vandal here?" Hudson was sniffing at a small pile of cedar chips, and the priest reached down to scratch the back of the dog's neck.

"This is Hudson, and his interests are purely carnivorous."

"I'm sure he's found plenty of trouble to get into over at the Crofts."

Ben's surprise must have registered on his face.

"We don't get many unexpected visitors up here, Mr. Tierney." He stuck out his hand. "I'm Father Caleb, and I've been looking forward to meeting you."

Ben took the hand offered to him.

Father Caleb started to make his way down the garden's central path, toward the cluster of stone buildings. He looked to be in his seventies, but he was straight as a weathervane. "Tell me about Charles. His transcripts were quite complimentary."

"Charlie's great. A really smart kid. Reads far above his age level. And he's enjoying it up here. I was worried he might not, but it's hard to keep him inside when there's so much for him to explore."

"Curious children are a blessing."

"I think so, too."

"There was some trouble at school in the city, though, wasn't there? The headmaster there was too discreet to say anything, but I've been doing this long enough to hear what isn't being said."

"Oh." Ben ran his hand through his hair. "There was some bullying."

"There was a note in his records that you'd hired tutors to school him from home for his last semester."

"He'd been roughed up a few times," Ben said. "His books had been stolen and ripped up." City schools could be tough, but even their short trip to Northbridge Day had gone poorly. When Ben thought of the place, he couldn't help but replay the way those three boys had turned on his son. The boys could tell that Charlie didn't watch the right cartoons or play the right video games or follow the right sports teams. They could smell it on him. The boys at Northbridge had found him out in half an hour.

"That can be very difficult," Father Caleb said. "On both the child and the parents."

"There was another incident. More serious," Ben said. He hated telling this story, but it had to be done. "I'd pick him up from the front steps of school every afternoon. One day he wasn't there, so I went inside. I looked in his classroom, talked to his teacher, went to the principal, but we couldn't find him anywhere. So we called the police. They started interviewing the staff members and Charlie's classmates and parents. An Amber Alert was issued. The FBI got involved. They sent his picture to every patrolman in the city. Still we couldn't find him."

"Oh, my," the priest said.

Ben cleared his throat. "Our other son was only two months old. And my wife was . . . still recovering. I didn't know what to do. Caroline sat by the phone with police and the FBI, but I couldn't stay in the apartment. So I walked and walked. I remember it was freezing outside. At some point, I got it into my head that Charlie would be okay as long as he wasn't taken out of Manhattan. There are only so many ways off the island, and the Holland Tunnel was the closest to our apartment; I just couldn't shake the idea that maybe he was being taken through it that moment. To New Jersey and then to who knows where. If they got him through that tunnel, he'd be gone forever. I was sure. So I stood there by the entrance all night, looking through the windows of cars for Charlie. It was impossible, it was stupid, but it was only thing I could think of."

"Where was he?" Father Caleb asked.

"Around ten o'clock the next morning I got a call on my cell phone from the school. The janitor had found him. Some boys from Charlie's class had taken him down to the furnace room and locked him in a closet. He'd been trapped in the dark for nineteen hours."

Sometimes, at night, Ben tried to imagine what that might have been like. He tried to build the closet walls around himself in his head, but all he could envision was a coffin. No wonder it was so hard to keep Charlie inside the house.

"That's ghastly," Father Caleb said. He rested a hand on Ben's arm. "I can't imagine how terrible that must have been. For everyone."

"The kids responsible had been questioned by their parents, the police, the FBI. They lied to all of them." Ben shook his head. "We couldn't send Charlie back there after that."

"We're very vigilant about things like that here, Mr. Tierney," Father Caleb said. "We have a zero-tolerance policy to make sure that our students respect their parents, teachers, themselves, and one another. Charlie will be safe here."

Ben nodded and turned away, pretending to look for Hudson.

Father Caleb showed Ben the classrooms, gymnasium, and cafeteria. Ben was impressed by how modern the facilities were. He'd never have guessed it from the medieval exterior. Many of the classrooms were outfitted with banks of flat-screen computers. The cafeteria was airy and welcoming. The only building they didn't visit was the chapel, as there was a mass in progress.

"Is that where the rest of the brothers are?" Ben asked him.

"Some of them; the rest are in Gracefield, setting up for the soup kitchen the parish there is hosting this weekend. Lots of people have been hit hard by the downturn." Father Caleb shook his head. " 'Downturn' doesn't quite do it justice up here, does it?"

"I guess if people didn't find comfort in euphemisms, we wouldn't use them."

"The priory is in good shape financially, thank the Lord, but a lot of families have been forced to make tough choices."

They had arrived back at the priory's front gates, and Ben again noticed the wall that encircled much of the campus.

"This looks more defensive than decorative," he said. "It reminds me of some old Italian monastery."

Father Caleb nodded. "It used to encircle the whole priory, and it was built to do exactly what most walls are meant to do. The foundations were set in the colonial period, when this whole area was frontier. Rough times, and rough country."

"It's still rough country."

Father Caleb laughed. It was deep and genuine enough to make Ben smile.

"That it is, Mr. Tierney."

They reached the Escape, and Ben opened the door to let Hudson jump in.

"I think Charlie could thrive here, but it would be nice to meet him, too," Father Caleb said.

"Of course. When would be the best time to bring him by?"

"I'm actually going to be near Swannhaven on Thursday. I could drop by the Crofts in the late morning, if that's convenient?"

Considering the state of the Crofts, Ben doubted Caroline would be thrilled by the prospect of receiving a visitor.

"The place is still a work in progress," he said.

"I don't mind in the slightest if the place is a disaster. But I don't want to put you out."

"Of course not. It's no problem. I think you and Charlie will like each other."

"Until Thursday, then," the priest said.

Ben climbed into the car. "Do you need directions?" he asked.

The priest shook his head and smiled.

"I know the way, Mr. Tierney."

11

Caroline admired the way Ben could turn a look of shock into a pleasant smile. He'd developed a thespian's finesse for such things. She didn't know how interesting the Preservation Society meeting would be, but the flash of surprise that lit his face when she told him she'd attend it alongside him had already made it worthwhile.

She enjoyed a chance to knock him off-balance. Ben was too confident that he had everyone around him figured out—as if they were characters in one of his books, amalgams of traits and quirks whose actions and dialogue could be predicted by anyone who knew enough of them. The only thing Caroline hated more than feeling like a foregone conclusion was knowing when she was acting like one.

But it felt nice to be on a family outing. The air was warm and the sky was clear, and she felt good today. Charlie sat in the backseat with Bub and read to him from *The Book of Secrets,* and Caroline enjoyed listening. She was glad to have a respite from *Hickory Heck.* He read faster than his usual cadence, his little-boy voice driven forward like a wave lunging for the shore.

Next to her, Ben was saying something about the Revolutionary War and the owner of the diner who'd invited him to the Preservation Society meeting. From what Caroline could gather, the woman's family had lived in the village for generations, and Ben believed that she knew all its secrets. Caroline had discovered over the years that Ben hunted mysteries in everything he saw. She might roll her eyes at him for these sojourns into fantasy, but this was a trait of his that she enjoyed. Because Ben didn't seem able to face the fact that life was, by definition, mundane, being with him had lent the world a vibrance it otherwise lacked. Caroline knew his childhood had a lot to do with the way he liked to live in worlds other than his own.

She'd first seen Ben during college orientation when they'd passed each other on a footpath. He was handsome, but the campus was filled with good-looking boys. Later, she decided that she took such an immediate interest because of the girl he was with—over the semesters, Caroline noted that Ben was always with one girl or another. It hadn't been the girl herself but the way Ben was with her. Completely absorbed. Breathing her in. He hadn't even glanced in Caroline's direction as she passed them. When Caroline tried to imagine the pure bliss of total engrossment, she'd come up empty.

Caroline liked the way Ben walked the university's halls and paths with a slight smile, how he tended to wear a scarf but not a jacket when the season started to turn. They began dating during their junior year, and Caroline had understood at once that Ben was different from her other boyfriends. More thoughtful and understanding. He listened. A man and not a boy, she thought—*finally*. Boys had demanded much from her. They needed to be entertained, they needed to be impressed, they needed to think that she needed them. Being with Ben had never felt like work. He was someone with whom she could be quiet, and yet he also made her laugh. For twelve years they had laughed so much. Twelve years of that—and the boys. She hadn't always *thought* it, but she'd known all along how lucky she was.

Bipolar had been her psychiatrist's diagnosis. She was told that the disease sometimes lay dormant like bulbs of spring flowers in the cold earth, awaiting the right conditions to sprout. For Caroline, the hormones from her pregnancy with Bub combined with the stress of losing her job had been the soil in which her condition had blossomed.

Between the diagnosis and her unemployment, Caroline had found herself spending more time with Ben than she had in many years. They'd had such busy lives that it had seemed a new thing to idle together, and she began to notice the changes that had accrued over the years. Her husband was not the way she remembered him.

She'd never paid attention to how Ben looked when he wrote, but now she had little more to do than study him. The way his face would tighten and then slacken, the way he would silently mouth the words written by him but spoken by another. Sometimes he'd fire an expression at the screen that she'd never before seen on his face.

Dr. Hatcher told her that this was simple paranoia, something that she had to be vigilant for. Nevertheless, a sense mounted in her that whoever Ben conjured in his head sat there in his chair, mouthing dialogue to the computer screen. Sometimes, when the words were working for him, she could almost see his creation, with its alien posture and phantom outline.

She could not arrest the thought that he wore an actor's smile when he played with the boys or held her close. As if another life—his real life—lay elsewhere.

"I thought this would be more popular," she said when they arrived.

The Preservation Society meetings were held at the little church in the village, and its parking lot held only six cars.

"This is probably, like, a solid third of the village's population," Ben said.

They pulled alongside a battered hatchback with a license plate two generations older than the one currently in use.

"Can I play out here?" Charlie asked them.

"Here?" Caroline asked as she slipped Bub into the BabyBjörn she'd fastened around herself. "What would you do out here?"

"I want to play in the park, then I can read for a while," he said.

Charlie didn't fidget, but Caroline had the sense that he thrummed with energy. He'd been like this for days now. Fueled with enough food and sleep, little boys were like engines without off switches, but the way he'd been acting struck Caroline as manic—something she knew a few things about.

"What park?"

"He means that broken plaza with the old fountain," Ben said. Caroline remembered it now. It was a broad space that once must have been the center of village life, but now it was overrun with trees and clogged with vegetation.

"You think it's safe there for him?" she asked. They'd agreed to give Charlie a longer leash up here, but some habits were hard to break.

"As long as he stays out of the streets. It's just on the other side of those trees," Ben said. He pointed to an outcropping of scraggly evergreens that leaned against the back of church.

"Take my phone." Caroline pressed it into Charlie's hands. "Call Dad if you have any trouble, and if you see anyone, run back to the church."

"Okay."

"Stay out of the streets, and don't leave the square, got it?"

Charlie nodded and ran for the plaza. Only an eruption of trembling fern fronds marked his way.

It was warm outside, but the inside of the church was stifling. Although the windows were open, there was little breeze. There were only ten rows of pews, but that was more than enough for today's crowd. Three women sat at a table facing the congregation, and four others occupied the front bench.

A large middle-aged woman rose from the table up front when she saw them enter. Ben moved to greet her, and Caroline guessed that this was the diner owner he'd been telling her about. Another of the women at the table stood up soon after the first. Mary Stanton, Caroline remembered. The chief of police's wife. She'd dropped off an apple pie as a housewarming present.

"So good to see you again," Mary said as she clasped Caroline's hands in her own. "Look how big he's gotten! What a beautiful little boy." She ran a finger across Bub's cheek. "Lisbeth said that your husband might come by, but I'm glad you came, too."

"Ben's eager to learn more about his family history, and I'd love to learn more about the village."

"We're so glad you're interested," Mary said. "Our history's very important to us. Do you know Lisbeth?" she asked. The heavy woman was still talking to Ben, and Mary put a hand on her shoulder.

Lisbeth turned around and Ben began to introduce them. The next thing Caroline knew, the older woman was hugging her. Embracing strangers wasn't high on Caroline's list of favorite things, but she allowed herself to return the hug. Making connections with the villagers was important, she told herself as the woman enveloped her. The success of their inn depended on it. *Everything* depended on it.

One by one, the other women introduced themselves. Mary Stanton seemed the youngest of them, and Caroline saw that she'd been correct to dress casually. They all said the right things, but Caroline couldn't help but think that some of them were more sincere than others. She didn't like the way their eyes held her gaze for only a moment before looking the rest of her over. *Paranoia,* she reminded herself; *something I must be vigilant for.* After a few minutes, everyone took their seats.

"We're very happy to welcome Mr. and Mrs. Tierney to our meeting today," Lisbeth said. "Mr. Tierney's grandmother was Alice Lowell," she said.

The woman who sat between Lisbeth Goode and Mary Stanton at the front table nodded at that. She was a wisp of a thing, and Caroline couldn't imagine her being a day younger than ninety. In a paper-thin voice, she'd introduced herself as Mrs. White. Caroline thought she might be the only one in the room old enough to have known Ben's grandmother personally.

"It's a rare thing to get fresh blood in this village, and rarer still for it to be blood of a familiar brand. Now, let's begin with a reading from Corinthians."

Lisbeth moved to the lectern while everyone else pulled out their Bibles. Caroline surreptitiously glanced at Ben. She hadn't mentally prepared herself for a religious component. Lisbeth began to read.

"Moreover, brethren, I declare unto you the gospel which I preached unto you, which also ye have received, and wherein ye stand; By which also ye are saved, if ye keep in memory what I preached unto you, unless ye have believed in vain—"

Caroline didn't consider herself a religious person, but neither was she irreverent. It just seemed to her the kind of thing politely kept in private.

Yet there was something soothing about hearing biblical passages read aloud. It reminded her of the poetry that Ben used to read to her years ago. Depending on the mood or season, he'd recite some Eliot or Frost or Keats. His voice would sound fresh and robust as he tried to get the inflections just right. But mostly it was the words themselves: worn and old, and stronger for it.

"Now, then, Mary, you brought the diary?" Lisbeth asked once she'd finished.

"I did," Mary Stanton said. She rose to take Lisbeth's place at the lectern.

"Most of you have heard this before," Mary said. "But this seemed like a good first step for the Tierneys to take with us. This is the diary of my Bill's ancestor, Margaret Stanton, who was only twenty during the Winter Siege." After clearing her throat, she began to read.

Caroline had never heard of the Winter Siege, and she wondered if this was one of the things Ben had been trying to tell her about on the drive down. The papers Mary read from were yellowed and loose. Caroline could hear them crackle as she turned the pages.

The diary chronicled a Native American attack on the village of Swannhaven during the Revolutionary War. The villagers who were able to flee escaped to the Crofts, of all places. There, they weathered a treacherous winter during which they were plagued with starvation and other misfortunes.

The material was chilling; each page brought a new horror for the people starving between the mountains. Margaret Stanton wrote with an unadorned prose that captured the terror of that season well. There were moments when the story was hard to follow, as if some pages of the journal had been lost. But none of that affected the tension of the narrative. Still, the story had to have a happy ending, Caroline thought. If their descendants still lived, then someone must have made it off the Drop. But in the part of the diary that was read, no such resolution was reached. The passage ended with a haunting description of the villagers huddled by a fire in the Crofts, listening to the screams of the forest caught in a winter gale.

"That always catches me short," Lisbeth said a few moments into the silence that followed. "What did you think, Ben?" she asked.

"It's quite a story," Ben said. "Very affecting to hear it from a firsthand source. Thank you for sharing that," he told Mary.

Caroline nodded in agreement and turned to Ben. He always seemed to know just what people wanted to hear, and his face matched his words: brows slightly furrowed in thought, lips slightly curved in gratitude. But these women didn't know his eyes, the way Caroline did. In his eyes she could see that he wasn't here at all. In his eyes she could see his gears whirring.

"Don't forget that it's your story, too," Lisbeth said. "That's why we three are sitting up here." She pointed to Mary and Mrs. White. "We're all descended from the Winter Families, just like you."

"I only married into one," Mary Stanton said. She raised her shoulders in humility.

"Well, maybe next time you should save *me* a seat up there," Caroline said.

The ladies, both those seated at the table and the ones in the pews, turned to look at her. It had been a joke, but she hadn't quite gotten the tone right.

"We're so grateful to be invited to this. I absolutely would love to come again," Ben said. He put a hand on Caroline's leg. "And I can see that the Crofts is a really important part of your history. We're in the middle of fixing her up, but as soon as she's in better shape we'd be honored to have you all up there."

"Might take you up on that," a woman seated in front of them said. She shifted her gaze back to Caroline before facing forward again.

"Yes, we're all excited to see the Crofts back to being a home," Lisbeth said. "And who better to—oh, now who's this?" she asked.

Everyone turned, but this time it was not to stare at Caroline. When she looked, she saw Charlie standing in the church's doorway.

"Can this be Charlie?" Lisbeth asked. Ben waved for him to come forward. "This is the Tierneys' eldest son," she said.

Charlie made his way toward their pew. He looked wary under the gaze of those eyes. As he got closer, the women stood to greet him. They patted his head and put their hands on his cheeks. The ladies had cooed over Bub, but Charlie had them transfixed. He was a handsome boy, with that combination of dark hair and light eyes that some people find so arresting, but Caroline had never before seen people so taken with him.

After a few minutes of this, Charlie began to look uncomfortable. Ben was too occupied talking with Lisbeth to notice. Caroline put a hand on his shoulder.

"I think it's time for Bub's nap," Caroline told Ben. She clutched the boy through his BabyBjörn as if this were the only thing that prevented him from crying.

"He does look spent," Ben said. He turned back to Lisbeth. "We should get going, but thank you again for inviting us. When's the next meeting?"

As Ben got his answer, someone tugged on Caroline's shirt from behind. She turned around to see Mrs. White beaming up at her with her wizened face.

"My dear, you are so beautiful, and so are your sons," she said, her voice as brittle as dried leaves.

"Oh, thank you," Caroline said. The first genuine smile of the day.

"The Crofts used to have the most beautiful gardens. Mine's not so grand, but many of my plantings trace their ancestry back to the originals from the Swanns' gardens."

"Mrs. White is being modest," Mary Stanton chimed in. "Her herb garden is the finest in the county. You ever have a problem, she can sort out anything from headaches to sleeplessness with her teas and tinctures."

"Really, how interesting," Caroline said. She'd planned to plant an herb garden at the Crofts so that the kitchen could use the freshest seasonings. Restoring the gardens with descendants from the original plantings would contribute a nice sense of authenticity and make good copy on the website and brochures. "I'd love to see it sometime."

"And I would love to show it to you," Mrs. White said. Smile still on her face, she turned to walk haltingly from the church.

At Caroline's side, Charlie was tugging on her hand. Bub lolled against her chest. She turned to Ben, who was still talking with Lisbeth. Whatever flutter of happiness Caroline had allowed herself to feel from the pleasant exchange with Mrs. White died at sight of him. Her husband's eyes sparkled, and his teeth gleamed through an easy smile. The indictment lay in the fact that it had been months since she'd seen his real smile. The one he used with her was fragile, the look in his eyes laced with fear and weariness. To see him use that smile so freely with strangers while withholding it from her—it made her feel utterly sunk.

"Ben, would you unlock the car?" she called over her shoulder. She tried to pitch her voice in a way that made it sound casual. She tried not to blink for fear that the tears that had suddenly sprung to her eyes would overflow. Used to be that years passed without her shedding tears, but they now turned in a daily performance. No wonder Ben's eyes didn't light up at the sight of her. She had changed on him as much as he had changed on her. Perhaps even more so.

"It was good to meet you, Caroline," Lisbeth called after her.

Caroline had already fastened Bub into his car seat by the time Ben caught up to them. She waved a fly away from her face. When she closed the door, she saw a swarm of them undulating over a dead raccoon, whose flattened body lay on the far the side of the road.

"That was interesting, wasn't it?" Ben asked her. "It's nice that people are starting to warm up to us."

"I guess so."

He smiled at her with a terrible facsimile of his real smile, but his eyes had that faraway look that told her that her husband was somewhere else entirely, thinking of things that had nothing to do with her.

They pulled out of the parking lot, and the dead raccoon was on Caroline's side of the car. The flies surged away from the body as the car drew near, but Caroline knew they'd be back.

12

The meeting of the Preservation Society had fired Ben's creative furnace. Revolution and loss. Wealth and suffering. Tragedy and love. Perseverance. In Swannhaven he'd found something he hadn't even known he was looking for.

He'd been imagining the conversation with his agent, telling her that the book he'd been writing wasn't working. He had 37,150 words, according to the counter at the bottom of the page. Months of work, months of his life, and it was dead on the screen. Somehow both meandering and inert.

Ben should have felt sick about this, but he didn't. He had a mug of fresh tea, a lively playlist humming in his ear, and a blank document on the screen in front of him. He'd also moved out of the kitchen and up to the attic. It was a vast, unfinished space comprised of many rooms. Ben had chosen a nook with a pair of broad windows set into the steeply pitched roof. The windows faced east and kept the room full of sunlight through the morning. A fresh start for a new book.

He rapped his fingertips lightly against the keys for a few moments before typing.

In God's country, the Drop seemed like heaven itself.

He read it aloud, testing it. Seeing what it conjured in him. The old Bible he'd found in the basement was one piece of the Crofts's hidden life that he'd already discovered, but the people who'd walked these halls over the centuries were the real prize. He thought again about those two spinster sisters who had died here, the last descendants of the Swann family, which had lived here from the beginning.

A family like that must have secrets to spare.

Ben had hoped to tell his agent something that would take the sting from the news about him starting over, and as he chewed on it he thought this new idea could be that good thing. A semi-famous writer who moves upstate and becomes so enchanted with his historic house that he sets his next novel there: That was a seductive hook. Ben understood the importance of such things. While his second book had been a hit, his first one had disappeared without a trace. With newspapers and magazines folding and book-review sections being cut, securing any measure of media attention for a work of fiction was a careful alchemy of black magic and divine luck. An angle like this gave the marketing and publicity teams something to hitch themselves to.

This was also something Caroline should be happy about. He doubted a bestselling author had ever set a novel at the bed-and-breakfasts in Exton or any of the other surrounding towns. This book would give their inn something that none of the others had.

Of course, Ben knew that good books were born of more than just a compelling setting and a hook. He needed his characters to be tested under stress. He needed danger and suspicion and horror and revelation, because these were the kinds of books that he wrote. But he had the feeling that a little research would be all the kindling he'd need to set the story ablaze.

He looked back at the sentence he had written.

In God's country, the Drop seemed like heaven itself.

The cursor blinked at him, and he began to type.

And for a time, it was.

13

Ben thought restoring the home of those who'd preceded him at the Crofts might help him understand the satisfactions and trials of their lives. He also hoped that making some tangible progress on the house would improve Caroline's mood. She'd been depressed since the meeting of the Preservation Society, eating little and sleeping less. It was not so deep as many of the episodes he'd seen her fall into, but he didn't like the boys to see her this way. He assumed it had been set off by the stress of meeting so many new people at once, but he couldn't be sure. Now Father Caleb's impending visit seemed to have her on edge.

He'd promised to keep the priest to the first floor, veranda, and grounds. This was why he'd spent the last two afternoons on his tractor, working to make the fields closest to the Crofts more presentable.

The rains had fed wildflowers along the edge of the forest, and the scent of the freshly mowed grass was intoxicating in the warmth of the day. It took Ben back to the summer afternoons of his teen years, to that feeling of anticipation that swelled in his chest as soon as he and his brother hit the sidewalk outside their house. Life back then had been far from perfect, but at least it had been uncomplicated.

Around he went in minutely smaller squares. He imagined the track he left on the ground looking like the minotaur's labyrinth from the air. By the time he finished, the sun was directly overhead, expunging the fields of shadow. Since leaving the city, he'd begun to notice such things.

He was trimming the edges of the gravel path when a shudder of movement drew his attention south to the tree line. A murder of crows rose toward the sky. As they flew for the valley, they darted and swarmed like smoke caught in the wind.

On impulse, Ben rerouted the tractor for the place where they'd taken flight. He was close to where he'd buried the dripping pieces of the deer two weeks ago, and his curiosity was piqued. It had been the shallowest of graves, and he wouldn't be surprised if the birds had been undeterred by the scrim of soil he'd shoveled over the remains.

A part of Ben hoped that scavengers had indeed uncovered what was left of the poor creature. He'd never seen an animal torn apart like that, and he was curious what it might look like after some time in the wild. It was sure to be terrible: rotting intestines, maggot-infested viscera, bones gnawed to the marrow. But for the kinds of books Ben wrote, every experience—especially a horrible one—was another card in his deck. Ben had to see it.

He pulled the tractor alongside the ruined outbuilding. As he stepped from the vehicle, he could already see a depression in the ground ahead where the soil had once been mounded. When he got to the hole, he saw it was empty.

Gone were the organs and bones; all that remained was sludge that had mixed with dirt and writhed with maggots. When Ben leaned in to take a closer look, the reek of it sent him back on his heels. It was the kind of stench that was less a smell than a feeling: a punch to the solar plexus.

As he backed away from the hole, Ben stepped on something that felt like gravel under his feet. It looked like stone, too, but when he picked up a larger chunk he realized that it was shattered bone. There were other pieces, closer to the trees.

A sound sliced through the quiet of the forest. Something like a scream, though there was nothing human about it. Ben peered into the dark maw of trees. A hawk, he thought.

He turned his attention back to the ground and began to notice tracks all over the wet earth. They didn't look much different from Hudson's, which made him guess coyotes. Coyotes wouldn't have had any more trouble sniffing out the dead deer than they would have had digging it up. They would have eaten the deer's organs, and Ben could also imagine them chewing up its bones. This explanation satisfied him.

Then that scream from the forest again.

There was something plaintive about it that tore at Ben. And as with the temptation of the deer's shallow grave, Ben couldn't help himself. He stepped into the trees.

The forest could have been a world away from the wide fields of the Drop. It lay in perpetual dusk, and the temperature was ten degrees cooler. Sounds were different, too: Some were soaked up, while others were given new prominence. Though the woods were so choked with trees and vegetation that Ben couldn't see more than a few yards ahead, they gave the impression of endlessness.

Moss was slick on the ground, while fungus studded the roots and trunks of trees. The air was heavy with the tang of vegetative rot.

Each time Ben ventured into these woods, he was reminded how different this place was from anything he was used to. It was the palpable age of the trees as much as their scale. Some of these oaks had been old back when the Swanns first set eyes on this valley. The creatures here were also a mystery. Ben knew their names and had seen their pictures in books, but it was hard for him to imagine what they did here in the dark of the forest, unimpeded by man.

The scream had a penetrating quality that made distance and origin difficult to pinpoint, but it was definitely getting louder. And there was a new sound: a rapping like branches caught in the wind.

The shrieks themselves sounded now like the panicked lowing of a cow, though that was unlikely. The closer Ben got, the less sure he was that it was a scream at all. The tapping sound was strange, too. It seemed to move in the dark.

"Hello?" Ben called into the trees. When he saw a clearing ahead, he found himself hurrying for it. There was something disturbing about the trees and the way anything might be hiding behind them. When Ben reached the clearing, he was startled to see a small gray face staring back at him.

It was the statue of an angel. She had wings spread as if about to take flight, the muscles of her calves tensed in preparation. Her head and shoulders were stained from the accumulated wear of bird and tree droppings. Thin scales of lichens stretched through the striations of her plumage.

Behind the angel stood a low stone wall with a single bare window. A chapel, Ben thought, or the ruins of one. He remembered seeing a cross etched onto one of the maps he'd found in the cellar. There wasn't much left of the little structure. The clearing was a mess of rubble and the detritus of the plants that covered it.

The tapping from the woods was insistent again, and Ben instinctively moved away from the trees. He could not imagine what made the sound, but he was sure it was following him.

He jogged to the far end of the ruin. He couldn't remember at what point he'd become afraid, but now his pulse drummed in his temples and his breath caught in his throat. There was a field southeast of here, where the cemetery was, but he would have to go through the trees in order to get away from them. He was trying to orient himself when he came face-to-face with a large plaque with an engraving of a creature.

The plaque was propped against the chapel's one remaining standing wall. The creature was a ferocious thing, formed in Gothic style. Ben could have fit his head in its mouth. It had sharp teeth and long nails, but except for the mouth and an oddly distended stomach, the figure looked almost human.

Any other time, Ben might have admired it. Now he hesitated to turn his back to it. Then the rapping sounded loudly from directly behind him.

"Hello?" he called into the trees. Someone was playing games with him. "Hello?" he shouted again. "Who's there?"

"There you are, Benj!"

Ben backpedaled and tripped over a root. He landed hard, knocking his elbow against the iron roots of a basswood.

His brother stepped out from the trees.

"Jesus Christ, Ted!"

"Jeez, so jumpy," Ted said as he picked his way toward him. In his Nantucket reds and Ray-Bans, he looked dressed for the beach. "I was trying to surprise you, but I was going more for *Surprise, I'm here!* than *Surprise, cardiac event!*" He helped Ben to his feet.

"Did you hear those sounds?" Ben asked. He worked hard to keep the fear from his voice.

"Yeah, that loud squeaking or whatever? What *was* that?" Ted stretched and ran his hand through his tousled hair.

"There was this tapping sound, too. Like someone hitting a tree with a stick." Ben scoured the tree line, but the tapping had stopped.

"It's a forest, man. Probably the wind. Or maybe woodpeckers? I don't know." Ted turned to the engraving of the monstrous creature propped against the wall. "Well, that's an ugly fellow."

"First the sound was over here." Ben pointed. "Then it was over there."

The scream sounded again, and this time it was directly above them.

The top of a spindly sugar maple had broken from its trunk and swayed by a few taut sinews. As it rocked in the wind, it filled the air with a piercing cry.

Ben felt stupid, but he also felt relieved.

Ted looked him over carefully. "You're not losing it, too, are you, Benj?"

"What are you even doing here?" Ben asked. He brushed leaves from his jeans.

"I saw you pull off the road in that tractor thingy and thought I'd follow." Ted frowned at him. "I feel like you're not happy to see me." He contrived an expression somewhere between a pout and a frown.

"You just surprised me," Ben said.

"Are you sure? I can find a hotel to stay at if you want. Or a motel. Whatever they have in a place like this."

"Now you're being ridiculous."

Ted looked at him for a moment, then grinned. "Come on, big brother." He stretched his arms toward Ben and beckoned with his fingers. "Bring it in, bring it in."

Ben let himself be hugged.

"It's good to see you, Benj," Ted muttered into his neck.

"You, too," Ben said, disengaging himself. "But you should have called. Or e-mailed, or texted—there are so many ways to not completely blindside people."

As they made their way out of the woods, Ben realized that he hadn't trekked as deep into forest as he'd thought. He wished his brother hadn't seen him so panicked. The trees and sounds must have disoriented him, and his imagination had done the rest.

Ted had pulled his silver bullet of a sports car off the road just behind where Ben had parked the tractor. The car's driver-side door was left open, its single gull wing gesturing to the sky.

"What is this thing?" Ben tapped the hood of the roadster.

"It's a McLaren—you've never seen one? What do they have up here? Pontiacs? Toyotas? That kind of thing?"

"It's yours?"

"God, no. A friend loaned it to me. But, hey, your ride's nice, too." He jutted his head in the direction of the tractor. "Gotta say that that's one long and tedious drive. But this is where our people are from, huh?" Ted turned to take in the view of the valley.

"Some of them."

They looked at the scattered buildings of Swannhaven, dilapi-dated even at this distance. "It's weird, isn't it?" Ted asked.

"You have no idea. Can your spaceship take us up to the house?"

Ben opened the passenger-side door and chuckled as it separated from the car's body and pivoted into the air.

"This is an absurd vehicle."

"You think *this* is absurd?" Ted asked. He swung himself into the car, shut the door, and peered up at the sprawling house between the mountains. "Oh, Benj." He shook his head. "What have you gotten yourself into?"

Ted watched Bub roll peas across the rim of his high chair and then drop them onto the floor.

"Young Robert likes his greens."

"Likes playing with them," Ben said.

"You think Caroline will be in bed long?" Ted asked. "Should we wait for her before we go to Grams's?" Ostensibly, Ted had come up here to visit their grandmother's run-down farmhouse.

"If she needs to rest, we should let her," Ben replied. Caroline had said hello to Ted but left soon after with a headache. Charlie had also made a brief appearance, but he'd already fled for the for-est. Ben had seen the red soil of the lakeshore on his bare feet, but he knew the boy could be anywhere.

"Is she still spending a lot of time in bed?"

"How about a tour before we head to the farmhouse," Ben said. "What do you want to see?"

"It is sort of amazing how much there is to choose from, isn't it? Oh, and before I forget, I have a box of books in the car for you to sign. Monica's book club is reading—did you ever meet Monica? I think you'd like her. Anyway, her book club is reading one of yours next month, so I thought she'd get a kick out of giving the girls signed copies. Never hurts to have an in with the friends, you know?"

"Which one are they reading?"

"They're all in the car." He hopped off the counter. "You think Charlie wants to go on the tour with us?"

"I've only published two."

"Come on, man, you know I can barely keep up with my blogs."

Ben doubted this was true. In their youth, Ted had been just as avid a reader as Ben—any chance to visit a world beyond their own. He tossed a hand towel at Ted, aiming for his head. "All right, I'm going to give you the abbreviated version, because we can only see Grams's place in the light." He pulled Bub out of his high chair and stepped into the hallway.

"This place looks like a museum," Ted said as he walked into the first room, one of the largest on this floor. Six windows probed its fourteen-foot ceiling, which was studded with medallion moldings, remnants of a past illuminated by a series of decadent chandeliers.

"None of the rooms on this floor are finished, except for the kitchen and a bathroom. We're thinking of making this a lounge. Maybe set up a bar over here with a few couches so people can enjoy cocktails before dinner."

"You have enough space for it."

The next room was smaller but had an opulent marble fireplace that came up to Ben's shoulders.

"We think this would make a great library," he said. "We've commissioned someone to build shelves into the wall. Maybe have them add a few of those sliding ladders so people can reach the books on the top shelves."

"You always wanted one of those," Ted said.

Ben stooped to peer into the fireplace's cold hearth, then ran a finger along the blackened stone. "A fire roaring on a winter's day. You're wearing thick socks, your feet up on an overstuffed ottoman. Little glass of port on the side table. Reading a book you've been meaning to read for a while, and wishing you hadn't waited so long. Can you see it?"

Ted nodded. "Music playing—fun but reflective. Something with the feel of a single but loose enough to be background noise at the right volume."

"Can you see it?" Ben repeated.

"I see it," Ted said, smiling at Ben.

They'd played the game in ten thousand variations when they were young. After school and waiting for their mother to go to work, they'd distract each other with the places they'd rather be. Their hands would be under their heads as they lay on their twin beds in the small room they shared. Once she was gone, the house would be theirs again, but until then they had any island or castle they could conjure. One of them would come up with a place of peace or fun or riches or just a place of their own, and the other would add to it until they could see it and almost believe they were there.

A version of the same game could be said to have led Ben and Caroline to the Crofts in the first place. *A fresh start in a new home. A place where Charlie can be himself and be safe. A place where the money we've saved can be stretched to last. A place where Caroline can heal herself with busyness and reap the satisfaction of work completed with her own two hands. Where Ben can spend his energy on his family and his books and not on the futile task of pretending that everything is okay. Can you see it?*

"Bub won't need the imaginations we had, will he?" Ted asked.

"I hope not." Ben smelled the baby's hair and savored the feel of it against his cheeks.

They briefly looked into the other rooms on the first floor, with Ben telling Ted what each would ultimately become. A large room with a set of French doors that opened onto the veranda would become the dining room, and a smaller room down the hall could become the professional kitchen. Ben envisioned one room for billiards tables and another as a card room.

Though the renovations to the second floor were closer to being completed, they breezed through the guest rooms and made right for the section of the house that they occupied. They stopped in front of the room Ben thought of as the Claret Room.

"Figured we'd put you in here," Ben said. It was one of the smaller rooms on the second floor, but it had a fireplace and enough room to comfortably place a king-size bed, a table, and chairs. Two windows faced east toward the verdant expanse of the Drop and the forest at the foot of the mountains. The red paint looked deep and rich framed against the glistening floor and stark white of the ornate molding. "I'm sorry it's not furnished, but we'll set you up with an air mattress."

"This is top-notch, Benj," Ted said. He stepped into the bathroom and looked over the wrought-iron fixtures and the steam shower. "This all looks new. Don't tell me that you—"

"I wish I could take credit, but we hired guys to add bathrooms to all the rooms that needed them."

"That's a relief. I was about to become extremely impressed."

"Can't have that, can we, Bub?" Ben said, though he was grateful for the compliment. Bub yawned but had the good manners to cover his mouth with a pair of little fists. "This one's flagging. Let's put him in for a nap."

Bub's room was just across the hall from Ben and Caroline's. It was an airy room painted a springtime yellow.

"Dream good dreams, buddy." Ben placed Bub carefully into his crib and clipped the baby monitor to his belt. He ushered Ted into the hall and closed the door behind him.

"Is this Charlie's room?" Ted was peering into the room next to Bub's. A single wall was painted blue, and a fish tank hummed against it. The floor was littered with the remains of an elaborate block structure.

"It's sort of a death trap. We make him clean it regularly, but it never takes."

Ted walked along the perimeter of the room and examined a jar on the floor. "He likes his creatures, doesn't he?" He held it up to the light from the windows and saw that it was filled with faintly green water and bubbles of small gelatinous eggs. "How's Charlie doing, Ben?"

"Really well. He loves the forest. Moving up here's been good for him," Ben said. He rapped on one wall that was built entirely of wood and studded with closet doors, display cases, drawers, and cupboards. "This room and Bub's were originally one enormous room," he said. "It must have been used as a parlor or a sitting room, because it was way too big for a bedroom. But we wanted the boys close to us, so we had the contractors add a wall of cabinetry here. Perfect for storing toys—in theory, at least. You'll like this." He stooped to open one of the larger cupboards, crawled into the compartment, and closed the door behind him.

After waiting for a few moments, Ted opened the door and peered into the empty compartment.

"What the—"

"Some of the cupboards open into both rooms," Ben said, surprising Ted from the door to the hallway.

Ted reached into the cupboard and tapped open the door on the other side.

"That's pretty cool. They'll have fun with this when Bub's older."

When they left Bub's room, Ben sent Ted downstairs while he checked on Caroline. The curtains in their room had been drawn, leaving the room dark and the air close. When he whispered Caroline's name, she didn't respond, though this didn't necessarily mean she was asleep. He left the baby monitor on her side table and shut the door gently behind him when he left. He hoped she'd be out of bed by the time they returned: Even under the best circumstances, it was going to be hard to show Ted that he had everything under control.

Ted said that he wanted to see the lake before heading over to the farmhouse. They walked upslope from the Crofts until the land leveled out and they could see the wild fields stretch across the plateau to the forest and the mountains beyond them. It was a relief to leave the house. "The locals call this the Drop," Ben told Ted. "The lawyer who showed us the place said that the fields used to go right up to the mountains, but the forests have reclaimed a lot of that territory."

"How much of this land do you own, Benj?"

"All of it up to the mountains." He pointed and spread his arm across the landscape. "The mountains are part of a state preserve. Then we own everything downslope until just before the county road. About a thousand acres is what they tell me," Ben said.

Ted shook his head.

"We got a good deal on the place, though. It's not as extravagant as it sounds."

"So you keep telling me."

"We can take this path to the lake." Ben indicated a trail between two clusters of hardwoods that skirted the edge of the south woods. "Caroline has an idea that we could eventually grow all our own food up here."

"That's a lot for her to take on, isn't it?"

"That's probably a couple years away. But it's something that'll appeal to our guests, too," Ben said. "You know, all organic, locally grown food. They can actually look around at the crops or maybe take classes on starting their own gardens. People love stuff like that these days, don't they?"

"What's that?" Ted had stopped walking and was shading his hand against the glare from the afternoon sun. Ben followed his gaze about a quarter mile to a tall and thin figure in white just inside the tree line on the far side of the lake. "What's he doing?"

Ben realized that he was staring at his own son, standing on the high stump of a broken tree. He stood in a patch of sunlight, and its glare off the boy's white T-shirt and the fact that he stood at the top of a four-foot pedestal of dead wood gave Charlie the illusion of height and ethereality.

"Just playing," Ben said. "You know how kids are." But he had no idea what Charlie was doing. His son faced the dark forest, utterly still, as if waiting for something.

"Is it safe for him to be there?"

"Why wouldn't it be?" Ben asked. They were far from the house, but Ben could still see the tops of the Crofts's towers. Technically, this was still within the perimeter he'd confined Charlie to. "We make him carry a whistle in case he runs into any trouble."

"Does he spend a lot of time out here on his own?"

"School starts in September."

"Right, right." Ted nodded and didn't say anything else, but Ben still heard the things his brother left unasked. Charlie was too quiet for an eight-year-old. Too serious. They'd had him tested in the city, and while it seemed that every other kid they knew had an ADHD diagnosis or was somewhere on the autism spectrum, Charlie was never labeled as anything more than "unusually interior." He'd even seemed oddly unmarked by the long night he'd been locked in the furnace room.

But at least he was interested in something up here. Spending all day in the forest had to be better than sitting alone in his room, as he had in the city.

Ben cast a last glance at Charlie, the white of his shirt just visible through the trees. *So still,* Ben thought to himself. He wondered how his son had ever learned to be so still.

November 24, 1777

Dearest Kathy,

 The bitterest of cold weather has fallen upon us. Game is nowhere to be found, as the conditions are too severe for both hunter and prey. William White has lost two fingers, and Matthew Armfield may lose an ear after yesterday's venture to the northern fields in search of deer.

 The last of the horses has been slain and its meat eaten. Now we must make do with griddle cakes and porridge made from last season's grain, but our stores have dwindled terribly.

 George and Bennett Townsend set out for the ruins of Swannhaven at first light in search of supplies that the Iroquois might have overlooked. Father thought them fools, but it is true that, save for some strange sounds from the forest, we have not seen the Indians since their attack. Nevertheless, George and Bennett left hours ago and there has been no sign of them. The sun has fallen behind the mountains, and we fear they shall not return to us.

 For our family, we have fared better than many. Emmett is sick, and you know how difficult the cold is for him. James has lost some weight, as we all have, but I now see beneath his childhood face the handsome man he will become. And our Jack is the bravest of the men, and no Iroquois hatchet can match the acuity of his wit. He keeps the men strong and can coax a smile from even Goody Smythe.

But as much as Jack keeps our spirits high, and Father's sermons keep our resolve strong, we worry about the winter, and we worry about the war. The fall of the fort at Ticonderoga still weighs upon us, and before the snows we learned the ill news that the British army that took New York has now seized Philadelphia from General Washington. Does the general still live? The men whisper of old rumors that more of the king's armies march on us from Quebec. I wonder if Boston has fallen, as well. I fear for you, sister.

The only solace is that it is difficult to think beyond the hunger that gnaws at us. Worries of the war pale beside the imperatives of our empty stomachs. The world has never seemed more far away. Pray for us, dear sister, as I shall pray for you.

Your Bess

14

"It's weird that she held on to this place for all those years, isn't it?" Ted asked. He'd insisted on taking the McLaren, and he drove too fast for the country roads. Every turn was executed too suddenly for the loose surface. "God knows there were times when she could have used the cash."

"We've had the place on the market for months without a nibble. Grams didn't want us to do anything with the farm but sell it, but she probably knew it wasn't worth anything. Turn left up here."

Ted took the curve and Ben winced at the cloud of dust and gravel he saw billowing in his passenger-side mirror.

"Remember the funny way she would talk?" Ted said. "All those old expressions? 'Keep up the light, Benjamin. Keep up the light, Teddy.' I kind of remember her telling us stories about a farm. The way the crops needed to rotate, how the hens clustered together in their coops, how cows would need to be marched back to the barn on a frosty night. How hard the winters were. Despite everything, I always assumed that she'd give everything to Mom, you know?"

"Whatever Mom got was a lot more than she deserved," Ben said.

By long-established habit, Ben had sheltered his brother from the details of his most recent conversation with their mother. All Ben had told Ted was that she'd finally signed the lawyer's documents and that Grams's estate was officially settled. "Here we are, on the right."

"Where?" Ted slid his Ray-Bans onto his forehead.

"Slow down. See the post?"

Ted pulled off the road just short of a crumbling stone gatepost. The ghost of a gravel path extended beyond it, barely discernible under the cover of wild grass. The low-slung remnants of a house sat a few hundred yards from the road. "So that's it, huh?" Ted asked. He turned the McLaren up the drive and pressed it forward in a crawl. The grass came up to the windows, and Ted arched in his seat, trying to see what he was driving over.

"I didn't know this car could move so slowly."

"I don't think the owner expected me to take it on safari. Can we walk from here? I don't even know if I'm still on the gravel."

Hudson was the first one out of the car. He dove headlong into the grass, sending a trio of chickadees chattering into the sky.

Ben waited while Ted checked his hair in the mirror, as if they'd arrived at a gallery opening instead of a derelict ruin. When he was ready, they lifted themselves from the car and looked at their grandmother's house. It was a small two-story stone saltbox with a single chimney and only a gesture of a roof. Its windows were narrow maws, their glass long gone. Its door lay on its side by the front steps.

The interior was cool and smelled vaguely of rot. The timbers supporting the second floor had collapsed it into the first. Patches of shingles from the roof were spread across the floor between thatches of ferns and other plants. Beams skewered what must have been the house's little sitting room, some of them embedded in what remained of the wood-plank floor.

"It's smaller than I thought it would be," Ted said, picking his way through the debris. He climbed over a pile of fallen masonry to the kitchen area. "Looks like they left a lot behind." He pointed to a brown wedge that was crushed under a timber beam. A bed of rusted springs was visible through the gauze of rotted fabric.

A couch, Ben thought.

The last time he'd been here, Ben had spent only a minute inside. Now that he took the time to look, he saw corroded pots and pans in the space where the kitchen had been. Fragments of shattered dishes covered one end of the floor. Pieces of broken chairs lay on the ground, alongside the empty husks of ruined oil lamps.

"Why would they leave all this here?" Ted asked.

"I don't know," Ben said. It seemed odd, now that he thought about it, that a family with so little would leave behind so much. For a moment the ruined farmhouse felt eerily like the Crofts: a place where possessions were left abandoned by suddenly absent owners.

"Why'd they move away from here, anyway?"

But Ben hardly knew anything about his grandmother's young life. His mom had said something over the phone about "demons in the wood and devils at the door," but she'd only been trying to ensnare him in conversation.

"Did you get down to the cellar the last time you were here?" Ted asked.

"I didn't see a way down other than jumping through the hole in the floor."

"Here's something, I think," Ted said. He pointed to a small alcove in the wall that was obstructed by tree branches and fallen timbers from the ceiling or roof.

Ted tried to maneuver a beam out of the way, and Ben grabbed its other side to help him.

"It's light," Ted said.

"It's rotted," Ben said. "Don't look down."

Ted looked down and dropped the beam onto the ground, where it landed in a cloud of powdered wood. He'd disturbed a nest of termites, and they welled out of the hollowed-out timber. Ted brushed his hands off on his pressed pants. "You enjoyed that, didn't you, Benj? I'm not exactly dressed for manual labor."

"Are you ever?"

Ted peered into the cavity in the wall. "The steps look like they're stone, so they should be safe. Might be something interesting down here." He squeezed between a broken beam and a sapling that had taken root in the floor.

The steps were dark and slippery, and Ben kept a hand against the wall for balance. The cellar was smaller than he'd thought it would be. The ceiling had caved in on the far side of the room. Decades' worth of rotting leaves and other vegetation along with this season's fresh additions made the floor feel soft underfoot.

Ted was right in guessing that they'd find something down here. There was enough clutter around the room for it to remind Ben of his own basement. The difference was that he could tell that this house's former inhabitants had kept the space orderly. Wooden milk crates were stacked along the walls, holding everything from folded clothing to sewing materials to empty mason jars. *So much left behind,* Ben thought. Every object that remained was an unanswered question.

"Knew there'd be something," Ted said. He showed Ben a wooden fire engine, its once-red paint faded to pink. "Wheels still work." Ted spun them around the screws they were fastened to. "You want it for the boys?"

"Sure." Ben doubted Charlie would be interested in the home-made plaything, but Ted's enthusiasm surprised him and he didn't want to quash it.

"I can't believe how little we know about these people," Ted said. "Do you ever wonder about them? Were they happy? Did their dreams come true?" He looked around the room as if trying to pull clues.

"Not if their dreams included living in a house with a roof."

"Who's going to remember them if not us, Ben?" Ted asked. "Don't you care?"

"I guess," Ben said. These people were gone, but their blood pulsed through his body with every beat of his heart. Compared to that, this place and these things were inert and meaningless.

"Who's going to remember us when we're gone?"

"Christ, Ted," Ben said. He should have known his brother's sudden sensitivity had a heart of narcissism. "Little young for a midlife crisis."

"What I mean is—family—we're supposed to be there for each other, right?"

"Sure."

"I know I can depend on you, Benj," Ted said.

Ben walked to another set of shelves, feigning interest in the contents of a mason jar.

"And you can count on me. For anything."

"Okay, Ted," Ben said. "Good to know."

"But I'm serious," Ted said.

Ben turned to his brother and saw the earnestness on his face.

"No matter what it is," Ted said. "I'm here to help."

"I get it," Ben said. He tried to keep the annoyance out of his voice. "I do."

"Okay," Ted said after a few long moments. He resumed looking through the shelf he was in front of. "This must have been hers, don't you think?" He handed Ben a faceless rag doll clothed in a yellow dress.

"Must have been," Ben said, though it could have been anyone's. He was just glad for a change in subject.

"Anything over there?" Ted asked.

"Old newspapers, some empty jars, old clothing, blankets and linens, that kind of thing." The closeness of the damp space was beginning to remind Ben of a mausoleum. He could envision skulls in the shadows of the wall and decaying bodies underfoot.

Ted pulled a folded bundle from a crate and shook it open, sending a cloud of dust into the air.

"Quilts," Ted said. The one he'd unfolded was composed of faded triangles of assorted fabrics. "Maybe her mother sewed this. God, I don't even know her mother's name."

Ben walked over and shook another quilt free of dust. "Here's your answer," he said after he looked at what he'd found.

Ted held the quilt taut and used the flashlight app from his phone to better see it. The quilt was a yellowing white except for light-blue patches that had been inscribed with names. "Her mother's name was Emily," he said. He was looking at the lowest branches of a family tree. "Grams was born in 1924. And she had a brother, did you know that? Owen, born 1928. This goes back to 1721. Jonas Lowell and Clara."

"They both died in 1777." Ben was still holding the quilt in front of him so Ted could see it. "Do we have any cousins?"

"Not as far as I can tell," Ted said.

Even from his poor vantage point, Ben could see that the Lowell family tree was an unusually narrow one.

"Not Lowells, anyway, assuming Grams's brother didn't have any kids."

The sun had fallen behind a bank of clouds or the house's crumbling walls, leaving the cellar in near darkness.

"You want to take this topside?" Ben asked him. "If you want to see the rest of the property, we should do it before the sun goes down."

They felt their way up the narrow steps to the first floor and climbed out of the ruin. Ben was relieved to be in the fresh air of the living world. The sun was stretching for the horizon, the light beginning to ripen.

Ben called for Hudson, and the beagle bounded out of the grass. He was covered in flaxen briars and dandelion seeds that he shook off in a fit of movement, sending his broad ears slapping against his head. He trotted to Ben, brushing himself against Ben's jeans. Ben gave him a vigorous rub and noticed how lean and muscular the beagle had become.

"Anything to see in particular?" Ted asked him.

"There's an old barn, but it's not much more than a pile of kindling. I could show you the land demarcations. The parcel's about eighty acres, according to the lawyer."

They made their way east through the tall grass. The cloying sense of discomfort Ben had gotten from the sad little house faded as they walked through the fields. The faint hum of insects and the whisper of wind through the brush were interrupted only by the shuffle of their footsteps. The grass had grown so long that it was beginning to seed. Ben ran his hands over the tops of the stalks as he walked, letting their silken pods brush against his palms. Hudson trotted a groove through the grass a few yards away, sending a flurry of insects aloft in his wake.

The late-afternoon light sat heavily atop the land, and Ben knew that if he'd been in the city the stratus clouds on the horizon would soon begin thickening to a mottled pink. But the air here was thin and clean. Here there was no single moment at day's end when a horizon of steel and glass blazed into a dreamscape of color. Only the long purple tendrils of loosestrife and orange thatches of butterfly weeds broke the monotony of the rolling grass.

"Neighbors, huh?" Ted asked after a few minutes, pointing ahead. They'd wandered closer to the road, and there was a small stone house on the other side of a post-and-wire fence, a few hundred yards away. It wasn't as run down as their grandmother's, but it was on its way. The low rise behind the house was specked with dozens of cows, the grass there cropped close by their grazing. Two little girls jumped rope not far from the house.

Ben waved at the girls. They stopped what they were doing, stared at him for a moment, and darted inside.

"Friendly kids," Ted said. He looked along the length of the property divider. "This fence is in good shape."

"It wasn't here last time," Ben told him.

"You know what they say about fences and neighbors."

"The guy called the cops on us the first time we came here," Ben told him. "Back before we bought the Crofts."

"You're kidding."

"He thought we were trespassing—reasonable enough, really."

"Did the cops give you a hard time? Can't imagine they love out-of-towners up here—unless they're pulling them over, of course."

"The deputy's a prick, but the chief's okay. He was pretty nice once he figured out who we were. He can't be much older than forty, but he knew exactly who the Lowells were."

"Small town, long memory."

"He liked that I was up here, checking out my roots." Ben pointed up at the mountains. "He's actually the one who told us that the Crofts was for sale."

From this distance, the Crofts was all granite walls, austere towers, and imperial windows. There were no rotten floorboards, loose windows, or cracked foundation. From here the house still appeared as its builders had intended.

Ted shook his head, staring at the house between the mountains. "Just look at that place."

Ben had had the same reaction when he first saw the Crofts, not far from where they now stood. From this distance, it looked awesome and terrifying, the kind of place where a princess is locked away in the remotest of rooms.

The two girls walked out of the little stone house. They stood side by side just outside the front door, staring at Ben and Ted. Ben waved to them again, but the girls didn't move.

The girls wore red sundresses with yellow flowers. From a distance the design looked familiar to Ben, and it was a few moments before he remembered the pattern from the boxes of children's clothes that he'd left with Jake Bishop.

"Company," Ted said. He laughed as he clapped Ben on the shoulder.

Ben turned to see a police cruiser pulling up onto the shoulder of the road.

"I guess they didn't recognize me," Ben said.

"Keep telling yourself that."

A tall man wearing a wide-brimmed hat got out of the cruiser's driver's seat.

"At least it's the chief," Ben said. He would have been in for an unpleasant time with Deputy Simms if he'd been by himself, but with Ted's mouth, there would have been an even chance of gunplay.

The chief took his time making his way to them over the wind-tossed fields.

Ben raised a hand, and the chief reciprocated.

"Howya, Mr. Tierney. I thought it might be you."

"This is my brother, Ted."

"The Lord's given us a right fine day," the chief said. "Bill Stanton," he said, shaking Ted's hand. He had a face made from wood and a smile that turned on a hinge.

"Sure beats the rain," Ben said.

"Hank Seward gave a call. Said there were some characters picking around the old Lowell place."

"Guilty as charged," Ted said.

"Folks aren't used to seeing people poking around that they don't know," the chief said.

"I thought he'd remember from last time."

"Think it was his missus last time," the chief said. He plucked the seedpod off a stalk of grass and ran it between his fingers contemplatively. "Here he comes now," the chief said.

A stout man in cuffed jeans and a sleeveless T-shirt had left the little stone house and was making his way toward them.

"Howya, Bill," the man said when he reached them. He had a ruddy complexion, the kind that was earned by outdoor work or too much whiskey, and small dark eyes that darted in their sockets.

"Ben and Ted Tierney here, Hank. They're the Lowells' kin."

Hank nodded in their direction. "Didn't know who they were. Gave my girls a scare," he said.

"I apologize for that, Mr. Seward. Just showing my brother around."

"New fence, Hank?" The chief tapped the top of one of the posts that separated Seward from the rest of them. "Hasn't been a fence dividing these fields since we were kids, has there?"

"Wasn't no point in building a new one while the Lowells were gone," Seward said. "But now they're back." He jutted his head in the direction of Ben and Ted. "Don't want my cows wandering someplace they're not wanted."

"Suppose not," the chief said. He flicked the seedpod into the brush. "Remember when we played ball here when we were boys? The stone in front of that old sealed well was home and any hit over the fence was a homer?" The chief smiled and rocked on the balls of his feet as if he were priming for a pitch.

"Sure I do," Seward said. He matched the chief's smile and raised him some.

"Hit a couple homers ourselves in our day."

"Frank Carson hit one or two out a game, I recall. Best batter in the county in his day. Coulda played for the Sox, I still say."

"All the Carsons were a force to be reckoned with on the diamond," the chief said. "Saw Molly Carson at Harp's week past last with little Danny in tow, wearing a ball cap. And him the spitting image of Frank. Takes me back, you know?"

"Sure do," Seward said.

"Thing is, Hank," the chief said, moving closer to the fence, "I can see the cap of that old well from here, and it's a good five hundred feet to the fence."

"You think so?"

"If not more." The chief nodded. "Fenway Park is three hundred two feet from the plate to the right foul post. You know that.

Now, you think we were hitting near twice that far when we were teens?"

"You want to say something, you can say it straight out, Bill," Seward said. The stocky man stretched his back to reach the full height available to him.

"No reason to get upset, Hank," the chief said, shaking his head. "I know the Lowells' land was a good feed for your cows—"

"And my daddy's and granddaddy's cows."

"—and with no claims on it, there was no harm in you using it, but it's not yours to use now."

"My cows can't live all year off just my acreage," he said shrilly. "And in my book the Lowells have no rights to that land no more, not after they—"

The chief clamped a white-knuckled hand on the man's shoulder, which brought him to a stop.

"It's not your place to tell people around here what rights they do or do not have. Next time I come out here, I want to see this fence at the legal boundary or nowhere at all. You understand?"

Seward swallowed and nodded. His face had lost its flush.

"Now, you give my best to Bessy and the girls, you hear?" The chief leaned back, and the smile returned to his face. "My Mary was just saying that she should fix our June up with Martha and Meg. Do you think they'd go for that? Play tea party or jump rope some afternoon?"

"Yes, Chief, I'm sure they'd like that very much," Seward said.

"Well, I'll make sure she gives her a call, then. And tending this land is the Lord's labor, but you don't work yourself to nothing now, you hear, Hank?" The chief started to walk back to his cruiser.

"You know me, Bill," Seward said.

"You take care, too, boys," the chief said, waving to Ben and Ted.

"Thanks, Chief," Ben said, then he turned to Hank Seward. "You know, I don't mind at all if you use this land for your cows. We're not using it for anything. You're welcome to it for as long as we own it," he said.

Seward's darting eyes twitched and grew hard. He spoke soft and rough, so that the chief wouldn't hear.

"Don't need charity from the likes of you," he said quickly, a faint mist of spit spraying from between his teeth. Then he turned on his heel and stalked back to his little house, where his daughters still watched silently from the stoop.

15

Caroline had made vanilla-bean French toast with strawberry compote for breakfast. This was a scaled-down version of an earlier meal in which each wedge of toast had been filled with sweetened cream cheese.

"Another?" Ben asked Ted, offering him a slice at the end of a fork.

Ted's eyes narrowed and he leaned toward Ben. "Don't need charity from the likes of you," Ted snarled. Then he fell back in his chair, laughing. Ted had found yesterday's exchange with Hank Seward to be the height of hilarity.

"More for me, then," Ben said, shucking the slice onto his plate.

"I think I'm going to hit Walmart," Caroline said. She helped herself to another spoonful of the compote. Ben was glad that her energy and appetite had returned. "I figure I'll say hello to the priest when he gets here, then I'll take off."

"I can give you a ride, if you want," Ted said. "Driving around in the McLaren is pretty fun. She really opens up on the interstate."

"I think I need something with a little more trunk," she said.

"I thought we just needed some diapers and milk," Ben said.

"I may as well stock up since I'm trekking over there," Caroline said. "I'm also going to pick up some paint samples from Home Depot. And there's an info session there on installing window treatments. They've got a garden center, too, and I want to see what kind of an herb selection they have. Also, I saw some recipes in *Saveur* that I thought I'd make for tonight. Pork loin stuffed with sausage, scalloped sweet potatoes, and braised Brussels sprouts. Might have a nice, light beef consommé to start. And one of the baking blogs I follow has a recipe for a great-sounding lavender crème brûlée. So I need to pick up quite a bit."

"That sounds"—Ted glanced at Ben—"*involved.*"

"It's my pleasure," Caroline said. She cleared her dishes and began rifling through the cabinets and making additions to her shopping list. "Entrées are important, but it's the sides that really tie a meal together." She headed for the pantry. "When's the priest due?"

"Soon," Ben said, checking the clock on the microwave. "You should get dressed," he told Charlie.

"I am dressed," Charlie said, rubbing his face with the back of his hand.

"I meant in something that you didn't sleep in. And how did your feet get so dirty?" he asked. The boy's feet dangled several inches above the floor, and their soles looked filthy.

"I don't know," Charlie said.

"I'm going with you to wash up. Right now. Let's go."

Charlie swung himself off his chair and started toward the stairs, dragging his black-soled feet.

"He looks like he escaped from a Dickens novel. Cee, when did he last take a bath? Do you remember?"

"Two nights ago?"

Ben also couldn't remember exactly when he'd last given Charlie a bath. Between diving into the new book and dealing with Ted, he'd been distracted.

He headed up the stairs and ran a bath in Charlie's bathroom.

"Charlie?" he called as he checked the water's temperature. "Char—" He turned around and was startled by his naked son standing not six inches from him. "Jesus," he said, "I didn't know you were there."

"Is it warm?"

"Feel it," Ben said.

Charlie carefully probed the water. The boy nodded and climbed into the tub.

"Do you want the battleship?" Ben asked. Charlie had a toy warship that they sometimes played with in the tub. The crew had had to deal with an astonishing assortment of problems. Torpedoes, sharks, icebergs, even bears. The captain was resourceful, and his men were brave, but the ship still sank several times an outing. It'd been a while since they'd played with it.

Charlie shrugged.

Ben squeezed shampoo into his hand and kneaded it into his son's hair. His hair was getting thicker every day, and it was in need of a cut.

"So Father Caleb's really nice," Ben told him as he worked up a lather. "And you'll like the school, too. It's on a mountain, just like we are, and they have lots of fields to play on."

"Is it in the forest?"

"Part of it is."

"Is there a lake?"

"Not that I saw, but there's a fountain. Close your eyes now." Ben dunked a cup into the bathwater and poured it over Charlie's head. "Scrub your feet with this." Ben handed him the soap. They used to play games with the bar of soap. Ben would pretend to fumble it and see how far he could send it flying when it slipped through his hands, but there was none of that anymore. "He's just coming up to meet you. It's not a test or anything." The water was starting to look dirty now, a ring forming at the upper reach of the waterline.

"What kinds of animals are in the forest?" Charlie asked him. This was familiar territory, something Charlie used to like to hear about when he was in bed, before the lights went out.

"Lots of animals. Too many to name. There are moles and voles and groundhogs under the fields, rabbits in the grass, and opossums in the trees. There are snakes and frogs and salamanders and newts around the lake; you can find them in the shallows between the stalks of cattails. There are deer in the woods, and—"

"How big are the bears?" Charlie asked.

"We have black bears up here. Not as big as the grizzlies they have out west, but they can weigh a hundred pounds more than me." Ben spread out his hand and held it in front of Charlie. "They have long hooked claws as sharp as razors."

"What animals walk around like we do?" Charlie asked him.

"Like we do?" Ben pulled a towel off the rack. "A bear can stand on two legs, but I don't think they go around walking like that."

"They're taller than you and have black fur?"

Ben pulled Charlie out of the water and wrapped the towel around him.

"There's nothing like that out there," he told him. Ben rubbed Charlie's head with the towel, sending droplets of water flying. The boy's eyes glanced past Ben's head. Ben followed his gaze but saw nothing.

"I was just wondering."

"Father Caleb's here." Caroline's head popped around the bathroom door. "Do you want me to take over?"

Because Caroline had worked long hours and Ben had worked from home, he'd always been the parent to make sure Charlie got to school on time and did his homework. He'd been the one who met with teachers on back-to-school night and the one the PTA called when they were looking for volunteers. He'd been the one who was called when something went wrong. There was no reason for this arrangement to continue now that they'd moved up here, but it had.

"Come down when you're ready, okay, buddy?" Ben tousled Charlie's damp hair on the way out of the room.

When he got to the kitchen, Ben found the old priest nodding at whatever Ted was saying to him.

"Don't believe anything he says, Father," Ben told him.

"I was telling him that I think you're nuts for living in this enormous place," Ted said.

"Oh, well, *that* may be true." Ben shook the priest's hand.

"I have to say that this is beautiful," Father Caleb said, gesturing to the kitchen. "So modern and lovely. I'm impressed and surprised."

"Well, prepare yourself to be less surprised by the rest of house. May I show you around?"

"I don't want to pressure you into a tour; I know you haven't been here that long."

"Charlie's not quite ready; it'll probably just be a couple minutes." Ben stepped into the hallway. He turned around on his way through the door. "Hey, Ted, feel free to load and run the dishwasher."

Ted, his mouth full again with French toast, gave Ben a salute.

"Younger brother?" Father Caleb asked when they stepped into the first room.

"Only by a year, though you'd think it was more, wouldn't you?" Ben said. "We're thinking about putting a bar in here. The light's stunning at sunset. A great view for cocktail hour."

Father Caleb walked to one of the middle windows and peered through its runny glass to the world outside.

"Do you believe in ghosts, Mr. Tierney?" the priest asked him.

Ben took a moment to make sure he'd heard him right. "I don't."

"Good," Father Caleb said. "Because, from what I understand, the Swanns were teetotalers. And the last thing you need is ten generations of them haunting you."

"Teetotalers." Ben shook his head. "How did they survive the winters?"

"It's a beautiful room," Father Caleb said. "Amazing ceilings."

"So you know something about the Swanns?" Ben asked. "I don't know much myself."

"The Crofts has a lot of history. I'm surprised that no one told you about it. Not even the realtor?"

"I'm not sure the guy handling the sale had even seen the place before I called him about it. I'd love to hear whatever you can tell me," Ben said.

"Well, I'm not originally from around here, and the folks in Swannhaven mostly keep to themselves—"

"I've noticed," Ben said.

"—but this place has always fascinated me. Did you know that a member of the Swann family lived here for nearly three hundred years, until just two winters ago?"

"I can't imagine many other places can make the same boast."

"Not in this hemisphere. They say the first foundations were set in the 1720s. The Swanns were one of the first families to travel this far into the interior. Some others had settled on the valley floor, but Aldrich Swann set his homestead up here on the Drop. He and his sons cleared the forest and planted their fields. The other families thought he was crazy at the time. They didn't see why a person would climb a mountain to knock down a forest when a whole new continent stretched ahead of them. But he said that he'd seen the place in a dream," the priest said.

"They say the Drop made good farmland," Ben said.

"The best in the county, maybe the best in the state. Within a generation, the Swanns were rich. When the village was incorporated in the 1740s, it's no coincidence that it was named after the family."

"I guess you'd have to be awfully rich to build a place like this," Ben said. "I just wish they'd been rich enough to keep it up."

"By all accounts, the Swanns only got richer in the nineteenth century. They helped build a railroad that ran through this valley, connecting the freight yards of New York to the North Country. Those were the boom years. I imagine that's how they could afford to expand the Crofts." He pointed to the ceiling, where the vestiges of once-grand chandeliers were still visible. "An old family with the purse strings of a robber baron."

"A family like that must have had some real characters," Ben said. He was practiced at drawing stories out of people, and the priest was a teacher. Teachers liked to talk as much as writers liked to listen.

"A mixed lot, I'm sure—like all families." The priest smiled at Ben. "I have to admit, I was hoping you'd know more about them, that maybe you'd found something of theirs? A journal or diary, or even old photos?"

"There are some portraits that I'd be happy to show you, and I found an old Bible in the basement."

"I'd love to see it sometime."

"Of course. It'd be good to learn something about it," Ben said.

"It's a big house, so maybe something else will turn up. If it does, you should take care of it. When people are gone, all we have left are the things they leave behind. Given enough time, almost anything can be forgotten. Such a shame," the priest said. "I'm sure the villagers will know more. Of course, getting them to talk to you will be another matter."

Ben was about to ask what he meant, when Father Caleb turned to the door. Ben followed the priest's gaze to the doorway, where his son stood in khakis and a light-blue polo shirt.

The interview went well. Charlie was polite if distant. The three of them walked around the house and into the northern fields as Charlie answered the priest's questions. Jake Bishop had mowed some of the farther fields. What remained of the stalks crackled underfoot. After thirty minutes, Charlie was dismissed and Ben was alone again with the priest.

"A fine boy," Father Caleb said.

"Thank you."

"Quiet and thoughtful. Rare qualities for someone of any age. He spends a lot of time alone?"

"He plays on his own most of the time. No neighbors, you know. Why?" Ben allowed a hint of defensiveness to enter his voice.

Father Caleb was silent for a moment. "It'll be good for him to be with boys his own age."

They had reached the edge of the most northeasterly fields, within the shadow of the forest. Ben had been here only a few times. The wind carried a musty smell. He was ready to head back to the Crofts, but the priest made no move to turn around. Ben turned to watch Charlie running past the house, toward the lake. Loping strides and pumping arms. Running as if the world hung in the balance.

"He loves the forest," Ben said.

"We can all find inspiration in nature's miracles," Father Caleb said.

Ben nodded. "It's a nice change from the city. The land feels so old here. Some of the trees by the mountains must have been here for centuries. Sometimes in the mornings, when the fog crawls up from the valley, it feels almost Jurassic."

The grass was stunted here and studded with bursts of starflowers. The woods stank of something—stagnant water or the putrid scent of a plant that Ben couldn't identify.

"The Drop has gotten under your skin, Mr. Tierney," the priest said. Ben could tell that the priest wanted to tell him something, but he was a man who took his time. "How are you getting on with the villagers?"

"You can call me Ben, Father."

"And you can call me Cal," the priest said. "Just not in front of the boys."

Ben nodded. "Some of the villagers have gone out of their way to help us feel welcome. Others . . . Are you familiar with the expression 'they wouldn't piss on me if I were on fire'?"

The priest laughed, a throaty sound that rang across the field and rebounded from the trees.

"I first came up here in '82," Cal said. He sniffed at the air, wrinkling his nose at the reek from the forest. "Smells like something died," he said before continuing. "It was a difficult year—maybe as tough as this year will be. Inflation and high gas prices coincided with a disease that cut down most of the milk herds. Before Thanksgiving, the wealthier parishes took up a collection to give away frozen turkeys in needier communities. Swannhaven was the only town to reject our help. And it's one of the poorest towns in a very poor county. We even gave away a dozen in rich towns like Exton and Greystone Lake. It made me curious. I wondered what kind of place it was where people wouldn't accept a gift as simple as meat for their Thanksgiving table."

"Farmers are proud people," Ben said. He thought of his encounter with Hank Seward yesterday.

"That's what I thought at first," Cal said. "So, of course, I redoubled my efforts. Christmas was coming up, celebrated around the world as the season when one can most easily get away with being a meddlesome priest. We had a great boys' choir back then, so I set up a free concert in the church in the valley."

"And no one showed up?"

"The concert never happened. By seven-thirty a handful of villagers had assembled, children mostly. They were thin as ghosts and half as haunted. Then, a few minutes before showtime, a man ran in to the church, wild with either horror or excitement. The Crofts was on fire. Of course, we all ran outside. The night was windless but unbearably cold. Between the mountains, there was a cloud of smoke hovering above the Crofts, tinted orange by the light of the fire below. I later heard people remark that they saw a pillar of flame billowing toward the sky"—the priest waved his hand above his head—"as if it were something from the Old Testament."

"Anyone get hurt?"

Cal cleared his throat. "Two of the Swann boys died in the fire."

"I thought the two sisters were childless," Ben said.

"The boys were their nephews. Their parents had died in a car accident years earlier, and the sisters cared for them. One of the boys was in his teens, and I believe the other was even younger."

"Terrible," Ben said. The night he'd spent thinking that Charlie had been taken from him was the worst of his life.

"The sisters had taken in foster children, and it was one of them who'd set the fire. A firebug from day one, apparently. There was an investigation, a trial, and the boy was taken away."

"Taken where?"

"Juvenile detention or some such place, I assume. Suffice it to say, this fire further piqued my curiosity about the town. I saw the looks on the faces of the villagers when it happened, and it just didn't feel quite right. I tried to find out more about the town and the Crofts. It had gotten under my skin, too—the way it sits between the mountains like a medieval castle. But small-town folk know how to keep to themselves. Their ranks grew even tighter after the fire. Even the county road closed for a few days. They said something about bad ice conditions, but the roads everywhere else were fine. Once it reopened, I tried to reschedule the concert, but they shut me out." The priest shook his head and looked at Ben.

"Is that all?" Ben asked.

"I assure you that, in my line of work, I don't encounter that behavior in people often, to say nothing of experiencing it uniformly across an entire community."

Ben nodded but felt dissatisfied. The priest's story was all dénouement. He raised his nose to the air. The stink from the forest had become too strong to ignore.

"That smell is really something," the priest said. What had begun as an unpleasant scent carried on the breeze was now a thick, oppressive stench.

"Might be stagnant water," Ben said, but he knew what it really was. On the opposite side of his property, the same smell had come from the hole where he'd buried the remains of the mutilated deer.

He peered into the dark wood as sweat pricked across his arms and forehead. His body wanted him to run for clean air, but Ben forded deeper into the smell.

"Probably," Cal said. He didn't sound any more convinced than Ben did.

Ben bent back a thatch of undergrowth and stepped under the forest's canopy. The sunlight-starved ground under the trees was soft with the last year's pine needles. "You don't have to come with me," Ben told the priest. He pulled up the collar of his shirt to cover his nose.

But the priest fell into step behind him, and Ben was glad for the company. They walked deeper into the terrible smell. Hudson would have known which way to go, but the stink had overwhelmed Ben's olfactory senses. Every direction seemed equally unbearable, and he began to breathe from his mouth.

His eyes and ears helped where his nose couldn't. The humming clouds of insects ahead blurred the air with their vast numbers.

The trench of a ravine or seasonal stream was ahead, and they climbed over the sprawling root system of a huge oak tree situated on its lip. It hadn't felt as if they'd walked far, but they were right up against the foot of the mountain.

The incredible number of flies made it difficult for Ben to understand what he was seeing. There were bones in the ravine. Dead animals, Ben guessed from the varying sizes of the remains. Stark white rib cages arced from the ground, some still draped with graying sinew.

Ben picked up a rock and pitched it into the ravine. Upon contact, there was a wet sound that made his stomach lurch. The insects momentarily relinquished their stake and diffused into the air in a pulse of movement. This sent the trees above him trembling, and Ben looked up to see the branches lined with hundreds of crows, silently watching him with their empty eyes.

"Looks like deer, mostly," Cal said.

Ben counted at least five large and separate rib cages. The ground beneath them writhed with maggots. Some of the bones were clean, others coated with torn flesh and gristle. It was a pit fresh from a Brueghelian hell.

"Maybe they fell into the ravine, broke their legs, and couldn't get out," Ben said. His voice was muffled from the sleeve he'd pressed over his face. The drop into the ravine was severe, and the bottom was littered with boulders. He could imagine a herd of the animals losing their footing in the dark of night.

"But there are smaller animals, too," the priest said. He pointed to a pile of rodent-like skulls along the rocky ledge.

Raccoons or opossums, Ben guessed.

"There are coyotes in the forest," Ben said.

"Coyotes don't gather their prey like this," Cal said. "And I doubt they'd have the strength to move a full-grown deer. Though the coyotes around here are bigger than they used to be. There's a theory that they traveled through Canada, breeding with wolves along the way before recolonizing the East Coast," Cal said.

"Interesting," Ben said. He hoped the priest had a Wikipedia entry's worth of information about coyotes. Anything to distract some of his attention from the grisly scene in front of him. Anything to postpone the obvious questions.

"Let's go," Ben said, turning his back on the pit of horrors. He got no argument from the priest.

Ben restrained himself from running out of the woods. He held his breath when he saw the tree line, promising himself that his first inhale would be of the sweet air of the living world.

Father Cal trudged out of the undergrowth a moment later, wiping his forehead with his sleeve. The Crofts was silhouetted against the verdant slopes of the mountains, and they gathered their breath, watching the fields ripple around the motionless house.

"That was appalling," Cal said after a few moments. "Why don't you seem more horrified?"

"I found a mutilated deer two weeks ago. At first I thought it was a bear or something, but . . ." Ben shook off the memory of those black eyes staring at him. "I think some of the locals are having fun with us."

"You think that the villagers filled up that ravine with dead animals? Why would they leave the creatures' bodies so far from the Crofts? If they wanted to harass you, wouldn't they put them in a place where you were sure to find them?"

"Could it just be hunters?" Ben asked.

"It's not the season, but even if it were, they shouldn't be trespassing. I can't imagine you'd want men hunting the forest with Charlie playing there."

"And I'd have heard the hunters' gunshots, right? Unless they hunt with bows; I know some people find that more sporting." He frowned. "Listen, I don't know, okay? But please keep it to yourself. Charlie's not allowed out of sight of the Crofts, and I don't want Caroline to worry. Honestly, we have enough on our plate right now."

They began the trek across the tall grass fields, and Ben told the priest more about the dead deer and the head on his doorstep.

"You're really not going to call the police?" Cal asked when they reached his car.

"I can't see how any good would come of it. And there was no harm done. We'll need the village on our side if this inn is going to work."

Father Cal looked as if he was going to pursue the point, but then he agreed. "Well, I can't say it was entirely pleasant, but we'd be glad to have Charlie in September. And it was good spending the morning with you, Ben. You take care of yourself and your family."

"Yes, sir."

Father Cal climbed into his sedan and stuck his head through the window. Ben thought he was going to say something, but he only stared at the Crofts for what felt like a minute. "It's a fine place, no mistake," Cal said. "But doesn't it ever frighten you to be alone in such a big house, so far from everything else?"

"No, Father, I'm not afraid," Ben said. He caught the scent of the pit as he shook his head. He would have to take a shower and launder these clothes. But he mustered a smile for the priest as he waved goodbye to him. "And I'm not alone."

He gave so much weight to the declaration that, for a moment, he even believed it.

16

Charlie stood at the center of the faerie circle, still as the trees that ringed it.

He tried to concentrate on the sound of the wind through the forest. He tried to hear past the rustling of leaves and the creaking of branches. He tried to listen for that which did not want to be heard.

It had been days since he'd followed noises up the mountain. Though he'd been grateful that the Watcher had finally revealed itself, their encounter had lasted only a moment. He'd gotten only a glimpse of it, silhouetted against the sun. It had stood there, the edges of its darkness catching fire. Since first seeing it, Charlie had replayed the sight constantly in his head. He thought about what it looked like, what it wanted, and what it would do next. It had summoned him to the mountain, and he had followed, and now it was the Watcher's turn once again. Charlie had only to be patient. This was why he waited here, still and silent as a tree. He felt sure that their game would soon continue.

Above Charlie, the birdsong stopped as the din from the forest changed. There was a new sound now. One that did not follow the rhythm of the wind or the sway of the trees. Charlie stepped off the stump to land in a crouch on the floor of pine needles. In his bare feet, he was as quiet as an owl gliding on a breeze.

These tapping sounds were the same as the ones he'd heard on the day he'd seen the Watcher. Explosions of noise across a range of pitches. Just as before, they lured him toward the mountains. He picked his way through the trees and underbrush as he ascended the slope. But the tapping from the deep forest never seemed to get any closer.

When the strange sounds stopped, Charlie stopped, as well. He stood in mid-step as the minutes stretched. He waited, but the sounds did not return. He wondered if he had done something wrong, but when he turned around, Charlie understood that he had done exactly what he was supposed to do.

Behind him, something was fixed to the silver belly of a mighty birch. It took him a moment to understand what he was seeing. It had been an opossum, Charlie thought. They were the only creatures with coiled muscular tails like that. Its head had been removed, its fur stripped. The creature had not just been skinned but disassembled; organs ranging in color from near white to darkest purple were staked carefully side by side among the animal's strewn musculature. The raw flesh glistened, but there was a strange absence of blood. When he looked closely, Charlie could see the way the pieces were linked by veins and tendons with the finest of textures. The animal's fur was staked to the tree just below its fleshy remains. It looked as if it had been unzipped and set aside like winter pajamas.

Two large block letters were inscribed between the two presentations of the animal. They were written in red, but Charlie thought it wasn't blood but a paste formed of mashed flesh.

GO, the letters read. Charlie frowned as he searched the trunk for other marks. Go? Go where? For Charlie, there was no place but this one.

Charlie turned his attention to the animal and touched a flap of its raw flesh. Though the opossum looked as if it had been bled dry, Charlie's fingertip still came away rimmed with scarlet. He smelled his finger before tasting it. He tried to imagine how a wolf or Hickory Heck or the Watcher itself might like the taste.

The opossum's blood was warm on his tongue, and that made Charlie smile. He smiled because that meant that the kill had been fresh and personal. It meant that the Watcher had indeed left the opossum just for Charlie. Most of all, it meant that their brief encounter on the mountain had not been the end of their games.

It had only been the beginning.

17

"Moving up here just seems like such an extreme reaction," Ted said. It was brutally hot outside, but they'd taken a jog with Hudson anyway. "It's not like you didn't already have your hands full."

This conversation had been wearying the first time, and by now Ben was thoroughly sick of it. Ted had been here nearly a week, and Ben had no idea how long he planned to stay.

"I mean, I could see Westchester or Connecticut, but—"

"I've run out of ways to say it," Ben said. "The city wasn't working for us anymore. We had to get out." Ben knew that with absolute certainty. For Charlie and Caroline's sake, they'd had no choice but to leave.

"Yeah, but you had *friends* there, Benj. You had a *life*. You had me."

"And how exactly *did* you help us when we were there, Ted?" Ben asked. He came to a dead stop in front of the Crofts. "Remind me again? Did you babysit Bub when I had to take Caroline to her doctor's appointments? Did you help look for Charlie when he went missing? You think this concerned-brother routine is helpful now that you *can't possibly do anything for us?*"

Ted stopped and turned around. He looked utterly stricken. Ben had a sudden vivid memory from one of their rare childhood tussles, when Ben had split Ted's lip. He remembered his feeling of horror at seeing the blood dripping down his brother's face and the way Ted had stared at him, too dismayed to cry. Ben hadn't meant to get angry.

"I was in L.A. when Charlie went missing," Ted said. "You know that."

"I know," Ben said. "I didn't mean to—" He shook his head. "But second-guessing every decision I make isn't helpful."

He turned away from Ted to throw a tennis ball for Hudson to retrieve. On their jog, Ben had made sure that they stayed far from the northeasterly fields. He'd woken up once in the night, imagining the stink of the pit on him.

"I get that you're stressed, Benj," Ted said. "Maybe you just need to slow it all down a little. Take some time off and relax somewhere, go on vacation or something. Caroline's trying to do too much at once."

"There's a lot to do."

"She's manic, Ben. Has she kept in touch with her shrink?"

"She checks in with her psychiatrist once a month to talk about the medications, but she doesn't want to find a therapist up here."

"Then you need to find someone for her." Ted put his hand on Ben's shoulder. "I'm serious. Don't you see how it's affecting Charlie?"

"Thanks for the advice, Ted." He shrugged out of his brother's grip.

"And whenever you don't have that dopey smile on your face, you look like you want to jump out of your skin. Like right now. Do you think I haven't noticed?"

"Got it." He accepted the soggy ball from Hudson.

"Come on, who knows you better than me, Benj?" Ben met his brother's gaze. Ted looked away first. "Fine. I'm not going to fight with you." Ted took off his T-shirt and mopped his forehead. "I think I'm going to take off after I shower."

"Don't be like that," Ben said.

"I have to make an appearance at the office at some point. And you've got that meeting, anyway." Lisbeth had called Ben the day before to tell him that there was another meeting in the village this afternoon. At first, Ben had thought that she was talking about the Preservation Society, but this seemed to be something else.

"Well, you should come back soon. Whenever you want."

Ted turned and took in the view of the Crofts for a few moments. "You got everything you ever wanted, didn't you, Benj? Your big house, your pretty wife and kids."

Ben paced his breathing so that he didn't say anything else he'd regret.

The kitchen door shut, and they turned to see Caroline walking down the steps with a bucket full of paint rollers.

"Ted's heading back to the city this morning."

"Oh," she said. "Sure you don't want to stay for lunch? I was going to make paninis with the leftover cheese and pork."

"Nah, thanks, though. I want to beat the rush-hour traffic."

Caroline nodded and headed back to the kitchen.

Ben threw the tennis ball down the field again and watched as Hudson bolted after it. He turned to his brother and was surprised to feel a pang of sadness when he looked at him. Despite everything, he'd miss Ted. He hadn't realized how much until this moment.

Ben helped Ted load his bags into the McLaren.

"Are you *sure* you don't want the quilt?" Ted asked, gesturing to the Lowell family tree folded on the passenger's seat.

"You hold on to it," Ben said. Caroline would be annoyed when she found out that Ben had given up this provenance of his local roots, but Ben wanted Ted to have something from the ruined farmhouse.

"Okay. You know, if you ever need a change of scenery, you can stay at my place," Ted said. He popped the trunk. "Even if I'm traveling, you have the keys. It's yours if you need it. If you need a break. A place to write or something."

"Thanks."

"And you should call. Me or your other friends. Sometimes you need to talk to an adult that you're not married to."

"Father Cal's a nice guy."

"I knew you'd like him when I met him. From your books, it's clear you have a weakness for old men who speak in aphorisms." He swung himself into the car, pulled the gull-wing door down, and stuck his hand out.

"A couple days ago you couldn't even tell me the title of one of my books. I thought you hadn't read them." Ben grabbed his hand.

"Of course I have, Benj." Ted squeezed his hand. "Every word."

18

You got everything you ever wanted, didn't you, Benj?

They'd parted on good terms, but Ted's words sat inside Ben like a shard of ice. He'd gotten everything he wanted, and look where that had left him.

It would be easy to dwell on the burdens he'd saddled himself with, but they'd bought the Crofts to avoid exactly this kind of introspection. They'd come here for unsullied horizons, new challenges, and fresh tasks. And Ben had more than just the house to occupy him. There was some time before the village meeting, and he decided to spend it doing research for his book.

In his attic nook, he clicked through pages of Google search results, but most that mentioned Swannhaven referred only to its dairy farms or budgetary shortfalls.

Eventually he came to a site with something, a link from the archives of the *Belleford Weekly*. Ben knew Belleford only as an exit off the interstate, about twenty miles south of Swannhaven. The article was entitled "Suspicious Fire Alarms Residents," and part of its final paragraph most interested Ben.

*. . . but there was speculation at the scene that an accelerant had
been used to start the blaze. If evidence is found to support this
claim, this will be the first act of arson in the county since the fatal
fire at the historic Crofts estate in Swannhaven in 1982. According
to the* Swannhaven Dispatch, *that fire—which resulted in several
deaths—was set by a troubled teenager "looking for attention."
With the surprise defeat of the Belleford Sergeants in Saturday's
football game against the Stoughton Minutemen, many wonder if
teens are also responsible for this week's fire.*

Ben found himself irritated that the reporter had referred to his
home as the *Crofts estate* instead of *the Crofts*. Then it occurred to
him that he'd never heard of the *Swannhaven Dispatch*. Google produced only a handful of links. Like the piece in the *Belleford Weekly*,
these were mostly articles from other regional newspapers that refer-
enced something that had once appeared in the *Dispatch*.

When it came time to leave for the meeting in the village, Ben
closed his computer and went to find Caroline. He'd succeeded in
distracting himself for a while, but now that restless anxiety had returned. He entered the second floor through one of the tower's ornate doors. The hallway on this floor had been sanded, stained, and
varnished. Each wide plank had been restored to its intended depth
and iridescence. The floor was beautiful, but something in the way
the dark muscles of wood meandered along the primed walls made
Ben think of a great serpent. He hesitated to step onto it for a moment, seized with the sudden thought that its planks would wrap
themselves around his foot and pull him down through their gleaming surface.

Caroline usually worked to music, but the second floor was oddly
silent. Headphones, Ben guessed. He did his best to ignore the
weighty quiet of the rooms, but when she wasn't in the room she was
supposed to be in, a worry began to grow in his gut.

"Caroline?" he called.

He quickened his pace as he headed down the hallway toward the rest of the rooms.

"Caroline?" Louder this time.

There were usually any number of noises in the house. The song of birds through an open window, the creak of old planks, the squeeze of water moving through pipes. This quiet was oppressive, as if something had gathered these sounds and crushed them.

His heart was pounding by the time he got to their bedroom. Then he saw her silhouetted against one of the windows.

"Why didn't you answer me?" he asked her.

"Bub's asleep. I didn't want to wake him," she said without turning around.

"Will you answer me the next time I call you?" As with the time he'd followed the sounds into the forest, he found himself suddenly afraid. In his voice, fear sounded like anger.

She turned around and he saw her face. She could have sliced through a tree with the expression she wore, but her eyes were red and swollen.

"Are you crying?" He moved toward her. He noticed that the bed was covered in papers: bills, bank statements, and forms from their investment-management firm.

"What happened?"

"Things don't always need to happen, Ben. And you don't get to yell at me, then look at me like I'm a lunatic. I don't always need your help."

"Cee, I was just worried because you weren't where I thought you'd be, and then when I—"

"Despite what you may think, the need to emote does not constitute a flaw. Not all of us have the talent of becoming whoever the situation calls for."

"I'm sorry," Ben said. He tried to calm himself. "Is there anything I can do?"

"I'm not sure how you'd be able to fit anything else into your day beyond holing yourself up in the attic, wandering the house, and driving across the countryside."

"Is there a reason why all this financial stuff is out?"

"You want to be the one to handle our finances now, Ben?" Caroline asked him. She scooped an armful of papers off the bed and held it out to him. Sheets fluttered to the floor around her.

"I came to tell you that I'm heading to that meeting in the village. Do you feel like anything in particular for dinner? I'm happy to make it. I can stop at the store if we're short on anything."

"What makes you think I'm not planning to make dinner myself? Don't I spend half the day cooking? What else could I *possibly* do with myself?"

Ben walked back into the hallway. He knew the longer he stood there, the worse it would get. There was no upside in engaging her when all she wanted to do was rage.

"Hopefully it won't take too long," he called over his shoulder. He closed the door gently behind him. When she was like this, refusing to argue with her was one of the things that made her the most angry, and he didn't want Bub to wake up, either.

He blamed himself. That fear that had suddenly gripped him when he couldn't find her was no less irrational than the fury she had leveled at him. He had raised his voice first. It might have been what woke the Wolf. He never knew what would do it.

Keep up the light, he told himself as he climbed into the Escape. His grandmother's old saying had crept back into his brain since Ted had reminded him of it. When Grams was dying, Ben had asked her what it meant. He had an idea from the way she'd used it over the years, but he wanted to hear it from her. She was in hospice then, her face heartbreakingly old. When she'd been healthy, her face was wrinkled, every crease a waypoint in the map of her life, but now she'd lost so much weight that her skin was taut, her bright-blue eyes as wide as a child's. It was as if she were transforming into an angel. Beautiful and only half there. He was trying to get a wise smile out of her with the question, but her mouth tightened and her eyes welled. "You know the right thing, and you know you gotta do it no matter what," she told him. She grabbed his hand, tears beginning to stream. "No matter what."

He shook off the image and started the car. Even when Ben was halfway down the gravel path, the Crofts seemed to take up the entirety of his rearview mirror.

19

Caroline took the hill with a vengeance. She slammed the balls of her feet into the turf as she launched herself up the Drop. Her face tightened as the burn in her quads flared into pain, then she pressed herself harder. Bub was napping, and while the baby monitor clipped to Caroline's waist had excellent range, she ran a loop that never took her far from the house.

She didn't need to look at her watch to know she was off-pace. If she was more than a minute off, she'd punish herself with something. Having left her personal trainer back in the city along with so much else, Caroline had become her own drill sergeant. Maybe she would do another hundred crunches or force herself to run a lap around the lake. She'd gone up there a few days ago, and the bugs had been terrible. The clouds of gnats went for her eyes while mosquitoes attacked her arms and neck. The shoreline was clotted with the fester of their larva. She didn't know how Charlie could stand it there.

Though Ben had recently placed limits on Charlie's exploration of the forest, Caroline still thought the boy spent too much time by himself. He'd always been a quiet child, but every day he seemed a little more remote. He was only eight years old and too young to become a stranger. And it cut her more than she'd admit that Charlie was growing into someone she didn't recognize. Growing into the kind of person who kept entire pieces of himself hidden. The idea that Charlie was becoming more like Ben made her pump her arms faster.

She wondered if Ben would be painfully careful around her when he returned from the village. Caroline wished, as she always did, that she hadn't yelled at him. Sometimes she wanted him to scream at her the way she did at him. Sometimes she believed that nothing could be worse than the way his mouth tensed when he smiled at her, curved with pity.

Her psychiatrist had told her that when she suffered an uncontrolled emotional reaction, she should examine the circumstances that surrounded it. It hadn't been a coincidence, she felt sure, that she'd yelled at Ben just after going through their most recent financial statements. They had not held good news. Most of the proceeds from the sale of their apartment and Caroline's severance had gone into buying and renovating the Crofts, but this was not nearly the end of their expenses. They hadn't yet begun to restore the grounds, and 90 percent of the house remained unfurnished. Without Caroline's salary, their financial resources were spread thin and becoming ever thinner. The fact that Ben had decided to scrap the book he'd been working on and begin another would also cut into their cash flow. But misplaced anxiety about this wasn't the only reason she'd lashed out at him.

Caroline tried hard not to resent Ben for the time he spent on his book and all the drives and meetings and other activities he claimed were related to his writing process. The new book he was working on could well be a tremendous resource for the inn. But the cavalier attitude with which he approached the Crofts bothered her. Sure, he was always game for a few hours of painting and sanding, but it was Caroline who worked long days, every day, to fix up the Crofts. When she wasn't restoring molding or varnishing floors or scrubbing away mold, she was coming up with a unified interior design, haggling with furniture manufacturers, or trying elaborate dishes for the restaurant's menu. Ben seemed to think that if the Crofts didn't work, they could simply sell the place and try city life again. He didn't understand that they didn't have the resources to do that anymore. He didn't grasp the fact that they didn't have the luxury to fail at this. That this wasn't *a* chance for them but *the* chance.

Mrs. White, the kind old woman from the Preservation Society, had dropped off a tincture of oils for bathwater that was supposed to promote relaxation. Caroline thought she might give it a try once she finished her run.

She wiped sweat from her eyes with the back of her hand. *So damn hot,* she thought.

Bub, her own personal angel, took delightfully predictable naps, so Caroline decided to risk a short detour into the forest. A few months ago, she could never have imagined leaving the baby alone for any length of time, but they were alone on the Drop and the monitor gave her a long tether—just another way in which their lives had changed since leaving the city. This new route took her north, along the top of the slope before it dipped into the woods. It was cooler here. Caroline darted over the bulging roots and between the coarse trunks with the fleet grace of a native creature. She followed the edge of a ravine downslope, the momentum and challenge of the course spurring her to run faster. This leg of her jog was reckless. The misjudgment of an inch could earn her a broken ankle, but she'd always been sure-footed, and running the forest's gauntlet made her feel invincible.

The forest air was wet and thick with solitude. Sound did not travel the way it was supposed to. But today Caroline only had ears for the pounding of her steps and the pulse in her temples. An undernote of smoke lingered on the breeze. It reminded her of her father's grill, of the long summer nights of her childhood, when a Popsicle and a running sprinkler were all she needed to be incandescently happy.

A flicker of movement to her right caused Caroline to turn her head. A large crow perched on the trunk of a fallen tree on the far side of the ravine. Its glossy black head shone blue in the scattered light, its onyx eyes watching her with a chilling predatory stillness. Her eyes were drawn upward, and she saw that the trees were full of the creatures. They stared at her as silently as gargoyles. She was so startled that she lost her footing. She tripped over a root and caught herself hard against the trunk of a massive oak. The baby monitor clipped to her waistband crunched in protest. The birds didn't move.

Now that she had stopped, she smelled the rancid stench of rotting flesh caught on the air. *Carrion scavengers,* she thought. Eaters of the dead. One of the creatures in the branches above her had a long rip of putrid sinew hanging off its beak. The sight of it, coupled with the smell, made Caroline gag, and she staggered along the edge of the ravine. She'd hurt her ankle when she tripped, and she tested it carefully, keeping one eye on the motionless birds.

Caroline limped away from the flock of birds as quickly as she could. The stench was terrible, and she couldn't tell if it was from the birds themselves or from whatever dead thing they'd found to feed on. She climbed over a fallen birch tree, her fingers finding purchase on the tangles of bark that had warped from its trunk. The regular course of her run would have taken her west, down the slope, but it was clear her jog was over. She wanted to get out of the forest as quickly as possible.

The light became murky as she picked her way to the edge of the woods, streaming in hazy beams through patches in the forest's canopy. She chanced a look over her shoulder at the birds, but she didn't see anything other than their dark silhouettes in the high branches. She was having trouble seeing anything with distinction. Her eyes watered, and she'd caught the tang of burning things again. An acrid taste collected in the back of her throat.

The fields were unrecognizable when she got to them. The clear summer's day had been replaced with the rolling fog of October.

Her eyes suddenly brimming, she squinted to make sense of what she was seeing.

It wasn't until Caroline saw the plume of black smoke billowing from the Crofts that realization ricocheted around her brain like a wayward bullet: the taste of smoke, the haze in the forest, her baby alone in his crib. That's when the pain in her ankle disappeared and Caroline rediscovered the pace she'd been missing.

20

Girded by mountains, the valley was shielded from the wind and left to bake in the July sun. With the rains of past weeks forgotten, the streets and buildings were glazed with sediment from the parched fields. Ben's Escape left twin burns of dust in its wake, as if it traveled five times its true speed.

Deputy Simms and Mose Johnson from the gas station sat outside Harp's General Store, facing the street and drinking something out of aluminum cans. Ben hailed them with an open palm as he drove by, but only Johnson waved in return.

Ben didn't know what this village meeting was about, but he was surprised that the church parking lot was even less crowded than it had been for the meeting of the Preservation Society.

"Shouldn't be too long," he told Hudson. He fastened a leash to the beagle's collar and tied it around a sapling on the edge of the thatch of trees. The dog tilted his head to one side. "Look, you've got shade and grass and everything," he said, scratching Hudson under his ear.

When he entered the church, Ben recognized nearly everyone there. Chief Stanton spoke to Walter Harp by the pulpit, and

Mrs. White and Lisbeth sat next to each other at the table up at the front. The only person whom Ben hadn't met was a prematurely bald man who approached him as soon as he entered.

"Roger Armfield," he said, shaking Ben's hand. Armfield was taller than Ben and thin as a lamppost.

"I thought there'd be more people," Ben said. The chief and Walter Harp waved at him across the pews.

"Oh, no, it's usually just us," Armfield said. "The Swannhaven Trust is made up of the heads of the, uh, the village's first families." Armfield looked about the same age as Ben, but his breathless way of speaking made him sound like an over-caffeinated adolescent.

"Is that the same as the Winter Families?"

"Oh, yes," the man laughed, looking relieved. "I wasn't sure you knew about that." He leaned closer to Ben. "We're the largest land-owners and we know the village best. The chief is the chief, and Walter Harp owns the store and acts as a middleman for most of the tenant farmers. Lisbeth Goode owns the diner and is our historian. The Goodes have always kept our records. And Mrs. White can fix up almost anybody with plants she grows in her garden. I'm the town veterinarian. Being a vet might not count for much where you come from, but this is a town that has fifty times as many cows as people." The man leaned back and guffawed.

Ben was beginning to wonder why he was here. As a descendant of a Lowell, he was technically a member of one of the Winter Families, but that didn't mean he belonged at a governing meeting for a village he'd moved to only a few months ago. Across the room, Lisbeth rose from the front table and began to move toward him.

"I guess that makes sense," Ben said. "Just doesn't sound very democratic."

"Oh, dear," Armfield said. A sheen of sweat sprang up across his forehead as he looked over his shoulder. People began to take their seats at the front table. "We're all properly elected. We have our quirks, but that's not one of them. After all, we fought a war over exactly that type of thing, didn't we?" His laugh became even more strained, and Ben was relieved when Lisbeth finally reached them.

"Glad you two have met," Lisbeth said. She put her arms around both of them. "Let's get started." Ben had planned to sit in the pews, but Lisbeth guided him to a seat at the table, between Chief Stanton and herself.

Everyone greeted Ben warmly, but he felt more out of place with every moment. He relaxed a bit when Lisbeth announced that they'd begin the meeting with a reading from the Bible. He'd come prepared for that, at least. Everyone else took out a Bible, and he pulled his from his messenger bag. The dragon-skin Bible shook the table when he placed it there.

"We'll take our reading from Job today," Lisbeth said. She began to read but hesitated. Ben was still flipping through the pages to find the right passage. It'd been a while since he'd had to locate a specific verse in the Bible, but he'd practiced the day before. He looked up when he was ready and saw that Lisbeth was staring at his Bible. Everyone was, except for Mrs. White, who looked only at him. When her crinkled blue eyes found his, a smile bloomed on her face. Ben was about to say something, but then Lisbeth continued with the reading.

When the passage was finished, Chief Stanton was the first one to speak.

"Where'd you find that Bible, Mr. Tierney?" he asked.

"In the cellar up at the Crofts," Ben said. "I was cleaning out some things and I found it locked in an old desk."

"It's a miracle you found it," Lisbeth said, shaking her head. "That's Aldrich Swann's Bible. One of the only things he took on the passage from the Old World."

"It looked old to me, but I didn't realize it was that ancient."

"Three hundred years if it's a day," Mrs. White whispered. The smile she'd set on Ben remained undimmed.

"I should be more careful with it," Ben said. He began to feel uncomfortable again. "Maybe I shouldn't have taken it out of the house."

"Nonsense," Lisbeth said. "Take care with it, to be sure, but the good book's not meant to die on a shelf. It's meant to live on a lap. It's right that you brought it, Ben," she said. "And it's good to have you here. Your kin used to sit at this table, and we invited you here today so you can see how the village operates."

"Great," Ben said, nodding. He took the opportunity to return the old Bible to his bag.

"Mrs. White, how are the Johnson boys?" Lisbeth asked. She opened her notebook and poised her pen above it.

Mrs. White had been treating Mose Johnson's sons for fevers, and they were coming along well. In her papery voice, she also reported that two of the farmers' wives were pregnant and that she thought one of them would have twins. Ben was surprised such things were discussed at a village council meeting, but he guessed that in a place so small, everything was of interest.

Lisbeth turned next to Walter Harp. He gave her a sheet that detailed how much milk the dairy farms had produced last month, where it had been sold, and for what price. He provided similar details for Swannhaven's chicken and eggs, corn and vegetables and fruit. Lisbeth and the chief compared this year's figures to last year's. Corn was up; chickens, eggs, vegetables, and fruit were about the same; milk was down. From what Ben gathered, most farmers who worked the valley floor rented their acreage from someone else— presumably from one of the families at this table. He didn't know if they paid rent but figured there was some arrangement. Walter Harp appeared to manage sales of milk and corn to purchasers outside Swannhaven. The rest of the production was sold via Harp's store to other villagers. In that way, the village seemed self-sufficient.

This brought them to Roger Armfield, who nervously related a spate of cattle deaths across the valley.

"A sickness tore through the milk herds back in the eighties," Lisbeth told Ben. "Lost half the herds. It began turning up again last winter. Hasn't gotten too bad so far because we've been careful to quarantine the infected," she said.

The discussion then moved on to a problem that some of the farms on the north end of the valley were having with well water.

The Swannhaven Trust meeting was like nothing Ben had expected. He was surprised by how interlinked all the families in the village were, but what really struck him was the way the village's services and economy were organized. It seemed to be a combination of feudalism and farming cooperative. He'd never heard of anything quite like it.

The meeting ended with a prayer, and the trust members began to leave. Lisbeth was quick to take Ben aside.

"That's how it's done in Swannhaven," she said. "What did you think?"

"I have to admit, that's not how I imagined a village council meeting," Ben said. "I didn't realize you'd be so involved in every aspect of the village. I guess I thought people just sat around talking about potholes and stop signs."

Lisbeth laughed at that. "We do things a little differently here," she said. "But only because we need to. Trading in kind and sharing what we can is the only way a small farming village like ours can survive these days. Gotta save what money we have for gas, electricity, heating oil, and the interest to the banks." She shook her head. "You can bet that no one in this village will hop into bed with a bank again. We need nobody but each other and the Lord. Speaking of which, you should come to Sunday service."

"I'll definitely come by," Ben said. He knew the Swanns had been religious folk, and he wanted to get a better sense of what that part of their lives had been like. "And I like that you all look out for one another."

"We've been through more together than most towns. Going all the way back to the Winter Siege during the Revolution so long ago. If you're trying to figure out this strange little village of ours, that one hard winter is all you need to know. Folks came out of it as close as family—*closer* than most, I'd wager." She suddenly smiled. "Speaking of families, I was right when I guessed that yours would be beautiful. Two handsome sons and a lovely wife for the full set. You should know that Caroline's welcome at all our meetings."

The others had already left the church, but Ben could still hear their voices.

"I'll tell her. She just wasn't feeling well today," he said. "She gets these headaches."

"That can be hard," Lisbeth said. "My late husband used to have something similar. The winters were always especially hard on him. Mrs. White used to fix him up with teas from her garden. It worked wonders on him."

"Really?" There was some commotion outside: shouts from excited voices and the rumble of cars accelerating.

Lisbeth's eyes also flicked toward the door as she spoke. "I know Mrs. White would be pleased to put something together for Caroline, if you like. See if it works? Always says that's what she was put here to do."

"I'll talk to her about it," Ben said. He didn't know how Caroline would feel about homemade therapeutic tea, but he'd try anything.

"Mr. Tierney." Roger Armfield had burst through the church door. "They need you," he said. He pointed through the doors.

"They?" Ben asked, as he walked outside.

He shielded his eyes against the sun as he stepped out. Something outside had changed. Loud voices came from Harp's General Store, and there was a vacant place where the chief's police cruiser had been. He could discern Deputy Simms's voice but not the words he shouted.

Two pickups had pulled in front of Harp's. Men from town squeezed into the seats and others piled into the back. Ben had never seen so many people gathered at one time on Swannhaven's streets. He wondered where they'd come from. Deputy Simms saw Ben and began to run toward him.

Ben didn't know what was going on, but he got the sense that he should be moving faster. He quickly untied Hudson's leash from where he'd fastened it and was about to lead him to the Escape when he felt a sharp rap against his shoulder.

Deputy Simms stood behind him. "Aren't you gonna follow them?" Simms asked, twitching his head in the direction of the two pickup trucks.

Ben frowned at the deputy, and the younger man pointed east. Ben followed his gesture to the place between the mountains, where a maelstrom of black smoke billowed from where his house was supposed to be.

21

The Escape shook from the irregularities of the broken roadway, and its tires shrieked on every turn.

Deputy Simms had managed to climb into the SUV before Ben floored the accelerator. He sat in the passenger's seat, with his face pressed against the glass of the window to keep an eye on the smoke. Ben was thirty miles over the speed limit, but Simms either didn't notice or didn't care.

"Call Cee," Ben said, punching the voice control on the car's steering wheel.

"Calling Cee," the car said.

"Fancy car," the deputy muttered to himself.

Ben listened to the series of rings until Caroline's voice mail kicked in. He disconnected and tried not to think about the questions posed by an unanswered phone.

"Did you get a call about it?" Ben asked Simms.

"A what?" the deputy turned to him.

"A call, a 911 call about the fire."

"Didn't need to. That smoke can be seen for twenty miles. Chief took off like a shot, soon as he saw it."

Ben clenched his teeth. If Caroline had called in the fire, that would have meant that she and the boys were okay.

"Were those men in the pickups the volunteers?" Ben asked. He'd passed the trucks filled with villagers the first chance he'd gotten, but he had no doubt that they were headed to the Crofts.

"Volunteers?"

"The volunteer fire department."

"No fire department in Swannhaven," the deputy said. "We'd have to call North Hampstead to get an engine over here."

"If they're not volunteers, then what are they doing?" Ben asked.

"What?"

Ben restrained himself from reaching across the gearshift and strangling the deputy.

"If they're not members of the fire department, then why are those men in the pickups heading to my home?" Ben turned off the county road and onto the drive that led to the Crofts.

"Well, damn, everyone loves a fire, don't they?" The deputy rolled down the window, and the air that rushed through smelled of burned wood and left a chemical taste in Ben's mouth.

Hudson began to bark in the backseat.

"Close it, will you?" Ben said. His eyes watered. He craned his head to get a better look out the windshield. He saw part of the house and thick black smoke but couldn't see any flames. It was hard to see much through the billowing darkness of the smoke.

"Pull 'er over here," the deputy said, his hand already on the door handle.

"I can get closer," Ben said. They were still a few hundred yards from the house.

"Too much smoke. This black and thick and you know something bad is burning. Don't wanna breathe that shit in."

Ben didn't want to follow any of Simms's suggestions, but he couldn't ignore the ringing in his head, and his visibility was virtually zero.

The outline of a police cruiser was just ahead, and he pulled in behind it. The deputy sprang from the car and jogged south, perpendicular to the flow of the smoke. Hudson didn't want to leave the car, but Ben hoisted him off the backseat and followed Deputy Simms as well as he could.

The air was relatively clean just a few yards from the road, and Ben dropped Hudson to the ground and coughed the noxious smoke from his lungs. He saw that the plume came from the shed just across from the kitchen. The shed was close enough to put the main house in danger, but Ben still couldn't see any flames. Upslope, out of the flow of smoke, he saw Caroline and Charlie standing with Chief Stanton. She held Bub tight to her chest. He ran toward them as she ran to meet him.

"Are you all right?" he asked before starting to cough again. He took Bub from her to make sure the baby felt the way he was supposed to.

"I'm sorry," Caroline said.

"What happened?"

"I don't know. I don't know," she said. Her face was pale, her skin like marble. But it crumpled as she began to cry.

Ben pulled her close. Her sobs set her body shaking, and she seemed thin and brittle in his arms.

"Hi, Dad," Charlie said. He pulled on the pocket of Ben's jeans.

"Are you okay, buddy?"

"Yeah," Charlie said. He wore his faraway look. He walked back a few feet and sat in the tall grass so that only his blue eyes and shag of black hair were visible.

"What happened?" Ben asked Caroline again. Bub smiled tightly, his little face intent upon the task of placing his lips on Ben's cheek.

"I don't know," Caroline repeated. She didn't look up from Ben's shoulder, where her head was still buried.

"That smoke's no good," the chief said. The chief had a dusting of black soot all over him. Ben saw that they all did. "What'd you have in that shed?" he asked.

"Tools, lawn equipment—we store all of kinds of things in there."

"Could be some varnishes caught on fire on account of the heat."

"You think so?" Ben asked.

"It's been known to happen. Especially anything with linseed oil if it's not stored just right."

"So damn hot today, too," Simms said. "Would'na taken much to set her off."

"The cussing, Simms," the chief said. He gave Ben an apologetic look.

"Sorry, Chief," Simms said, and spat into the grass. "You think we need an engine out here?"

"I called 'em, but that shed's a goner no matter what."

"Could be worse," Ben said, more to Caroline than to anyone else. "Could be a lot worse."

The pickups from the village began to arrive. They parked downslope from where Ben had pulled over.

"Get rid of them, Simms," the chief said.

"They're just tryin'a get a better look, Chief," Simms said.

"This isn't the circus," the chief said. "They're not going to be any help with a fire like this, and this smoke's probably toxic. Tell 'em that, and see where it gets us."

Simms headed down to the trucks.

"Much smoke inside?" the chief asked Caroline.

"The air-conditioning was on in the south part of the house, so the windows were closed. And I turned off the air before we came out here."

"Smart thinking," the chief said. "If the air's still good in there, why don't you head back in with the boys? Thank the Lord, they're safe."

Caroline nodded. She took Bub from Ben and threw him over her shoulder. "I'll make something to drink for everyone."

Ben squeezed her arm as she moved away from him.

"I know they'll appreciate that, ma'am."

Caroline pulled Charlie up out of the grass and started to make her way back to the house. She gave the smoldering shed a wide berth.

"Engine should be here in twenty minutes," the chief told Ben.

"That long?" He watched the shape of Caroline diminish as she trudged for the house.

"Things are far apart up here. They take longer to happen, especially if you're in a spot like this—a place in between places."

A *place in between places* described it well, Ben thought. He wondered if the Swanns had ever thought like that when they first settled the Drop. He wondered if they also sometimes woke up in the dark of night forgetting where they were and why they had come here.

"I'm so sorry that this is so much trouble," Ben said. The sky above the mountains was heavy with smoke. He saw more cars from the village heading up the drive. This was the most exciting thing to happen in Swannhaven in a long time.

"These things happen. Likely just an accident. But we'll poke around tomorrow to be sure."

Ben nodded. "You should know that this isn't the first strange thing to happen to us up here." He wanted to believe that the fire happened precisely the way the chief guessed, but he couldn't take the chance that there was something more to it. He told the chief about the eviscerated deer.

"Maybe coyotes," the chief said.

"Then its head showed up on my doorstep that night."

The chief nodded. "A prank. I can talk to the boys. Even with all the trouble with the cows, there isn't enough to do around here."

But when Ben told him about the pit in the north woods, the chief's eyes widened.

"A lot of carcasses?" he asked.

"At least five deer and dozens of smaller animals."

"The boys might be poaching," the chief said. "If they have

blinds nearby, they might skin and butcher their kills in the woods and throw the rest into the ravine. Never an excuse for trespassing, though. And not safe for your little ones. Yep, I'll have a long talk with them, Mr. Tierney."

"Thanks, Chief." It had been a relief to talk to him about it. "Please call me Ben. And my wife doesn't know anything about any of this, so if we could keep it between us . . . I don't want to frighten her if it's just some guys blowing off steam in the forest, you know?"

"Misleading the womenfolk. Ugly business, but sometimes necessary. You don't have to worry." Chief Stanton smiled and put a hand on Ben's shoulder. Ben turned back to the Crofts. He hoped to glimpse Caroline and the boys making their way home, but he couldn't see them through the haze.

When he turned back to the chief, he saw that the older man's eyes had strayed to mountains. His hand remained on Ben's shoulder, but the smile had fallen from his face.

III

LOST *and* NOW RETURNED

DECEMBER

December 10, 1777

Dearest Kathy,

Jack is gone, and I do not know what to do.

He stood the watch at the edge of the south woods with Stephen Harp and William Lowell. The men fear the south watch and most draw lots for it, but it did not bother Jack to go. After midnight they heard a high-pitched chattering noise from the wood. You know how the sounds from the trees play tricks in the cold empty spaces here, but they say that this noise was of a different quality. At first it sounded near, and they moved beyond the tree line to observe its origins. William Lowell said that they walked into the wood, listened to ascertain the direction of the sound, and then walked a bit farther, then listened again.

Lowell does not know how long they went on like that, but they soon found themselves lured beyond the edge of the Drop. And when they dared not go any farther, a hint of smoke and meat tempted their noses. We have eaten nothing but small measures of wheat flour for some days now, and I know well the craving of which Lowell spoke. My mouth waters at the thought of it.

*It was then that they came upon a clearing with the embers of a fire
still smoldering. It had been an Iroquois encampment, but the Indians
were dead. They counted the remains of five. Our men searched the camp,
suddenly so hungry for meat that they could scarce think of anything else.*

*The site stank of food, but they could not find the source. Only then
did they examine the bodies of the Indians, thinking that one may have
fallen into the fire. The corpses were torn apart, with ragged pieces ripped
from the legs and chest. Lowell believed it to be the work of wolves. It is
the hungry season, and all creatures are emboldened by necessity. Upon
looking at a body, Jack cried out. By some miracle, one of the Iroquois
still clung to life. The man's lips were stained with blood, but he tried to
speak, his eyes rolling to their whites. The men clustered around him.*

*Lowell's account becomes confused here. He said that Jack bent down
to listen to the man's last words, and the Iroquois bit deep into his
forearm. Startled by the attack, Harp fled into the woods. Lowell struck
the Indian with the butt of his musket, and Jack was able to tear himself
free. Then the Iroquois faced Lowell and bit his leg. I have seen the
wound. With his uninjured arm, Jack threw the creature off Lowell, and it
turned upon him. Lowell says the Indian tore out our dear Jack's throat
with its teeth, and when that happened, Lowell ran, following the noise of
Harp's escape from the woods.*

*Father has not left his study since Lowell was brought to him. I have
comforted Mother and little James and Emmett as best I can, but you and
Jack were always better at that than I. I've told them that I believe he
didn't suffer, our Jack. A throat wound is so very swift a death. I've told
them that he registered a moment of surprise and a brief sensation of
pressure on his neck before unconsciousness took him. This is what I have
told them.*

*If you ever read this, sitting in the sun on a cobblestone street in free
Boston, you will think me mad, dear sister, and you may be right. Like
hunger, once madness is in the air it is likely to take root anywhere.
Perhaps my madness might be in continuing to write these letters. For all
I know, Boston, New York, and Philadelphia have all burned and this*

war has been the undoing of us all. What else is there to think with demons at our door and our beloved brother taken from us?

Pray for our dear Jack, Kathy. Pray for all of us, as I shall continue to pray for you.

Your Bess

22

Caroline held the brittle nook of Mrs. White's arm as they surveyed the frost-glazed garden. The fall herbs had long since been harvested, but trudging through the rows was a habit they'd carried from warmer months.

"Birthroot," Mrs. White said, pointing at one bed. In its prime, the plant had boasted beautiful crimson blooms, but it was now little more than a frozen stub of frayed leaves. The garden had been glorious in the summer and fall, but the weeks of cold had beaten most of the plants back into the earth. "When eaten, it speeds a baby along. And in a salve it clears insect bites right quick."

Caroline hadn't known anything about herbal medicine before spending time with Mrs. White. But over the course of many visits, she'd become a convert. Specially blended teas had eased her moods, broken her headaches, and calmed her nerves. These remedies had proved so effective that Caroline had completely phased out her medications a few weeks ago. Gone were the feelings of flatness and suffocation she sometimes felt on the drugs, and gone, too, was the sense of victimhood that came to her each time she had to obediently count out her pills. The transition hadn't been entirely smooth, but she and Mrs. White had experimented to find a combination of herbs, teas, and tinctures that worked. Ben's head would probably explode when he found out, but Caroline didn't plan to tell him until they'd gotten all the kinks worked out.

"For every problem, God offers a solution," Mrs. White said.

Lately, her soft voice had dropped to the volume of rustling leaves. Caroline was not the only one for whom the dark days of winter were difficult. Under the spell of cold, Mrs. White had withered along with her plants.

"I meant to tell you, that balm you made for Bub's teeth has been a blessing. He's sleeping right through the night again."

"Such a darling baby," Mrs. White said. "And how is Charlie?"

"He's fine," Caroline said. Maybe this wasn't strictly true, but he was Charlie. There was no easy answer.

"And Ben?"

"A bit distant, but he's always like that when he's working on a book." *Unfortunately, he's always working on a book,* was what she didn't say. Mrs. White had become the only person she could talk to about such things, though she tried not to complain much about Ben. Caroline didn't want to be one of those women who constantly whined about her husband. It wasn't appropriate in so small a village, especially considering that Ben and Mrs. White were both active in the Preservation Society and the Swannhaven Trust.

"It's a hard season," Mrs. White said. Caroline had often heard that said about the holidays, and she couldn't disagree.

After negotiating a good rate with a manufacturer, Caroline had ordered dozens of beds, tables, couches, and dressers for the Crofts. She'd also commissioned larger pieces of furniture for the rooms on the first floor. As much as they'd already bought, they still needed linens, rugs, curtains, dishes, towels, art—and that was just for the interior. Though Caroline had big plans for an herb garden and other landscaping, she and Ben hadn't even begun working on the grounds. And unless it involved moving furniture or holding picture frames against the wall, she knew Ben would be of little help. As usual, Caroline would find herself shouldering the burden. It would take a massive amount of time to get everything right. Time and money. Always money.

"I like the holidays," Caroline said—though saying this aloud made her remember that she still needed to cajole Christmas lists out of Ben and Charlie, buy the presents, wrap them, get more ornaments for the trees, bake cookies, bake more cookies, plan a menu for Christmas Day, write out cards, address the envelopes, and decorate the house nicely for the kids. The Christmases of her youth had seemed magical, and she wanted her sons' to be the same. If she couldn't be a banker, she was going to be the best mother anyone had ever seen. She wanted the holidays to be perfect, just as she wanted the Crofts to be. Ben thought that this was part of her problem, but Caroline believed in striving for excellence. Still, that left her with a lot to do and little time in which to do it. They hadn't even taken their Christmas card photo yet.

"It's right to look forward to happy times, but the winters here have their hardships, too," Mrs. White said. Coming to the end of a row, they turned back to Mrs. White's small house, where they would share a cup of tea before Caroline headed home.

Whenever Caroline visited Mrs. White's cottage, she felt as if she were stepping into the pages of a fairy tale. Inside, the embers of a fire glowed in the hearth, and the ceiling beams burgeoned with bundles of dried herbs. A wall was covered with narrow shelves that held an entire apothecary's worth of tinctures, oils, tonics, and balms.

Mrs. White fired the stovetop for the kettle and examined the small mounds of bespoke teas on her workbench. Caroline knew hers would have St. John's wort and lady slipper for anxiety, while Mrs. White's often had some milkweed and yarrow for her arthritis.

"Maybe you should include some blessed thistle and wormwood in yours," Caroline said. "For appetite."

Mrs. White nodded. She had grown frighteningly thin.

"It's nice to be by the fire," Caroline said. "I wish we had fires more often at home. Ben usually makes them only on special occasions, but they're so comforting."

"Best way to beat the cold," Mrs. White said. "Now, I've made you a new blend, dear. Something that will chase those December blues away." She took the whistling kettle off the stovetop but, in doing so, knocked over a plate. It shattered against the floor like an eggshell.

"No, no, let me," Caroline said. She practically dove for the shards to keep Mrs. White from bending over.

"So sorry, dear. Must be a little light-headed."

"You're so busy taking care of everyone else that you forget to take of yourself," Caroline said. She brushed the broken fragments from her hand into the garbage. It was a relief, really, to be able to dispose of a mess so easily.

"It's a hard season," Mrs. White said again. She handed Caroline a steaming mug. The old lady had also repeated herself many times on Caroline's last visit as well as confided that she'd been getting confused at night. Caroline hoped this wasn't the beginnings of dementia. "Up here, the winter months are filled with trials. But our days in the sun wouldn't count for anything if we didn't know what life was like in the shadows. And always remember that for every problem, God provides a solution." This was Mrs. White's mantra, and one that Caroline had tried desperately to believe. It was good to think that she only had to find the right way to repair herself and her family. It was good to think that it wasn't impossible for them to have it all again. She sipped at the tea and winced at its bitterness.

"The hard times make the happy times better, I think," Mrs. White said.

Caroline sighed. If contemporary misery was a down payment on future contentment, then she could look forward to some very good times indeed.

23

Ben leaned in to the chain saw even as the blood glazed his eye guard.

"That's good," Jake yelled behind him. "You can cut bigger, if you like."

Old man Robards had called in the carcasses at noon, and Ben and Jake had been the first to arrive. Five Holsteins in a rough circle, frozen solid to the ground, their puddles of icy guts and blood glowing like red glass in the sun.

Ben had been helping with the cattle cleanup for the last month. Some days, cows at four or five farms need to be chopped up and hauled away. If they'd lain there through the night, the coyote packs left their marks. They tore chunks from the hulking bodies, emptying their contents onto the frosted grass. Tangles of intestines often trailed for many yards toward the trees, as if they'd tried to haul their mighty bounties back to their lairs.

The carcasses couldn't be left for the forest animals and were too heavy to lift, so they had to be cut into more manageable sizes. The cold didn't make any of this easier. Even after Ben sawed through the leg, it stuck up from the glaze of frozen blood as if it had been sunk in concrete. Jake had brought a sledge for such work.

Five dead cows was a high toll for one farm during a single night, but last week eleven had been struck down on the Wyatt parcel. Like these five, they hadn't been found until morning, their bodies frozen to the ground, their blood and viscera mingled in a crimson lake that filled the spaces between them. The coyotes must have thought they'd died and gone to scavenger heaven. Gas was treasured in the remote valley, but gallons had been spent in burning the bodies where they lay.

Ben pressed the blade down again and watched as blood misted the nearby tufts of grass red. The spines were always tough.

As Ben went for another pass, a white pickup pulled alongside his car, with a battered black truck following close behind. Roger Armfield raised a hand in greeting as he got out of the white vehicle. These cleanups had an ever-shifting cast, but as the town veterinarian, Armfield was a constant presence. Two younger men, the Connelly brothers, hopped out of the black truck.

Greetings were exchanged in the local parlance—head nods and evaluative squints.

Reaching the first carcass, Armfield clucked to himself. "Rheumy eyes, swollen tongue, bloodied saliva." He ran through a checklist of symptoms. Not being a cattle owner himself, Ben hadn't made a study of the sickness, but it did seem strange to him how it killed in clusters. The townspeople were exceedingly diligent in their quarantine procedures, and yet this appeared to have little effect.

Armfield moved on to examining the predatory element of the grisly scene. He spoke in staccato observations, as if summarizing the autopsy into a recorder. "Seven to eight individuals. Large hunting pack. Unusually large for coyotes. Lupine hybrid? Highly socialized. Scat suggests—" Armfield had misjudged the slickness of the icy blood, and his feet flew out from under him. He landed hard on the gory field.

Ben bit down on a smile, but the others didn't bother to hold back. Ben offered his hand as the gangly man unfolded himself back to his full height. As he did, Armfield clutched his head, leav-

ing a crimson swath across his bald pate. Ben almost felt sorry for
him.

As the vet staggered away from what was left of the Holsteins,
Ben revved the chain saw and resumed his cutting. With the Connelly brothers here, he could cut larger pieces, and their pace quickened.

Months ago, Ben couldn't have seen himself chopping up frozen
diseased cattle with a chain saw. But he needed to feel what it was
like to be a part of this place, to be a member of this raw and austere
world that the Swanns had lived in. In this valley, he'd learned, your
hands sometimes got dirty. Sometimes they got bloody.

The chief or Armfield might throw the boys a twenty or two at
the end of the day, but the cleanup crews practically worked for free.
Ben had heard his share of clichés about rural living, and every one
of them had rung in his head in the months he'd spent here, but there
was something about watching a small, isolated community like
Swannhaven pitch together in a crisis that made him feel as if this
was how things were meant to be.

Arms thrumming from the machine, face and clothes splattered
with crystallized blood, Ben cut and the boys hauled. Somewhere
nearby, milk was bottled and eggs were cleaned, grain was ground
and bread baked. Even in the frozen stillness of December, the little
valley hummed onward.

It was inspiring, but it sometimes filled Ben with envy. If only his
own household ran with such elegance. Free of acrimony and
stripped of cross-purposes.

Ben sliced into the bowels of one cow, and the air shimmered
with fumes. This one hadn't frozen all the way through. The smell
was as horrific as the scene itself, but Ben was careful to keep his face
as expressionless as those of the other men. There would be no eye
rolls at the unpleasantness of the task. Here, Ben had learned that
all work was stoic's work.

Ben felt his phone buzz in his pocket but ignored it. He was covered with blood, and he was pretty sure there was no provision for abattoir damages in his service contract.

With the additional help, the work sped by, and in no time the beds of the two vehicles were filled. The bodies were gone but the patch of blood would remain, and Ben wondered if it would poison the ground or fertilize it. Sometimes death begat more death; sometimes it made new life possible.

When he was finished, Ben stripped off the long raincoat he'd worn for the occasion. He did his best to knock the gore from his boots. Jake did the same before getting into the Escape.

"Might finish the roof today," Jake said as Ben pulled away from the field. The fire had totally destroyed their old shed, and Jake had been building them a new one. Except for the shingles, he was nearly finished, and just before the full brunt of winter came crashing upon them.

"You've done a great job on it," Ben said.

"Incoming call from Cee," the car announced.

"Ignore," Ben said. He'd be at the Crofts in five minutes, anyway.

The Robards' farm was on the south edge of the valley, but already Ben could see the Crofts between the mountains. When November passed, it took the fall's blazing forests with it, but what color the forests had lost, the rooms of the Crofts had gained. Cracked plaster and faded wallpaper had been replaced by drywall and paint in empire blues, deep sea greens, noontime yellows, and day-end reds. The floors had been sanded, stained, and waxed to a brilliant depth.

When Ben turned from the country road onto the gravel path, he accelerated into the slope.

"Why is that the only tree out there?" Ben asked Jake. He jutted his head toward the great elm on the lip. It was a beautiful tree. It reminded him of the giants that flanked the Literary Walk in Central Park. When he stared out of his windows, he often found himself wondering about it.

"The elder tree," Jake said. "They say that when Aldrich Swann first cleared the woods from the Drop, he kept that one tree there to remind everyone of how great the forest once was."

Ben nodded. From what he'd gathered, the Swanns had been an eccentric bunch.

When the Escape was parked, Jake headed for the shed, while Ben made for the kitchen. Bub toddled up to him in lurching steps when he entered the kitchen. The baby had started walking a few months ago and now careened around the house with all the grace of a clubfooted drunk. Ben swept him up and kissed him on his forehead.

"I called you," Caroline said. She was chopping leeks on the island. "More than once." She wore khakis and one of Ben's old oxford shirts. Back in the city, this wouldn't have qualified even as weekend wear, but now every day was the same for them. The chores demanded of him were the only things that changed.

"Had my hands full," Ben said.

"Too bad dead cows take precedence over your own son."

"What are you—" Then Ben noticed the clock on the microwave. "Oh."

"What is this? The third time this week you've forgotten him?" She made a sound with her tongue.

"Don't. Please." Ben closed an open drawer with more force than was necessary.

In his father's arms, Bub began to fuss.

"If only you could get out of your head for long enough to—"

"The last time I checked, I wasn't the only one in this house with a driver's license," Ben said.

"Good. I'd been trying to figure out how this was actually my fault." She slammed the chef's knife into the cutting board.

Bub began to squall, his lungs now as strong as his little legs.

"Hush," Ben said as he bounced him. The baby wasn't as easy to wrangle as he'd once been. Ben could tell from the quality of his cries that Bub was ramping himself up to an inconsolable level. "Where's Hudson? *Hudson?*" he bellowed into the house.

"Forget the dog!" Caroline told him.

"Bye-bye," he told Bub, trying to pry him from his arms. The boy, now hopelessly distraught, shrieked for him. He arched his back in that way that made everything impossible. But Ben forced the baby to the floor, near where a Fisher-Price airport had collided with a parking garage.

He jumped into the Escape and took the gravel drive at a reckless speed. Fallen leaves from the forest danced in his rearview mirror.

Ben punched up the volume on the stereo. He was playing another one of the albums that Ted had sent his way. The vocals were angry, but they fit him fine.

The priory bused many of the boys, but Charlie was the only student from Swannhaven, and the little village was too remote to warrant a bus route. Ben rarely minded driving him, though he hoped that everyone had exaggerated the treacherous winter weather.

Some students still loitered around the school's front steps when Ben pulled up, but Charlie wasn't among them. He parked the Escape and walked around the cluster of buildings to the athletic fields, where a soccer practice was in session. The priory ran a winter soccer program that competed against nearby private schools. The boys were running passing drills in two lines, from one end of the field to the other.

Ben found Charlie watching from one of the small metal bleachers that flanked the field.

"Hi." He sat next to his son. "Sorry I'm late."

"It's okay."

The boys who had completed the drill started doing tricks with the balls. They bounced them off their knees and knocked headers between them. Ben could feel the cold from the bleachers through his jeans. He watched Charlie's eyes follow the boys showing off to one another.

"I bet you can juggle the ball better than any of them. I should get you one so you can try it."

"I have one already."

"Well, we should play with it more. Did you know that I was on the soccer team when I was your age?"

Charlie shook his head.

"I was pretty good, too." Ben saw Father Cal walking through the priory's garden, and he raised a hand to him. "I was a forward. You know what that is?"

Charlie shook his head again. His eyes were still on the field, but Ben sensed that his thoughts were far away.

"It was my job to score the goals."

"Oh."

Father Cal reached the bleachers and shook Ben's hand. "Getting chilly."

"I can't believe they're still wearing shorts," Ben said, nodding to the boys on the field.

"The young don't stand still long enough to feel the cold," Cal said. "Hello, Charlie. Do you mind if I borrow your dad for a moment?"

"Okay," Charlie said. His eyes did not stray from the soccer players.

"Is everything okay?" Ben asked Cal as they walked toward the garden. He talked with the priest every few days, and Cal had never hesitated to speak in front of Charlie.

"Charlie's doing exemplary work in all his classes. He's a bit shy, but that's not unusual since he's still new and he's been through a lot recently."

"Switching schools is hard," Ben said. "But after the last one, this place must feel like a relief." He kept up with the priest's casual tone, but Ben had plotted enough dialogue in his time to already dread where this conversation would take them.

"Moving here from the city is a big change. Getting a new brother can be traumatic. And having Caroline around more is something else he's had to get used to. There was also that business with the fire over the summer."

They skirted the edge of the garden to head toward the buildings. "That could have been a lot worse than it was." The fire in the shed had been a near thing; if the wind had been any different, they could have lost much more than its four walls and some lawn equipment.

"Some events latch on to children and don't let go. Who can say why? But it's best that they're brought into the light, rather than left to grow in the dark."

"What exactly are we talking about here?"

"His art teacher, Miss Woods—you may remember her from back-to-school night? Lovely woman. They've been doing pastel work in Charlie's class, but Miss Woods sensed that they needed a break and gave them a free drawing period."

"I'm not going to like this, am I?"

"It's a small thing, Ben," Cal said. "But a thing that shouldn't be ignored."

They entered one of the low stone buildings on the edge of the school's campus. Student artwork was on display along the walls of the hallway. Watercolors of the seasons, colored-pencil renderings of pilgrims and tall ships.

When they reached the classroom, Father Cal announced their presence to the young woman updating the bulletin board.

"Hello, Mr. Tierney." A smile lit Miss Woods's face. "It's nice to see you again."

"Likewise," Ben said. He tried to return the smile.

"Well, as I told you at conferences, Charlie's great." She gathered a sheaf of papers from her desk. "He's very careful and doesn't cause any trouble—which, I can tell you, is a characteristic I appreciate in kids of any age."

Father Cal remained standing, but Ben settled into a desk in the third row that he remembered was Charlie's.

Miss Woods recounted what Father Cal had already told Ben about the free drawing period. She pulled a page from the pile and showed it to them: a jungle scene with a child's stab at giraffe shapes and elephant impressions. The second sheet she showed them depicted a figure standing on grass, with rows and rows of multicolored circles in the background. "I think this one is of a soccer stadium," she said, before setting it aside. She removed the top few pages from the pile.

"Charlie always does things a little differently—which is one of the things I most enjoy about teaching him." She began to lay the pages out on her desk. "A different perspective is invaluable. It gets the other students thinking and certainly keeps me on my toes, too."

Charlie's drawing was comprised of six sheets of paper, arranged in three columns. The left column was a stark outline of the Crofts, executed in sharp black strokes, its towers pressing all the way to the top of the upper sheet. The right column was of the forest, an impenetrable bank of overlapping trees rendered with the same clear purpose as the drawing of the house. With a medieval sense of proportion, Charlie had given the two subjects an equal presence. Taken together, the drawing's two outermost columns had a stark elegance to them.

The center column was the problem. The shed, half the height of the Crofts itself, was ablaze—the vivid red of the conflagration the only color on any of the pages.

"And the smoke, do you see it?" Father Cal asked.

Ben did see it: The way the smoke coiled and curved like a dark halo above the blaze. The way its tendrils looked like two arms and two legs. The way the cloud of smoke at the uppermost edge of the page looked like a featureless face.

"Okay." The word came out cold and tight.

"I asked him about the man in the smoke, but he didn't answer me," Miss Woods told him. "He gets quiet sometimes."

"Yeah." Ben ran his hands over the unblemished wood veneer of Charlie's desk. He didn't need to look at the desks around him to know that they were etched with half-formed words and scratched by restless pens.

"We thought it best to point it out to you, Ben," Cal said. "It's normal for a child his age to have lingering anxiety from witnessing a fire like that. Everyone processes these things differently—children often deal with fear or trauma in unanticipated ways."

"I didn't realize it was still on his mind," Ben said. He'd never tell them, but he couldn't recall ever discussing the fire with Charlie. He remembered that afternoon, with his son sitting in the field watching the fire, his dark tousled hair and unblinking blue eyes immobile among the waves of grass. "Sometimes it's hard to guess what he's thinking."

"It's probably a small thing," Cal told him again. "We share a counselor with another school who's trained for this, if you'd like Charlie to see her."

"Thanks." Ben rubbed his eyes with his hands. "I'll talk to Caroline about it."

"Good," Cal said. He smiled and straightened his back, his duty done. "Thank you, Miss Woods."

"Yes, thank you," Ben said, and stood up.

"How's everything else?" Cal asked once they were out of the building.

"Fine. Busy, you know." He was happy not to have to talk about the drawing or the man in the smoke.

"I'm sure."

"Caroline's still upset that we weren't able to open in time for the foliage."

"You've both accomplished amazing things in such a short amount of time."

"I've tried to tell her that, but she's back to the pace of her finance days. She can never admire the things she's accomplished. The tasks left undone are all that matter."

"And it's not as if the Crofts is your only project. Have you heard back from your editor?"

"Yesterday," Ben said. He stopped at the path that would lead him back to the athletic fields, but Cal moved to walk deeper into the dying garden. "I should probably head back to Charlie."

"Indulge me for a moment," Cal said. "I learned something that I think you'll appreciate. And I'm dying to hear what your editor said."

"Oh, he said he liked the pages." Ben had also used the opportunity to ask his publisher to release part of his next advance payment early. He hated asking, but Caroline said they were having "liquidity issues" and that an early payment would help keep them going for a while longer. Ben hadn't been in a position to argue, but it was still hard for him to believe things had gotten so bad so quickly.

"Congratulations!"

"Thanks." He'd been happy with the pages he'd sent in, but lately the words weren't flowing as easily as they had been. "He said he'd feel better if I sent him an outline for the rest of it, but he knows I don't really work that way." He forced himself to smile. "But I couldn't have done it without you," he told Cal.

The priory had extensive if unorganized records that dated to the colonial period, and Cal's curiosity about the Swanns and their home had prompted him to sniff out some intriguing details about their history. While Ben had gained a valuable perspective by attending the Preservation Society meetings, Cal's research had proven just as useful. As arresting as Chief Stanton's ancestor's account of the Winter Siege was, the ones shared in later meetings of the Preservation Society were very similar. Terrible strife and losses followed by faith, cooperation, and—ultimately—salvation. The story had a pleasing arc, but there was something missing from it. Ben had sensed this same weakness in his own book. He didn't know how to fix it.

"That's very flattering," the priest said.

"I mean it," Ben said.

Cal waved him away, but Ben knew the older man was pleased. They stopped in front of the mosaic of St. Michael and the dragon. With the bite in the air and waning forests all around, Ben thought that today the dragon might hold the advantage.

"Yesterday I was in the archives to see if there was any mention of the railroad that passed through Swannhaven in the nineteenth century. Jamison Swann had been one of the railroad's founders in the 1840s. It was an exceedingly lucrative venture until the railroad collapsed in the 1870s. Does this ring a bell for you?"

"Of course. It's all anyone talks about."

"Those were tough times, and I was genuinely surprised to discover amidst the priory's accounts of good works that one of our chapter's favorite bits of lore is more fiction than fact. When I first showed this mosaic to you, I was under the impression that it had been created by a talented brother who'd lived here."

"And?"

"Most artists sign their work, don't they?"

Ben dutifully moved closer to the mural to examine the edge of the mosaic. The tiles that made up the piece were exquisitely fitted. In order to achieve such a sense of dimension against such a dark palette, the artist must have expended great effort to make use of every nuance of color.

"I don't see anything."

"Anything out of place?"

"The Socratic method, is it?" He panned the shadows of the wall twice before he found it in the right corner of the foreground: a curved neck and ebony beak, the carefully wrought texture of feathers. "Is that . . ."

"A swan," Cal said. "A black swan. A perplexing addition to the scene, until you realize it's also a signature."

Ben stepped back and looked at the mosaic again. In the slanted winter light, the ripple of gray mountains lined up behind the beast like waves approaching the shore. *A swan?*

"Joseph Swann, age sixteen, begged hospitality from the brothers at St. Michael's soon after his family's railroad went bankrupt," Cal said.

"Why?" Ben couldn't imagine what would bring a Protestant heir to a Catholic monastery.

"Family troubles of some sort. His older brother had passed away, and the two of them had apparently been very close. He remained at the priory until he matriculated at Harvard. After graduation, he moved to New York, where he became an artist quite in demand among the city's gilded class. He returned here later in his career, creating the mosaic as a gift to the priory."

Ben moved closer to the mosaic. His eyes ran along the contours of the land, and a knot began to tighten in his chest.

"It certainly is something, isn't it? Perhaps there's another novel in his story. Perhaps a sequel to your tale of troubled Swanns?"

Ben hardly heard him. A chill slid down his neck as he traced the lines Joseph Swann had crafted to form the unbroken ranges of distant mountains. He squinted at the way he had articulated the slow slope of the land that fell into the valley beyond the dragon. The way he had placed a single great tree in the mural's foreground.

Ben agreed with Father Cal that Joseph Swann had possessed rare talent. He had captured the vista perfectly. Ben knew this because he woke up to that precise view every morning.

24

In the car, Ben attempted conversation with Charlie. He asked him questions about his day, about his vocabulary words, about the owl pellet his class had found in the forest. He asked his son questions because that's what he was supposed to do. Charlie answered them for the same reason. For the most part, Charlie stared out his window as intensely as Ben stared ahead.

The first time Ben had seen the mosaic in the monks' garden, he'd assumed it depicted the valley upon which the priory perched. It made sense that the artist would portray the brothers as St. Michael, their patron, combating the dragon. But the view Joseph Swann had perfectly captured was of Swannhaven's valley as seen from the Crofts. The infernal creature that he'd given such power rose from where the village stood, poised to strike out at the Drop.

As he drove down the empty county road, Ben imagined a giant beast galloping alongside the Escape, just beyond the tree line.

The light had faded. The clouds were stygian streaks above them. It had been getting dark early, but Ben must have spoken with Father Cal longer than he'd realized. He could see the outline of the Crofts up on the Drop. Caroline would be in the kitchen now, but Ben couldn't see that side of the house from here. The unlit towers and soaring roofs looked black against the purpling sky.

Ben felt a grip on his shoulder: Charlie had grabbed him. He looked forward and saw a figure standing in the road. Ben slammed on the brakes and spun the wheel. The car screamed to a stop when they were abreast of the person in the road.

"You okay?" he asked Charlie.

"Yes."

"Stay here." Ben got out of the car.

The figure hadn't moved from its position in the middle of the road, but in the dusk it seemed to have turned to them. In the flash of the headlights, Ben had thought he saw a woman, but he wasn't sure.

"Are you all right?" he asked. "Ma'am?" He walked around the car to where the figure still stood. He was sure it was a woman now; a breeze had caught the wisps of her white hair.

Ben came alongside her. She wore a breezy housedress that was too thin for the cold day, and she still hadn't acknowledged him.

"Do you need help?" he asked. It was only then that he realized it was Mrs. White. He hadn't seen her in a few weeks. In the past her hair had been tied tight behind her head, but now it billowed around her like white flames.

Her mouth moved, but Ben couldn't hear what she was saying. Finally, he reached out to touch her shoulder and saw her face clearly for the first time. He wanted to let go, but instead his grip on her shoulder tightened. She had wide almond eyes and a face that had grown gaunt enough to erase her wrinkles. For a second she looked so much like his grandmother that he couldn't breathe.

"Get your hands off her." A man's voice came from the woods.

Ben pulled his arm back. He heard footsteps along the side of the road, and soon he saw the man attached to them. He was about Ben's height and in his sixties, powerfully built. A shotgun was slung across his chest.

"You're going to scare her," the man said.

"She was standing in the middle of the road," Ben said.

"All right now, Mama?" the man asked the old woman. "Wandered away, didn't you?" The man slid his shotgun so that it hung across his back and gently picked the woman up in his arms. The man looked strong, but from the ease with which he did this, it was clear Mrs. White was nothing but skin and bones.

"It was a miracle I didn't hit her," Ben said.

"I'd kill you," the man said. He said it evenly enough for Ben to believe him.

Ben knew enough to back down from a confrontation with an upset stranger, but he had his son in the car, and now he was angry, too. He stalked back to his car door. "If you're so attached to your mother, keep her from walking in the middle of the road in the dark. Not everyone's going to stop."

He got into the Escape, slammed the door, and took the road as fast as it would let him. He watched the figures in his rearview until they melted into the dark.

"Sorry about that," he told Charlie after he'd calmed down. He slowed the car to the limit.

"She shouldn't have been in the road," Charlie said.

"No, she shouldn't have been. But she's a nice old lady. She's Mom's friend, the one who gives her that tea she likes. She must have gotten lost." They were almost to the Crofts. The county road ascended just before their turnoff.

"She looked sick like Grams," Charlie said. "She looked hungry."

Midway up the gravel drive, Ben saw the lights from the south end of the house. For the first time, the place almost felt like home.

The kitchen was warm and smelled of the soup Caroline had simmered through the afternoon. Jake sat by Bub, trying to coax a spoonful into the baby's mouth. Ben was relieved to see the young man there. The Wolf rarely made an appearance when they had company.

"Bub tired himself out with a meltdown, and I wanted to get some food into him before putting him to bed," Caroline said. "What took so long?"

"We watched soccer practice for a while," Ben said. "And almost hit Mrs. White. She was wandering down the middle of the street."

"Are you serious?" Caroline asked. Her hand went to her heart.

"Yeah. It was close. She must have gotten disoriented. A guy— her son, I guess—is taking care of her."

"She seemed a little off this morning," Caroline said. "I thought maybe she was coming down with something. She'd told me she gets confused at night. But wandering in the dark and cold—and on the road!"

Charlie hoisted his backpack off his shoulders and onto the floor. As he neared the table, Hudson let out a low growl.

"Hudson, do I need to put you in the hallway again?" Ben asked him. Hudson bared his teeth for moment, then settled back down to the floor. "She put you on dribble detail?" Ben asked Jake.

"I think some of it's going to the right place," Jake said.

Caroline ladled soup into bowls, while Ben began sawing through a loaf of peasant bread. She'd made potato-leek and garnished it with rashers of bacon.

"Did you ask your dad about dinner?" Caroline asked Jake. From the brittle smile stretched across her face, Ben knew she was trying to change the subject from poor Mrs. White.

"He was tickled. Said he hasn't been up here in years."

"Tell him that we're really excited to have him," Caroline said. Their dining room furniture was arriving any day now, and Caroline felt obligated to invite some of the locals up to the Crofts for dinner. She'd never taken to many of the villagers, other than Mrs. White, but she thought showing them the renovations and treating them to a nice meal would be a smart way to strengthen their ties to Swannhaven.

"Is he feeling better?" Ben asked. Jake's widower father often seemed to be ailing.

"His back doesn't seem as bad. Was down at the Picket place last week, helping with the cleanup."

"Would you take him some soup from us?" Caroline asked.

"Thanks; it's real good," Jake said. "And the shed should be finished tomorrow for sure. Got to get that roof on before the weather turns."

"Then what? Back to the orchard?" The pained smile was still on Caroline's face, and she had bolted her soup with frightening speed. Still, it was good to see her eat.

"Better leave that till spring. I cleared the big brush, and the cold should take the fight out of the rest. I'll clear what's left after the snowmelt. You gotta decide what to replace the dead trees with. Got about twenty that are still kicking."

"And the lake?" Caroline asked. She never let up, but it didn't seem to bother Jake.

"Don't really know where to begin with the lake, is the honest truth. But you could lay the lines for the herb garden. Could take a look at some of the outbuildings, too," Jake said. "See if anything can be saved. The old stables could be fixed up if they're not too bad off. Maybe the shed by the road, too. Probably too late for the others, though. The cider house and the chapel were wrecks last I saw them, but that was when I was a kid."

"There's a chapel?" Caroline asked.

"What's left of it is pretty deep in the woods now, north of the cemetery," Jake said. "Visited it once in school, back when the Swanns were here."

Ben remembered stumbling upon the ruins of the chapel over the summer. When he thought of the terrible creature he'd found carved on the plaque there, it reminded him of the man in the smoke from Charlie's drawing.

"Did you know the Swanns well?" Ben asked Jake. The young man had been a good source of information about Swannhaven, but Ben had learned to spread his questions around. The villagers tended to clam up in the face of too much curiosity.

"The aunties?" Jake asked. "They were good women. Eleanor, the younger one, was still beautiful, right to the end. And Miranda was so old you'd think she was born that way. Used to deliver their groceries," Jake said. "Didn't leave the Crofts too much, not after the fire." He stood up to clear his dishes.

"When the Swann boys died," Ben told Caroline. "Mark and Liam."

"Horrible," Caroline said. Ben had told her Father Cal's story about the night of the fire. "They had foster children, too, right? What happened to them?"

"Moved to other homes, I think—I only heard, because I wasn't even born yet. Then there was that one that was sent away."

He meant the boy who'd set the fire.

"What happened to him?" Ben asked.

Jake shrugged. "Wherever they put the bad ones, I guess. A hard lot the Swanns had to shoulder," he said. "Real saints, though. Were always nice to me."

"I've learned a lot about the village from the Preservation Society, but I still feel like there's so much I don't know." The more Ben found out about Swannhaven, the more he realized how much remained to be discovered.

"I'd guess Lisbeth Goode and the Preservation folks know all there is to know," Jake said. "The Goodes have kept the records for this place as long as there've been records to keep. Lisbeth's father, old August Goode, ran the *Swannhaven Dispatch* until he died."

"Right, the *Dispatch*." Before he'd decided that his book would focus on the Revolutionary War period, Ben had been interested in tracking down back issues of the old town paper. "She must have an archive or something. I'll have to ask her about that."

"The village's history means a lot to us," Caroline told Jake. "I think its backstory will really help distinguish the Crofts from the inns and hotels in Exton. It'll make great copy on the website and in promotional materials. And it's exactly the kind of thing that appeals to travel magazines."

"Sounds good," Jake said, putting on his jacket.

If that was the pitch she planned to use on the villagers at dinner, Ben thought it could use some work.

"It must have been shocking for the village when the sisters died, what, two winters ago now?" Ben said. "Had they been sick?" Ben and Caroline had speculated about this since they first visited the Crofts.

"Nothing like that," Jake said. "That winter was colder than most, and the whole house couldn't be heated. Such a big old place. That's why you had to go and get a new furnace and all the rest. The aunties spent most of their time in the kitchen." He pointed to the stone fireplace on the far wall. "Story is that one night the fire wasn't enough."

"What do you mean it wasn't enough?" Caroline asked.

"The cold," Ben said. He leaned back in his chair. They'd imagined a dozen scenarios but nothing like that. "They both froze right here in this room."

25

Ben had been in bed for an hour, and still sleep did not come.

When he closed his eyes, he saw the face of Mrs. White. Her lips mouthing something he could not discern. The news that the Swann sisters had died in the kitchen also troubled him. He'd assumed that they'd died in their home; that was where old women died. But to think that this family had survived sieges and depressions, wars and pandemics, only to be finished by a cold night . . .

He threw himself onto his side and tried to stave off thoughts of the old sisters, imagining in their place Swannhaven against the blank slate of fresh snowfall near the end of the blood-soaked year of 1777.

At the time of the Revolution, there had been no more than a handful of buildings clustered around the village square and a dozen farmhouses spread throughout the valley. The snow on the fallow fields gave the view from the Crofts an unfinished look, as if the artist had been retained only to depict the valley's human contributions.

Just before dawn, the air cold and still, the Iroquois came from the south. Most arrived on foot, but some rode horseback along the flanks. By the time the sky had ripened, a group had detached for the southmost farmhouse, while the rest surged for the village. The snow began to mirror the amber sky. A beautiful morning.

Ben decided that the Swanns had woken at first light. By then, two of the farmhouses had been set alight. The Iroquois went from building to building along the village square, their guns shattering the morning. Up at the Crofts, where they could see but not hear the attack, the Swanns stood at their windows and watched their valley burn. The only daughter at home, Elizabeth, would have comforted the twins, James and Emmett, while Jack, the eldest son, would have grabbed his musket and run to rouse the tenant families on the Drop.

Their father, Henry Swann, had woken in the still of that morning knowing something of the day that awaited him. His grandfather Aldrich Swann had once told him that he had seen the Drop in a dream and known from that moment the wealth of land and family that God would grant him. Henry Swann had also dreamed in the restlessness of the night, but it had been no vision of comfort. And so he sat on the edge of his bed in his nightclothes for a time, feet stung by the floor's cold, praying for the courage to stand and walk to the window. He peered beyond the rime of ice and saw dark figures walking across the stark white fields with otherworldly grace. In a moment Henry imagined the full arc of the thing. He knew the horrors that flashed through him were a promise. The bill for his grandfather's dream had come due, and Henry wondered if God had played any part in it.

A noise tore Ben back to his own bedroom. A scream came from the attic.

The wind played all sorts of tricks when it found a way in. He and Jake had worked hard to seal the upper floors, but they could locate the drafts only when the wind was brisk. It was an odd sound, a warbling whistle. He stared at his ceiling, listening to the rhythm of the noise. It tapered to almost nothing, and just when it had nearly disappeared, it came surging back.

He closed his eyes again and searched his mind for the snowy village that burned in the valley, but the attic noise had pulled him too far out.

"Okay, I'm up," Ben said to himself. He swung his legs off the bed. Caroline turned over and muttered something. He remained motionless until her breathing settled.

He grabbed a sweater off the back of a chair and eased himself into the hallway. Using small steps and memory's projection, he felt his way down the hall, not flicking on the light until he got to the tower stairs. There were naked bulbs here, the cold light of cork-screw fluorescents. He shielded his eyes against the glare, knowing now that it would take him forever to fall asleep. On his way up the stairs to the attic, he caught his reflection in one of the windows. In the morgue lighting, he looked thin and startled.

Tracking a phantom sound in a house as large and old as the Crofts was a frustrating exercise. The acoustics of the building were strange. At times he could hear a noise in his bedroom and be certain it came from upstairs, only to ascend the stairs to find the place deathly quiet. He assumed it had something to do with the air vents that ran through the walls, the fickle wind from the valley, and the fact that the house had been constructed in stages. So when he opened the door to the attic, he wasn't surprised to find the room utterly silent. This was a game he'd played before.

With the exception of the nook where he wrote, the lighting in the attic was poor. There were just a handful of bulbs to light the immense space. He flicked them on and grabbed a roll of duct tape, a candle, and some matches from where they sat on a table near his desk.

The next room was in the center of the attic. He was sure this was where the noise had come from, but the way the scream ricocheted confused his senses. He rarely ventured beyond his writing nook and was struck by the emptiness of the space, which seemed to have grown in the dark.

A draft raised the hairs on his arms and sent a whistling cry through his ears. He quickly lit the candle to track the sound. He'd

hunted gaps in the ancient windows enough to know not to waste
the evidence left by a strong gust. The flame blew east, so he headed
to the windows on the western wall. One by one he traced the frames
with the candle. While he checked the last window, the flame was
blown out by the wind. Ben felt along the side of the window: The
current was cold fire on his fingertips. He ripped off a measure of
duct tape to mark the spot and unfastened the lock on the window.
Sometimes fiddling with the window was enough to temporarily dis-
rupt the wind's noise.

The window did not want to be opened, but Ben coaxed it halfway. The breeze from the valley tore through his hair and filled the
room. The chill from the December wind was as complete as a
plunge into the ocean. It was a bell-clear night, the sky an unfathomable blue, with only the boldest stars visible beyond the immensity
of the waxing moon. It could still catch him off guard: how beautiful
the world could be when no one was there to see it.

The sound was gone now. The attic was still in the new silence of
the night.

As he reached up to close the window, a flash of movement pulled
his gaze to the ground. Something ran through the dark.

It was a person, he was sure. He caught flashes of pumping arms
as the figure loped through the ghost-lit field.

Ben was on the tower stairs before he realized he was running. He
thought of poor lost Mrs. White and her son with his shotgun. He
thought of the man in the smoke from Charlie's drawing and of the
mutilated deer and the pit in the north woods. Death and violence
and blood. Ben thought of his boys asleep in their beds. He had an
abstract thought that this was the point in the story when the man
got his gun. But he had no gun. When he reached the kitchen, he
crashed through the baby gate they kept on the stairs, sending it spi-
raling into the counter. On his way to the door, he pulled a knife
from the rack.

He burst out of the house.

His heart thudded in his chest, but beyond the rustle of grass in the wind, the world was quiet. Walking quickly in front of the house, he ran his eyes over the Drop, searching for movement. He looked down at the knife. In the story, the knife would seize a malicious gleam from the moonlight; in his hand, it looked as dark as the sky.

The fields had been tamed by the morning frosts, and the grass was half its summer height but still tall enough to hide a man who did not wish to be seen.

"Hey!" he screamed. He screamed again before taking the time to consider whether this was a good idea.

He turned to the south woods and saw someone running toward him. Announced by ripples of windswept grass, the figure ran with the beat of the land. Its footfalls punctuated the gusts from the valley and matched the cadence of the forest's swaying trees. Ben dropped the knife.

"What the hell are you doing out here?" Ben shouted.

Charlie slowed to a stop in front of Ben.

"It was different in the dark," Charlie said. His little chest heaved as he tried to catch his breath. "Everything was different."

Ben knelt down to grab the boy at the shoulders, to force his son to look him in the eyes. "You can't be out here by yourself. It's too dark; it's too cold."

"Yes," Charlie said. He turned to the valley. "It will get darker."

"You could trip and hurt yourself out here. And we wouldn't know, because we'd assume you were in your bed, because that's where you're supposed to be. If you were out here alone all night, you'd die of hypothermia, except you wouldn't be alone because of the goddamn coyote packs." Ben realized he was screaming.

The sound of barking made Ben turn around just in time to see Hudson speed by him, a blur. The dog moved so quickly that Ben could only watch as the beagle launched himself at Charlie, knocking the boy to the ground.

"Hudson!" Ben shouted. The dog stood on Charlie's chest, growling, inches from the boy's face. Ben grabbed his collar to lead him away. "What's wrong with you?" He tried to get the dog to shift his focus to him, but Hudson would not stop. "Are you all right?" Ben asked Charlie.

"Yes," Charlie said. He got to his feet slowly, rubbing his side.

Spikes of grass lit up around them as light burst from the kitchen windows.

"What are you two doing out here?" Caroline called from the kitchen door. Her voice was nearly lost over Hudson's growling. She wore a red robe that turned a shade closer to black with every step she took from the house.

"Did you *see* him?" Ben asked her. He still had a grip on Hudson's collar.

"I heard *you*," Caroline said. "And Hudson. What's going on? Are you okay, Charlie?"

"I want to go inside," Charlie said. He let Caroline press his head against her hip.

"He's been running," Ben told her. "Running around. Out here. In the dark. I don't even know for how long." Ben could not remember ever being this angry. He didn't know what to do with it. It was a river burning inside him with nowhere to go.

"You can't be outside at night by yourself," Caroline told Charlie. "We need to know where you are, okay? You know this, honey. You're shaking, so go warm up. You're filthy, too. Wash your feet before going into bed." They watched Charlie run back to the house.

"What's wrong with Hudson?" Caroline asked Ben. The dog was now barking at the forest. Ben still had a grip on the beagle's collar, and it was hard to hear Caroline over the sound.

"I don't know. Charlie has everyone worked up. He's *unbelievable*," Ben said. "I'm up in the attic and see this . . . *thing* sprinting across the field. I don't know whether to call the police or *The X-Files*. But, no, it's not a yeti, it's my eight-year-old. He's not even wearing shoes."

"Neither are you," Caroline said. She was talking about his feet, but she was looking him in the eyes.

Ben couldn't read the expression on her face.

"Can we go inside now?" She sounded tired.

"This is *really not normal*. We have to do something." Ben remembered the quirks of Caroline's that he'd overlooked and knew all too well where ignoring them had gotten him. He could not live in a den of wolves.

"You know how he is. He just needed to be specifically told that he's not allowed to go out alone at night. We should keep better tabs on him, anyway. We've been too lenient about letting him play out here by himself."

After so many years of certainty, Ben was bewildered by what a puzzle Caroline had become. This was a woman who'd barely left her room for a day after he'd come home with a bucket of the wrong shade of ecru, so how was she not as upset about this as he was?

"It's not only that," Ben said. "At school, he drew this picture of the shed burning down, and there was this big black man in the smoke. Hudson!" The beagle leapt toward the forest, and Ben nearly lost his balance. "Calm down, buddy."

"What does that even mean?"

"The smoke from the shed was made to look like a man. Arms, legs, a face. It was *disturbing*. I'll show you the drawing." They were nearly to the kitchen door. "I think he should talk to someone. A counselor. The school has someone they think might be able to get him to open up." Ben knew this would be delicate territory for Caroline. She did not like therapists.

"Because of a drawing?" Caroline asked.

"It's probably just his way of processing the fire, but they could help him work through it. One evaluation session." Ben realized he was nearly pleading with her. "They'd pull him out of class for an hour. If everything's fine, like we think it is, then that'll be it." Ben didn't know if that was how it worked, but he needed her to agree to this.

"I don't know, Ben," Caroline said. She opened the door and held it for him. In the kitchen light, Caroline looked as tired as her voice sounded. Worn through.

"Please," Ben said. "What harm could it do?"

As Ben ascended the steps, Hudson twisted out of his grip and bolted for the moonlit fields.

"Hudson!" Ben called after him. The beagle howled his hunting cry into the night. "Hudson!"

"Ben, I've got to go to bed," Caroline said.

"I can't leave him out here," Ben said. "It's too cold." He had no idea how he was going to get the beagle back into the house. Hudson had never acted like this before.

"It's too cold for anyone to be out," Caroline said.

"I'll get my coat and boots," Ben said. He followed her inside. Maybe Hudson had sniffed out a coyote pack. This thought did not make him feel any better.

Caroline had already made her way to the tower stairs. Ben caught his reflection again in the glass. He was still thin and startled-looking, but now he seemed weary, too. And it was not the kind of exhaustion that could be fixed by a full night's sleep.

26

Charlie ran up the steps to his room. It was warm here, yet he trembled.

He had to clean off the blood first, in case Mom checked on him. The blood had looked like mud in the dark, but Hudson knew the difference.

While the Watcher had left Charlie the gifts of many arranged creatures in the forest throughout the summer and fall, it had rarely let itself be seen. But twice Charlie had spied it by the lake from the blind that he'd constructed in the branches above the faerie circle. Both times it had been trying to catch fish with its hands but had been doing it wrong. Charlie knew this because *The Book of Secrets* had a chapter on all kinds of fishing. He'd left the book by the lake, with a bright maple leaf to mark the page. The book was gone the next morning, but the day after that, Charlie had found it placed in the center of the faerie circle, ringed with the heads of five raccoons.

The game he played with the Watcher had changed over the months. At first it had seemed like a kind of tag, or a treasure hunt, but now it was a game of hide-and-seek, in which they both hid and searched at the same time. Charlie thought the rules to their game had changed, but watching the blood slip down the bathtub drain, he wondered if there had been any rules in the first place.

Charlie ventured into the night only when the moon lit the land. Caught in the wind and its cold light, the fields of the Drop ebbed and flowed like an ocean. Tonight was chillier than his other watches had been. He had worn a coat but no shoes so as to cross the land without a sound.

A family of deer had been drinking at the south end of the lake. They had paid Charlie no mind as he slid into the faerie circle and up the rope ladder that led to the platform from which he watched. As he climbed, he heard coyotes in the distance. He'd heard them many nights, but they never ventured into this part of the forest. This part of the forest had already been claimed.

Once up in his blind, Charlie searched the contours of the lake and saw that the deer were gone. The Drop was different at night. Sometimes he saw bats flutter against the stars and heard the mourning of owls from deep within the woods.

Charlie had learned things about the dark during that long night in his old school's furnace room. He knew that the dark was not one thing but many. Like layers of fabric stacked upon one another, each with its own texture. The longer he watched, the more these layers fell aside to reveal something more of the world beneath.

A loud crack shattered the silence. Charlie sat up straight; this was new. The first sound was followed by three more. The noises seemed too loud for broken branches. There was a sickening quality to them that Charlie could not place. The sounds had to be the work of the Watcher, but still he could not see anything.

While Charlie sat on his perch and wondered if he was supposed to follow the sounds, he heard more noise: a rustling followed by an urgent pattering. He could not imagine what made these sounds, but it was coming closer.

It was then that the massive bulk of the Watcher became visible. Charlie had never been this close before. If he had draped his arm off the platform, he would have grazed the creature's bristling head.

The Watcher was entering Charlie's faerie circle. And it wasn't alone. It took Charlie a second to understand that it was dragging one of the deer, a full-grown doe. Charlie hadn't realized it was a deer at first, because of the way it was crumpled against the ground. As the Watcher pulled the animal into the center of the circle, its legs dragged behind, splayed at terrible angles. Its useless feet pawed hopelessly at the frozen ground.

"Soon," the Watcher said. Its voice was deep as the mountains and broken from disuse. Charlie had never heard the Watcher speak; it had not occurred to him that it could. He knew it could write and read, but to hear the sound of its voice filled him with wonder and horror. The Watcher propped the deer against the stump in the center of the faerie circle, stretching its neck so that Charlie could see the profile of the doe's face. Short puffs of panicked breath clouded the air around its blinking eyes.

Though Charlie thought himself well hidden, the Watcher turned toward him. Without breaking their gaze, it plunged something into the deer's neck. A gush of blood arced high into the air, followed by another and another.

"Soon it will be you," the Watcher said. The pale eye of the moon shone in the sheet of crimson that rippled across the ground. The doe's breathing slowed. "In the cold, in the dark," the Watcher said. The deer twitched, and became still. "All alone. That's when you die." The Watcher's frozen face changed for a moment before turning away. It let the deer's limp body slump against the ground.

The Watcher disappeared into the woods, leaving Charlie with the dead deer. After a time Charlie realized he was shaking. He'd thought himself immune to the cold, but now it was all he felt.

He staggered down the rope ladder and into the wide pool of congealing blood. Once through the tree line, he began to run. Past the lake, he darted back into the trees. He wanted to purge the cold from his bones and the drying blood from his feet. When he turned back for the Crofts, he saw the illuminated windows of the attic and his father's silhouette against the light.

Even now Charlie's hands trembled in the heat of the faucet's stream. He would have to hide these pajamas. They were splattered with blood. As he took them off, he tried to imagine what the Watcher wanted.

The match between them was uneven; Charlie realized that now. Charlie could run and hide and search and watch, but if the Watcher in the forest decided to do something, Charlie knew that he could not hope to stop it.

27

Ben paced the edge of the forest for an hour, calling Hudson's name. When he became too cold to continue, he sat in the kitchen, listening and hoping for the beagle's scratch at the door.

He woke just before five, his face smeared against the table, his spine a tangle of pain. Outside, the moon had set; the land lay under a thicket of total darkness.

Ben returned to the forest, to walk along the trees and shout for Hudson. He shone a flashlight into the maw of the woods. Still no sign. The beagle might have found a quiet burrow in which to sleep through the night. This was possible, and this was what Ben made himself believe as he trudged back to the Crofts. After breakfast, Hudson would scratch on the kitchen door, 100 percent okay and in need of a bath.

Since this was going to be just another normal day, he should begin it in the usual way, Ben thought. He made coffee and brought his laptop down from the attic. By the time he got settled, the eastern sky had begun to lighten. Along the Drop, the fields were glazed with frost that gleamed purple in the day's nascent light.

Ben tried to immerse himself in his book. Sometimes, this part of his day filled him with dread, but today he was thankful for the distraction. He'd reached the book's second part. The Revolution had begun, the snows had fallen, and he had finished the chapters that played through his mind the night before: the action-filled scenes of the Iroquois attack. Now he was up to the difficult middle pages: the morning after the winter morning that changed everything.

Ben had set the stage and introduced the players in the first part of the book. Henry, the strict and religious patriarch. Elizabeth, the kindhearted but weak-willed daughter. He'd also set out some of the backstory of how the Swann family first found themselves in the house between the mountains. This was all essential to understanding their actions during the long disaster of the Winter Siege.

What, exactly, that long disaster entailed had somewhat eluded Ben. He knew that there would be death and that there would be terrible cold and even more-terrible hunger. But from the accounts Ben had heard at the Preservation Society, when the snows finally melted, the Iroquois were simply gone. Not much of a climax. And difficult as that winter must have been for the surviving townspeople, it did not seem quite so significant that it would still play such a part in their lives. The valley's entire political and economic structure appeared to be informed by the events of the winter of 1777, and Ben could still not make sense of why.

This was why the words had not been working for him. He typed himself in circles as the sun crested the horizon. After a time, creaks sounded from the floors above. When he reached for his coffee to find it empty, the mug ice cold, he discovered that hours had passed.

He put on some more coffee and made waffles. Bub liked waffles.

"You didn't come back to bed," Caroline said from the doorway. Bub writhed in her arms.

"I couldn't find Hudson," Ben said. "I thought if I stayed in the kitchen, I'd be able to hear him paw at the door."

"He spent the night out there?" Caroline asked. She put Bub in his high chair. "What are you going to do?" The alarm on Caroline's face somehow made it more real to Ben. Hudson was supposed to be here right now, curled at his feet.

"I don't know." He paused to let the lump in his throat recede. He supposed he could search the forest tree by tree, but Hudson knew how to get back to the Crofts. Beagles did not get lost. And if he'd hurt himself, Ben thought, he'd still be able to howl or bark. Yet the forest's silence had been unyielding. He refilled his mug with coffee. He moved to fill Caroline's, but she stopped him.

"Mrs. White gave me a new batch of tea that I wanted to try." She sighed as she filled up an infuser with the latest concoction. "I was thinking I'd bring her some leftovers today. Last night must have been so frightening for her. I hope it's not a sign of things to come."

"Tell her I said hi," Ben said. It felt like a decade had passed since he'd encountered Mrs. White in the middle of the road, but it was good to change the subject.

"I got an e-mail. The furniture's coming today," she said.

"Great." He wondered what beagles might eat in the wild.

"I'm going to a fabric store in Gracefield," Caroline said. "But I should be back in time. If not, I'll tell you."

"I'm meeting with Lisbeth Goode at around eleven." The night before, Ben had made an appointment to look at her archives of the *Swannhaven Dispatch*. He hoped that these papers might shake something loose and get him back on track with his book. "And I need to pick up Charlie at three."

"The big table's supposed to be in this shipment, so I thought next Friday would be a good day for that dinner with the villagers."

"That soon? I thought maybe we could do it after Christmas." This morning, the idea of playing host filled Ben with dread.

"Christmas is the perfect excuse for a dinner party. And we may as well get it over with."

"If you don't want them to come over, then why invite them?" He didn't understand what drove Caroline to continuously add stressful new items to her list of tasks. Between the house and the holidays, taking on anything else seemed like a self-inflicted wound.

"The only thing that matters is the inn, Ben. We need them to support it. Now, we were going to invite the Swannhaven Trust plus the Bishops?"

"Yeah," Ben said. He was sure he could count on Lisbeth Goode, the Stantons, and the Bishops coming, but he didn't know about the others. Walter Harp was always polite enough, but Ben had never gotten the impression that Harp had warmed to him. They would love for Mrs. White to come, but they'd have to see how she was doing. And Roger Armfield always seemed to be flustered to the point of incoherence around him—then again, for all Ben knew the man was like that all the time.

"What about Father Cal? Having another non-villager would be nice."

"I'll ask him."

Bub threw a waffle slicked with syrup at Ben. It left tendrils of stickiness clinging to his sweater when he peeled it off, but all Ben could muster was a sigh. He could feel Caroline staring at him.

"If we're both going out, you should make sure that Jake knows about Hudson so he can keep an eye out," she said.

"What about Hudson?" Charlie asked. Ben hadn't heard him come down the stairs. He moved as quietly as a ghost, and this morning he looked as pale.

"Hudson ran out last night and didn't come back," Caroline said. "You're late, but I'll fix a waffle for the drive to school, okay?"

"He went into the forest?" Charlie asked.

"I'll cut up half a grapefruit, too," Caroline said. "You need your fruit."

"He was there all night?" Charlie asked.

"He ran into the forest right after you went inside," Ben said. "I looked for him but couldn't find him." There was much he wanted to say about last night's excursion, but right now he didn't have the energy.

"You went into the forest?" Charlie asked. His face was taut: an expression that Ben couldn't read.

"I called from the edge of the trees," Ben said. "Why?"

"You can help Dad look for Hudson after school, can't you, Charlie?" Caroline said.

"In the forest?" Charlie looked as if he'd slept as poorly as Ben had, but there was something off about him that could not be explained by fatigue.

"Where else?" Ben asked. "You like the forest, don't you, Charlie?" He watched his son carefully.

"Better run and get your things now," Caroline told Charlie.

Charlie looked from Caroline to Ben. He opened his mouth once before closing it and heading back up the stairs to his room.

"I'd like to tell Cal to schedule that session with the school counselor," Ben said once Charlie was out of earshot.

"I think it's an overreaction," Caroline said. She picked up her mug, cradling it in her hands for a few moments before taking a sip. "But if it will make you feel better."

"It will." He'd expected another fight but was happy to be wrong.

Charlie came down the stairs, his backpack listing from side to side as he walked. He had the face of a prisoner awaiting execution. He let Caroline kiss him before heading outside. The door banged on his way out.

Ben put on his jacket and moved to follow him.

"I'm sure Hudson will show up, Ben," Caroline said.

Outside, Charlie stood by the Escape. He looked even paler in the bright morning light. Before school Ben often found him staring dreamily at the trees, but today he was fixated on the car door, pulling urgently at its handle, waiting for Ben to unlock it.

28

Ben had not been gone ten minutes when the ladies arrived. Some-times Caroline thought they purposely waited until he pulled from the drive. This morning it was Mary Stanton along with Ruth Wyatt.

"Good morning, Caroline," they chirped from the doorway. Caroline let them in, wishing she'd had the foresight to stuff Bub into a jacket when she'd first heard their car doors slam.

"Mary, Ruth," Caroline said. "How nice."

"I wanted to thank Ben for his help during last week's cleanup at the farm," Ruth said. Even in a coat three sizes too big, she was all angles. She thrust a pie toward Caroline as Mary stooped to the floor to greet Bub.

"That's so kind of you," Caroline said. She took the pallid thing by its sweating aluminum foil pan. "Ben was happy to help."

Caroline had originally been pleased when Ben volunteered to help the villagers dispose of the plague-stricken cattle. Community integration was essential. But he spent so much time lugging around chopped-up cows and working on his book, Caroline had to prod to get him to do anything around the house. She hated being that kind of wife, but he seemed to demand it from her.

"We missed you at last Sunday's service," Mary said. She pursed her lips in a way that was somehow both conspiratorial and admonishing.

"Oh, I know," Caroline said. She shook her head in mimed exasperation. "Bub's been out of sorts with the teething, and Charlie's been off, too. And Ben—well, he probably didn't even notice it was Sunday." Not lies, exactly.

They'd gone to Sunday services at the small church in the village several times. These had been bleak affairs, filled with interminable dirges and brimstone sermons from the town's elders. The village was a dire place and had a religion to match.

Ben had gotten a kick out of it, but, then, he got a thrill from everything these people did. *"That was interesting, wasn't it?"* he'd invariably say at the end of the service. As if it were performance art and not part of the actual life they were living.

For him, Swannhaven was a time capsule stuffed with colorful anecdotes that would someday fill an acknowledgments page. To Caroline, the village's claustrophobic society grew less endearing by the day.

"I just have a few minutes before I need to run some errands," Caroline said. "But maybe you'd like a cup of something? Some of Mrs. White's teas? Or coffee, if you'd prefer?" Hospitality was a virtue the region seemed to value above all others, and Caroline did her best.

"Maybe a little coffee," Mary said, looking at Ruth.

"But we won't keep you," Ruth added.

Promises, promises, Caroline thought, as she got two mugs from the cabinet.

"How's Ben doing?" Mary asked.

"Oh, fine," Caroline said. "Busy. We're always busy around here," she laughed. She gave the women their coffee and made herself more tea.

"And his new book, it's going well?" Ruth asked.

"Absolutely," Caroline said.

She hadn't dared talk to Ben about it, but she actually got the sense from his mood that the book wasn't going well at all. This, his usual flakiness, and the masculine sense of entitlement that came with the work of the cattle cleanups was not a winning combination. If poor Hudson was really gone, Caroline could only imagine the nightmare the holidays would be.

"It must be very hard to write a book and fix up a house at the same time," Mary said.

Yes, impossible even, Caroline thought. "Well, at least he's not entirely on his own with one of those projects," she said.

"Poor dear. You must end up doing just about everything around here," Ruth said.

"Well, I wouldn't say—"

"We're all wives here, Caroline. We know who ends up doing the real work around a home. But it's important not to overexert yourself," Ruth continued.

"You have to think of your health," Mary said.

"My health?" In the corner of the kitchen, Bub crashed a toy airplane into a firehouse, shouting the delighted sounds of explosions.

"If you ever need a break, someone to watch Charlie and Robert— you know you can count on us," Mary said.

Caroline smiled. She didn't know if they were referring to the pressures every mother had or the particular troubles she suffered in addition to these. But how could they know?

"And the holidays can be so stressful," Ruth said. There was something in the woman's gaze beyond concern. Something Caroline had recognized so often in the faces she'd found across from hers, something she dreaded more than anything else: pity.

Caroline's mind rattled.

Could Ben have said something? Maybe at one of those town-council meetings. The kind of joke a man tells about his wife to get a laugh and a little sympathy. She tried to imagine Ben talking to these people about her.

Paranoia—something I must always be vigilant for.

"Are you all right, dear?" Mary asked.

Caroline realized she was massaging her temples. An ache had set in behind her eyes. She must look every bit the crazy woman they now knew her to be.

"Fine," she said. "Thank you so much for your offer. I'll be sure to keep that in mind. And if you two need a break from your kids, I'd be happy to help you out, too. Sometimes an afternoon to ourselves is all we need to recharge our batteries, you know?" she said.

"Exactly, exactly," Mary said.

Caroline sat around the island with them, chatting and smiling and sipping. Saying all the things she was supposed to say in just the way they were meant to be said. But she was thinking of Ben. She thought of him splattered with blood, sweating with the other men on those frozen fields. She tried to imagine him betraying her, telling them all her problems. *Yeah, she seemed a good purchase at the time. I just wish I'd sprung for the ten-year warranty.* Ben could always get a chuckle from a crowd when he wanted one.

When Caroline asked herself if it was possible Ben could betray her, she found that the answer was yes.

By the time the ladies finally finished their coffee, Caroline's headache hummed like a drill. Luckily, Mrs. White had a treatment for this, too. It required an entire garden's worth of herbs for the crazy woman between the mountains to maintain a grip on herself.

"So good seeing you, Caroline," Ruth said on her way out. "You keep up your strength, now."

As soon as she shut the door, Caroline fumbled through the drawer where she kept the salves. Shopping for fabrics in Gracefield was the last thing she wanted to do, but she was determined to be strong. She had to be strong, for Bub, for Charlie. Even for Ben. She'd be strong for Ben, even if just to spite him.

Finally she found the jar she'd been looking for. As she watched the women's cars descend the gravel path, she dabbed a pat of ointment on each temple.

When the ladies were out of sight, she dumped the pie they'd brought into the trash.

29

When Ben returned from dropping Charlie at school, Caroline's car was gone and Jake's pickup was parked by the shed.

He spent the hours before his meeting with Lisbeth calling for Hudson and searching the south woods. He didn't have any luck, and he was beginning to admit to himself that he hadn't expected any. When he told Jake about Hudson running off, the kid had managed to smile, but Ben could tell it was forced. A beagle was not going to survive a December night in the forest, the look on Jake's face told him. Now that Ben thought about it, Charlie's face had held much the same expression.

To think of Hudson alone or dead in the cold made Ben's insides hurt. But he had no idea what else he could do.

Hudson would have fought to be included on this trip to Lisbeth Goode's home, but Ben pulled up to her house alone. She lived in an old Victorian not far from the village's overgrown square. It might have been a handsome house once, but time had caught up to it. The paint was well maintained, but the roof was patched with mismatched shingles. The wooden steps to the house felt soft under his feet.

Lisbeth answered the door almost immediately.

"Hello, sugar; you come on in," she said. Her voice was welcoming, but Ben did not miss the strained smile on her face.

"I'm sorry, bad time?" he asked. A part of him would have been grateful to reschedule.

"It's been a day for the devil, but I'm glad you're here," she said. "Now, let me take your coat. Oh, you need a much thicker coat. Tea?"

"That would be great, thank you." Her home had a nice-size foyer and living room, but they were so cluttered with furniture and their walls were so heavily laden with photographs that the space felt constricted.

Lisbeth walked down the hall toward what Ben assumed was the kitchen.

"Was over at the Kirkwoods'—you know them?" she called over her shoulder.

"No," Ben said. He chose one of the armchairs in the living room and sank into it. Its fabric was worn, but it was comfortable. A battered butter churn was on display in the corner of the room, and ancient oil lamps were arranged carefully in the breakfront.

Lisbeth's voice came from the kitchen. "Bank finally had it with them. Looked like they were going to get another month, but someone somewhere figured another month wouldn't matter any. Not to anyone but the Kirkwoods, that is."

She bustled into the room with a silver tea service. The tray and its vessels looked freshly polished. Biscuits, milk, sugar, and lemon slices were arranged carefully around the teapot.

"I wish you hadn't gone to such trouble," Ben said.

"Any excuse to use the thing," Lisbeth said. "Makes me think of my grandmother. Now, what was I saying? Oh, the Kirkwoods. Shame, too, because Lord knows the bank will never sell that land to anyone else. Makes more sense to let the Kirkwoods have it and pay what they can when they can, rather than leave the place empty. But, then, I didn't ever really have a head for business."

"I thought most of the farmers around here leased their land from the Winter Families," Ben said. That was the impression he'd gotten from the Swannhaven Trust meetings he'd attended.

"Used to be the case for all of them. But times come in both good and bad. All the families have had to sell some land over the years. Think of the Swanns: once the richest in the land, but in the end the bank got it all. Fortune comes hand in hand with misfortune around here. But *you* know that," she said. Ben looked up at her. "You live in their house. Wouldn't you say they had a taste of both?"

"Yes, that's true," Ben said. "Sorry to hear about the Kirkwoods' troubles, though."

"Well, everyone's got some of their own, I suppose. The sorry year we're having, it's a wonder that the bank hasn't taken half the land in the valley. The town's bleeding money as it is. We can't afford to lose any more taxpayers. You know it as well as I from the trust meetings. This year's worse than last, and last year was mighty bad. Especially with the sickness still hitting the herds. Don't know how we're going to keep everything running. Some say we should ask North Hampstead to annex us. Sure, it would save us a pretty penny, but it's still hard to believe it's come to that."

"It won't come to that," Ben said. Now it was Lisbeth's turn to look at him. "Swannhaven's been through a lot in three hundred years. It's going to take more than a burst real estate bubble to finish it off."

"It warms my heart to hear you say so." Lisbeth smiled. "Now tell me how things are going for you."

Ben didn't bring up Hudson; he told her about the progress they'd made on the house. He also mentioned how his book was going, but he was vague on the details. Swannhaven was a private place, and he didn't know how the villagers would react to the subject of his novel. He mentioned that his brother would be staying with them for Christmas, though Ted traveled so much for work that Ben wasn't sure when he'd be coming up.

"Must be a success, too, then. Must be in the blood."

"Were the Lowells a success?" Ben asked. The ruins of their dreary farm did not speak of any great achievements. The people there might have been happy and proud and good, but he had not sensed accomplishment.

"Oh." She squeezed a wedge of lemon into her tea. "The Lowells were always well thought of around here."

Ben noticed a yellowed front page with a huge headline framed and hanging on the wall behind Lisbeth. The Great Fire, it read.

"How bad was that?" Ben gestured to the frame.

"The Great Fire of 1878. Let's say there used to be a lot more buildings in town. Used to *be* a town, for that matter."

"That was around the time the railroad went under, too?"

"That's right," Lisbeth said. "Though I don't remember that coming up at the Preservation Society."

"I've been doing a little research on my own," Ben said. He reached for the milk and he felt her eyes on him. "Oh, and before I forget, Caroline and I are having some people over next Friday— we're inviting everyone from the trust, and the Bishops will be there, too. We'd love for you to come."

"Lord knows I've been half-dying to see what you've done with the place."

"We're hoping people can come over between six and seven o'clock; can you get away from the Lancelight by then?"

"It's the slow season. This time of year, one of the girls could work the register, walk the floor, man the grill, and still have enough time to do her nails."

"That's great. We're both excited to show you around."

"Likewise. Now, should we get down to business? I could jabber on all day, but the old copies of the *Dispatch* are in the cellar." She got up and Ben followed her into the kitchen.

The steps to the cellar were narrow and steep. As they descended, the air became colder. The tight, damp feel of the space reminded Ben of the old Lowell farmhouse.

"You're welcome to look at anything down here," Lisbeth said.

They'd reached the bottom of the stairs, and the cellar was larger than Ben had expected. There were cardboard boxes piled against three sides of the room and a small desk and chair arranged along the remaining wall. A few framed portraits were hung above the desk. "You won't find everything in here, but you'll find everything that survived. Between fires, floods, and careless clerks, you're sure to see a couple gaps here and there. You know what you're looking for?"

"I guess I'm most interested in the major events that the village has been through. It seems to have a more action-packed history than most."

"That's a pretty way of phrasing it," Lisbeth said.

"I'm still curious about the Winter Siege, but I guess the *Dispatch* doesn't go back that far. I'd love to learn more about the Great Fire that the issue upstairs mentioned, or anything else that you think is interesting."

"There was a problem with poisoned water during the Depression." She moved closer to the stack of boxes. "The Black Water. The crates should be labeled with the year of the issues inside, but I wouldn't count on much more organization than that. I'd try '33 for that one. The Great Fire was in 1878. And there was also the sickness that cut through the milk herds; '82 for that calamity."

"That's the same thing that the cows are getting now?" Ben asked.

Lisbeth nodded. "Still hasn't gotten as bad as '82, though. Not yet, praise God."

"I'd love to know more about that. And I'm interested in the fire at the Crofts that killed the Swann boys in the early eighties."

"We seem to have trouble with fire, don't we? That was also '82." Lisbeth raised her head to look at one of the framed photos on the wall: a formal black-and-white photo of a handsome teenage boy with porcelain skin, a shock of dark hair, and silver eyes. "Even back as far as the Winter Siege, all the buildings in the valley were burned by the Iroquois, and the homes on the Drop didn't fare much better. All but yours, of course. Spared by the grace of God."

She pointed up to the photograph she'd been looking at. "There's Mark Swann, one of the boys who died in the fire at the Crofts in '82," she said. "What a terrible night. One of those things that—" Her voice caught. Ben saw that she was struggling with tears. He approached her, but she waved him off. She rubbed the sleeve of her blouse over her eyes and collected herself. "A night like that changes a place forever, is what I wanted to say."

"Did you know him?" He felt bad to press, but he wanted to know.

"It's a very small village, sugar."

"Of course. I'm so sorry."

"He was a beautiful boy, as you can see." She ran her hand in front of the other images on the wall. "Here's Philip Swann; he was taken in 1878. He was just eighteen." She slid her fingers along the frame of the large portrait.

"The same year as the Great Fire?" Ben asked. He remembered that Joseph Swann, the artist, had moved to St. Michael's after the death of his brother.

"That's right." The next one she came to was a large painted portrait. "And you know James Swann from the Winter Siege." The boy depicted shared the same fine features as the others. "I'm named after his sister, Elizabeth."

"They all died so young," Ben said. In his portrait, James Swann looked no older than Charlie.

"They used to say that the Swanns were cursed and blessed in equal measures. But I think someone had their finger on the scale."

The last of the prominent photos was of an even younger boy. A year, *1933,* was scrawled on its corner.

"Well, I have some paperwork of my own to get through," Lisbeth said.

"Why do you have these hung here?" Ben asked as Lisbeth headed for the stairs.

"They're beautiful and sad, aren't they? I have them here so that we can remember. Remember those who were taken before their time. Remember how blessed we are to still be here, and remember how quickly those blessings can change."

Ben turned back to the portraits of the Swann boys, their likenesses frozen in youth like a thing caught in amber. Striking young men, all of them.

"Well, you have me feeling just about low enough to stick my head in an oven," Lisbeth said. "I'll leave you to it. I'm trusting you to take care with the papers, now. They're the last of their kind. When they're gone, it'll be as if all of this never happened." Ben heard her slow steps as she began to heft herself up the stairs. "And it wouldn't do to forget," she said. "Even if that'd be the easier thing, we can never let ourselves forget."

30

Ben spent hours at Lisbeth's house. When it came time to pick up Charlie, he took three boxes from the *Dispatch* archives with him: 1878, year of the Great Fire; 1933, year of Black Water; and 1982, year of the fire at the Crofts. Each issue was slim, no more than three pages folded into one another, thin even for a local weekly. While they primarily contained weather forecasts and the kinds of things you might find in a farmer's almanac, each usually had a couple of news articles, as well. He hoped there would be something in them to jump-start his imagination. At the very least, they'd be useful examples of the local vernacular, something upon which he could model his characters' dialogue.

He'd known from the beginning that the novel he was writing was different from his others. There was a piece of him in every character he'd ever written, but he felt a special kinship with the people in this book. Living at the Crofts, as the Swanns had, made for a strong connection. And his people, the Lowells, had been one of the first families here: They'd survived the very Winter Siege that he wrote about. He'd known this in an academic kind of way, but the more time he'd spent with the Preservation Society, the Swannhaven

Trust, and the men from the village, the more Ben realized that a part of him had been woven through the whole arc of the narrative from the very beginning. Woven through by both will and blood. Even if it turned out to be a dark and unhappy story, it was one that had always been his to tell. He guessed that this was one reason why it had become so difficult for him to write it. It might also account for why he had become so certain that something was still missing.

When Ben got to the priory, its pathways were quiet, its grounds still. Early for once, he decided to take advantage of it by telling Father Cal to set up a session between Charlie and the school counselor.

He found the old priest's office empty, but a young woman at the administrative desk directed him to the archives in the subbasement. The stairs she sent him down terminated with a single unmarked door.

Ben had a romantic's image of the archive: Leather tomes carefully shelved on heavy wood bookcases that stretched to the ceiling. Thousands of books, each one a mysterious bud waiting to flower. A smell that combined desiccated paper and incense with the dusty notes of neglect. *Can you see it?*

Ben knew better than to expect an Alexandrian labyrinth, but he was still surprised by the state of the place. Fluorescent lights flickered overhead. Banks of large metal filing cabinets broke the room into narrow corridors that stretched the length of the floor. Sheaves of paper and accordion files were piled high on top of them. Father Cal poked his head between two of these stacks and saw the look on Ben's face.

"It's a disgrace, I know," Cal said. "One of the reasons I've never taken you down here. Someone was tasked with straightening this room out in the seventies, so they brought in all these horrible filing cabinets. But if you thought their notion of filing meant anything more than shoving papers into drawers to keep them out of sight, you'd be mistaken. I've been trying to discern some logic from the organization, but it has thus far eluded me."

"I had no idea you had to ford through all this," Ben said. He pulled open a filing-cabinet drawer. It was wedged so tightly with reams of yellowed paper that he could barely close it.

"I knew what I was getting myself into when I offered to investigate down here for you."

"It's a shame. There must be some interesting things in here."

"Interesting for some, but not for most. More than two centuries of accounting notations and meeting minutes. No wonder no one else seems to care about the place. All the records we keep these days are digital. But, if nothing else, there's a principle at stake. Monasteries a thousand years older than this one manage to have a well-organized vault of records." Cal picked a manila folder off the floor. "Of course, when a seeker is forced to deal with chaos like this, it's that much more rewarding when he's able to turn something up." He handed Ben the folder. "There's probably little here that you're not aware of, but it was satisfying to find it all in one source."

Ben opened the folder to find a tree of names that began with Aldrich Swann and his wife, Sarah, at the top.

"A partial New World lineage of the family Swann," Cal told Ben. "You'll see that Mark and Liam Swann, the ones who died in the fire, aren't noted here, so this must have been written before their birth. Carlisle Swann was the boys' father, who passed away some time before they did."

Ben had already put together a short family tree that covered the first four generations of the Swanns, but it was good to have a more complete record. At the bottom, Ben recognized the old sisters, Eleanor and Miranda, alongside Carlisle, his wife, and some half-siblings, Emily and Washington. Above them were Dorothy, Tucker, Huntley, some of their spouses, and dozens of other Swanns.

Whoever had compiled the document had included many of the years of birth and death; Ben had been missing a lot of this information. "This is fantastic. Thank you so much."

"My pleasure." Muted church bells sounded from the world

above. "Final bell," Cal said. He flicked off the lights and held the door open for Ben.

"By way of insufficient thanks, Caroline's having a dinner party next Friday. We'd love for you to come."

"How wonderful. I'm so looking forward to seeing what you've done with the place." Though Ben had told him about the renovations they'd undertaken, Cal hadn't been to the Crofts since the summer.

"It's coming together, slowly," Ben said. "Caroline thought it'd be a good time to show some people what we've done. A very select group, of course." He smiled.

"I'm so flattered to be included," Cal said. They reached the ground floor and began walking to the door where Ben had entered the building. A towheaded student walked by them, wobbling under the strain of a large book bag. The young boy smiled at them as Cal greeted him by name. It was a sweet smile, but Ben's spirits deflated when he saw it.

"Caroline and I also discussed Charlie's drawing," Ben said. "We agree that he should talk to someone about it. She's on board for one session, but I don't know if I can talk her into more without a really good reason."

"I already checked with the counselor's office, and she's able to talk with Charlie, also next Friday. I'll call to confirm and explain Caroline's concerns."

"Thanks. Actually, if you could send me the counselor's number, I'd like to fill her in on the family history before she meets with him." Ben knew that children could be strange. He knew that they had phases and idiosyncrasies that they would grow out of. But if there really was something wrong with Charlie, Ben wanted the counselor to have all the relevant information.

Through the door's pane of glass, Ben saw cliques of boys jostle one another, laughing as they ran along the pathways to the buses.

Then he saw Charlie and his tousled black hair, walking slowly and alone, staring at his feet.

31

The fabric store in Gracefield carried many patterns but nothing Caroline liked.

The headache that had sat behind her eyes surged under the fluorescent lights. Bub was wrapped around her left leg, his feet on top of her own, his face buried in her pant leg, making kissing sounds into the crook of her knee. She waved off help from a salesperson for the third time and began to have difficulty discerning white from ivory. She felt too warm, and the harsh light seemed to accrue a physical weight.

Caroline slung Bub over her shoulder and returned to her car. She sat in the driver's seat, out of breath. It struck her as wet outside, though it had not rained. She listened to the sound of traffic in front and the toddler talk behind. She'd been feeling steadily worse since the ladies had left. She paced her breathing, trying to slow her heart rate.

Ben was the problem. The idea of him talking behind her back had made her sick. She'd also slept fitfully after last night's activities, and it had caught up to her. She could still summon the sound of Ben shouting at Charlie as it rang through the windows and pulled her from sleep. He almost never yelled, but he was wound tighter than she'd ever seen him. Tears swelled her eyes when she thought of what a stranger he'd become.

Stop, she commanded herself. Pull yourself together. The websites she'd read advised to break a task down into manageable parts if she began to feel overwhelmed. She stuck her key in the car's ignition and turned it.

Bub said something to her, and Caroline tried to smile at him through the reflection of the rearview mirror. The websites also recommended that she visualize a wall between her and her troubles. She should construct this wall from bricks, each of which represented something that strengthened her. Bub was one of the bricks that she could always count on.

Yes, for every problem, God offered a solution. Caroline just had to be aware of her state of mind, take her herbal treatments, and muster her strengths, brick by brick. By doing this, Caroline could handle not only the holidays and the Crofts but also her problems with Ben and her worries about Charlie.

In the backseat, Bub muttered something in the neighborhood of his brother's name, and Caroline realized she'd been talking aloud.

"You won't leave me, will you, Bub?" she asked the baby. "If you wandered in the dark alone, you would tell me about it, right? If you spent all your time in the forest, you'd invite me along sometimes, wouldn't you?"

She began to cry then. The tears came in a torrent, and sobs racked her chest. The car lurched, and when she looked up she was surprised to see that she was stopped in the middle of the Crofts's gravel drive, just past the ruined outbuilding. The sky had seemed bright a moment before; now it was a study in gray scale. Behind her, Bub was wide-eyed. She looked at the clock and saw that almost two hours had passed since she'd walked out of the fabric store. She could not account for the lost afternoon.

Caroline tried to shake her head clear. She tried to stack her bricks of strength. She and Bub were safe. And Ben would be home soon with Charlie. She would have some tea and share a biscuit with her baby while she waited for them. Sometimes pretending everything was all right made it so. Maybe she would take a bath when Ben came home. She would light some candles. Vanilla made her calm. Maybe she would bake two pies with the pecans they had in the pantry. One for Mrs. White and one for Ben. Ben loved pecan pie, and it would make her happy to make him happy. A happy husband would never spread his wife's secrets.

But Caroline wondered why she'd parked here in the middle of the gravel path. She noticed Bub studying her carefully through the rearview mirror. "Boom!" the baby shouted. He slammed his palms together with a noise that startled her.

Dread began to churn in her chest. She could suddenly feel very clearly that something was wrong. Standing made her light-headed, and she braced herself as she got out of the car.

"Hello?" she called out to the frozen reaches of the Drop. She must have had a reason for stopping here. Had she seen Mrs. White wandering around? As she turned toward the forest, Caroline thought she saw a flash of movement in the darkness beyond the trees, but she dismissed this as a trick of the wind.

She began to walk back down the gravel drive, intending to peer into the old outbuilding, but she didn't get farther than the rear of the car.

The remnants of the animal were spread over several feet. Split almost perfectly in half lengthwise, it seemed too big to be a raccoon or squirrel. Viscous red sludge filled the treads of the Escape's left rear tire, and Caroline remembered the sickening lurch that had shaken her from her reverie. Her horror mounted as she realized that the animal had been so crushed that it appeared to have been turned inside out. Shredded intestines and crushed organs were fully on display, but she could hardly see a scrap of fur.

Caroline had seen roadkill but nothing like this. It was hard to believe it was possible for an animal to be so obliterated by a set of tires. Then Caroline saw the dog collar and nearly fell to her knees.

"Hudson," she whispered to the remains. Tears sprang to her eyes again, but she wasn't sure for whom. The only thing she was sure of was that Ben couldn't know. No matter what, he could never find out.

Deciding this gave Caroline strength. She broke the task into manageable parts. First she would get a shovel and put poor Hudson in a plastic bag. Then she would dispose of the bag someplace where Ben would never find it. Ben hadn't really believed that Hudson had survived the night. He didn't need to find a body. It was better this way, better for him to remember Hudson as the dog he had been. She'd have to hose down the Escape's tires.

Caroline drove up to the Crofts to get started. I can do this, she told herself.

Then she saw two white trucks drawing slowly up the gravel drive toward her, and all the bricks that she had so carefully collected throughout the afternoon came tumbling down.

32

"Whoa," Ben said when the Crofts loomed into sight. Even Charlie sat up in his seat to get a better look. Two large moving trucks had pulled alongside the house. Dozens of large boxes were piled behind the trucks and along the front of the Crofts. Men in pairs shuttled back and forth on their way to the front door, struggling under their burdens.

Bub was in the kitchen by himself. He banged his cup against the top of his play parking garage in time to the thump of the delivery men's boots, which resonated from the floor above.

"Big commotion, huh?" Ben asked the baby. He scooped Bub off the floor and wiped the beads of water off his chin. Charlie breezed past them to the kitchen stairs.

"Watch the floors!" he could hear Caroline scream. "And the walls!" The Wolf was in her voice.

With Bub in his arms, Ben jogged to follow the sound of her shouting. He found her on the second floor, berating a group of men.

"They're slamming into every corner they come to," Caroline told him when she saw him. Her voice trembled with rage, but she looked close to tears. The wildness in her eyes made the bottom drop out of Ben's stomach.

"It's okay," he told her. "That's why we kept the extra paint. And, remember, we chose a semigloss for the halls and stairs because we knew they'd get a lot of wear and tear. We planned for this. It's okay."

"And the floors," she said, closing her eyes.

"These scuffs?" He bent down to an ugly black mark that arced across several planks of molasses-colored wood. "They're from the work boots. They'll rub right off."

He stood up to hug her. Her body went rigid when he touched her, but he felt her shoulders relax when Bub, in his other arm, kissed her on the cheek.

"Just go downstairs and tell them where you want everything. I'll stay up here to make sure they put everything in the center of the rooms—well away from the walls. Okay?"

Caroline disengaged herself from his arms and nodded. She brushed past the men and made her way down the main stairs.

With the help of the foreman, they worked out a system in which Caroline marked each box with a note that told Ben where she wanted it; then he made sure it got there. It was near dusk by the time all the furniture was settled into the correct rooms.

The pieces for the upstairs rooms remained in their boxes, but the men had assembled the tables and arranged the new couches and chairs that Caroline had purchased for the main floor. There was a grand mahogany table in the dining room with matching buffets and breakfronts. Classic leather and microfiber couches now stood in several of the rooms, and the library had a trio of red settees squaring off in front of the fireplace.

After Ben had tipped the men and seen them off, he fixed the boys up with something to eat and began cutting the boxes away from the upstairs furniture. He called for Caroline, but she did not answer. After he put Bub in his crib and got Charlie settled, he took the house room by room, looking for her. He found her sitting in the dark, on a large chocolate-colored couch in the room where they hoped to one day add a bar.

"You okay?" he asked her.

"How could I not be?" she asked. There was an open bottle of red ice wine on the floor, a glass in her hand.

"Do you have a glass for me?" he asked. They rarely drank during the week, and they'd been saving that bottle for a special occasion.

She didn't answer, so he went to get one from the kitchen. He pulled a glass out of the cabinet and considered whether or not to join her. He wanted to look for Hudson again, but there was something about Caroline that made him not want to leave her alone. When he returned to her, he filled his glass and sat beside her. The room's huge windows looked out upon the bloody remains of the day's last light.

"I love all the couches," he said. "Comfortable and just the right color."

"Sorry about yelling at the men up there," Caroline said. "Thanks for talking me through it." Ben never knew what to expect when she was like this. "I don't know why I got upset. Everything was fine, then . . . I don't know. The next thing I know I'm screaming."

"There was a lot going on at once, and you were by yourself. It was completely normal to feel stressed out."

"I used to run a division that rang up billions of dollars in transactions. I know how to deal with moving pieces. I used to be able to handle all this." They sat in the dark except for a few candles on the table. The light flickering across her face made her look tired.

"But this is your money—your home," Ben said. "It's natural to be passionate about something you're so close to."

"I hate having to need you. I hate being managed."

"We came up here for a new life, Cee, one that we make the rules to. We just have to find our equilibrium. Right now everything is crazy, but we'll figure it out."

"I'm not happy, Ben. And I haven't been happy in a long time."

Ben let this hit him in the face, but it slowed him for only a moment. "Are you keeping up with your pills?"

"Those goddamn pills."

"Do you want to talk to Dr. Hatcher?" he asked.

"No."

"He said that the talk therapy is important. Lot of people who—"

"I'm not interested in being one of those people."

"No, I guess not," he said. He hadn't seen his anger coming. Like the night before, it had begun as fear, but now it flamed to fury and it was too late to stop it. "You're a person who enjoys being miserable. Who wants everyone around her to be just as unhappy, because you're either too proud or stubborn or stupid to do anything about it. You want to *wallow* in it. You want to wrap it around yourself like a blanket and twist it tight enough for it to strangle you. You want to martyr yourself with your own misery." He got to his feet and stood in front of one of the windows. A strand of red clouds scorched the dark sky.

"When I was twelve, there was this boy, a little older than me, who lived a few houses down," Caroline said after a few moments. "He had white-blond hair and eyes the color of the Caribbean. One day I paged through one of Mom's magazines, looking for the perfume samples, and I saw this ad for Aruba. I'd never seen anything like it. White sand and blue water. That was the color of Paul Cole's eyes. God, I loved him. I didn't know what it was at the time, but it was like . . . gravity. I was just drawn to him whenever he was close."

"Why are you telling me this?" Ben asked.

"I guess every neighborhood has a dream boy like that. My neighborhood also had a block party on the Fourth of July. Everyone outside, grilling and playing and talking. It'd start in the afternoon and last until after the fireworks. Kids jumped through the sprinklers, and I did, too, even though that summer I was too old for it. And Paul Cole walked down the sidewalk, carrying buns for the burgers his dad was cooking. I remember seeing him there. I couldn't help myself. I ran up to that boy, got on my tiptoes, put my hands on his chest, and kissed him. Right there on the mouth. In front of half the neighborhood. I hadn't kissed anyone before. I didn't know what I was doing. But his incredible eyes opened and his face broke into a shy smile. The best kind of smile I could have hoped for." She was crying now, the tears rolling from her cheeks to her blouse.

"Why are you telling me this?" Ben asked again.

"I thought you should know."

"What? Why?"

"Because that was the last time I was happy."

Ben looked at the glass in his hand for a moment. He thought about it, then threw his arm back and launched it against the wall. The glass shattered; diamond fragments of it skidded across the floor with the rattle of falling hail. The wine punctuated the wall with the arc and drip of crime-scene evidence.

He left the room. He wondered if the couch was made of a kind of fabric that got stained by water. He wondered if her tears would ruin the cushions just as his wine had ruined the wall. A matching pair.

He got a flashlight, put on his coat, and headed back into the night. He made for the lake, to look for Hudson in the parts of the forest that came up against the mountains.

In the dark, he spoke to his missing dog.

"You're going to be okay," he said. "Just come home." The freezing air seared his throat and burned his eyes. "You're going to be okay."

December 14, 1777

Dear Kathy,

 Mother will not leave her bed. Only after coaxing will she take even the smallest bite of flour. Father still does not leave his study. Sometimes, I listen at the door and hear him talking, but I do not know with whom he thinks he speaks.

 The other men have pulled their watch away from the forest. After hearing William Lowell's account, I cannot blame them for being afraid. Without Jack, our spirits have grown black. Emmett has taken to sleeping in my room. He is fearful, and I try to be brave for him, but the truth is that I am as thankful for his company as he is for mine.

 It is strange how one gets used to things. In Boston, such effort was spent considering the London fashions and the list of households to call upon through the day. Now it is different, but it is also the same. Instead of dresses, we speak of food. How little is left, and how it should be apportioned. In place of soirees and society connections, we track the noises in the night. Sometimes sounds come from the trees, and sometimes they come from somewhere nearer. And the hunger, Kathy. You cannot imagine the terrible hunger.

More of the tenant families have moved into the Crofts. Few of them leave here, even the men, even during the day. None but little James ventures into the dark of the forest, though this has been forbidden. I've seen him go there when he thinks no one watches. The wind wipes aside his footprints as soon as he leaves them. He is like Jack in so many ways, but he, too, has grown quiet.

I know it is selfish, but I wish you were here. You would know better than I what to do. I do not know how to comfort James and Emmett. I do not know what hope I can give them, when I have none for myself.

Pray for us.

Your Bess

33

Ben woke to an empty bed: another night of broken sleep. He shuffled down to the kitchen and poured himself coffee from the cooling pot. He already dreaded the day. Hudson was gone, there was no more avoiding the fact. Hudson was gone and Ben did not know what to expect from the Wolf.

Outside, the slamming of a car door. Caroline entered the kitchen, carrying a bag from Home Depot. It was Saturday, Ben realized.

"Where were you?" Ben had wanted to punish Caroline for the night before. He'd wanted her to feel what it was like to be made to suffer at the hands of someone you loved. But holding on to anger was not one of his talents.

"Had to pick something up," she said.

"I wish you'd told me. I didn't know where you were."

"Well, you might remember that we're planning to have a dinner party now that the house is coming together and we finally have some furniture. Just one problem: A deranged individual threw a glass of red wine at one of our walls last night, and we didn't have enough spare paint in that color to redo the entire wall. So I bought some."

"What else do we need to do today?" Ben had been up for ten minutes and he was already exhausted. It was easier to capitulate. It was easier, but it also made him loathe himself. For the first time, he realized that he and Caroline could not go on like this forever.

But he asked all the right questions about how he could help Caroline realize her vision for Friday's dinner party.

"You firm up the guest list and I'll work on the menu," she said. "I might want to do a dry run on some of the dishes before the event."

He was going to say something about not going overboard with elaborate dishes but knew it would only enrage her. Ben realized that he didn't care anyway.

Creaking came from the floor above, which meant Charlie was up there. Ben looked at the clock. Usually, Charlie would have been in the forest for hours by this time.

The front bell rang, and Ben went to answer it. It was UPS, with a package unwieldy enough that it was difficult to maneuver through the door.

Ben slit the tape along the edges and yanked out the Styrofoam packing material. It was a picture frame. With some difficulty, he pulled it out of the box. He removed the thin padded sheet that protected the glass.

It was the quilt of his grandmother's family tree. Framed and handsomely mounted. He searched for a note but couldn't find one. It didn't matter, because he knew who had sent it.

"Ted sent it back," Caroline said from the hallway. She appraised the quilt through the glass. "We can definitely find a place for this."

"It'll mean something to the villagers, too," Ben said. "It means that we're supposed to be up here." He ran his eyes down the length of the tree and felt a sudden wrenching sadness.

He set aside the frame and looked at his wife, who was still looking at him. He tried, but he couldn't think of anything else to say.

34

In the days before the party, Caroline kept Ben's time filled with tasks. Despite this, he rose early each morning to search the grounds for signs of Hudson, and he stole the odd moment to work on his book. It was good to be busy. Everyone knows it's a bad idea to slow down while driving through a bad neighborhood.

Caroline was pulling out all the stops for their dinner. She was serving smoked trout on endive, caviar canapés, and fig and goat cheese crostini as appetizers. The entrée would be game hens stuffed with apricots and wild mushrooms, served with marinated beets and roast potatoes. She wouldn't give Ben details about the dessert, but earlier in the week he'd signed for a package containing packets of gold leaf. He had a feeling this would be an event to remember.

In terms of attendees, Walter Harp and Roger Armfield had sent regrets, and he'd heard through Lisbeth that Mrs. White would not be well enough to attend. In addition to Lisbeth, the confirmed guests were Father Cal, the Stantons, and the Bishops.

"That makes eight," Caroline said. They were in the dining room, setting the table for tonight's gathering. "We'll be spread thin along the table, but if we open the guest list much beyond the Swannhaven

Trust, then everyone will expect an invite. I thought these place mats went well with the carpet, but now I think the red is too bright." Caroline took a place mat and knelt on the ground to compare the reds. She tilted it to test the color in both light and shadow. She was on the floor long enough to make Ben feel uncomfortable.

"What are you doing? It looks fine. Cee?" She stood up slowly and almost lost her balance in doing so. Ben grabbed her to steady her. "Are you all right? Here, sit down."

"Just got dizzy. Stood up too quickly," Caroline said. Her voice sounded thick. "With only eight of us, we'll be spread thin along the table."

"Yeah, you said that already. Are you sure you're okay?"

"I'm fine; stop asking me." She sat down anyway.

The front doorbell rang.

"Must be the flowers," Caroline said. She began to massage her temples with her fingers.

This was the first Ben had heard about flowers. He went to answer the door.

"Morning, Ben," said the chief. "Sorry to drop in unexpected."

"Please, come in." The outside air was below freezing. "Can I get you some tea or coffee?"

"Appreciate the hospitality, but I'm not alone." He thumbed over his shoulder toward a pickup idling on the gravel drive. Ben recognized it as one of the trucks that had sped up the Drop from the village to gawk at the shed fire back during the summer. The truck's cab was similarly crowded today. "Tommy White called for help finding his mother. Apparently she wandered off again. He said you ran into her a couple days ago?"

"Just missed her, but I know what you mean."

"Seems she tends to head toward the mountains. Gathered up some men and thought we'd look for her through your woods up here, if that's okay with you."

"Of course." The air from the open door had begun to numb his bare feet. "I hope she's dressed better than she was when I last saw her." Thinking of the old woman in the cold reminded Ben of Hudson. How he must have been cold and frightened at the end. It didn't seem fair, a lifetime of comfort wiped away in a burst of terror and pain.

"Tommy said she took a coat, so that's something," the chief said. He looked gaunt and tired under his winter hat. "Already got some boys looking through your land along the road. Should have asked your permission for that, too, but small towns sometimes gotta make their own rules. She's a good God-fearing woman." He sniffed at the air in a way that also reminded Ben of Hudson. "Storm's supposed to hit soon."

"How much snow are we expected to get?"

"Not too much tonight, six to ten inches. But a bigger storm will hit Sunday. That one could drop twelve to eighteen, but you never know. You ready for it?"

"I think so. I bought a plow for the car, and the furnace has been running fine. Got lots of hot cocoa," he said.

"The Crofts has survived worse than a nor'easter." The chief slapped his palm against the frame of the door. "Doubt you'd even notice if it weren't for the wind."

"The boys will like the snow. The Drop seems made for sledding."

"You keep an eye on them, though. Kids can get lost in the drifts. The winter here doesn't forgive mistakes."

"I'll make sure they're careful," Ben said.

"Mary is really looking forward to tonight," the chief said as he turned to go. "Sure do like their dress-ups, don't they? Been too long since an invitation has gone out from the Crofts."

"You've both been so welcoming," Ben said, but the chief waved him away.

"Just being neighborly. I better get the boys settled. See you tonight."

Ben closed the door and rubbed his hands together to warm them. He thought about going back to Caroline, but he guessed she would be occupied in the dining room for a while, making minute changes to each setting. He decided to take the chance to slip away unnoticed.

He'd taken brief notes from articles written about the Great Fire of 1878, but it was the fire at the Crofts in 1982 that had most attracted his attention.

Ben had heard people talk about only the death of the two Swann boys, but he'd learned that three others had also died in that fire. He was tempted to ask Lisbeth Goode and Chief Stanton tonight about their personal recollections of the event, though he doubted Caroline would think the subject appropriate for dinner.

The other matter of interest was the newspaper's coverage of John Tanner, the foster kid held responsible for the fire. Over the course of three months, the *Dispatch* had referred to Tanner as being *disturbed, schizophrenic, depressed,* and *a pyromaniac,* which made Ben wonder where he could find an official evaluation of the boy by a real mental-health professional.

Ben was nearly to the tower stairs when Caroline called down the hallway.

"Was it the flowers?" she asked.

He turned on the ball of his foot to head back the way he'd come. "Chief Stanton. Mrs. White wandered off again, so they're going to search our woods for her."

"Again? Why isn't someone watching her?" Caroline said. "I went to her house yesterday, but she didn't answer the door."

Ben reached the dining room and saw that the place mats were all over the floor and the silverware was back in a pile at one end of the table.

"No one's going to want to sit down and have a meal while one of their friends is missing in the cold. And I can't blame them; I feel the same way." Caroline slammed the stack of plates she held onto the table. "What was I thinking, inviting people up here before everything was ready? And in the middle of a blizzard! It's like a nightmare." She was actually wringing her hands.

Ben knew that this was the moment to reach across to her, but he was so tired of the endless tiptoeing and glad-handing that had become necessary to their daily life. On Monday he'd call Dr. Hatcher to figure out how to get her to go back into therapy. She'd hate him for a while, but he was out of ideas.

"It'll be fine," Ben said. Hosting a dinner party was the last thing he wanted to do, and he wondered how on earth *he* had become the one to assure *her* that everything would work out.

"I guess I should get started on the stuffing," Caroline said.

"It'll be a great night," Ben said as she walked out of the room. His words sounded wan, even to himself. "One we'll make sure they never forget."

35

Everyone at school was excited for the snow. Everyone except Charlie.

Mrs. Crane drew a diagram with the clouds and the wind and the sun on the board to explain it. Charlie did his best to listen to her, but he could not stop looking out the window, trying to imagine what the forest would look like under a blanket of white. The thought of it tied his insides into a knot.

In the cold, in the dark. All alone. That's what the Watcher had told him.

A lady Charlie didn't know came into the classroom. Charlie thought she might be someone's mom. Sometimes moms came into class if something bad had happened. But then she called Charlie's name, and Mrs. Crane told him to go with her. This had never happened before, so he moved slowly to make sure that he was doing what they wanted him to. He put his workbook in his backpack and zipped the bag all the way closed before standing up.

The lady had a nice smile and smelled like something baking in the oven. She told Charlie her name and shook his hand, like Dad's friends from the city used to. He followed her to the building where the teachers went at the end of the day. The doors here were all open. It smelled like coffee, and that reminded Charlie of the name of the lady's smell. The lady smelled like vanilla.

She took him to a little room with three big green chairs. She told him to sit wherever he wanted. He sat in the one closest to the door. It was strange to sit on the soft chair, because the chairs in the classrooms were wood and metal.

"Charlie, did your dad tell you that I was coming to talk to you?"

Charlie shrugged. He wished the room had windows. Though he couldn't do anything to stop the weather, he felt it was important to know when the storm began. The storm would bring the kind of cold and dark that the Watcher had spoken about.

"Well, I just wanted to see how you were doing, Charlie," the lady said. "You're not in trouble or anything like that. Your teachers say you've been doing great in your classes. You're a very smart boy." The lady looked at Charlie as if he was supposed to say something, but he hadn't heard a question. "But I know it must be a big change coming up here from the city. Wow. What a difference! I love New York. Have you been back to visit since moving up here?" she asked.

Charlie shook his head.

"Do you ever miss it?" she asked.

"Maybe," he said. He'd never been afraid of the cold or dark in the city.

"Can you tell me about your house up here?"

"It's old," he said. "The stone it's made from came from the mountains. The wood in the floors came from the forests. The walls are thick to keep out the cold, but the cold comes in anyway." It got colder every day.

"Stone houses are very nice," the lady said. She smiled at him, and Charlie could see himself in the shine of her eyes. "And you're right, old houses can be very drafty. Must be a really big change from the city. But I bet you get to play outside more, right?"

Charlie nodded.

"What kinds of games do you play out there?"

"I like to run and sit and watch."

"Oh, me too. What do you see out there?"

"In the summer there are bullfrogs in the lake, and herons, too. There are rabbits and moles and voles and mice and groundhogs in the fields. There are deer in the forest and chipmunks, squirrels, opossums, and raccoons in the trees. There are hawks and coyotes and crows and turkey vultures, too. But some of them only come out when it's warm. The winter is different."

"Yes, it's too cold for a lot of those animals now, isn't it? And how about your family? How do they like it up here?"

"I don't know."

"Well, you'd probably know if they were unhappy, right? How about your little brother?"

"Bub," Charlie said.

"Bob?" She reached for a red folder on a side table.

"Bub," Charlie said again.

"That's an interesting name."

"It's not his real name. I called him Bub when he was born, and my dad liked it, so we call him that now."

"Does Bub seem to like it here?" she asked.

"He's a baby."

"I know, but is he a happy baby? Does he cry a lot or cause trouble? I have two little brothers, and they were always causing trouble."

"He's nice. When he kisses me it tickles."

"That sounds very sweet. He sounds like a nice baby."

The lady returned the red folder to the table. She turned the back of her neck to him as she leaned down, and that reminded Charlie of the position a deer might be in before you slit its throat.

"How about your mom? She used to have a big job in the city, right?"

"She was a banker." Charlie imagined the deer thrashing its broken legs and tossing its head. Blood had sprayed from its neck to cover the ground, but it had never made a sound.

"And what does she do now?"

"She used to like going to parties, but she doesn't do that any-more. She used to like food, but now she cooks for us and doesn't eat a lot." The lady's pencil tapped against her notepad.

"And your dad's a writer? That must be neat. Have you ever read anything he's written?"

"When I was little, he wrote me stories and drew pictures on the pages, like a real book."

"That sounds fun. Do you play with your dad in the forest?" the lady asked.

Charlie shook his head.

"You play in the forest by yourself? Alone?"

"Not alone, not always."

"With friends, then?"

"No, but . . ." He had promised himself to never tell.

"But what?"

"In the forest . . ." He'd learned from Dad that there were all kinds of stories. Some were filled with monsters and villains, and some had happy endings while others had sad ones. The trouble was that it was hard to tell what kind of a story it was when you were in the middle of it.

"Yes?"

The Watcher would know if he said something. Charlie *knew* it would know. His head began to feel warm.

"It's hard," Charlie said. He did not know how to answer the question and keep the promise to himself. "The winter. It's hard. It's cold and dark. But I wouldn't want to be alone. Not ever. I know that now."

The lady wrote something in her notebook. "You just have to find some friends. There are good people up here, and soon you'll find some nice friends."

Charlie shook his head. His shirt felt too tight around his neck. He wondered if it had started to snow yet. He wondered if it was beginning.

"It's okay, honey. Do you want some water or—oh, let me get you a tissue."

Charlie reached to touch his nose, and his hand came away streaked with blood.

His head felt warm again, and he looked for the lady but couldn't find her. He saw nothing but darkness; then he felt the rough carpet on his cheek.

"It's okay," he heard the lady over him. "Just stay down there a little bit. Got to get the blood back to your head."

Charlie could see again, and he looked up at the lady. He could feel the blood from his nose slide past his eyes.

"It's okay," she said again.

But Charlie thought of the forest between the mountains. He thought of the winter and the snow and the cold and the dark, and he knew that she was wrong.

36

The *Dispatch* had devoted an entire issue to the fire at the Crofts, and its aftermath was abundantly covered in the issues that followed. The incident had taken place on the evening of December 21, 1982, during a Christmas party being thrown by the Swann sisters. Back then, the village had its own fire truck, so they were able to mobilize in time to save the bulk of the house. The paper included a list of fatalities from that night: Claire Armfield, age 51; Jason Armfield, age 18; and Arthur White, age 27. Mark Swann had been 15 and his brother, Liam, had been 11.

There was a murky black-and-white photo of the fire; all you could see were the snowy outlines of the mountains and a flare of white in the center, but it appeared in every issue. There were no quotes from Miranda or Eleanor Swann, but considering the circumstances and the sisters' status in the community, this didn't surprise Ben.

The most concise account of what had happened was a synopsis written by Lisbeth's father, August Goode:

While the official cause of the fire at the Crofts has yet to be deter-mined by the county investigators, there is little doubt as to the conclusion they will reach. Survivor accounts uniformly agree on a great many facts, and the police investigation also supports the view of the tragedy that has emerged.

Dinner was served in the dining room at approximately 7:00 p.m. There were 25 adults and 12 persons under the age of 18 present. With respect to the privacy of those in attendance, this publication has decided to withhold the party's guest list at this time. At 7:20, most of the children excused themselves from the room, while the adults remained at their tables.

According to witnesses, it was at this time that John Tanner, age 16, separated himself from the rest of the children and entered the home's exterior supply shed. Mr. Tanner had lived in the Crofts as a ward of Miranda and Eleanor Swann since 1976 and was familiar with the house. It's believed that, once in the shed, he wrapped a large rag around the head of a rake and drenched it in kerosene. It appears that he then returned to the house and entered a back parlor, where a fireplace had been lit in preparation for the coffee and desserts that would be served there after dinner.

Mr. Tanner lit the kerosene-soaked rag in the fireplace and set the draperies in the parlor ablaze. He then ran to the room next door to set its curtains on fire.

It is unknown how long the fire burned before the adults in the dining room became aware of it, but most agree it could have been only a few minutes. However, the Crofts being an old structure, these few minutes were enough for the fire to burn deep into the floors and climb the wood panels of the walls. When the adults discovered the blaze, the hallways were already thick with smoke.

At this point, accounts diverge due to the chaos of the situation. While the guests of more advanced age began to leave the Crofts, others rushed to find the remainder of the children and escort them to safety. It was at this point that Mr. Tanner and his burning rake were found. Upon discovery, the teenager ran out of the house, attempting to hide in the estate's south woods.

While the children were being counted and escorted from the

house, other adults attempted to extinguish the blaze. By most accounts, they initially succeeded in stemming the spread of the conflagration. At the time, they were unaware that the fire had already pressed inside the walls and reached the second story. Just minutes before the Swannhaven fire volunteers arrived, the wood-beam supports in the affected section of the house collapsed, crushing several in the wreckage.

In the articles Ben had read, John Tanner was never depicted as anything more than a caricature. Ben didn't find this surprising. A story like this needed a villain. Tanner was put through the usual paces and sent to the Lockwood Institute, a state psychiatric facility.

Ben was about to Google the Lockwood Institute when the nurse from the priory called his cell phone. "A nosebleed and a fainting spell" was how she described what had happened to Charlie.

When Ben found her, Caroline was still in the dining room. She sat at one head of the table, contemplating the grain of its wood. He was relieved to see that the place mats and silver had all been rearranged, but for some reason the forks were on the wrong side of the plates.

"The nurse from school says Charlie's sick, so I'm going to pick him up," Ben said. Charlie hadn't been sick for years. Children his age were walking petri dishes, but he'd seemed impervious.

Caroline turned to him and shook her head, as if roused from sleep.

"What?"

Ben told her what the nurse had told him.

"Poor little guy," she said. There was a slur to her voice, as if she were drunk. "Did the flowers come yet?"

"I didn't hear the doorbell ring."

"Can you call them from the car? The number's on a card on the kitchen table. If they haven't left, you can pick the flowers up on the way back from school."

"Where's the florist?"

"In North Hampstead." Caroline stood up haltingly from the table.

"That's sort of in the opposite direction from the school."

"Hopefully they're on their way, then." Caroline looked and sounded disoriented, and Ben wondered if she, too, was coming down with something. A household brought low by the flu: a fitting way to cap off the year.

"The forks go on the left side," he said. He left her frowning at the silverware.

Something sweet was baking in the kitchen, and the smell reminded Ben that he was hungry. He'd had an early breakfast and it looked as if he was going to have a late lunch. On his way out the door, he picked up an apple along with the florist's card.

Outside, the wind had started up again, and Ben remembered the storm. He tightened a scarf around his neck and wondered what the Drop would look like under the blankness of the snow. Leaving the Crofts without Hudson still felt like venturing into the world without a limb. Ben tried not to think about it.

The Escape's steering wheel was like ice. He held the florist's card with one hand, activated the car's voice dialing, and began reading the number aloud. Halfway through, a flash of movement drew his eyes to the windshield.

He swore and slammed on the brakes. He heard the spray of gravel rattle across the road's surface.

Mrs. White stood by the path, staring at him.

She was on the side of the road this time, so he wouldn't have hit her, but she'd still scared the hell out of him.

"Mrs. White!" he called as he jumped from the running car. "Are you all right?"

The old woman shook her head. Her lips moved, but, like last time, Ben couldn't hear her. Her hands fluttered at her sides. She wore a man's plaid hunting jacket, and beneath it she looked as frail as a skeleton.

"How about you get in the car and get warmed up?" He stepped a little closer to her. "Come on, now." He had the idea that she might bolt if he moved too quickly. She continued to mouth something. Though her mind was lost, her milky-blue eyes still held a startling lucidity.

When he got close enough, Ben dipped his head to bring his ear closer to her trembling mouth. It was the same word again and again. After listening for a few moments, Ben understood.

"Swann? Do you want to go to the Swanns' old house?" he asked. Mrs. White shook her head slowly.

She reached for him, and her mouth stopped moving. Her well-used face still reminded Ben of his grandmother's, but the resemblance was diminished in the light.

"Are you hungry?" he asked. He took the apple out of his jacket pocket. He held it out to her and her fingers grazed its green skin. Then her eyes widened and she whipped her hair around as she ran back into the trees.

Ben called after her, but she didn't stop. She darted through the forest, gliding through its pillars with barely a rustle. He cursed and hurried back to the car to turn off the engine and put it into park. By the time he'd turned back to the woods, she was hidden from sight. Ben picked his way after her, first jogging and then running as best he could around the trees. The forest here was dense, thick enough to crowd out the sunlight no matter the hour. Sometimes Ben thought he caught the flash of the woman's coat through the shadowy trees, but then it would disappear just as quickly.

Eventually he stopped. He'd lost his bearings in the dark forest, and Mrs. White could be anywhere. The wind didn't penetrate this deep into the wood, and as Ben noticed the stillness, he got the disconcerting sense of being watched. He spun around, but all he saw were the expanding rings of trees and the shadows that bound them. Clouds of tiny crystals exploded from his mouth with every breath. Ben looked up at the gray sky through the barren branches; he didn't know what to do but turn around.

———

"Hi, buddy," Ben said when he saw Charlie.

The nurse's office had a partitioned section with three small beds. Charlie was lying on the farthest one, staring out the window.

"Hi," Charlie said. "Your face is red."

Ben had called the chief on his way out of the forest. By the time he got back to the gravel path, the chief and a pickup of men from the village had already pulled up near the Escape. Ben pointed them in the right direction. He would have liked to continue the search for Mrs. White, but Charlie was sick and waiting for him.

"It's cold outside," Ben said. "Are you okay?" The rings around the boy's eyes stood out against the pallor of his skin.

"I feel okay," Charlie said. "I don't know what happened."

"You're all right. I'm going to take you home." Ben held his palm against his son's forehead.

"Mr. Tierney?" The nurse spoke from a separation in the partition. "Could I borrow you for a moment?"

"Be right back, okay?" Ben said. He put his hand on Charlie's chest and felt the rapid thrum of his heart. The nurse waved him into the hallway.

"Charlie was in his session with Mrs. Fraser when he passed out," the nurse said.

"Mrs. Fraser?"

"The school counselor. She's with Father Cal right now. They're waiting for you."

They found Cal at his desk. A heavyset woman in a tight white blouse sat in one of his chairs. When she saw Ben, Mrs. Fraser introduced herself.

"Well, I spoke with Charlie, Mr. Tierney, and I think he's a very sweet and smart—"

"Thanks," Ben said. "But tell me what happened."

"He got a nosebleed and then fainted," Mrs. Fraser said. "He didn't hit his head or anything."

"Did he eat breakfast this morning?" the nurse asked. "Low blood sugar could explain it."

"Of course. I mean, I think so. Is there anything else?" He just wanted to take Charlie home.

"He was acting a little oddly before he passed out," the counselor said. "Said some strange things." She looked at her notebook. "He said, 'The winter. It's hard. It's cold and dark. But I wouldn't want to be alone. Not ever. I know that now.'" She looked at Ben. "I thought he sounded frightened."

Cal asked a question, but Ben only half-listened. *It's cold and dark. But I wouldn't want to be alone. Not ever.* Why did Charlie think he'd ever be alone? And what about the cold or dark could have frightened him? That didn't sound like him at all.

The counselor left, and the nurse went to check on Charlie. Ben had intended to follow her, but something kept him rooted where he stood.

"Did what he said mean anything to you?" Cal asked.

"I don't know," Ben said. It was the truth. Still, there *was* something in what Charlie had said. Something that brushed against the edge of Ben's mind, but something he couldn't quite get a good look at. "I didn't even ask how the rest of their talk went."

"I don't think they got a chance to speak about the drawing. Mrs. Fraser said he passed out only a few minutes into the session."

"Just as well, I guess," Ben said.

"One thing at a time," Cal said.

"Would that I were so lucky." Ben rubbed his eyes. He wanted to stretch out on the floor and fall asleep, but he forced himself into motion. "I'm going to take him home. See you for dinner?"

"Absolutely."

"And we might not want to get into any details about what Charlie said," Ben said. "No reason to get Caroline worried."

"Whatever you say, Ben," the priest said. "I'll see you tonight."

Ben nodded to Cal and returned to the nurse's office.

"How are you feeling, kid?" he asked Charlie.

"Okay," Charlie said. "Better." Ben thought he looked the same.

"Let's head home. You let me know if you feel like you might pass out or anything like that, okay?"

"I need my jacket," Charlie said. "It's in my cubby."

"Okay, I'll get it. Put on your shoes," Ben said.

The nurse gave him directions to an enclosed walkway that connected to a neighboring building. Flurries had begun to collect against the glass.

The walkway opened into a corridor that was still and quiet. All the rooms along it had their doors closed. Ben could imagine the teachers at their boards and their students staring out the windows, watching the first snow of the season.

He found Charlie's jacket in one of the wooden nooks along the wall near his homeroom. Peering into the other cubbies, Ben saw shin guards, comics, and other artifacts of boyhood, but there was nothing like that in Charlie's. A few books, a sweater. He pulled out one of the books, a worn oversize hardcover. When he read the frayed spine, Ben was surprised to see that it was *The Book of Secrets*, the book he'd bought for Charlie back in the summer. Its pages were loose and stained, as if they'd been read every day for a hundred years.

"What did you *do* to this book?" Ben murmured to himself.

Ben smiled as he paged through it. He wished he'd had a book like this when he was little—one of the reasons he'd bought it for Charlie in the first place. It had illustrations, maps, and instructions about all the things that lit a boy's heart. If they'd had a copy, he and Ted could have found themselves some real trouble.

He stopped on a page that had a diagram of how to climb a wall and safely walk on a roof. "How to Make the Night Your Own" was the title of the following section. It gave tips on amplifying night vision, techniques on how to move quickly and quietly in the dark, and demonstrated how to navigate by the stars. "How to Build a Fire Anywhere" was another chapter. It illustrated how to kindle and grow a flame in any conditions you might find, from the rain forests to the Arctic.

But something began to gnaw at Ben when he reached the topic called "The Buffalo Jump," which described how Native Americans had herded buffalo over the edge of cliffs in order to kill them. Ben thought of the broken rib cages that arced from the bottom of the pit he'd found in the north woods.

The next section had detailed diagrams on how to skin a small animal and properly prepare its meat. Many of the book's pages were stained through much use, but one chapter, on fishing, was streaked with brown residue. There was a thumbprint twice the size of Ben's on one corner of the page.

He shut the book, suddenly out of breath. He pulled Charlie's jacket from its hook, and a small skull fixed Ben with its sharp-toothed grin.

Ben put the battered book back into the cubby. He stared at it a moment longer before returning to the walkway. On his way, he tried to think about what he'd need to do when he got home. He tried to think of the batches of cocktails he'd store in the freezer and how he would prepare the smoked-trout appetizers. He tried not to think of the deer's head that had been displayed on their steps. He tried not to think about the carcasses he'd found in the north woods. He tried not to think about the fire that had burned down their shed or the skulls at the bottom of the pit, which looked just like the one Charlie had in his cubby.

He tried hardest not to think of the man in the smoke from Charlie's drawing and how his hands were twice the size of Ben's own.

37

When Ben and Charlie returned to the Crofts, Caroline was stuffing the game hens. Her apron was smeared with the juice from wild mushrooms, and her hair smelled like apricots. She hugged Charlie and made him grilled cheese sprinkled with the extra mushrooms. She even let him have one of the macaroons they'd picked up in Exton. She looked much better than she had when Ben had left her, but he could take little pleasure in it now.

"You don't look so good, either," Caroline told Ben. She was covering a tray of the stuffed birds with plastic wrap.

"No?" He felt a bit light-headed. Charlie had been his usual quiet self on the ride back, and Ben hadn't felt like talking.

"You're not catching what he has?" she asked.

"I don't think so."

"Okay, because I need you tonight. Did Father Cal seem excited about dinner?"

"I guess."

"Good. The flowers came, and I'm on schedule as far as the food goes. The beets should be done soon. I want to serve those at room temperature. I think the cake turned out well, too. I have it in the cellar, where it's cool."

"Great."

"Are you sure you're all right?"

"Are you just going to keep asking me?"

"Were you going to make some cocktails?"

"Yes, I can do that." Ben tried to focus. "Manhattans? Good in cold weather."

"What if you serve them and they don't know how strong they are? Maybe some specialty drink that's not too strong. Something they might get a kick out of. The bar's full, right? We have Apple Pucker and liqueurs like that?"

"Sure, I can make appletinis. But if I knew the night's theme was 1998, I would have also bought some Red Bull."

"Fine, make your Manhattans. Just remember we'll have a priest and a lawman in attendance. We should probably salt the gravel drive, too. And could you give Bub a bath? I figure we'll put him to bed a little early, but people will want to say hello to him, and I want him to be as fresh as possible."

"Sure."

"Same with Charlie, don't you think?" Caroline asked.

"You want me to give him a bath, too?"

"I mean we should parade him around a bit, then send him up to his room. I hate the way the ladies dote on him. And he's sick, anyway. If he needs us he can call, but he can probably take care of himself up there until it's bedtime, right?"

Ben turned to where Charlie sat at the table, methodically chewing his lunch.

"Yes, I'm certain he can take care of himself."

Ben held Bub's hand as the baby hoisted his leg from one step to the next. It was slow going; Bub's knees only came up to the top of the step in front of him. It looked exhausting to Ben, but he liked the way the baby's grip on his hand tightened each time he undertook a new step.

"You're getting to be a strong little boy, aren't you?" Ben asked him. Bub looked at him and turned his grin all the way up.

Bub loved his baths, and Ben spent more time than he needed to playing with the floating dinosaurs that Bub liked to dip in and out of the water. Ben lurched the brontosaurus around the tub so that its neck cut through the water as if it were the Loch Ness Monster.

It occurred to Ben that he'd never gone swimming with Bub. When Charlie was a baby, they'd rented a house in Montauk, right on the ocean. The Atlantic had stayed cold that season, but he'd taken Charlie in a few times. He liked how Charlie's eyes changed to match the gray green of the ocean, and he liked the surprised look that flashed across his face whenever salt water splashed into his mouth. The cold of the water made Ben's skin dance, and the feeling of Charlie's small body clutched against his chest made his heart swell. He could have stayed there all afternoon, just the two of them, bobbing in the waves.

Ben wondered when he'd have the chance to swim with Bub.

"Maybe we can go on vacation someplace by the water," he told Bub. He pulled the baby out of the tub and rubbed a towel over his shoulders. "You'd like the Gulf Coast. Great shells there. And lots of animals. Colorful birds and rays and fish."

"Ish," Bub said. He reached a hand to touch Ben's face.

"But would we have to shut down the whole inn to take some time off?" He ran the towel over the baby's head. The season had turned his hair darker. "And what time of year do we do it? The fall's going to be the busiest season. But there's skiing in the winter and lots of outdoors stuff in the spring and summer. It's not like there's a clear off-season, you know?"

Ben couldn't make out Bub's answer, but he nodded to the boy. He didn't even know if they could afford to take nice vacations anymore.

"Right, I'm sure we'll figure it out. Tons of people own small businesses, and they must take time off, right?"

"Who are you talking to?" Charlie asked from the doorway.

"Your brother."

"What is he saying?"

"Can't you understand him?"

"No. You can?"

"Of course." Ben finished drying Bub and wrapped the towel around him.

"I try to understand," Charlie said. "I know he wants us to understand."

"Maybe you should try being a better listener. You're supposed to be in bed."

"I was in bed at school."

"We can't have you passing out again. What if you hurt yourself?"

Charlie didn't say anything and didn't move from the doorway. "Who was the lady I had to talk to today?" he finally asked.

"A counselor. Didn't she tell you that? I know I told you someone would be talking with you."

"You didn't say why."

"Oh, there are a couple reasons," Ben said. He stood up, lifting Bub with him. "Mostly because of that picture you drew of the shed burning down. Do you remember that one?"

Charlie nodded.

"Well, some people found the man in the smoke you drew kind of disturbing."

"The man in the smoke," Charlie repeated.

"They think you might have unresolved issues having to do with the fire."

"What does that mean?"

"It means that they think there's something you're not telling us. Is there something you'd like to tell me?"

"Like what?" A frown creased the boy's face.

"Like anything."

"You're mad at me."

"No, I'm not." Ben looked away from Charlie and kissed the top of Bub's head.

"You are. Sorry."

"Sorry for what?" Ben looked at Charlie and thought of Hudson. After tackling Charlie, Hudson had run into the forest howling at something. That very same something had kept him from ever coming home.

"Sorry you're mad at me."

"Is that an apology or a recrimination?" Ben asked.

"I don't know wh—"

"I have to get Bub dressed, Charlie."

"Do you still want me to go to bed?" he asked.

Ben studied his son. He still looked like a little kid. A pale and sick-looking kid. But Ben saw someone older in those gray-blue eyes. In their reflection he could imagine the dead animals in the woods and the fire in the shed. They made him think of huge men lurking in the forest. They made him wonder about his dead dog. They made him think of secrets that no child should be keeping to himself. When he looked at Charlie, he felt more things than he could sort.

"Do whatever you want to do," Ben said. He maneuvered past him. When he turned in to Bub's room, he could still feel Charlie's gaze on his back.

Ben had just gotten Bub dressed when he heard Caroline call for him. There was something strange in her voice, but it wasn't the Wolf.

He slung Bub over his shoulder and headed downstairs. The chief was sitting in the kitchen, his shoulders powdered with snow. Caroline leaned against the counter, gray-faced.

"What happened?" he asked.

"We found Mrs. White," the chief said. "Not far from where you told us to look. Found her up in the cemetery. She passed, I'm sorry to say."

"She's dead?"

The chief nodded.

"God," Ben said. He sat in the chair next to the chief's. "She didn't look that bad when I saw her. I mean, she was disoriented, but she was also sprinting through the forest."

"The cold can catch up to you fast," the chief said.

"I don't know what to say." Ben felt sick, and he felt naked against the eyes that were on him. "I ran after her, but I lost her." Saying it aloud only made Ben feel worse; how hapless would a man have to be to be outrun by an arthritic ninety-year-old?

"She say anything to you when you saw her?"

"No," Ben said. "She was totally out of it. And she was so thin. I offered her that apple—I thought she must be hungry—but that's when she took off." He shook his head. "She was muttering something to herself, but she had almost no voice. It sounded like 'Swann.' She said it over and over again, but I didn't know what she meant."

"She said 'Swann'?" the chief asked. "You're sure?"

"That's what it sounded like to me. I figured she was remembering that the Swanns used to live here. Could it mean anything else?"

"Her mind was gone," the chief said. He scribbled something in his notepad. "Coulda meant anything at all."

"She froze to death?"

"Hypothermia's our guess. Book says we gotta take her to North Hampstead for the autopsy."

"She was such a sweet lady," Caroline said. "I really can't believe it." She looked down at the counter.

"I don't know what I could have done differently," Ben said. "I searched for her and I couldn't find her."

"No one's blaming you, Ben," the chief said. "She's with God now."

"What about her son?"

"You let me worry about Tommy." The chief stood up to leave. "Sorry to give you this kinda news before your party."

"Don't worry about us, Chief," Caroline said.

"Yes," Ben said. "Our sympathies are with the family."

"In a village this small, we're all family," the chief said. He put on his gloves. "Now, you remember that. We all got to stick together up here. The winter's too hard to do otherwise. I'll see you tonight." When he opened the door to leave, the room filled with icy air.

"Are you all right?" Caroline asked.

"Yeah, it's just—yeah, I'm fine," Ben said. "I'm sorry, I know you and she became close."

"Do you think we should cancel the party?"

Ben would have liked nothing more. But one look at her face told Ben that wasn't what Caroline wanted to hear.

"You've already made so much food," Ben said. "It'd go to waste."

Bub pounded against Ben's chest with one tiny fist.

"I'll get the boys dressed then start the fires," he said. Ben sensed that Caroline needed to hear something more from him in this moment—almost any bromide would do—but still, he couldn't find the words she needed. He left her in the kitchen, staring at the granite counter.

Ben got the boys ready, got himself dressed, then started the fireplaces in the lounge, library, and dining room. His hands smelled like charred wood when he assembled the smoked-trout appetizers.

Caroline changed into a green velvet dress with a gold belt that matched her hair. She looked as if she'd stepped off the cover of a magazine, but she picked at her cuticles as she paced the halls. When she left the kitchen to light the candles in the lounge, Ben poured a measure of vodka into a water glass.

Outside, the snow fell. Several inches covered the ground, and the wind had already built drifts against the walls of the Crofts. The monochromaticity of the storm turned the contours of the Drop into an alien landscape.

Staring at the strange blankness of it, Ben decided he didn't want to spend Christmas here after all. Not in this place where women froze to death, dogs vanished, and wives and sons turned into strangers. He'd tell Caroline tomorrow. They'd visit with Ted in the city instead of the other way around. Caroline would protest, but she thought only in time and money. Ben could no longer ignore the fact that every problem they'd come here to solve had gotten worse. Like the oblivious frog being boiled on a stovetop, Ben thought that maybe a week or two away from this place would give him perspective on just how hot the water around them had become.

You got everything you ever wanted, didn't you, Benj?

Ben saw the flash of headlights pulling up the gravel drive. He finished his vodka and waited for the doorbell to ring. When it did, he listened to Caroline's hurried steps to the front door.

He heard Lisbeth's voice before he set eyes on her. He was glad that she was the first to arrive. Caroline was anxious enough, and Ben thought that Lisbeth would be able to put her at ease.

". . . about the snow and everything," he heard Caroline say.

"Don't be silly, sugar. Folks around here have been itching to slap the chains on their tires for weeks. There he is now," she said, seeing Ben. She pressed her palms against his face.

"No trouble finding the place, I hope?" he said. The cold of her hands brought the blood to his cheeks.

"Hundred and one laughs, isn't he?" Lisbeth's smile lit the hallway.

"Please let me take your coat," Caroline said.

"Look at these floors!" Lisbeth said, looking down. She took in the walls and the foyer's chandelier. "Everything is so beautiful!" Her compliments seemed genuine, but her face was drawn and tired. Ben wondered if she'd already been over to Tommy White's place to lend comfort to him, the same way she had to the family whose farm had been repossessed.

Caroline started to leave with the coat, but Lisbeth stopped her.

"Wait, just stand next to each other," she said. She nudged Caroline into Ben. "Closer."

Ben put his arm around his wife. They posed like actors facing a photographer. An actor was exactly what he was, Ben realized as he donned his smile. When you came down to it, the language he spoke and the air he breathed was that of pretending.

Lisbeth looked them over and shook her head. "What lucky and beautiful people you are."

Father Cal arrived next. When Caroline walked off with Lisbeth to get a bottle of wine, Ben lowered his voice to tell Cal about what happened to Mrs. White.

"How perfectly horrible," Father Cal said.

"I hate to mention it at all, but when the others get here they might say something about it, so I wanted you to know."

"Are you all right?" the priest asked him.

"She was a very nice lady. Caroline knew her better than I did, though," Ben said. "But it's still hard to process, because—"

"You were the last one to see her," Cal said. He shook his head. "Another grim story for this old house."

The doorbell rang again. Ben opened the door to find both the Stantons and the Bishops standing on the veranda.

The chief had shaved, and the skin of his face was tight against its bones.

"Please come in, everyone," Ben said. "And sorry about the snow."

"Don't expect you to control the weather, Ben," Mary Stanton said.

"If only all wives were as reasonable as you, Mary," he said.

He introduced himself to Jake's father, Henry. They'd spoken on the phone before but had never met. Other than their wide-set eyes, father and son looked nothing alike. Jake was tall and broad, while his father was short and wiry.

Ben brought the Bishops and Stantons to the lounge, where Caroline was showing Lisbeth and Cal the room's architectural details. He tracked back and forth from the kitchen with drink orders, and on his last trip he came upon Charlie and Bub holding hands in the lounge doorway. Charlie wore gray pants and a black sweater over a white collared shirt; except for Ben's tie, they were dressed identically. Bub was dressed for bed, in red pajamas with feet.

"Look who's here," Ben muttered to himself. He could hear Lisbeth cooing from down the hallway.

Caroline left to check the dinner as Ben passed out the drinks. When he was finished, he found himself next to Cal, while the Bishops, Stantons, and Lisbeth stood in a group by the doorway with Charlie and Bub in the center. The villagers were craned over Charlie, asking him questions and patting his shoulders. Bub stood behind Charlie, somewhat ignored and becoming agitated because of it. Charlie nodded and smiled, but even across the room Ben saw something wild in his eyes.

Looking at his son, he could not imagine a single thought that might be running through his mind. Perhaps this was what it meant for a child to grow up, but Ben didn't think so. His own mother would have brutalized him at the slightest whiff of deception, but maybe Ben had erred too far in the other direction. As he watched Charlie wield his frozen smile, Ben decided that he'd been passive for too long. Since finding the bloody fingerprint in *The Book of Secrets,* Ben's fears and suspicions had not coalesced into anything more than a profound sense of wrongness. There was something wrong with this place, and there was something wrong with his son. Tomorrow he'd find out what the boy knew about what was in the forest. He'd ask about the pit and find out what had happened on the day the shed went up in flames. Maybe he would find out what happened to Hudson. Then they'd all take a break from the Crofts over the holidays.

"I think it's just about bedtime for the boys," Ben said. Charlie was still holding the baby's hand. Ben pulled Bub away from him.

"I can put him to bed," Charlie said.

"I got him. But it's getting late for you, too," Ben said.

"I'm not tired," Charlie said.

"He had to come home sick from school," Ben told the villagers.

"Hope you feel better, sugar," Lisbeth told Charlie.

"Mom's in the kitchen. Now, go say good night to her," Ben said. He met Charlie's stare until the boy did what he was told. "You say good night, too, Bub." He waved the child's hand for him while he watched Charlie make his way down the hall.

"Good night, boys," Mary Stanton said. "You have beautiful sons," she told Ben.

Bub lay heavily against him as Ben made his way up the stairs to his room.

"They tired you out, didn't they, buddy?" The baby had his eyes closed before he hit the cushion of his crib. Ben switched on the monitor and clipped the receiver to his pocket. "Would you dream a happy dream for me?"

38

It felt strange to be seated at the head of such a large table. The meal was perfect, and the room glistened with candles and Christmas trees and cascades of poinsettias. It was beautiful in the way a movie set would be. And sitting there smiling, laughing, telling stories, Ben felt it again: an actor. Everyone was gracious and said polite things, but the night felt like a performance.

"Will anyone be able to come to the restaurant, or would you need to be a guest?" Mary Stanton asked. They had peppered Ben and Caroline with dozens of questions about the kind of inn the Crofts would become. Ben could not tell whether these were asked out of interest or simply to prevent the table from falling into silence.

"Eventually we'd like to open it up to everyone," Caroline said. "We have a space for a professional kitchen. The pipes and wires and gas lines are all there, but we don't have the equipment yet."

"Well, I may need to make myself a regular," Lisbeth said. "These beets are like a dream."

"You gonna run this place on your own?" Henry Bishop asked. It was clear that none of the guests had explored the full extent of the

Crofts in a long time. The house cut an imperial silhouette against the mountains, but they'd forgotten the sprawling massiveness of the place. The tour Caroline gave had been limited to the first two floors, but Ben watched their eyes widen every time they turned a corner to reveal a different section of the mansion.

"At first we'll need at least a couple of people to clean the rooms," Caroline said.

"You'll need some bodies for the kitchen, too," Lisbeth said. "A cook and a prep, at least, I think. Then someone to run the tables."

"And eventually we want to grow most of our food," Caroline said. "Turn the Crofts back into a working farm. Then there are the stables. And we're talking about restoring one of the outbuildings, making it into a spa." She glanced at Ben. This was the first he'd heard of it. "Then there's all the landscaping and grounds maintenance."

"Thought I had that covered," Jake said. Jake had barely said a word all night. He'd seemed fine the day before, but Ben wondered if he had whatever was going around. He didn't look as if he'd been sleeping well.

"You do, but you can't do it all on your own. You'll need help," Caroline said.

"Don't worry, we'll give you some fancy title so everyone knows you're in charge," Ben said. "Executive Groundskeeper. Living Resource Management Director. Estate Director. Unless that sounds too much like an undertaker." He regretted the words as they left his mouth. Mrs. White had been the ghost in the room all along.

"Ah, poor Tommy White," Lisbeth said. She dabbed at her mouth with her napkin. "God bless the boy."

"Hard season," Henry said, nodding.

"And it's only beginning," the chief said. He looked to the windows, but they'd been frosted by the storm's onslaught. "Hope the road stays open."

"The county road?" Ben asked.

"Enough snow and the south pass gets closed up tight. Probably won't get enough for that tonight, but the ice on the turn before the pass can be murder, too."

Ben vaguely remembered Cal saying something about the county road closing for a few days after the fire in 1982. He tried to imagine what they would do if a time came when they needed to leave the valley, and couldn't.

"Told Simms to keep an eye on it."

"Ben, you look like someone ran over your cat," Lisbeth said. "Even if the south pass closes, the north pass almost never does. Isn't that right, Bill?"

"You'll get used to it up here," Henry told them. "The winters are hard, but they make the rest of the year seem that much easier."

"I look at the calendar and I know we haven't been here long, but some days it doesn't feel that way," Caroline said.

"Just means you must feel at home," Lisbeth said.

"And you've been working so hard and pouring your heart into this house," Mary Stanton said.

"It's been a busy time." Caroline nodded. "And there's a lot more to do."

"And you like it up here, too, Ben?" Henry asked. "You don't miss the city?"

"Sometimes." He thought back to New York: drinking coffee on marble steps while reading the paper, lowering Charlie's feet into fountains, drinking beer with friends on rooftops. His memory of the city was frozen in spring and sunlight. "That life seems like a long time gone."

"That's 'cause this is where you belong," Lisbeth said. "Place wasn't right without any Lowells." She turned to the chief. "Isn't that right, Bill?"

"Lisbeth has it right. The village is small and gets smaller all the time. We've lost a lot of good people, and it's a nice change to have some of them come back. And it's good to have a family at the Crofts again."

"And doing so right by it," Mary said. "How you turned this old place into something like from out of a magazine, I'll never know."

"We're so pleased you like it," Caroline said. "It means a lot to hear it from you. Ben's been reading up on the history of the place, so we know it's important to the village."

"Not writing a book on us, I hope," Henry said.

"From the moment I saw this place, I knew it had a story," Ben said. This was a chance for him to change the subject, put his guests more at ease, and possibly even stop lying to them for a minute. "Actually, Chief, you were there. Remember? We were at the old Lowell farm, and Hank Seward called the station on us for the first time."

"That grass-eater," Henry said.

"Then you told me the place between the mountains was for sale."

"Did I?" the chief asked.

"You did. You're the reason we're all here," Ben said. He raised his glass.

"Oh, you don't need to." The chief held up a hand. Ben toasted him anyway, and the rest of the table joined him.

After they'd finished their meal, Ben led the guests into the library. This wasn't a room Ben had spent much time in, but the new couches made it a comfortable place. He had bottles of port, sambuca, and brandy waiting, and he offered glasses to everyone. The fire here had burned down to embers, and he threw another log on.

"Do you think Caroline needs any help with the dishes?" Mary Stanton asked from the couch. "I feel like a heel, living it up in here while she's in the kitchen." She gave Ben a nervous smile that showed her incisors.

"She's just clearing the table for dessert," Ben said. "And don't worry about it; you're our guest." He filled her glass with sambuca. "I'm going to check on the coffee. I'll be right back."

"I thought they'd eat more," Caroline said when he got to the kitchen. There were mountains of leftovers on the counter, but Caroline always made too much.

"But they definitely liked it. Everything was fantastic." He began slotting glasses into the dishwasher.

"Well, I hope they brought their appetite for this," Caroline said. She opened a cabinet to reveal the dessert: a huge two-tiered cake iced with dark chocolate. Its sides were decorated with a pattern made from gold leaf.

"Each tier is three layers. White cake with whipped ganache filling," Caroline said. "I made it for you."

"It's beautiful," he said.

She'd outdone herself with this one. Even among the spectacular cakes she'd made for his birthdays, this was a standout. He remembered how he used to look at those birthday cakes and feel the time and love that had gone into their perfection.

"I'm so sorry about Hudson, Ben. I really am."

He turned to Caroline and saw her eyes brimming with tears. There was a time not long ago when this would have filled him with sympathy, but now he felt something closer to disgust.

"You didn't have to bake me a cake," Ben said. He turned away from her and the dessert. Why she thought this was a good time to mention Hudson, he had no idea. "Do you want me to make the coffee?"

"I almost forgot," she said.

"I'll take care of it." He wanted a few minutes to himself. He was so tired of pretending. "Have some port and sit by the fire. I'll let you know when it's ready."

While Ben's hands were busy with the coffee brewer, he felt Caroline watching him from the doorway. A moment later he felt her lips on his cheek. Months ago, his heart would have hummed at such spontaneous affection, but it was not that kind of kiss. Long after her footsteps faded down the hall, the feel of her mouth lingered alongside his, sitting there like an exhausted goodbye.

Ben picked at the cake as he emptied tumbler after tumbler of brandy. This evening could not end soon enough. His thoughts had turned as dark as his mood.

"The Swanns didn't drink, you know," Henry said.

"I'd heard that," Caroline said.

"It must be about two years," Ben said.

They turned to him.

"Since the Swann sisters died," he said.

"Shame the aunties couldn't see the place like this," Lisbeth said. "Doubt it looked this fine even when they were children." She shook her head. "There were times when the wind was howling that I was afraid the roof would fall in on them while they slept. But two nicer ladies you couldn't find."

"Everyone has very nice things to say about them," Caroline said. "Jake told us how they died. Such a tragic accident."

"It was their time," Mary said.

"And we can't go around second-guessing God's plan," the chief said. "Isn't that right, Father?"

"It's hard to make sense of so many of the things that happen in this world," Cal said. "Terrible, unthinkable things happen every day. It's faith that sees us through. Faith that there's something better waiting for us."

"Those dear sisters," the chief said. "They are missed, but they are also remembered. Isn't that right?"

The others all nodded at that.

"In the end, maybe that's the best anyone can ask for," Ben said. He drained his glass.

"What's that?" Lisbeth asked.

Everyone at the table turned, and at first Ben thought that they were looking at him. Then he pivoted to see an orange glow lighting the room's large windows. He walked to the nearest window, but the glass was too heavily frosted for him to see through it.

"We haven't been here all night, have we?" Henry joked. He looked at his watch. The light looked like the sunrise, except it came from the west.

"Ben?" Caroline said from her seat.

"I'll look," he said.

The dining room had French doors that opened onto the veranda, but they were locked and Ben didn't have the keys with him. He headed for the front door. Jake, Cal, and Chief Stanton followed him.

"Looks like a fire," the chief said. "But I can't guess what could be burning out there."

"The elder tree," Jake said. "That's what's out there."

"What's that?" Cal asked.

"Our oldest tree. Been here since the beginning. Since Aldrich Swann cleared the rest of the forest," the chief said.

Ben pulled open the door to see that Jake was right.

The great elm on the lip of the Drop was on fire. Orange flames washed over its branches like infernal foliage. Even at the distance of a hundred yards, Ben could hear the tree crackling. The snow danced in the unexpected light. An hour ago the Drop had seemed as stark as a charcoal sketch; now it blazed.

Ben looked down and realized he'd run out into the snow toward the tree. The snow was almost to his knees. The tree had been the size of a torch from the veranda, but the flames now encompassed most of his field of vision. His face burned, but his feet were cold. He felt a hand yank him backward.

"Too close," Cal said. "One gust of wind will send the flames into us."

Chief Stanton helped pull Ben back. "Can't do anything about it," he told him. "Lucky it's too far from the house to be a danger."

"Lucky it's not summertime, with the grass all long and dry," Jake said.

"What did this?" Ben asked. "Lightning?"

They all looked at the sky. The stars were hidden by clouds, but there was no evidence of electrical activity.

"Woulda heard the thunder, wouldn't we, Chief?" Jake asked.

"Weather's strange on the Drop," the chief said. Ben watched as the man's eyes wandered to the edge of the north woods.

"Should I call 911?" Ben asked.

"Call them." The chief began to walk around to the other side of the tree. "Tell them I'm here and to send the North Hampstead volunteers over."

Ben pulled out his phone and began dialing.

"Strange, isn't it?" he heard Cal say. "Oddly beautiful. The flames and the snow and the darkness."

"I'm seeing it with my own eyes and I can't believe it," Jake said. "That tree was as old as the mountains."

Ben spoke to the 911 operator, pacing as he talked. Wetness from the snow climbed the legs of his pants. He figured he'd ruined these shoes. The operator said they were sending an engine over.

"This place has some trouble with fire, doesn't it?" Cal asked him.

Ben felt something in his chest shift position. It was one thing to burn a dry shed at the height of summer, but could anything in *The Book of Secrets* advise someone on how to set a frozen tree ablaze? The Crofts glowed with reflected light as he searched its windows for small faces. Some of the guests approached through the snow. They'd taken the time to put on their winter gear, and Ben felt colder looking at them.

"How? How?" was all Caroline was able to say when she reached him.

"I don't know." He glanced back at the Crofts, but it revealed nothing. "The fire department is coming."

"Footprints here," the chief called. "Don't get too close now. Evidence."

Ben followed the chief's own tracks in an arc around the burning tree. When he got there, he could see two sets of footprints. One led to the tree, the other headed away, toward the north woods.

"What size would you say?" Ben asked.

"Fourteen or bigger," the chief said. "Some big feet."

A blast of static came from the baby monitor on his belt.

"It sometimes acts up if I get too far from the house," Ben told the chief. Then he heard Bub crying. The boy hardly cried, even when he woke up in the middle of the night. He usually talked to himself until he fell back to sleep.

"No reason for all of us to be out here," Ben said. "We should at least get our coats."

Another sound came from the monitor. A man's low growl: "It's okay, baby. Be quiet, baby."

Ben and the chief both stared at the monitor. The chief took off first, running for the house. Caroline asked Ben a question as he ran past, but he didn't hear it. The house seemed far away, and the snow slowed them.

He saw Henry Bishop by the front door in his jacket. The man's head was jutted forward, trying to make sense of what he was seeing. He opened his mouth as the chief approached him, but something he saw made him shut it again.

Ben got inside just after the chief.

"Which room?" the chief yelled. His face was red enough for it to be on fire, and his eyes blazed, too.

Ben took the lead up the central stairs. They ran down the second-floor hallway for Bub's room. When they got there, the room was empty. Ben ran to the crib, but it, too, was empty.

"What about Charlie?" the chief asked.

"Next door," Ben said, pointing. He couldn't feel his legs.

Charlie's room was also empty. Ben ripped through the bed-clothes, looking for him.

"Gone," he said. "They're both gone."

There was a creak from the wall of cabinets. Ben unfastened a telescope from its tripod and held it like a baseball bat. The chief took a large geode from the bookshelf. One of the cabinet doors inched open. Ben could see the rims of two pale eyes watching him.

"Dad?"

"What are you doing in there?" Ben dropped the telescope and heard its lens shatter against the ground.

"Hiding," Charlie said. He climbed out of the space.

"Where's Bub?" Ben asked.

"He took him."

"Who—"

"Where did he go?" the chief asked. "Which way?"

Charlie pointed the way they had come, and the chief took off running again. Ben stared at Charlie. This would have been the time to hug his son, but he didn't.

"Who was it?"

"*Him,*" Charlie said. He wouldn't look at Ben.

"Look at me!" Ben shouted at him. "*Who?*"

"The man," Charlie said, wiping at his face. "The man in the smoke." He stared up at Ben, and his face shone in the light. Ben saw that he was crying.

Ben staggered back into the hall. For a moment he forgot which way the chief had gone. He began to follow him, then stopped.

He wouldn't believe it. He went back to Bub's room. He looked under the crib and under the blanket. He lifted the cushion and tore through the laundry.

But he was gone. Bub was gone.

IV

KEEPING UP *the* LIGHT

DECEMBER, DARKEST

December 18, 1777

Dear Kathy,

I know now that these letters will never be sent, but what have I to do but write them?

We have eaten the last of the flour. Now nothing remains for us but to wait. The hunger that has taken us is strange. It is not of the same kind as when a meal is missed, nor is it like the pangs one feels upon waking after a long sleep. It is a cloak that encloses me, like a husk of corn. Sometimes warm and sometimes cold. Sometimes it is heavy enough to press me into bed, and sometimes it is so light that I imagine I could fly if only I moved my arms swiftly enough.

There are dreams, too, bright and wild, though they are not always bad. It is only upon waking that I regret them. They sit upon my chest like a sin.

Goody Smythe has perished, and so, too, has little Susie Harp. The Coxes died last night. Their stove was extinguished in the night; we do not know whether on purpose or by accident. Martha Goode found them frozen together in one bed. She said that they looked at peace.

Now all of the families stay in the Crofts, as it is the farthest dwelling from the trees. The forest seems to get louder each night, as if the trees themselves are demons. It is difficult to sleep. And when we sleep, the dreams give us no rest. All of us are sacks of bone, except for James. The men watch him to see if he has hidden a store of food for himself. One of them caught him going into the forest last night. I do not know why he goes there or how he still looks so well. He was never a conniving child—had he found food, he would tell us, would he not? But the time here has made us all strange. Men so placid in the warm months have grown violent, and the kindest of women have become cunning. I can now imagine that any terrible thing is possible. Mother has left her bed and tells us that God speaks to her, and she asks us to remain faithful to Him.

Father has also returned to us with renewed vigor. He gives a sermon every morning and every night. His subjects are of the Old Testament, of the tests given the faithful. There is a new light in his eyes since Jack was taken. Sometimes I am myself fired by it, but other times it frightens me, when I did not think I could be frightened any further.

And perhaps he does indeed know what must be done. Are we not the only ones who live while so many are dead? Is that alone not a sign of God's blessings? What else is there to believe when our own forest has turned against us? But I fear the time is coming when unthinkable things will be asked of us.

I have nearly knocked over my candle laughing, dear sister. People such as you say "the unthinkable" as if there is but one unthinkable thing. But I tell you they are legion, and I come to know a new one each day.

Your Bess

39

Caroline heard it again.

Her ear pressed against the wall, she filtered out the sounds of the heat and plumbing. It was there, she was sure, just beyond the hum of electricity.

Behind her, Charlie tugged at her shirt.

"Come here, honey," she said.

She hoisted the boy onto her knee without removing her ear from the wall. Normally Charlie would have squirmed under her grip, but all their normal days had been spent and he was docile as a lamb. She pressed his little head against the wall.

"Do you hear it?" she asked. His thick hair still smelled of Johnson & Johnson, just like his brother's would have.

"I don't know," Charlie said after a few long moments. "Is it . . . is it kind of a scratching?"

"It does sound like scratching sometimes," Caroline said. "But it's more of a creaking, I think. And sometimes—"

"There are mice," Charlie said. "I've seen them in the cellar."

"Not big enough to make that creaking noise. And sometimes

there's another sound, too. If we listen carefully enough, I know you'll hear it."

They leaned there like that for a few minutes, their ears pressed against the wall that separated Bub's room from the hallway.

Caroline tried to focus the entirety of her attention on the noise in the wall. Over the last day she'd discovered that it was a tricky sort of sound, the kind that knew just when your attention began to wander.

It was poor planning that she hadn't put her other ear against the wall. If she had, she might have been able to see the window and guess what time it was. It was too late now: She didn't dare move and risk missing the sound. Something in the room's shadows made her think it was morning again.

Caroline had searched with Ben and the others through the first day. The ice-glazed trees were terrible in their beauty, the air in the forest cold enough to make her teeth hurt. Full-grown adults swaddled in down and neoprene lasted barely a half hour outside, and yet that's where they thought Bub was.

Charlie had trudged through the snow between them. They were not about to let him out of their sight. Not now. Not ever, probably. The little man hadn't uttered a word of complaint. Had not said a word of any kind that Caroline could recall. He wanted to find his baby brother as badly as anyone, but it was clear he was too small for the search. The drifts in the woods were too deep and the wind was too cold. Caroline decided to stay at the Crofts with him. This might have been the most important decision she'd ever made.

After Caroline made hot chocolate for Charlie and some tea for herself, they'd gone upstairs. She'd meant to get Charlie dry socks, but they ended up in Bub's room. Clothes covered the floor, emptied drawers lay against the walls, and pictures hung askew on their nails. Ben had torn the place apart looking for Bub, and so had Caroline.

Still ajar was that cabinet that swung into both Bub and Charlie's rooms. Caroline checked it again, just in case. Then she made Charlie scamper through it into his own room, and she watched as he retrieved fresh socks from his dresser. When he returned through the cabinet, she made him sit between the two doors. While Charlie stayed there, she'd looked at him from the doorway of Bub's room, then walked down the hall to his own room's doorway to examine him from that vantage point.

It struck her as so strange that a boy could be in both rooms at once yet in neither one at all. She checked from both doors again and then joined Charlie in the cabinet that was in both rooms or in neither.

That's when she'd first heard it.

Charlie had been right next to her, but he hadn't caught it that time. They'd sat there through the night, and each time Charlie seemed to miss it. Between the howling wind and all the noises of the old house, it was a hard sound to grab hold of.

She'd tried to get Ben to hear it, too, but had no luck there, either. This wasn't much of a surprise. He'd come in, stubble glazed with frost, skin raw from wind. So cold that his breathing was practically the only thing she could hear.

When he couldn't hear what she heard, Caroline was sure she knew what would happen next. *Time to call Dr. Hatcher,* he would say. *Have you been keeping up with your pills?* he'd ask, with that pitying smile that he thought looked kind. But it hadn't gone like that at all.

"Good," he'd said. "That's real good. You look in here and I'll look out there. We're doubling our chances. We have to try everything."

That was the first time she'd considered letting herself cry since the night of the abduction. *Finally,* she thought, her insides swelling with gratitude and love. He'd hugged her then as fiercely as he used to. Not as if she was broken but as if she was the only thing he had left to hang on to. *Finally.* She'd flushed, thinking of the terrible things she'd said to him a week ago, about not being happy. She had come to feel besieged, she knew, by the rough acoustics of everyday living; every perceived slight, every misjudgment of tone was a dissonant note that could not be unheard. Each little failure building upon the others until you couldn't hear a thing over the cacophony. But that was Before. She remembered now that Ben was *the root* of her happiness. Ben and Charlie and Bub were her reasons for living.

Then Ben had gone outside again. He was going to find their baby if she didn't find him first.

Ben was depending on her to search the house, and that's what Caroline would do. She was sure that the sound in the walls would show her the way. All she had to do was stay focused and—

"There!" she said. A cry from somewhere behind the drywall. She was sure of it. "Did you hear it?" she asked Charlie.

"I don't know," Charlie said. "Maybe."

"It was definitely from this wall." Her ear rang as she pulled it from the wall for the first time in many hours. Some pictures hung above her: a photograph of Bub and Charlie in front of Belvedere Castle; a watercolor of a line of elephants holding one another's tails. She tossed them into a corner, the shattering of their glass adding more voices to the conversation that rang through the hidden spaces of the Crofts. "But how do we get to him?"

"But . . . but how could he have gotten in there?" Charlie asked.

She smiled at him and ran her fingers through his hair. The boy was so young, but a child should know better than anyone. Impossible things happened all the time. No better proof of this than the fact that Bub had gone missing in the first place.

There was a grate by the door between Bub's room and the hallway. Some kind of heating vent.

The vent's grate was fastened into the wall. She could have pried it from its brackets with a screwdriver, but she didn't have a screwdriver. She picked up a rocking chair and used one of its angles to batter the grate.

After a few tries, the vent's cover finally buckled. Caroline kicked aside the warped metal and brushed away fragments of drywall.

I knew it, she thought as she peered into the opening. This was part of the heating system their renovators had added. This was why the wall's original plaster had been replaced with drywall.

"Bub?" she yelled into the space. The vent was made of slick aluminum. "Bub!"

Faintly, a call came from the distance.

She hammered at the drywall. When the rocking chair came apart in her hands, she picked up a large geode from the floor and used that. Cracks spread across the wall as the grate's housing came loose. The vent was far too narrow for her to get into, but if she dislodged it she might be able to access the main duct connected to it. Once there, Caroline thought, she might be able to tell if Bub was above or below her. Figure that out and she'd finally be making some progress.

She cut her finger on a prong of bent metal. In the shadows, the blood looked black. But Caroline found herself choking back a laugh. All those people in the woods, and Bub had been here the whole time.

She slammed the geode against the wall with all her strength. Flakes of yellow paint and fragments of crystal rained onto the carpet. When Caroline succeeded in widening the hole, she tore at its edges with her hands. Sinewy clumps of drywall collected at her feet. Once she'd cleared enough room for her shoulders, she forced herself into the space between the walls.

This house had taken her baby, and nothing was going to stop her from getting him back.

40

Seized with cold, Ben stood in front of the bathroom mirror. His hands trembled under the water from the tap. The flow from the faucet felt like a blowtorch, but it was the fastest way to get feeling back into his fingers. In the cold room, the water created billows of steam.

He wiped the fog from the mirror and was surprised by what he saw. Other than his greasy hat-pressed hair and two days of growth, he looked the same. Tired around the eyes, but it was still him. It didn't seem right.

That night, after Charlie told them where the man in the smoke had gone, Chief Stanton ran into the night. The tracks he'd found led him to the edge of the forest before he lost the trail. The snow had been too powdery to hold any footprints for long. The chief had called in the abduction, and the FBI arrived early the next morning.

The agents had been most interested in Charlie's story, but Ben doubted they'd be able to do much with it. Charlie had told them that he woke up to Bub crying, and Bub hardly ever cried. So Charlie went into one of the cabinets that connected their rooms. He'd wanted to see what was wrong with Bub. That was when he saw the man. Charlie had remained hidden in the cabinet when the man went into his room, looking for him. He'd stayed there until Ben and the chief arrived.

The agents had Charlie sit down with a sketch artist, and the result was a drawing of a gaunt, heavily bearded man with wild hair, who looked like a character from any child's nightmare. The agents hadn't questioned how an eight-year-old had gotten such a detailed look at the face of a man he'd seen in an unlit room through a crack in a cabinet door. Ben doubted they would have gotten a satisfactory answer if they had asked. Ben knew he would have to be the one to get it out of Charlie.

The FBI also had a lot of questions for Ben and Caroline. Most couple's children did not suddenly go missing, and this was the second time in just over a year it had happened to the Tierneys. Whether this was terrible luck, incompetence, or something else entirely was of understandable interest.

The agents had taken rooms in Exton and were coordinating with the state police, while Chief Stanton assumed control of the searches of the Drop for traces of the kidnapper. Yesterday's searches had been fruitless, but the chief pushed for them to continue. If they discovered the kidnapper's trail, they might learn something about the vehicle he drove, which would give the investigators something concrete to work with.

It had taken Ben more than a day to reach his brother. Ted was in Los Angeles, but he promised to get to Swannhaven as soon as he could. Ben wanted him to take Charlie back to the city: someplace where Ben knew his son would be safe.

This morning, Ben had been out before the sun. He thought the predawn silence might tell him something. The snow had made the forest strange. There were no birds, but the woods were alive with sound. From the ground, the rapping of icy branches across the heights of the ancient trees was disorienting. The shrieks of broken treetops punctuated the morning.

With a flashlight, Ben had walked the edges of the forest. From the ruined outbuilding by the gravel drive, up and around the lake, and down the Drop beyond the charred husk of the elder tree. He'd returned to the Crofts as the first angels of dawn tested the sky.

While drying his hands, Ben could hear the sounds of Caroline breaking through the walls of the floor above him. Like Ben, she hadn't slept or eaten since Friday. She'd become convinced that Bub was trapped somewhere within the Crofts. Of course it was insane, but it was no more crazy than standing outside the Holland Tunnel all night, searching each passing car for a child's face. A week ago, Ben might have tried to stop her, but if this was how she needed to look for Bub, he wouldn't stand in her way. If it came to it, he'd help her tear this place down to its foundations.

In the kitchen, Charlie was at the sink, standing on a chair, trying to do dishes. The kettle went off, and Ben saw that Charlie had boiled water for tea.

"Should I go to school tomorrow?" Charlie asked.

"Do you want to go to school?" Ben asked.

"No."

"Good, because I don't want to drive you." Between the police, search parties, and FBI, yesterday had passed in a whirlwind. Ben hadn't yet asked Charlie the questions that had to be asked. With Charlie, they had to be asked in just the right kind of way. Now they festered in Ben's chest, to the point where he almost feared letting them out. "Did you eat any fruit for breakfast?"

"This is breakfast."

Ben looked at the clock on the microwave and saw that Charlie was right. It was nine o'clock in the morning. He had lost all track of time. "I'll get out the applesauce."

The sledgehammer blows thundered from the ceilings.

"Mom's making holes in the walls," Charlie said.

"It sounds that way."

"I want to help you today."

"You want to help." Ben rolled the words around in his mouth. He ladled a few spoonfuls of applesauce onto a plate in front of

Charlie. As he did, he hit the spoon hard enough against the plate to make the boy jump. "How do you propose to do that?"

"I want to go with you. Into the forest," Charlie said. "To look."

"It's really cold out," Ben said.

"I know the forest."

"The snow is deep in places."

"I'll be careful. I'll step in your footprints."

"Uncle Ted's flying from Los Angeles," Ben said. "He's coming to take you back to the city tomorrow."

"Why?"

"It will be better there."

"I want to stay with you."

"It's just for a little while," Ben said. He looked at Charlie when he didn't say anything. His son's eyes had flooded with tears. Ben wondered if the boy would begin to cry again.

"But I can help you today." Charlie choked out the words.

"Fine," Ben said. He looked at his son's plate and wondered if he should eat something. But he was too tired to eat and too afraid to sleep. All he could do was search.

Ben put on a long-sleeved shirt over his T-shirt, slipped a heavy sweater on, zipped up a track jacket, then wrapped a scarf around his neck before putting on his winter coat. Charlie wore long underwear underneath his snowsuit.

"You have to tell me if you get too cold," Ben told him.

"Okay."

They stood on the steps outside the kitchen and looked at the vast white world.

"Where are we going?" Charlie asked.

"You tell me," Ben said. "Where did you see him?"

Charlie stared at his feet.

"The man in the smoke. I know he's real. I saw *The Book of Secrets*. I saw his fingerprints on it."

"I—" Charlie started. He glanced up at Ben. Today his eyes were gray like the sky. "I didn't know he'd take Bub. I didn't know that's what he wanted."

Ben looked out over the valley's dusted treetops.

"The lake," Charlie said. "Let's go to the lake."

They climbed the slope to the lake. When they got there, they were met by the flat white plain that the lake had become. A rim of dead cattail husks was the best evidence of its outline.

They walked along the woods to the east of the lake, picking up Ben's footprints from earlier. Ben was so exhausted that moving his feet felt like hoisting stones. Charlie stopped at the tree line, just outside a small clearing.

"I saw him here last time. At night."

"What was he doing?" Even his speech was slurred with fatigue.

"He scared me. He—he killed a deer. He said I was going to die, too. Alone in the cold and the dark." Ben saw Charlie shiver. "I didn't know what to do, because he wasn't scary before. He'd leave me dead animals, like a cat does. Like they were presents. I'd find them sometimes when I followed the sounds in the forest."

"He left you dead animals?" Ben asked. He tried to keep his voice even as he processed what he was hearing.

"Sometimes." Charlie pointed farther along the lake. "I saw him try to fish once, but he was doing it wrong, so I let him borrow *The Book of Secrets,* because Hickory Heck and Shoeless Tom always helped each other in the forest. You're supposed to help people when they need it, aren't you?" Charlie asked.

"Tell me everything, Charlie." Ben didn't want to know, but he *had* to know.

"He used to write things like *go* and *leave* by the dead animals," Charlie said. "He'd write it in blood or with their insides on the trees where he staked pieces of them."

"Pieces? He *mounted* them?" Ben asked. He'd lost the fight for calm. He tried to push images of Hudson far from his mind. Within him, a pendulum swung from exhaustion to adrenaline-fueled terror.

"But it didn't make sense, because why would he give me gifts and tell me to leave at the same time? I thought it was part of the game."

"*Jesus,* why didn't you *tell* me this?" Ben asked him. "Why didn't you tell me that some crazy man in the woods was mutilating animals, delivering death threats, and telling us to leave the Crofts?"

"Because I didn't want to go," Charlie said. "But—but now I know I should have told you. I'm sorry." The boy was again on the brink of tears. He'd been like this since Friday. No one could doubt he was sorry.

Ben peered into the thicket of trees on the far side of the clearing. The forest went all the way to the mountains and then continued into the state forest preserve. If there were still traces of Bub or his kidnapper out here somewhere, it would take a search party of hundreds to cover those many miles of dense wood. Ben wondered if the FBI had simply given him and the villagers the task of searching here in order to keep them out of the way of the real work. Ben wondered if a person could survive finding the pieces of his baby mounted to the trunk of a tree.

"Why did the man take Bub?" Ben asked.

"I don't know. But the last time . . ." Charlie trailed off.

"Last time what? You have to tell me *everything,* Charlie."

"Last time I felt like he didn't want to kill the deer. He didn't do it carefully, like with the others. Hickory Heck would only ever kill something for a reason. For food or clothes. The man wore their fur just like Heck. But it was different with this deer. I had to think about it, but now—now I think he did it to scare me, because I think he was scared, too," Charlie said.

"You were here when he killed it?" Ben asked.

"I was in my hiding place."

"Show me," Ben told him.

They pushed into the clearing. Charlie grabbed a braided rope from the air. It was threaded through whittled branches in a makeshift ladder. Charlie began to pull himself upward. Ben watched him scramble onto a platform a few feet above his head.

Ben tested his weight against the ladder. The structure above him creaked, but the rope was thick enough to hold him. The platform was not high. Ben thought it was less than ten feet off the ground. When he got to the top, he saw it was constructed from only four planks propped up by a large forked bough. There was enough room for Charlie to sit comfortably, but Ben had to rest on his stomach with most of his legs dangling off the side. Branches framed the view of the lake like a picture window. The frosted tops of the trees in the south woods were behind it, and he could see the frozen valley beyond.

"You built this?" he asked Charlie.

"*The Book of Secrets* showed how. Making the ladder was the hardest part. And learning the knots. The knots were hard."

"How did you get the planks up here?" Ben asked.

"I tied a rope to my foot when I climbed the tree. I threw one end over the branch, then I went back down and tied it to a plank. I pulled on the other end of the rope to lift up the plank, and when it was high enough, I tied my end to a root. Then I climbed up and put the plank in the right place."

"Did you ever learn anything else from *The Book of Secrets*?" Ben thought of the worn book's blood-streaked pages.

"I liked the chapter on animal tracks and reading about the stars. And I learned how to see better at night and how to walk without making sound. It was good for watching animals."

"There's a lot of other stuff in the book, too," Ben said. "Like how to make a fire and catch animals." Even before finding the man's bloody thumbprint on the book, Ben had often wondered what Charlie did when he played in the forest. He thought of the burned shed and the piles of carcasses in the pit.

"I made the boats from bark and leaves and put them in the creek," Charlie said.

"Did you ever start a fire? Did you ever try to catch animals?" Ben asked.

"I had those caterpillars once. And the frog eggs in the jar. I mostly like to watch the animals," he said. "They're happier then."

"Yeah." Ben lowered his head to the plank platform. He lay there for almost a minute with his eyes closed, letting the cold wood sear his cheek. "Are you cold yet?"

"No."

"Okay, let's walk around a little more."

Ben rolled onto his side, looking for the rope ladder. When he did, he turned toward the trunk of the tree. RUN was carved into the bark, in deep block letters.

"Did you write that?" Ben asked Charlie. Charlie craned his head to see what Ben was looking at.

"No." He spoke the word so softly that it was barely there.

"Let's get down," Ben said.

"We can pull the rope up," Charlie said. "I do that when I'm up here."

"We have to get down, Charlie," Ben said. He knew the man in the smoke wasn't there. Even if he was, Ben wasn't afraid. The man should be the one to be afraid. "He's not here. I'll go down first."

Ben lowered himself a few rungs, then jumped the rest of the way to the ground.

He looked around and saw nothing but trees. Charlie started to climb down, and Ben helped him, even though he didn't need it.

"I don't think he's here," Charlie said.

"No, but we can go back to the Crofts, if you want."

"Not yet," Charlie said. "Do you want to check the creek?"

"Sure, let's do that." This time they walked side by side through the forest. The trees by the mountains were some of the oldest ones on the Drop. In the spring they shut the light away from the ground, but now the corridors were wide and bright between their columns.

The creek flowed from the mountains, but even at the height of the melt it was only two feet deep. Rounded stones stuck from its white course like a broken street.

The trees here had been glazed in a thin coat of ice, which made the stretch more dreamlike than the other places they'd seen. The low winter sun hadn't picked up much beyond the horizon, but it lit the space like a hall of mirrors.

Ben put his hand on Charlie's shoulder. Other than helping him down the rope, it might have been the first time he'd touched him since finding that book in his cubby.

"I'm sorry, Charlie," he told him.

"For what?"

Ben could only shake his head. He didn't know where to begin.

He felt cleaved by the guilt of what wild things his imagination had spun about Charlie's role in all this. In the short hours between finding *The Book of Secrets* in his son's cubby and Bub being taken, Ben had wondered if Charlie had burned the shed, killed animals, hurt his dog, or merely been an eager accomplice for the man who wandered their forest. When Hudson attacked Charlie, he must have smelled the man's scent on him and mistaken the one for the other. Ben was guilty of the same mistake.

"No matter what happens, we're going to be okay. I want you to know that."

"Okay."

But Ben knew there were hard days behind him and worse ahead. He felt this in the pulse of his neck and heard it in the current of the wind.

41

Their search proved useless, and Ben wasn't surprised. For him, useless endeavors had become something of a specialty.

"What should we do now?" Charlie asked once they'd returned to the Crofts.

"How about you make sandwiches for the three of us," Ben said. "I need to make a quick phone call. I won't be long."

Caroline had moved to the third floor. The sounds of splintering wood led him right to her. Fragments of what had been the hardwood floor were heaped along the hallway like drifts of leaves.

"Where's Charlie?" she asked when she saw him. She pried an ax head out of the gleaming mahogany.

"In the kitchen, making food."

"I can't eat, Ben. I just can't," she said. Caroline had peeled up a fifteen-foot span of the flooring, exposing a splintered subfloor. She'd spent days testing colors for this floor. They'd spent a week sanding, staining, and waxing it. It had all been undone in a few hours. The hallway was ruined and the ceilings of the floor below would soon follow, and Ben didn't care.

"Me neither," he said.

Neither of them had found Bub, of course, but Caroline thought she'd traced the sounds to this part of the third floor. She was nearly certain of it. And Ben had his own hunch to follow.

Ben took the tower stairs to the attic, thinking of the man in the smoke.

The man was clever. He'd set the elder tree on fire to distract them while he took Bub. They'd found empty jugs of gasoline that he'd taken from the shed. The fire had been ignited by some kind of homemade fuse so that the man would be well away by the time the gas caught. But instead of escaping downslope to the county road once he had Bub, the man had headed for the forest.

The FBI assumed that the kidnapper had run into the forest in order to confuse his pursuers and then made for the county road or one of the access roads and driven Bub elsewhere. But if the man really lived in the forest, maybe Bub had never left the Drop in the first place. Ben left the chief a voice mail, asking him to call him back so he could share this theory.

Ben also thought the man must have some kind of connection to the Crofts. He seemed to know the place too well to be a stranger. And from the messages the man had left Charlie alongside the mutilated animals, it seemed clear that he wanted the Tierneys to leave. He could have been the one who'd set fire to the shed back in the summer, to scare them off. He could have mutilated the deer whose head Ben had found just outside the door and left the carcasses of the animals he lived off to rot in the pit in the woods. He might have been the noises in the night and the eyes they felt coming from empty rooms. They might have been living with the man all year without knowing it.

Ben still had the box from the archives of the *Swannhaven Dispatch* in the attic. He checked his notes against the newspapers. John Tanner, the boy who had set the fire at the Crofts in 1982, would be in his late forties now. The man in the sketch Charlie had helped with could easily be that age.

He glanced through the newspapers again to confirm that Tanner had been sent to the Lockwood Institute in 1983, after spending some time in a juvenile detention center. Ben called Lockwood and was told that Tanner had been released last year and sent to an assisted-living facility.

Ben took down the number for that facility and was about to call when the faint ring of the front bell sounded through the attic floor.

He ran to the foyer and saw Charlie talking to Chief Stanton in front of the open door.

"Anything?" Ben asked.

The chief shook his head.

"Charlie, wait for me to answer the door, okay?" Ben said.

"But I know him."

"Just do it for me, okay?"

"Okay, Dad," Charlie said. "I made peanut butter sandwiches for us."

"Thank you."

"He's a good boy," the chief said after Charlie had left the room. His voice splintered in his throat. The man looked worse than he had the day before. Ben guessed that he hadn't slept or eaten since the day of the dinner party, either. "I was already headed here when I got your voice mail. Mary sent me up with one of her casseroles." He handed Ben a bag heavy with Tupperware.

"Nice of her," Ben said.

"And Caroline?" the chief asked.

"She's holding up," Ben said. The ax blows from the third floor were barely audible from here.

"Good. You're not on your own with this, Ben." The chief rested a hand on his shoulder. "The whole village is behind you. The biddies too old to search have been holding prayers at the church since yesterday. In today's service we talked about nothing but you folks. Now, what did you call to tell me?"

"I got something more out of Charlie. He just needed to find a way to tell me."

Ben told the chief about Charlie's previous encounters with the man.

"I've been asking myself why the man would go deeper into the forest after taking Bub. Why he spent so much time at the Crofts through the summer and fall. I think we're dealing with someone who exists in a world in which the Crofts is the center," Ben said. "How much do you know about John Tanner?"

The chief looked at him with an expression as close to astonishment as his ashen features could muster.

"What is it?" Ben asked.

"JoJo's all I've been thinking of since I saw that sketch yesterday," the chief said.

"How well did you know him?" Ben asked. He and the chief were halfway to the far end of the lake, to Charlie's blind. The chief told Ben that he'd called Lockwood yesterday and gotten the same information Ben had learned today. He'd also checked in with the assisted-living facility. They told him that John Tanner had been in residence there for two months when he disappeared, in the middle of December of last year. They hadn't heard from him since.

"He was a year ahead of me in school," the chief said. "That was before they closed it down and started busing the kids to North Hampstead."

"So you knew the Swann brothers, too."

"In this small a village, all of us know one another. Have since we were in diapers."

"But Tanner was a foster kid, wasn't he?"

"But he was from Swannhaven. The Swann sisters took him in when his parents passed."

"What was he like?"

"Called him JoJo. Big guy. Was always big. Could have made a go of football if he knew which end of the field to run for."

"Not too bright?"

"We didn't have names for all the problems kids have now. But the boy wasn't right. Never was. You only had to look in his eyes to know something inside him had gone all wrong."

"Why do you think he set the fire?"

"Lots of theories on that one. Could have been that the other kids were teasing him and he was acting out. Could have been that he wanted some attention. Could have been that he just got it into his mind that he wanted to see something burn."

"Should we tell the FBI, too?" Ben asked.

"We can. But, to put all the cards on the table, I don't think they sent their best and brightest to work this one."

"Really?" Ben had thought they were sharp enough.

"When they're good, they're the best, but they're stretched like everyone else these days. If it is JoJo, well, we know these mountains as well as he does. The feds know it, too. That's why they left it to us to search the woods. Those FBI agents can send out their APBs and Amber Alerts and keep tabs on the staties, but send them trudging through these woods in this snow and they'll just ruin their shoes."

"It's in here," Ben said, ducking into the trees. He followed Charlie's and his footsteps to the rope ladder. When he found it, he handed it to the chief. Ben waited as the man lifted himself up to the platform. After a few moments the chief had his feet back on the ground. He'd seemed exhausted on the walk over, and the climb had winded him.

"What do you think?"

"Charlie built this himself?" the chief asked.

"Yeah, he loves it out here, the animals and trees and everything. He's sort of obsessed."

"He ever mention anything strange about the Drop? Or about the village?" the chief asked. They started to walk back to the Crofts.

"Well, I thought him having clandestine contact with a large man dressed in animal skins was pretty strange." Ben sensed that the chief was watching him closely. "If it was JoJo, what do you think he meant by carving *run* into the tree?" he asked.

"Sounds like he's taunting Charlie."

"Or could it be a warning?" Ben asked. "The man in the smoke kept telling Charlie to leave, then said he was going to die. But what if it wasn't a threat but a warning? As if he thought it wasn't safe here."

"Sounds to me that he wanted you folks out so that he could have the Crofts to himself."

"Yeah," Ben said. "I guess it could mean anything." They began to work their way out from the trees. "But it's not safe for Charlie here. My brother's coming up to take him back to the city."

"When's he coming?"

"Hoping to get here tomorrow."

"Charlie would be just as safe at our place. There's plenty of room, and it'd give us the chance to repay your hospitality."

"Thanks, but a change of scenery would be good for him right now."

"Not sure that teaching a boy to up and run when things start getting hard is a good lesson," the chief said.

Ben had to look at him to realize that he was serious.

"It's not safe for him here," Ben repeated. He wondered if he'd offended the chief by declining his offer to take Charlie in, but he couldn't possibly generate the energy to care about the man's feelings.

"You know best," the chief said. But Ben could hear the clench of the man's jaw in every word.

"The FBI is operating as if this is a conventional kidnapping, right?" Ben said. "But if it's JoJo, we don't understand his motives. What does that mean for us? What should we do differently?"

"We're gonna try our best to find the baby, Ben. But not every story can have a happy ending," the chief said. "You gotta prepare yourself for that. It's a hard life up here for most folks in the village, always has been. And you're one of us again. But hard things happen to good people because the Lord knows they can take it."

"What are you talking about?" It sounded like something straight from one of the village church's dour sermons.

"It's life and death, Ben. Does it get any bigger than that? Man does what he can, but in the end, it's not *our* will that matters any."

"Chief, you need to get some rest," Ben said.

They were still a long way from the Crofts, and Ben began to pick up the pace.

42

The Crofts was cold and filled with sounds. Charlie imagined each creak as a footstep; every howl as a scream. He didn't want to be here anymore.

Dad had gone outside with the chief. While they were out there, Charlie helped Mom by breaking holes in the walls of the third-floor bedrooms so that they could hear Bub better. Charlie didn't know why the man would put Bub in the wall, but Mom was sure he was here, and Charlie did what she said, like a good son. If he'd been a better son—if he'd been a better brother—Bub would be playing in the kitchen right now instead of being stuck in the walls or cold in the snow.

Mom had used an ax to open a tear in the hallway at about Bub's height. When she called into the walls, she and Charlie were quiet so they could hear Bub answer.

Charlie had given Mom the sandwich he'd made for her, but she took only a bite. She looked as tired and hungry as Dad did, but she didn't stop or slow. She attacked the walls and the floors like an opossum caught in a trap. It was scary, but Charlie thought it was good, too. If he was ever taken like Bub, he would want Mom and

Dad to look just as hard. He thought Bub and he must be very lucky to have a mom and dad like this.

"Did you hear that?" Mom asked, turning to him. This time he *had* heard something, a bang that came up from their feet. Mom got a crowbar to pry loose the planks that were where the floor had been. At first she had been tearing at the walls and floors with her hands, but Dad had brought her gloves, an ax, a crowbar, and a big hammer. Still, Charlie could see red where the blood from her hands had soaked through.

"Any luck?" Dad asked from the stairs. The bang had just been Dad, coming upstairs from the kitchen.

Still, Mom pried at the floor. "I think we're getting somewhere," she said. Sweat speckled her lip and breath rushed from her mouth as if she'd been running.

"Good," Dad said. He was still in his coat. Inside his coat, Charlie knew, he was thin and cold. He carried mugs that clattered in his shaking hands. Tea for Mom, coffee for himself, cocoa for Charlie.

"The chief's leading the villagers on a search of the south woods again," he said. He put Mom's tea down where the floor used to be and put his hand on her head. "I'm going to warm up in the attic before I head out again."

"The chief?" Mom said. "What about the FBI? Shouldn't they be in charge?"

"I think they're chasing other leads," Dad said.

"Can I go with you to the attic, Dad?" Charlie asked.

"Be my little listener while you're up there," Mom said. "There isn't as much insulation, so you might hear something."

"We'll both listen real hard, Cee," Dad said. "We promise."

Mom smiled at him almost as if none of the bad things had happened.

When Dad and he reached the tower stairs, they heard a shriek of wood as Mom tore out another chunk of the floor. She was hurting the house, and this seemed like a good thing.

"The villagers are searching the woods," Dad said again when they were on the stairs. He pointed out the window where they could see rows of cars parked along the gravel drive. Flakes of snow hit the glass without making a sound. Charlie noticed little figures walking in a long line through the forest. It was strange to see people among the skeletons of the trees. Something about it didn't seem right, but Charlie knew they were trying to find Bub.

"Does the chief know the man?" Charlie asked when they got to the attic. Dad's walk with the chief had not lasted long, but Charlie thought something had happened.

"If the man is who we think he is. The chief recognized him from your sketch, and I remembered reading about him." Dad flicked on a space heater and shuddered when the orange glow lit his face. "He used to live at the Crofts, but he started a fire. It was a long time ago, but people got hurt. We think he might be sick. He might be angry at us for living here."

"I didn't think he was angry," Charlie said. "He seemed sad." He had been thinking about this a lot. Over and over, he'd tried to remember the man's face. Charlie was still afraid, but he wasn't sure anymore if the man was what frightened him.

"You don't have to worry about him. He's not going to get you," Dad said. "He's not going to get you." He said it again as he rubbed his hands in front of the heater. "He's not going to get you."

Charlie saw that Dad hadn't shaved, and he brushed his hand against his cheek. The bristles were sharp and his hand came away wet from the places they'd thawed. Dad didn't move when Charlie touched him, but he stopped saying the same thing over and over.

"He wouldn't hurt me," Charlie said. "I don't think he'd hurt Bub, either." If the man had wanted to hurt him, he could have at any time.

"But he took him," Dad said, turning to Charlie. "He stole him from us."

"I don't know why he did that," Charlie said. "But maybe he's not bad."

"Charlie, people can't take children away from their families.

That's what bad people do." Dad was starting to sound more like he was supposed to, and that was good.

"Maybe he had a reason."

"No reason could be good enough. You understand that, don't you?"

"He shouldn't have taken Bub," Charlie said. This was true. Bub belonged safe at home. But maybe doing something bad didn't always mean that you *were* bad. There was an old couch by Dad's desk, and Charlie lay down on it. He had to think more about this.

"Are you tired?" Dad said. "You can go to bed if you want."

"I don't want to sleep. I feel . . ." He did not know how to tell him. Feelings moved inside him, and they came together in ways that made him forget their names. Feelings that came from what had happened and what had yet to happen. "Like when the phone rang that night when Mom was sick and Grams was in the hospital," Charlie said.

"When she died?"

"Yes. It made me feel . . . *tight* inside."

"Like you were nervous?"

"Like when you know something bad's going to happen," Charlie said. "I heard the phone and I knew you would be sad. It made me tight inside."

Dad looked sad now. Charlie wondered if, when Dad thought of Grams dying, he now also thought of Bub.

"Bub's not dead, Charlie. You can't even think it," Dad said.

Charlie wondered if he had been reading his mind. Sometimes Dad could do that.

But Bub *could* be dead. He could be dead, and they wouldn't even know.

Tears pushed at Charlie's eyes, and he looked away so Dad wouldn't notice. From the windows here, he could see all the way to the top of the mountains. Even the tallest trees looked like toys compared to the mountains. The world was so big, and Bub was so small.

Even with Dad here and Mom downstairs, Charlie was afraid.

He'd been afraid ever since he saw the man kill the deer in the faerie circle. Maybe ever since he'd been locked in the furnace room back in the city. Maybe even before that. Fear had sat next to his heart like a seed waiting for water as long as he could remember. Like a strange flower that waited until the worst of winter to bloom.

"Why did we come here?" Charlie asked, as he tried to bury himself in the couch's cushions. He hadn't meant to say it out loud, but he could tell from the way Dad startled that he had.

43

"Why did we come here?" Charlie asked.

Ben flinched, because the same question had rung through his mind since Friday night. *Why? Why? Why?* was interrupted only by *How? How? How?*

Everything that happened had a cause. Maybe the reason seemed insufficient or unfair, but there always was one. It wasn't fate that brought them to the Crofts any more than it was chance that Bub had been abducted. *Why did we come here?* was a good question, but *why did we stay?* was a better one. The former had a dozen answers, but the latter had only one: They'd stayed here because Ben was a fool.

Though he'd done his best to try, he had no one to blame but himself.

One of many flaws he had, he saw now in the ice-cold clarity of hindsight, was that he'd seen himself as the unerring protagonist of this story when he was at best the unreliable narrator.

Since Caroline got sick, Ben had been convinced that she would be their undoing. He'd even faulted Charlie for a while, holding him responsible for some of the things that happened around the Crofts.

Confronted with his family's flaws, Ben couldn't look at them without revising their characters to the way he wished they were. But it turned out they weren't the problem in the first place. If Ben had gotten out of his head for ten seconds, he might have seen that. If he hadn't been so critical of those closest to him, if he hadn't fixated on the quirks of their tight familial unit or been so absorbed in his stupid book, he might have noticed the signs of things going catastrophically wrong all around them.

Now his mistakes had cost them something that could never be replaced.

You got everything you ever wanted, didn't you, Benj?

"I'm sorry, Charlie," Ben said.

"It's not your fault," Charlie said. He turned away from the cushions with red-rimmed eyes.

But it was. Ben knew that it was.

Feeling had returned to his hands, and he groped in his desk drawer. He had a present for Charlie in here somewhere. It was hard to believe that Christmas was a few days away. He could see it sitting like a tombstone at the end of the calendar for the rest of his years.

"I got a book for you," Ben said when he found it. It was set in postapocalyptic America, a place where every bad dream had come true. He was glad that Charlie had grown out of the saccharine fables that populated the bookshelves of less-advanced readers; a narrative from the wasteland of the future seemed more instructive.

Charlie accepted the book and looked over the jacket illustration.

"Thanks," he said.

Contents of the crates from the *Swannhaven Dispatch* archive lay spread across the table by Ben's desk. Three years' worth: 1878, 1933, 1982. Bad years all around, and worse in Swannhaven. Just like this one, Ben thought bleakly.

He brushed the brittle yellowed papers through his hands absentmindedly as he watched Charlie start to pick through the book he'd given him. He told himself that Charlie would be safe in the city by this time tomorrow. One less person to worry about. One less person to disappoint.

Then his eyes strayed to one of the 1933 papers' headlines. BOY LOST IN STORM rang out at him in thick lettering. He thought of Bub, and his stomach clenched.

He had to read only the first sentence for his head to catch up to his gut.

BOY LOST IN STORM

> On Thursday evening, Peter and Emily Lowell of Swannhaven reported to authorities that their son, Owen, aged five, was missing.

Peter and Emily Lowell were Ben's great-grandparents. Owen was the great-uncle Ben hadn't heard of before finding the ancestry quilt in the Lowells' basement.

> Mrs. Lowell informed police that she put the boy to bed at seven o'clock in a room that he shared with his sister, Alice, age nine. Owen was found to be missing at ten o'clock, when Mr. Lowell returned from his work in the family's dairy farm.
>
> Police Chief Edward Stanton reported that the boy appeared to have left the residence by his bedroom window. Upon discovering the boy's footprints in the snow, investigators tracked them to the forest on the west end of the family's land, where, due to weather conditions, they were unable to continue following the trail.
>
> Chief Stanton confirmed that Alice Lowell had not woken during her brother's disappearance, making the possibility of an abduction unlikely.

"We do not believe that the boy was forcibly taken from the residence," Chief Stanton said. "Based on the evidence and interviews with the family, it is likely that he snuck outside to play in the snow. He must have become disoriented in the dark and wandered into the forest."

With temperatures as low as twenty degrees below freezing, the probability of the boy having survived the night is considered remote.

The article was thin and perfunctory, but it still left Ben shaken. He wondered if his great-uncle's body had ever been found. There was a photo of Owen above the headline. It was hard to make out between the yellowing paper and the faded ink, but Ben could see that the boy was not smiling.

For the hundredth time that day, Ben wished that his grandmother were still alive. She'd been nine when Owen died—not much older than Charlie was now—but that was old enough to remember the death of a brother. Ben wondered about Owen, if the boy had spent his hours playing among the trees. He wondered if his parents had ever found him in the fields at night, running to the beat of the land.

Through the attic windows, Ben watched snow whirl through the air. From where he stood, he could see Charlie in profile as he read his book. Ben would have to go outside again soon. He would need to find some way to flush the man from the forest. That's when he realized that Charlie hadn't been reading his book at all. His pale eyes were focused above the page open before him. He was watching the mountains.

"Do you have him?" Ted asked.

"No," Ben said. "Not yet," he corrected himself. He could hear Ted's exhalation rattle through the receiver. "Where are you?"

"Cleveland," Ted said. "There's a lot of weather along the coast.

There's still a chance flights will start up again, but if not, I'll rent a car in the morning and start the drive."

"Thank you, Ted." Charlie was on the other side of the attic, and Ben tried to keep his voice from breaking. "You don't even know what it's been like. You have no idea. I don't even—I don't even understand how this is happening again."

"I'll be there tomorrow even if I have to walk, Benj," Ted said. "I'll get Charlie out of there so you and Caroline can do what you have to do." He cleared his throat. "How is Caroline?"

"The same way anyone would be," Ben said. "Tearing the place apart." He had to clamp down on a hysterical laugh that had fluttered up his throat. "I guess you were right about me, Ted. Right about this place. I got everything I ever wanted, and look at where it's landed me. I'm such an idiot."

"What are you talking about, Benj?" Ted said. "Look at everything you've done, coming from the place we came from. You can do anything. Anyone would tell you that. You're only an idiot if you can't see that."

Ben found himself dangerously close to tears.

"I'm proud of you, big brother," Ted said. "Remember, you're not in this alone. Hold it together a little longer. I'll be there soon."

They said their goodbyes and Ben found himself unmoored, reeling from emotion to emotion and always perilously close to panic. What was he going to do? *What was he going to do?*

The phone was in his hand, and by the time Ben's mind caught up, his fingers had already dialed.

"Hello?"

"It's Ben, Mom." His voice sounded like a rusty door.

"Ben?" she asked. One syllable, but it was all he needed to determine that her blood alcohol level was above the legal limit in every state. "What an early Christmas present this is," she said. "Twice in one year! I wonder if even the pope is treated this nice. You see much of your brother? Haven't heard a peep from him in years."

"When I can." He'd never called her from his cell phone before because he'd never wanted her to have his number. Another of his ridiculously invented problems of Before.

"He doing okay?"

"He's great. We're all great." He just wanted to hear her voice. He just wanted her for one moment to be a tiny fraction of what a mother was supposed to be.

"It warms my heart to hear it." Over the line, her voice was not cruel or ingratiating, only faintly ironic. She didn't know why Ben had called but didn't yet realize that he wasn't entirely sure himself.

"I told you I visited Grams's family's old farmhouse."

"The place she left to you boys and not to me, her own daughter? The one you seem so sure you'll never see a red cent for? She used to talk about that old place, your grams. I always asked her why they left. We had that sweatbox of an apartment in Weehawken—nothing like the nice neighborhood where you grew up. I used to imagine I could have been some kind of dairy-land princess if they hadn't left that farm."

Demons in the wood and devils at the door: That was what she'd told him last time. Ben hadn't asked her about it then, and maybe he should have. If he had, maybe things would be different.

"What did she say?"

"What did she usually say? Something about the water being bad. Also said that her daddy had gotten tired of farming. Though I can't imagine working at a gas station could have been much more glamorous."

Demons in the wood and devils at the door: Of course she'd been making it up.

"You okay, Benj?"

"Yes, I'm great."

"How is your wife?"

"She's fine."

"And the kids?"

"Couldn't be better."

"How many do you have now?"

"Two."

"Right. Charlie and . . . what do you call the other one?"

"Robert."

"Two boys. Just like you and Teddy. Would you send me a picture?"

"Sure. I gotta go, Mom." Ben wasn't sure what he'd needed from her, but now he knew he wasn't going to get it.

"You still in the city?"

"Not anymore."

"Where are you?"

"We got this place upstate."

There was silence on the line.

"Ben, do not tell me that you moved to that village," she said flatly.

"What village?"

"You *know* what village." The way she said it made him jump. She used the voice that had yelled at him for eating too much or not enough. It had berated him for running or for not getting somewhere fast enough. "Grams's village."

"What's wrong with the village? You just told me that they left because they were tired of farming."

"Didn't you ever hear her when she'd get into her cups? Singing her lullabies?"

"Grams didn't drink."

"Maybe not when you knew her, but she had her day. You think my thirst invented itself? You think she was a saint? She was the saint and I was the demon? Well, she was no saint."

"What did she say about the village?"

"A million reasons to leave, to hear her tell it. Said the woods were haunted and the village was worse. Said there was a curse on the place. It took her brother. My uncle. After Grams tied a few on, she'd sing the lullabies she used to put him to sleep with. For hours, sometimes. Well, he didn't need the lullabies anymore, I'd tell her."

"Why didn't you tell me this the first time I asked?"

"You have kids now, Benj. You know why. I bet you're a good dad. Isn't most of it trying to pretend the world isn't half as bad as it really is? If they knew it all up front, what kinds of people would they grow up to be?"

"Which half of the world's horrors were you protecting us from?" She laughed and then began coughing.

"You always hid razors in your words, Benj. And you've done all right with them, haven't you? And what were the odds that you'd move there? Of all the miserable places in the world, how could I know you'd choose that one? Now, are you going to tell me what's wrong?"

"I'm fine."

"You're not fine, Benj. Why else would you be calling?"

44

Ben left Charlie with Caroline as she took apart the upper story of the central staircase.

She fought like a locomotive against the Crofts, but Ben got the sense that what powered her impossible energy had begun to flag. They'd both been awake for over forty-eight hours, and Charlie needed an alert set of eyes on him, so Ben had called Father Cal. Ben recalled only pieces of the hours that followed Bub being taken, but he could still feel Cal's firm grip on his shoulder. He knew he could count on the priest.

Ben decided that when Cal arrived, he would set up in Charlie's blind to watch for the man. Charlie had seen him up at the lake more than once, and waiting for him there was the only thing Ben could think to do.

While the priest braved the roads, Ben took another lonely sojourn into the woods. The villagers' cars were gone from the gravel path, except for a battered sedan far down the slope.

Though the gravel path was nearly empty, he'd never seen the county road along the edge of the valley so busy. The sight of two vehicles at a time had been a rarity, yet nearly a dozen now drove along where the road hooked like a question mark around one of the foothills that framed the valley's north pass.

From his high vantage point, Ben could make out rows of cars parked in front of the church and gas station. It was Sunday, but the chief said the service had already concluded.

Ben tried not to worry about why all the villagers were gathering. There was no reason to assume it had anything to do with him. If it did, it might just be because the chief had a new plan for searching the Drop for Bub. He had to keep his imagination in check. He had to think straight and not let his mother's words get into his head. *Demons in the wood and devils at the door.* A world without sense and trust and security was her belief, not Ben's. As he walked down the Drop, Ben watched more cars wend their way from the far corners of the valley to the village's little church.

Ben would have asked his mother more questions if he'd thought that she had the answers. But if she'd known any details, she would have released them in a barrage at the height of her rant. Instead, she'd begun to repeat herself. This is what she did when her ammunition ran out before her fury. She spouted platitudes of fear and paranoia that meant nothing yet still managed to fill him with dread.

He hadn't salted the gravel drive since the dinner party, and the surface was slick. Ben realized he recognized the old Toyota ahead, along the hulk of naked trees. It was pulled off just to the side of the road, and he thought that, without four-wheel drive, Lisbeth would have a tough time getting out of the snow. She'd dropped off some food the day after Bub went missing, but Ben hadn't seen her since. This seemed strange now that he thought about it.

Ben followed Lisbeth's footprints through the trees. The deeper he got, the better idea he had of where he was headed. After a few minutes he sensed the clearing ahead of him. He parted the branches, and the stone angel welcomed him.

Lisbeth stood facing the statue.

"Heard you coming," she said. A bouquet of dried red wildflowers lay at her feet. Their crimson petals lanced the snow with their color.

"It could have been anyone," Ben said, but Lisbeth shook her head.

"I've been praying for you, Ben. For you and your family."

"I could use all the prayers you've got." Ben had many questions, but he didn't know how to ask them. They had been building in him throughout his months between the mountains. He had a queasy feeling that giving them voice would give them substance, and they were the kind of questions that, once asked, could never be taken back.

Lisbeth nodded. "Life can be hard, but we're never given anything that we can't handle. Gotta keep strong, gotta keep faith. Gotta do what has to be done."

"Gotta keep up the light," Ben said.

"What's that, now?"

"Something my grandmother used to say. Keep up the light. To do the things that have to be done, no matter what."

"I know the expression," she said. She turned her head toward him, and he saw her face for the first time. She looked tired. "You never know what you're capable of surviving until life demands it of you."

The flurries drifting from the empty patch of sky above the ruined chapel had burgeoned into full snow. Ben walked along the edge of the clearing until he came to the frightening carving that had been propped against the chapel's sole remaining wall.

"What is this thing?" Ben asked. The creature had the eager claws and hungry jaws of a gargoyle but seemed somehow too human.

"That's the wendigo."

"Isn't that Native American?" Ben asked. He vaguely remembered reading a story about it, years ago. "Some kind of a demon?"

"In a way," Lisbeth said. "It's a person so consumed by hunger and fear that it becomes the very terror it dreads."

Ben expected her to continue, but she didn't. "Funny thing to have in a church," he said.

Still the woman said nothing.

"Storm's supposed to hit soon," Ben said. "You should be careful out here."

"It's a hard season."

"I'm starting to understand that."

"My own granny used to say that winter brings out the ghosts. The snow quiets the forest enough for us to hear voices from the world that was."

The conversation was being carried out in a cipher that Ben didn't understand. He imagined getting into bed and letting the world carry on without him.

"I think JoJo Tanner took my son," Ben said. His voice came out in little more than a whisper, but Lisbeth heard him fine.

"Bill Stanton told me," Lisbeth said. "I'm sorry."

"I think Bub is still in the forest somewhere. I can't leave here without him." Ben felt his throat tightening, but he refused to give in. "After that, we'll go back to the city."

Lisbeth looked at him as if seeing him for the first time. "You would leave?"

He could not read the expression on her face.

"Ben, we've told you about our village," she said. "Swannhaven is special. You see that, don't you? How else could we have survived that terrible winter so long ago? Times can be hard here, but they can be good again, too. We need only survive the days that seem the darkest. It will be hard; it wouldn't count for anything if it weren't. A price has to be paid. Some need to pay more than others, it's true. But we're strong together. You've seen that from the meetings, haven't you? How we all work together to put food on everyone's table? I hoped that you would see that. It's the same with every necessity. We do not live on bread alone. Sometimes we need more than eggs and corn and heat to make it to tomorrow. But if we stick together, everything will be all right. We tried so hard to help you understand," she said. "Tell me that you do."

"We don't belong here," Ben said. He shook his head. "This isn't the place for us. I understand that much."

Lisbeth studied him with sad eyes.

"That's not it at all, sugar." She shook her head and looked at the ground. When she finally raised it again, he saw little trace of the kindly woman who'd once cajoled him into eating two slices of pie. "You do belong here. You always have."

45

The day crept toward dusk, and the wind whipped dark clouds through the sky. But even a blizzard wouldn't get in the way of Ben looking for the man by the lake. He knew the likelihood of seeing him was slim, but it was all he had to hold on to.

Snow was falling heavily by the time Father Cal arrived. Ben answered the door with his coat in hand. The priest was a shock of black against a field of white.

"Could you help Charlie get packed?" Ben asked. He slid a hat over his head. "Just a few days' worth of clothes. He can get whatever else he needs in the city." He stepped outside, and it was all he could do to keep himself from sprinting from the Crofts for the lake. The man might be there right now.

"You're leaving?"

"My brother will be here tomorrow, and he'll drive Charlie back to the city. Caroline's resting upstairs." Ben had found her when he returned from his encounter with Lisbeth; she'd passed out on the stairs, utterly exhausted, the ax still in her hands. He'd carried her to their bedroom, where she slept like the dead. He'd tried to pull off her bloody gloves, but her torn hands had scabbed them fast to her skin.

"Caroline and I are leaving, too, but only for Exton." He'd decided this on his walk back from the ruined chapel. This would be their last night here. "We can't go back downstate until Bub is found, but we can't stay here."

"But, Ben, why would you leave the Crofts?" Cal asked.

He didn't know how to explain his fears to Cal, because he couldn't yet articulate them to himself.

"I have to go." Now that the priest was here, the idea of delaying his search for even one more moment made him want to tear his own face off.

"Will your brother be able to get up here tomorrow? We're supposed to get two feet."

"I don't know." Ben shook his head. He couldn't consider that possibility right now. "But I have go. I shouldn't be more than two hours."

"Two hours? There's no way you can stay out there that long. The storm will kill you."

"I need to try everything I can think of." Ben struck out in to the frozen world and he knew the priest wouldn't try to stop him. Cal dealt in the coin of the human condition. Tragedies might be bursts of misery, but regret was forever.

Ben seemed to walk against the wind no matter which direction he moved, but he realized how cold it was only after he'd settled himself into Charlie's blind. When he stopped moving, he felt the cold begin to creep past his clothes and into his skin. Soon it had dug into his bones. His toes became numb in his boots.

Ben flexed his muscles to keep his blood circulating. He kept his eyes on the lake and watched the storm unfurl around him. The great heads of clouds that had billowed over the horizon in the afternoon were lost in the blur of snow. He could see the near edge of the lake clearly, but there was no trace of the far shore. The footprints he'd left on his way to the tree line were already gone.

He knew that men who fell asleep in the snow did not wake up, but he was so tired. He let himself lay his head against his arm as he watched for the man. He could feel the beat of his heart in his ears. After a while, Ben began to feel like a tree or a rock or another immobile piece of the forest.

Through the snow, the trees swayed. The wind howled and the land turned indigo in the dying light. Eddies of snow swirled into faces against the lake's frozen outline.

He strained to focus his attention. He tried to watch for the man, and he tried to catch what the wind was saying. He let himself close his eyes. He could hear the beat of his heart keep time with the wind as it sounded through the planks beneath him. He could hear it in his ears and feel it ebb into the tree where he lay and into the ground in which his tree was rooted and into the mountains against which the ground was nestled.

A hand tapped his leg, but he shook it off.

All right, now, Benjamin, his grandmother said. *Time to shine.*

Ben whirled around and saw nothing. The forest was dark, and there was only the wind in his ears. He groped his pocket to check the time on his phone and saw that two hours had come and gone. He pulled himself into a seated position.

He'd surely have died if he'd slept much longer. But he wasn't dead. He was still alive, and Bub was still missing. He turned back to the lake, but it was too dark to see anything. If the man had come, then he'd missed him. He closed his eyes and caught a hint of the rose scent from his grandmother's soap, but when he searched for it again, it was gone. He tried to remember his dreams but couldn't. Something about the forests and the mountains. There had been the sense of something important ending.

Ben was so disgusted with himself that he almost rolled off the platform. He felt like falling through the icy air and landing on the frozen ground below. From this height, he thought, he might break his arm or at least dislocate a shoulder. Something like that would make him feel better.

Instead, he reached for the rope ladder and lowered himself from the tree.

He made his way out of the clearing. Beyond the tree line, the wind was a muscular and serpentine thing. It worked its way around his arms and up his jacket, plying his spine with a frozen tongue. He had a flashlight, and he used it to search for footsteps along the shore of the lake. His own steps were whipped away by the wind as soon as he left them, but he looked anyway.

46

Hope sometimes came to Ben in the morning, but not today.

A twinge went up his back when he turned toward the window. He'd spent the night on a comforter in front of a love seat he'd pushed against his bedroom door. Murky light doused the room in shadows.

He stood to stretch. Charlie was still in bed next to Caroline. When Ben looked at him, his eyes were already open.

"Hi, Dad."

"Did you sleep okay?" Ben asked.

"Yes. Did you?"

"Yes." This morning they were both liars.

"When's Uncle Ted coming?"

"Depends on how bad the roads are." Ben checked his phone, but there were no messages. He pulled aside one of the window's curtains. The snow had stopped, but the land and sky were a single gray color.

"Is there a lot of snow?" Charlie asked.

"Looks like it," Ben said. He decided that if Ted couldn't get here today, then all three of them would move to an inn in Exton.

Charlie picked through a bundle of bedsheets to look for Caroline's face.

"Just leave her be," Ben told him.

He shoved the love seat away from the door and peered into the hallway.

Ben had locked all the doors that connected the stairs to this floor and propped water glasses on top of the knobs. It was something he'd seen in a movie, but he'd tested it and it had worked. If someone tried to get through a door, the glass would fall to the ground. Ben checked the glasses, and they were all just as he'd left them.

When he got to the kitchen, Ben shoveled coffee into the machine. He turned to find Father Cal in the doorway. By the time Ben had finally returned to the Crofts from the blind, the roads were so bad that Cal had to stay the night. While Ben warmed himself by a space heater, he tried to explain to the priest what he'd learned about JoJo Tanner.

"I don't think you're going to make it to school today," Ben said.

"We're closed. You should be getting a text and an e-mail any moment now," Cal said. "To be honest, I always thought it was a bit cruel to be open at all on Christmas week. May I help with breakfast?"

Ben had forgotten about breakfast. "Charlie should eat fruit. Would you mind slicing up a banana? Where did he go?"

"He scampered past me on the stairs. He said he was going to get his book. How's Caroline this morning?"

"I'm going to let her sleep as long as she can."

"They're both lucky to have you."

Ben looked out the window and saw the husk of the elder tree. Its black skeleton marred the vast white space.

"Cal, did you know that the mosaic Joseph Swann created for the priory was based on the view from this house?" The sight of the elder tree had reminded Ben of this. It looked like a withered hand clawing its way out of the field of endless rolling white, as if a giant beast waited underfoot.

"I thought it was of our valley."

"The dragon is perched right on the edge of the Drop. The tree in your mosaic is now a blackened wreck on my lawn," Ben said. "You said Joseph stayed at St. Michael's after his brother died, around the time of the Great Fire and the railroad collapse. There's a photo of Joseph Swann's brother, Philip, on display in Lisbeth's cellar. She had other photos and paintings of young people who'd died here in Swannhaven. It was strange."

"Sounds a bit ghoulish," Cal said. He handed the plate of sliced bananas to Ben. "By the way, I hope you don't mind, I took your Bible to bed with me." The priest had brought the dragon-skin Bible down with him. "I can't remember the last time I saw such an old Bible."

"They say Aldrich Swann brought it over from England," Ben said. "His grandson, Henry, was a pastor during the Winter Siege. I assume he's the one who wrote the notes in the margins."

"Yes, the notations were what attracted my attention. Very much of the 'Sinners in the Hands of an Angry God' variety, especially in the books of the Old Testament. For instance, here in Job, he writes, *True faith thrives when tested by ailments of body and spirit. No torture is undeserved. No torture cannot be survived if he wills it.* And here, in Genesis in the story of Abraham . . ." Cal flipped the pages of the Bible. *"All that he demands must be surrendered, as all is his to claim. Nothing is truly lost, as heaven possesses every necessity for body and spirit. We shall see him again. We shall see them all again,"* Cal read.

"As a rule, religious fundamentalism sort of terrifies me," Ben said.

"Still, it gives a fascinating sense of the zeitgeist. Think how dangerous this country was back then. A poor harvest, a hard winter, angry natives, the frontier, war. Any one thing could have spelled disaster for them. Rich soil for the hellfire-and-damnation religious movements that thrived up here. It's no wonder their faith was so strong. It might well have been the only thing they could depend upon."

"Faith," Ben said. "Bad times are worse up here." Someone had told him that once. He looked through the window, searching for something more than the charred tree and the interminable blanket of white.

"Bub is all right, Ben," Cal said.

"Isn't that risky for you to say? Aren't you supposed to say, 'The Lord works in mysterious ways'? Or 'Hard things happen to people with hard lives because the Lord knows they can take it'? Isn't that the line? It's what everyone else up here says."

Cal took off his glasses and rubbed the sides of his nose.

"Dark thoughts lead to dark paths," he said. "Don't let that happen, Ben."

"Keep up the light," Ben said.

"Yes." Cal nodded.

Ben closed his eyes and then willed them open again. He pulled his coat from its hook.

"Aren't you eating anything?" Cal asked.

"I have to do something first."

Outside, Ben looked for the gravel drive but could not find it. The Drop was an uninterrupted field of white.

He made for the south woods.

Trekking across the open was difficult. The storm had left the snow in drifts. In some places it reached his waist; in others it barely covered his knees. But it wasn't as cold as it had been. The wind had dropped off. When he reached the forest, the woods were quiet. Only the very tops of the trees rattled.

The snow had taken him off course, and he looked back to the Crofts to find his bearings. Against the snow, the house was a dark hulk.

A nice home for a young family. A place where good work is both undertaken and rewarded. His sons, happy and thriving. *Can you see it?* It seemed harder with every step. Ben had wanted a house with a story, but this one had too many of them. The place was too big and too old. Ben didn't know what they'd been thinking, moving here. Everything about it had been wrong from the start.

He walked south through the woods until he thought he was well beyond the old chapel. The fresh snow should have covered the bouquet of flowers that Lisbeth had left at the stone angel yesterday, but if it hadn't, he knew the sight of snow stained red would be more than he could bear. He turned east, into a steep slope. Soon he was on the very edge of the Drop, nearly on the side of the mountain. He had to brace himself against roots and rocks to keep from slipping. When he looked up, he saw the spiderweb silhouettes of naked trees against the sky.

Finally, the land leveled out and Ben saw the cemetery. He hadn't been here since the summer. Its stones weren't buried as deeply as he thought they'd be.

Thinking of poor Philip Swann and the other dead boys on Lisbeth's wall made Ben realize that this was a village where children died long before their time. Even Ben's great-uncle Owen had died here. He tried not to imagine an image of Bub hanging alongside theirs in Lisbeth's cellar.

The gravestones were organized chronologically, with the newest ones on the west side of the clearing. Miranda and Eleanor Swann's headstones might have been carved yesterday, and Mark and Liam's did not look much older.

Ben began at the back, where the stones were too worn to read. The first had been rubbed to a thickness of only an inch. He walked the lines until he reached one with an inscription he could make out. The stone was for Ruth Swann, who'd died in 1852. He found Philip Swann's marker not far from there. There was a prominent death's head at the top of the stone, and Ben had to clear away the snow to read the inscription.

MEMENTO MORI
In memory of Mr. Philip Jackson Swann, son of
Carter Allen Swann, who departed this life on
A.D. December 21, 1878 and died with
hope of happy immortality.

Ben noticed that the date was the same as today's. The Great Fire of 1878 had been earlier that year.

He found himself back among the newest of the stones. Mark and Liam Swann were buried next to their father and mother, Carlisle and Sara Swann. According to the parents' tablet, they'd died in 1974. Their marker had a more modern style than Philip Swann's, but they had retained the inscription of *memento mori*. Remember death.

Ben knew that Mark Swann had been fifteen when he died, but he couldn't remember Liam's age. He went to check the dates on his gravestone. The boy's date of birth had been 1971, but it was reading his date of death that made Ben feel as if someone had reached into his chest and squeezed his heart.

Mark and Liam Swann had also died on December 21. Today.

He'd read the articles about the fire, but the date of it hadn't stuck in his head.

"What does it mean?" he whispered into the cold air. He backed away from the grave markers and nearly fell into a drift. "It doesn't matter." He shook his head. Maybe it meant something and maybe it didn't. All he knew was that he had to find Bub. When Charlie had gone missing, the FBI told him that the first seventy-two hours were essential. He had to find him today.

He began his trudge back to the Crofts. When he got there, Ben would make sure Charlie was packed. When Ted arrived, Ben would see them off, then he'd walk the forest until the sun closed the day. When he'd fallen in the dark too many times to keep going, he'd pack a bag for Caroline and himself and they'd go to the inn in Exton. The Crofts didn't feel safe anymore. He'd sit there in the dark of his rented room and think about what the rest of his life would be like.

It took him twenty minutes to get through the woods, but his brain spun enough that they passed quickly. Before Ben knew it, the Crofts was in front of him again.

In the gray light, it struck him as a desperate place. It was vast and opulent, but that didn't mean anything to the mountains. It sat between them like a bauble. They had only to fold their hands to crush it.

Ben exhaled heavily into the freezing air. His breath clouded and dissipated like a ghost caught in the light. Now that he was out of the forest, Ben could see the full dome of sky. A thick crust of angry clouds stretched from horizon to horizon. For all the talk of the weather, Ben hadn't watched a report. He hoped that last night's snow had been the extent of the nor'easter, but from the look of the sky, he doubted it.

A hawk carved a gyre through the clouds above him. Ben wondered what the bird saw that he couldn't. He followed the arc of its course. When it glided east, Ben saw a plume of black smoke skirting the treetops along the slope of the north mountain.

He watched it for a few moments to make sure it was real and not a trick of the wind and murky light. Then Ben began to run toward it.

There was someone in the woods.

Ben ran. His feet ached from his hiking boots, and his chest burned when he breathed. He was already to the slope of the mountain before he considered what he was going to do when he reached the fire. As he climbed, Ben looked for sticks. Soon, he found one that felt like a short baseball bat in his hand. The chief had said that JoJo was a big man, but Ben knew he was a careful one, too. He wouldn't have revealed his presence unless he wanted to be found.

Ben could smell the smoke. The slope was steep and icy and thick with spindly conifers. He had to kick the toes of his boots into the frozen ground to grab enough traction to propel himself forward. The wind carried a sound that could have been crying.

The terrain finally leveled out. The fire was close now. His eyes began to sting. Ben pressed aside the branches of a pine tree to reveal a small clearing with a smoldering pit at its center. He moved past the tree and into the clearing.

He'd forgotten the stick in his hand, but now he held it in front of him like a sword. Like St. Michael confronting the beast. Ben walked around the smoking fire, challenging the trees and rocks. When he saw that he was alone, he kicked the fire pit. Orange sparks flared from his shoes. Someone had covered the fire with wet leaves, which had built the smoke up to a thick black.

Ben heard the high-pitched crying again and this time knew that it wasn't a trick of the wind. A series of large rocks abutted the side of the mountain, and when Ben inspected them, he saw that he could fit between the boulders. He threaded his way in. His boot became wedged between the rocks, but he was able to force it loose. The air had an animal smell to it.

The rocky passage was no more than ten feet long, but it took Ben almost a minute to traverse it. When he was through, he stepped into a small den not much larger than the couch Caroline had bought for the living room.

Wood coals glowed from a depression that had been dug into the ground. The space was surprisingly warm. Animal furs roofed the den and covered the walls. Ben recognized the skins of deer and bear. The hooked prongs of dozens of antlers were piled at one end of the cleft. In the scant light, he saw that there was thick-blocked writing scratched onto the deerskin in front of him. Ben would have read it, if not for the dark and the mewling bundle of fur that wiggled at his feet.

He picked it up and turned it around and saw Bub's red face looking up at him.

———

Alive! Scared but alive. Ben ran his hands over his son to make sure he was real.

Bub's eyes were swollen, his nose and cheeks covered in mucus. Ben could hardly believe it: this gift, this miracle, sobbing in his arms. This year had been an endless slow-motion train wreck, but that didn't matter now. All those setbacks were erased by a single luminous fact: Their baby was alive.

Bub stopped crying when he realized it was Ben who held him, then his face collapsed and he cried louder than before.

"I know, I know." Ben choked out the words and soon he was crying, too. Finally holding Bub made Ben realize that he'd never really expected this reunion. *Thank you* was all he could think. *Thank you.* Bub began to cough, his little body racked by it. *I will be better now,* Ben swore. *A better father. A better husband. I don't deserve this, but I swear I will make myself into someone who does.*

"You're a little sick, baby. But you're going to be fine. I'm going to take you home." He pressed his face into his son's, where their tears mingled.

Ben wedged Bub under his arm and started to work his way back down the rock passage. Bub was wrapped in some kind of home-made swaddling. It was constricting, but it looked warm. Ben wondered how he was going to get him down the mountain. He didn't know how he was going to get through all the snow to find a doctor. But his son was alive and in his arms.

He still had a foot in the fur-lined space when he remembered the writing on the wall. His eyes had adjusted to the dim light, and he could read it easily now. It was scrawled with charcoal in letters five inches tall.

IT IS NOT SAFE.

YOU MUST GO.

IT IS NOT SAFE.

47

Elation and euphoria. Tears and long embraces.

But even in his own room, atop a pile of family, Bub wouldn't stop crying. He wailed in a hoarse scream that made Ben shiver. Spasms of coughing shook his little body, and his every breath came as a tortured wheeze. Ben tried every trick he knew to get him to laugh, but Bub found nothing funny.

"He's really sick," Ben told Caroline. "Listen to his breathing. I think we have to take him to the doctor."

"We just got him back." She hadn't let go of Bub since laying eyes on him. Between her torn hands, tearstained face, and unwashed hair, she was a mess, but still beautiful.

"I know," Ben said. "But look at him."

"We'll all go," Caroline said.

"One of us needs to pack." Morning had seemed to pass in an instant, and suddenly they found themselves with only scant hours of light.

"Ted called and said the roads were bad," Caroline said. "Would it be safer to stay here?" It would be easier, a lazy few days spent in happy reunion. But Ben had made a promise to be better than he had been. *Better* and *easier* were almost never the same thing.

"We can't stay here, Cee," Ben said. "JoJo Tanner is still somewhere in the woods. And I don't know what's going to happen next. I don't *want* to know. I'd rather sleep off the side of the Thruway than spend another night here."

"You're right," Caroline said, nodding. "We need to get the hell out of here. You take Bub and I'll pack."

"We can switch, if you want," Ben said. Today, laughing and crying together had felt like old times, and he didn't want to mess that up again.

"No, you drive him." She hadn't said anything, but from the way she winced at the light, Ben was sure she had a headache. He'd asked Father Cal to make her some of Mrs. White's special tea. "When you get back, Charlie and I will be ready to go."

In Caroline's arms, Bub began to tire himself out. His cries had faded to whimpers and his eyes began to droop.

"When are they going to leave?" Caroline asked, tilting her head toward the floor. Ben could hear the murmur of voices from downstairs. When he'd returned to the Crofts with Bub, the villagers had been about to start another search. While the search for Bub had ended, the search for JoJo continued, and they'd been using the Crofts as a base of operations.

"We shouldn't kick them out," Ben said. "JoJo's not going to try anything else while they're here." The villagers' presence around the property was the only reason he'd consider leaving Caroline and Charlie behind.

"I'd feel better if they left," Caroline said.

"I swear I'll get back here as quickly as I can." He hoped he wouldn't be gone long; for all Ben knew, Bub might have to go to a hospital.

"All right," Caroline said. "I'll find something warm for Bub." His clothes were strewn across the floor from when they'd ransacked his room. All the drywall on one side had been torn out, its remains in a heap that spilled into the hallway.

"Where's Charlie?" Ben asked. The boy had also tried to soothe Bub, but had eventually left it to Ben and Caroline.

"He went to get something to eat," Caroline said.

"I'll check on him." He kissed Bub on the head and Caroline on the cheek and headed downstairs. Chief Stanton, Jake, and Cal were in the kitchen. The chief and Charlie sat at the table while Jake and Cal leaned against the counter.

"Swannhaven's very special in the winter," Ben heard the chief tell Charlie. "It's like no other place on God's earth."

"Did you call the FBI?" Ben asked the chief.

"I did. They're mighty glad the boy's safe. They'd be on their way here, but their cars are buried in the snow."

"Okay," Ben said. "Where are you looking for JoJo?"

"Sent a crew to the den you found in the mountain. Just about to head there ourselves." The chief stood up from the table and smiled at Charlie. "Glad your brother's safe, aren't you?" he asked him. "You see where your prayers can get you?"

The chief went for the door, and Jake followed him. Jake hadn't said anything to Ben since he'd arrived, and he left without a word.

Ben saw Father Cal's eyes also following the men out of the room. He wondered what the older man was thinking. He wondered what else Chief Stanton had said to Charlie as they sat at the table.

"Charlie, see if you can help Mom pack," Ben told him. "We're getting out of here."

"Okay," Charlie said. It was hard to tell with a face like his, but Ben thought he looked relieved.

"I'm sorry, Ben," Cal said when Charlie left. "I'm starting to understand what it must be like to live here. Demons in the wood and ghosts in the parlor."

Demons in the wood and devils at the door, Ben almost corrected him.

"Even the living are—" Cal shook his head. "Chief Stanton thinks you should stay here over Christmas, but I think you're right to leave for a while. And I'm sorry to add to your burden, but this tea—" Cal opened the canister of Mrs. White's tea.

"Right," Ben said. "Caroline's head is bothering her, and I thought a cup of it would even her out."

"There are some things in here that shouldn't be," Cal said.

Ben looked at him.

"Well . . ." The priest reached into the canister to take a handful of the tea. "There's some St. John's wort, which is fine, and some lavender for flavor. Lady slipper, too, if I'm not mistaken. But this . . ." He pulled a brown shaving from his hand. "This is valerian root. It can be a pretty powerful sedative if it's prepared in a certain way."

"Mrs. White designed the tea especially for Caroline. To help with her moods."

"It can also cause night terrors and disorientation. And this . . ." He plucked a withered white petal. "This looks like hellebore. We grow it at the priory but only for aesthetic reasons. It's quite toxic. It can cause stupor, vertigo, and any number of other problems. People can die from eating it. I can't even identify some of these other things."

Ben took the canister from Cal. He wondered if old Mrs. White had lost her grip well before she began to wander in the forest. If Cal was right about the herbs, this explained much of Caroline's erratic behavior over the last few weeks. He tried to imagine how many cups of this tea she'd made for herself—how many he'd made *for* her. Yet she'd still managed to drive around, continue renovations, plan and execute an elaborate dinner party, and all without Ben noticing that something was seriously wrong. Had he really expected so little of her that he didn't even notice when she was being *poisoned*?

He shook his head at himself, disgusted. *Better.* He emptied the tea into the garbage. *You have to be so much better.*

"Ben?" Caroline called him from upstairs. He could hear Bub

screaming again. The raw sound of it made the hair on his arms stand up. He had to get him to a doctor.

"I have to go," he told Cal. "Thank you for everything. Really. I can't make it up to you." He grabbed the priest's hand. "I'll be in touch, okay?"

"Are you sure there's nothing else I can do?"

"No, no, you've done so much. I'll call you when we get to the city," Ben said. Cal's weathered face was still etched with worry, and that was how Ben left him when he ran back up the kitchen stairs. He found Caroline coaxing gloves onto Bub's tiny hands.

"Do you want me to patch you up before you go?" she asked. Ben had cut his forehead and torn his hands on his way up and down the mountain. He hadn't realized the damage until he'd seen himself in the mirror.

"No time," he said. One of Bub's eyes was encrusted with mucus again. Ben felt more terrified every time he looked at him. With Bub on his shoulder, he turned to where Caroline stood in the doorway. "Maybe when I come back."

"It's a bad cut, Ben," Caroline said, frowning at his forehead. "I'm just going to put some Bactine on it. It'll only take a second." She ducked into the hall, and Ben could hear the gentle thuds of her jogging to their room.

Ben wiped Bub's nose for the hundredth time. When he turned around, Charlie was standing behind him. Ben noticed that he was dressed to go outside.

"Why are you wearing your boots?" Ben asked him.

"Aren't we going?"

"I have to take Bub to the doctor first."

"We should all go," Charlie said. "We should all go now." The boy's face was inscrutable.

"He gave him back to us, Charlie," Ben said. "He's not going to take anyone else."

"I still feel tight inside," Charlie said. He touched his heart with his finger.

"I'm not going to be long," Ben said. "Bub really needs medicine. Look at him." Ben had to quench the sudden panic that surged within him.

"Bub got sick, so he gave him back for us to take care of him," Charlie said. He walked over and held Bub's hand.

"We're all leaving here," Ben said. "He's getting what he wanted. I just have to do this first."

Caroline returned with the antiseptic. She had a gentle touch, but it still stung.

Charlie hadn't let go of Bub's hand. The baby's body was convulsed by another series of coughs. They had a dry, rough quality that made Ben grit his teeth.

"Charlie, I have to take him now. It's going to be a tough drive. But, listen, if you get scared, if you feel strange"—he tapped the boy over his heart—"Mom will drive you away." Ben nodded to Caroline. "That goes for both of you. If anything doesn't feel right, just forget packing and *leave*. We'll meet up on the road, okay?" Ben didn't feel good about Caroline driving anywhere if she still had that tea in her system, but he didn't like the look on Charlie's face, either. And he needed to get Bub help *now*.

A tightness clenched Ben's own chest as Caroline wept her good-byes to Bub. He could not say whether it was stress, or panic, or something else that was not so easily named. He let Charlie kiss Bub on his forehead, and he pretended not to notice the shine left on the baby's face where Charlie's tears had fallen.

Ben fit the Escape into the treads left by Cal's car. The packed snow was slick under his tires. He was just turning down the gravel drive when something pounded on the side of the car. The sound was loud enough to shock Bub out of his wailing.

It was Jake. Ben slid his car window down. The young man's face was as white as the snow.

"Taking off?" Jake asked. He tried to smile but didn't quite pull it off. Through Ben's window, he peered into the backseat. His face fell when he saw what was there.

"I'll be back," Ben said. "They're packing, but I have to get Bub looked at."

"Thought you'd all be leaving together."

"Jake!" Ben heard the chief bellow from up the road.

"It'll be dangerous if it gets too late," Jake said. "The snow and the ice and the dark."

"Jake! The trail's growing cold, if it isn't cold already," the chief said.

Ben turned to the sound of the man's voice and saw him a few car lengths away.

"Just telling him to be careful, Chief. He hasn't had to drive much with the roads icy like this," Jake called back to him. "You should leave before nightfall," Jake said to Ben, lowering his voice. "The way becomes dangerous in the dark."

"Jake!" the chief shouted.

"Don't forget now, boss," the young man said, his eyes wide and unblinking in their sockets. "Don't forget."

The county road was in bad shape. A plow had shuffled walls of snow onto the shoulder, but the wind had undone much of its work.

Bub's pediatrician in North Hampstead was expecting them, and Ben drove as fast as he could for the south pass. When he got there, he wasn't surprised to see that the road was closed. Wooden police barriers were set up across both lanes. Cal would have taken the northern gap, so maybe that route was still open. But Ben was in the mood for neither a detour nor a roadblock. And the road ahead didn't look any worse than the road he'd just driven down. He moved aside the barriers and then replaced them after driving past them.

Ben wanted to press the pedal to the floor, but he controlled himself. He forced himself to focus on the icy road. He didn't know what Jake meant when he told him that he had to hurry, but it didn't matter, because he intended to.

He and Bub were the only ones on the road. No one ever had any reason to go to Swannhaven except for the people who lived there. And Ben thought that most of them were probably as happy as a bear in a cave, because the storm had finished what geography had begun. For a while, no one would intrude upon them in their valley.

Fallen trees had closed a number of streets in North Hampstead, including their main street. Ben had to carry Bub three blocks to the pediatrician's home. The baby had finally fallen into a restless sleep, but Ben did not know if that was a good thing or not.

Despite the freezing conditions, many people were outside. Some worked to shovel their sidewalks and others walked around in their snow gear, taking in the strange beauty that had descended upon them. Neighbors waved to one another across the street and gathered around broken trees, shaking their heads and looking to the sky. Children tried to sled down their meager hills, and others waged snowball fights that spanned lawns.

Stuck in Swannhaven's strange little world, it was easy to forget what life could be like. Being among these happy people in their unhaunted town, Ben tried to remember.

48

Charlie watched the window as Mom counted underwear across the hall. She seemed better than when she'd been fighting the house. Dad seemed better, too, but still things did not feel right. A knot of something hard and cold hurt Charlie inside his chest.

He understood why Dad had gone away with Bub, but Charlie did not think Dad should have left Mom and him here. When he thought about it, he felt the knot tighten.

The man was still in the woods. But it wasn't the man that Charlie was afraid of.

The others were in the kitchen and in the living room. More came in cars from the village. They were dark specks pulling up the long white slope of the gravel drive.

Charlie thought about going downstairs to see what they wanted. But he was afraid. When the chief had spoken to him, there was something in his eyes that Charlie hadn't understood. But he knew that Hickory Heck would not have been so afraid.

He crept down one of the back staircases. He heard voices in the rooms. Some he recognized, but not all.

Someone was in the bathroom in the hall. The door wasn't closed all the way, and Charlie looked through the opening.

It was Jake. He was at the sink, washing his face. Blood flowed through his fingers. Charlie thought of the deer he'd seen the man kill. He thought of the way the knife had slipped into its neck and how its fur was lost under a sheet of crimson. Jake's face was not as bad. His eye was bruised and there was a cut on his forehead. His lip was swollen. Red splotches stained his undershirt.

Charlie leaned against the door to get a better view of Jake, and Jake saw the door move. Their eyes met in the reflection of the mirror. It was strange: They looked each other in the eye, but they weren't looking at each other at all. Jake turned away and mopped his face with a towel. The towel came away stained pink. Then he glanced back at Charlie in the mirror.

He mouthed a word. Charlie stared at his swollen lips. He thought of the way the deer's tongue had flicked against its teeth when it died. When Jake mouthed the word again, Charlie left him and made for the stairs.

He wore only socks, and he knew that the others in the rooms wouldn't hear him.

Now he knew what he had to do. He knew where he had to go.

Mom was in Bub's room. She was still packing, but there was no time for that now. Charlie wondered if he could make her understand. He did not know if he understood himself. What he did understand was that the man had been right from the beginning. They should not have come here. They should not have waited so long to leave.

Charlie knew he would convince Mom, because he had to.

He thought of what he should say to her, but all he could think of was that one word. The man had said it to him, and now so had Jake. More than that, he knew it was the truth. It screamed through his mind and flowed to every part of his body.

Run.

49

It was nearly dark by the time Ben returned to the barricades at the south pass. Crimson clouds seared the sky like a wound.

He'd left the pediatrician's with antibiotics, eye drops, and a list of instructions. It was painful for Ben to see Bub in such discomfort, but the doctor had given him medicine, cleaned out his eyes, flushed out his nose, and had not seemed as worried as Ben had been. Still, a pit of foreboding remained in his chest. He knew he wouldn't feel right until he got his family out of Swannhaven.

From a rise just beyond the pass, he saw that the village was dark and quiet. Though the valley was already cast in shadow by the western mountains, Ben could not see even a glimmer of light from the isolated farmhouses. He wondered if this was how the village had looked when the Iroquois attacked it centuries ago. On a night like tonight, it felt as if little had changed here since that long-ago winter.

The icy snow gleamed in the fading light. The frosted limbs of the tallest trees caught the last flames of sunset. It was almost beautiful.

The Crofts was dark when Ben reached it. There were a dozen cars parked along the drive behind Caroline's Escape, but not a window was lit. Outside, the air was brutally cold. It burned Ben's cheeks and hands as he pulled Bub from his car seat.

It was little warmer in the kitchen. He tried the light switch; it gave him nothing but a hollow click. They kept a flashlight in one of the drawers, and Ben tripped over something as he went to look for it. The thing on the floor was heavy and immobile, and it sent a jolt through his leg when he knocked into it. He dug through the drawer but was unable to find anything more useful than a matchbook. Through the flare of a match, he found a candle to light and used its glow to survey the kitchen.

The kitchen table held several mugs of half-drunk coffee. Ben felt the mugs, but they were as frigid as the air. He could not guess how long ago the Crofts had lost power. Without heat, the house would have quickly succumbed to the terrible cold. Clouds burst from his mouth with every breath, shining like nebulae in the flicker of the candle. Ben wondered if the entire village had lost its electricity. It would not have taken more than a single ice-laden tree collapsing against the lines for the valley to revert to a time of darkness.

Bub was still asleep in his arms. The cold was no good for the baby, but Ben didn't plan to linger.

The chairs around the kitchen table had been pushed away, as if their occupants had left in a hurry. Ben had expected Caroline and Charlie to be waiting for him in the kitchen, but losing power might have slowed their packing. This is what Ben told himself. There was no sign of the villagers. They might still be searching the forest for JoJo, though Ben did not know what luck they could expect in the dark.

As he headed to the staircase, he noticed what he had tripped over. It was a thick coil of iron chain. Its links were rough and hand-hewn, each the size of Ben's fist. It caught the candle light dully across its timeworn shine. Red blooms of rust flecked its surface.

Even if he hadn't had a sleeping child in his arms, Ben would not have called out for Caroline and Charlie. There was something about the cold quiet of the house that demanded silence. This feeling became even more pronounced as he walked the halls and stairs and peered into the chasm of the Crofts. Without the hum of the furnace, the house was as still as a grave. With his own footsteps as the only sound, it was as if the Crofts itself were holding its breath.

Caroline and Charlie were not upstairs. Ben checked all the bedrooms and found nothing more than half-packed suitcases. Fear fluttered in his chest. He called Caroline's phone and heard a chirp from across the room. Her phone lay on the floor by their bed.

He held Bub close. He did not know what to do.

The tightness in his chest told him that nothing was more important than finding them, and the pounding in his heart came from the fact that he had no idea how to do that.

Charlie had told him that they should leave, but Ben hadn't listened. And now they were gone.

Even if they were somewhere in the house, it would take him forever to search the place room by room. He wanted to scream into the emptiness of the Crofts, but he didn't. If Caroline and Charlie had left the house, it had been for a reason. If they were hiding, then there must be something here that they were hiding from.

Ben's gaze wandered to a window. In its frozen valley, the village was so dark that it might have vanished. The snow was stone gray in the light of the moon and the color of sapphires where the trees cast their shadows. The wind kicked up loose snow as it ravaged the fields, glazing them in an icy mist.

The ceiling above him creaked.

He froze and turned his eyes slowly upward. With the horrors dancing through his brain, Ben prepared himself for anything. He half-expected to see some abyssal creature poised on the ceiling, peering through lidless eyes at him. But there was nothing other than an inert chandelier and the shadow of his own hand warming itself over the candle's fire. Then there was another creak.

Slow footsteps made their way across the floor above him.

Ben headed for the stairs. Anything could be waiting for him on the third floor, but he chose to believe that it was his missing wife and son.

It would be interesting, he thought, to write all this down one day. Perhaps then he would see where the facts and his fantasy parted ways. He'd heard it said that the difference between fiction and non-fiction was that fiction had to make sense. It would be satisfying to impose order on the series of unfathomable events his life had become.

He opened the door into the drafty expanse of the third floor and came upon a tall, solitary figure bundled against the cold.

"Oh!" said Roger Armfield. "Ben, hello! You startled me." His voice was muffled by the scarf he wore around his face. He stood in the puddle of illumination left by his flashlight. All Ben could see of his face were his eyes, which darted in their sockets.

"Where are my wife and son?" Ben asked.

"That's why I'm here," Armfield said. "I'm looking for them."

"Why? Why are you in my house?" Ben didn't remember the hapless veterinarian helping with any of the searches for Bub.

"The chief asked a bunch of us up here to help search the forest for JoJo Tanner," Armfield said. He paused, expecting Ben to say something, then continued when he didn't. "Then your wife and Charlie went missing. We don't know where they are. The chief is searching the forest, but I thought I'd have a look around here."

"Why would they be hiding?" Ben asked.

"Hiding? Oh, I wouldn't say they're hiding. We know your wife hasn't been well; maybe she got confused." There was something different about the vet. His words had often tripped over themselves, but now there was a kind of mania to them.

"Confused," Ben repeated.

"We want the best for them. It's just that sometimes what seems

like the right thing isn't the right thing. Do you know what I mean?"
Armfield pulled off his scarf. Under its striped wool, his face was
gaunt and unshaven.

"No."

"That's why we need to find him," Armfield said. "We have to do
the right thing. Even if it seems hard. Especially if it seems hard. If
it weren't hard, then it wouldn't count for anything."

"Where's everyone else?" Ben growled. "All we want to do is get
out of here."

"I know, I know," Armfield said. "And I'm sorry, I am. It must be
so confusing. But I know someone who can help." He stepped past
Ben and started down the stairs. "Come on," he said.

Ben followed him down to the first floor. Before they reached the
library, he saw the orange flicker of a fire dance across the hallway
ceiling.

Lisbeth was staring out the window at the blank fields. When she
turned to him, the flames from the fireplace threw into relief the hol-
lows of her face.

"I need to find my family, Lisbeth," Ben said.

"We all do, Ben. This won't take long, and that's God's truth. To
tell it right might take longer, but the time for that has passed, and
I'm sorry for that."

"What's that supposed to mean?"

"Have you ever tried to tell a story to a child and had to leave out
the ugliest parts of it?" she asked him. "But when you make it easier
to swallow—to protect their precious ears—the story just doesn't
quite mean as much. Sometimes the savage parts and the important
parts are the same. You can see that, can't you?"

"What are you talking about?" Ben asked.

"Your questions, Ben," Lisbeth said. "You must have them, sure
as I have the answers to them, even if it'd be an easier thing not to
have to hear them."

She pulled a sheath of handwritten pages out of her jacket. They were protected in a plastic folder, but Ben could still see that they were written in the hand of a woman who'd been taught penmanship with a flourish. He recognized the dates at the top of each letter and the signature at the bottom. Ben remembered that Lisbeth had told him that she was named after Elizabeth Swann.

December 21, 1777

Dear Kathy,

At last we have found salvation, Kathy.

Father has told us again of the Coptic saints, who sustained themselves in fierce deserts by faith alone. Through the purity gained from that sacrifice, they achieved true communion with the Lord. These ancient saints could not eat less than we do, and I cannot conceive of a place less fit for man than these frozen mountains. It is no wonder that the Lord in His wisdom has acted through us, as well.

Mother and Father have heard him, and so have many of the others. I, too, have heard voices in the night, but I confess that I cannot discern the words, though I try so hard to.

James has been bound to the elder tree. He alone of us has persisted in bodily strength, and so God has set him apart from the rest. It is wondrous to behold God's work in this, Kathy. Skin peels from the rest of us in sheets, and hair falls aside in clumps, but James is at his most handsome. They have bound him with chains to the elder tree. No less *was demanded of Abraham when he was commanded to deliver unto the Lord his only son.*

I hear him call to me from the cold, and his cries cut me like a blade. This is as it should be, for if we did not suffer, then our sacrifice would count for naught. We cut out the best part of ourselves to demonstrate our faith. Our strength comes from our suffering.

I look at my calendar, and I cannot credit that a mere ten weeks have passed since the attack. Everything about that old world is gone. It is a dream brought to waking. Gone is our country, gone is our village, gone is our beloved Jack, and gone are so many of our dear friends. How else to explain our sudden misfortune than by the intervention of the beast? But now the Lord had returned to show us to salvation.

Though we are proud to fight as his soldiers, it was a folly for our ancestors to come to this place, Kathy. It was arrogance that led us into this winter. I have read Grandfather's journals. How blessed he must have counted himself to believe that we alone in all of history are a people untethered by the past. That we are creatures of splendor, forging a new country in a new world. How wrong he was.

We shall remember James always. Faith and memory are what shall ever keep this valley from the beast's grasp.

You cannot fully understand what has transpired here, Kathy. It is a thing not seen since the time of Christ Himself. That is how important our part is. Does that sound like blasphemy to you, sister? Perhaps it is, but, then, what wisdom did not first begin as such blasphemy? As hard as our lot is, we between the mountains cannot tread wrong in His service. Not where demons desecrate His land, and much-loved children are laid out in offering.

Have faith, Kathy. Only the strongest can keep up the light in a world that has become so dark.

Your Bess

50

Spare me your horrified looks, Ben. Truth is, we in this valley might well be the last people in all the world who haven't lost our minds. Think on what greeted the first Christians when they delivered the word to the heathen lands: ridicule, torture, and death. So save your smart talk. Do not pretend that this hasn't happened before.

We've told you of the Winter Siege. The hunger and the cold. What the Iroquois didn't take, the demon in the woods tried to make its own. The Iroquois called it a wendigo: a starving man in thrall to a spirit with a hunger so great it cannot be slaked. The Indians worship false gods, but their demons are as real as ours. What can't you believe? If your twenty-first-century mind needs a twenty-first-century answer, imagine it as an Indian brought to madness by unspeakable hunger. Your kind wraps the old illnesses with words long enough to disguise the fact that you know nothing about the darkness that can grow in the human heart. Whether the man was ill or possessed by a creature from the abyss or taken by the very shade of Lucifer himself changes nothing.

What matters is that the beast tried our faith that winter as he once tested Job's. And our faith did not fail. God tested our obedience as he once tested Abraham's. And our obedience did not falter.

Our ancestors made terrible sacrifices because that was what was demanded of them. God's will be done. Remember that this life is fleeting. The pain suffered here? The barest of shadows on the face of eternal salvation. How do I know? Because God accepted their sacrifice.

James Swann was given unto the Lord on the winter solstice, a thumb in the eye of the beast who so thrives during winter's darkest days. The thaw began no later than the next day. The winds died down, and the forest became silent for the first time in memory. A holy calm spread across the valley. From the Crofts, the men spied deer on the Drop. Our people ate well that night for first time in many weeks.

We returned to the burned remains of the village to see that the Iroquois had gone. Our valley was restored to us by the grace of God and our mighty faith in him. In praise of him, the Winter Families formed a covenant. Swannhaven would ever be God's country. No matter what hardships he asked us to endure, we would endure them happily.

Our ancestors pledged on behalf of their progeny to carry out God's will if called upon. We have been promised to keep up the light. A sacrifice, if demanded, was to come from the Swann family, for it is right for the greatest of us to offer the most. They pledged forevermore their eldest son. A most worthy offering. Something for which they would suffer greatly—but if they did not, it would not count for anything.

And tested again we were. Do you remember the pictures in my cellar, Ben? This was what I tried to tell you. James Swann's portrait hangs there to be remembered forever for his sacrifice during the Winter Siege. Recession and fire were the enemy's next weapons. You know of the Great Fire of 1878, and you've seen Philip Swann's portrait next to James's. It was dear Philip who delivered us from ruins of the Great Fire.

You've seen how the Swannhaven Trust administers to the village. During a year in which we are tested, the heads of the Winter Families fast through December. Each day we eat a cup of rough wheat flour and no more. Our ancestors' suffering and hunger brought them close to God, close enough to hear his voice. And so it is for us. Your wife's cooking smelled of heaven's own banquet table, but it was another of the beast's temptations. We are used to them. Their seduction is swept aside as easily as food into a pocketed napkin.

It was once a rare thing for God to demand a great sacrifice, but the pace has quickened with the foulness of the world around us. We have grown so much more important to him. We must be ever ready to do his will.

James was first, and Philip was second. They were good boys, their sacrifices given gladly and accepted gratefully. Yes, Mark Swann would have been an offering, too. Mark would have saved us all from the fuel shortages and the sickness that plagued our herds. But that big foolish boy ruined it. Our offering could not be made after Mark was killed in the fire that JoJo set. JoJo had meant to take him away from us, but he only succeeded in killing both Mark and his brother in the blaze. We believed then that the line of Swanns had finally come to an end and that our village was doomed.

And yet some of us continued in our faith. And have we not been mightily rewarded for it?

But I must tell the story right. That was my mistake with you in the first place, and for that I am sorry.

Our third trial was during the Depression, when we were again tested by hunger and also by the Black Water. So many of us had died. Perhaps no test was more difficult than the Winter Siege itself, but this time the Swann family had no male heir to offer. But God does not offer a problem that faith cannot solve. A daughter of the Swanns had married into one of the families in the valley. A Winter Family itself, as providence would have it. You shake your head, but you already know what I'm going to say. You've seen his portrait in my cellar with all the other brave boys who gave their lives for our village, for this one flame of light in all the darkness of this bleak earth.

Your great-grandmother was Emily Swann before she was Emily Lowell. Her son, your great-uncle, Owen, was given unto the Lord in 1933. You're as much a Swann as you are a Lowell, Ben.

I told you before that names are nice, but it's the blood that matters.

51

The forest shifted in the night. The moonlight wove shadows of skeletal branches onto the icy ground.

In front of Caroline, Charlie disappeared in a puff of snow. She hoisted him out of the drift by his waistband, and they continued their silent escape through the frozen trees.

Charlie had not had the words to explain, but he hadn't needed them. Her son was not a liar, and the look on his face told Caroline what she needed to know. In a strange way, this wasn't news so much as it was confirmation. Their strange religion, their self-contained valley, their intractable attachment to their grim history, the unsettled feeling she'd get in her gut when one of their stares lingered upon her: Caroline had known for a while that something was wrong with the people of Swannhaven. What exactly it was, she didn't know, and at present it didn't much matter. What she knew was that Charlie and she had to get away from the Crofts.

They'd taken the steps down from the north tower. Once outside, they'd ducked along the rear veranda to hide themselves from anyone watching from the windows. It had not been the perfect escape: She'd forgotten her phone and wallet, but she did have her car keys.

Not that they would help her. When she and Charlie got to the cars, Caroline saw that the villagers' vehicles had boxed her Escape in. This was not an accident, she realized. Maybe there were no accidents here between the mountains.

There were villagers in the woods, she knew. They had been there to find JoJo, but now she was sure that they hunted Charlie and her, as well. What they needed to do was get to the county road and stop Ben before he returned to the Crofts. Once in the car, they'd be fine, they just—

An arm stretched from a tree trunk and caught Caroline in the throat. This slammed her flat on her back into the snow, her vision shifting from land to sky in a swift and shocking dislocation.

"Dangerous to be out in the snow, Mrs. Tierney."

Caroline blinked the tears from her eyes to see a stout man step from between the trees.

"*Run,* Charlie!" she cried as she tried to bolt to her feet, but the fall had rattled her brain and the man was on her in a moment. She gasped as he caught her from behind in a sleeper hold.

"Time to head back to the Crofts now," the man told Charlie.

The boy stood a few yards away, still as if frozen, eyes as bright as the moon.

"Don't want your mama to get hurt, do you? No, you're a good boy. You'll come back to the Crofts with me, won't you?" Spots swam across Caroline's vision. Though his face was behind her, she now placed the man's beady eyes and florid complexion. Seward, she thought, the man who lived next to Grams's old farmhouse.

"No," Charlie said. The word was only a whisper, but it sparked with defiance. Even with the breath being choked from her, Caroline felt pride. Her little man was strong. He got so much from his father, but he got this from her. This had always been true, even if lately it had become easy to forget.

"Come on, now, you're a good boy, aren't you?" Seward asked again, his hot, rank breath on her neck.

He *was* a good boy, Caroline thought. The best sort: the kind that might not give a parent what they wanted but always what they needed.

Caroline shifted her center of gravity, slammed her heel down hard onto Seward's foot, and delivered a blow to the bridge of his nose with the back of her hand. It had been years since she'd taken a self-defense class, but still the movements were rote. Seward's hold broke and his screams were muffled slightly by the hands he'd reflexively pressed over his face. Caroline spun around to knee him in the groin. The man groaned and bent over. As Seward vomited into the snow, Caroline kicked him in the ribs and face until he went down.

Caroline stopped when the man made no further move to stand. She turned to Charlie, and the boy nodded.

But there was no time for self-congratulation: Seward's first scream had echoed through the forest's icy corridors. The rest of the villagers would be coming for them now. They had to move faster than ever.

52

As he ran, Charlie tried to see which shadows swayed with the wind and which moved on their own.

It was hard to run for long in the thin, cold air. Beside him, Mom was out of breath, too, her face bright red above her scarf. He didn't know if the man had hurt her badly, but even if he had, Mom had hurt him worse. She had broken him like she'd broken the house, and it made Charlie proud. But the fight had made her tired, and the hunters were close.

The man's scream would have told the others where they were as clear as the North Star on a cloudless night. But Charlie knew what to do from *The Book of Secrets*. He had quickly broken two wide limbs from a red spruce. Dragging these behind them through the cold, dry snow had helped hide their trail through the night. It would not stop the hunters, but it might slow them.

There was a noise, and Charlie turned around to see a flutter of snow fall from a disturbed branch. The villagers would be upon them soon, but he'd finally found what he'd been looking for: an old oak with a hollow large enough to fit a grown man.

"Hurry," Charlie whispered to Mom.

Once they'd both squeezed into the hollow, he propped the spruce branches in front of the tree's opening. They could still see through the frosted needles, but they were hidden from the ones who chased them. They had been lucky that Charlie knew this tree, but, then, no one knew the forest as well as he did.

Almost no one.

Mom hugged her arms around his chest as they waited in the close space. The clouds of their breath burst and faded in the weak light.

A branch snapped to the right of their tree, a beat out of rhythm with the sounds of the overhead branches. A moment later, a boot crunched into cold snow to their left. Charlie watched as shadows separated from shadows. Mom's grip on him tightened.

Three men stood in front of them. Charlie could not be sure who they were. Two of them searched the snow with flashlights, while the third sniffed the air. They spoke to one another in low voices that Charlie couldn't hear.

Their beams of light crossed over the branches and burned across the white ground. Not long now before they were found, Charlie thought. He wondered if they wanted only him or if they would hurt his mom as the other man had. He began to consider giving himself up. Maybe if he did that, they wouldn't search the hollow for Mom. Maybe she could get away and bring back help.

But he knew Mom would never let the men take him without a fight. She was a very good mom. If Charlie showed himself, though, it might give them some time. Light from the flashlights gleamed through the tree's rotted bark as the men examined its trunk. Charlie realized that their luck had run out.

He squeezed his mother's hand and was about to move aside the pine boughs when the rattling of a stick against a tree sounded through the forest. The beams of light turned toward it, and the two men holding the flashlights ran toward the noise. The third man looked in the same direction and sniffed at the air again. It was this third man who scared Charlie. He seemed human in shape only. He tested the air and moved with the care of a predator. The man took one last look at the trees before following the others. He slid through the night like a fish speeding through water.

Charlie waited a few minutes, until he could no longer hear the men's movements through the wood. The cold had soaked into his joints and stiffened his legs. He was grateful to move again.

He helped his mom up, and they moved in the opposite direction from where the men had gone. Charlie knew that they had to leave this valley tonight, but they now had to go back up the Drop, farther from the road. He did not think that Mom and he could survive the cold night, but he knew that, even if they did, the villagers would find them in the light of morning. He wondered what Hickory Heck would do. Dad would also know what to do. Charlie wished he were here.

As they slowly made their way upslope, Charlie wondered about the noise from the forest that had sent the men scrambling. He had heard it before, during his long afternoons in the woods.

Charlie was thinking about this when he walked right into a man who stood as still and as tall as a tree. Charlie looked up and saw the one who knew the forest best: the one who moved through the trees like the wind and made a noise only when he wanted to be heard.

53

Simms and Harp stagger through the dark with their flashlights, but I see better by the light of the moon. They trample the undergrowth and clutch at the frozen trees, but I pick my way through without a falter or a sound. I am a forest creature.

The air is clean between the mountains. Clean and pure as my fasting soul. That is what happens when you do not eat. The excess of this ugly world burns away and takes with it all of its doubt and distractions. You reach a place, beyond the hunger, where everything is clear. You see the Lord's language everywhere. You can read it in the flutter of a crow's wing. You smell it in hints left by the cold east wind. He is everywhere, and he sees our every weakness.

The boy is ahead. I can smell his mother, and he would keep her close. He's a good boy. They all were.

Simms says something smart, and I grip his neck in a move fast enough to make his eyes bulge. The boy is too close for us to risk making any noise. I show my teeth and know that Simms can feel the low growl building in my chest. He remembers what I did to the Bishop boy.

The elders doubt that the youth of this village possess the strength to do what must be done. Will they be able to carry our burdens once we have gone? I wonder if my own grandpappy had such worries. Still, the blame for their weaknesses is not theirs alone. Our young people were not raised the way we were. They do not yet understand the importance of this village to his plan. They have not yet seen how we are tested in this in-between place, this cold valley between heaven and hell.

But they will.

Time was that every Sunday sermon would be of the Winter Siege and of the sacrifices of the Swann family, but that fell away when Mark and Liam died in the fire. We thought the line of Swann to be at an end, and we despaired and believed we had failed him. We believed that the unredeemed world had grown too corrupt to save. In our anguish, some of our old ways fell aside. Our village withered like an unwatered field. Some families died, others moved away. We did not teach our children all of the things they should have known. But our greatest failure was to doubt him. Through his providence, the line of Swann has been restored, and so has our chance at redemption. We will not fail him again, and we will again teach our children the ways of our forefathers.

When the time comes, I will have my June tighten the chain around the boy's bare chest. I will let him fix his tearstained face upon hers to beg for his life. I will have her watch as the cold slowly takes its grip. In the morning, I will have her help unclench his frozen fingers from the unyielding iron and carry his rigid body to the cemetery of his ancestors. Then she may truly understand and one day teach her own children.

The boy is close now. The mother's scent lingers in the cold, thin air. Simms and Harp shine their lights over the wood. They mutter to each other and look at me from the shadows of their faces. I watch the branches sway and wait for the wind to whisper me its secrets. A pain surges from my stomach. This suffering builds my determination. The pain makes me stronger.

And you will be rewarded, says the wind. I smile at the darkness.

Through the forest, a noise rings out: a rattling among the trees. Simms and Harp chase after it. Perhaps this is the reward the wind has promised. Harp has fasted, and so has Simms, but not the way that I have. My line has ever heard his word with great clarity. Perhaps the boy is deeper in the woods, or perhaps he lingers here with the scent of his mother.

The road to salvation is not straight. It is broken with trials and stained with blood. Perhaps the time for the boy to be found has not yet come. Perhaps it is God's will that we follow this noise in the dark.

What have we poor men ever been but wanderers in the dark?

Moving through the trees, I soon catch up to old Harp. He pants like a broken plow horse. I feel the flush of his face through the sharp air. He has misused his body, and now it takes little for it to fail him. He smells of cigarettes and liquor, though they are forbidden in this season. He turns around, disoriented in the dark because he does not hear the Lord's voice. How could he, with a mind so weak and a body so corrupted? A disgrace to his family.

Harp stops and tears the scarf off his neck, gasping for air. The artery beneath his chins throbs in the moonlight. It would not be a hard thing to take his life from him. His jowls are weak; my teeth are strong. It would be a mercy. Not all of the old ways have survived, but perhaps they should live again. It is not strictly true that our ancestors survived their terrible winter by wheat flour alone.

If I close my eyes, I can already taste the metal notes of his blood. I can feel the slick of it as it overspills my mouth to drench my chest.

Simms stumbles over a root ahead of us, and I remember our task. I shake my head free of this latest temptation. Perhaps there will be time for Harp later, after we find the boy. Perhaps he will be the reward the wind promised. Perhaps he will be how I break my fast.

54

Ben stared at Lisbeth in the silence that followed her declaration. In the gleam of the fire, he saw only hunger and madness in her eyes.

He bolted from the room. Roger Armfield stood in the doorway, his arms outstretched as if to stop him. But Ben did not slow. As he ran down the hallway, he registered Armfield's lanky form crashing to the floor behind him.

If you're trying to figure out this strange little village of ours, that one hard winter is all you need to know.

He had to find Caroline and Charlie.

Images flashed through his mind. Mrs. White, who had looked so hungry because she had been fed nothing more than a cup of flour. When she'd seen him, she whispered, "Swann." He hadn't understood that she had been naming him. Perhaps her naming him had been all that the other Winter Families needed.

Ben remembered his great-uncle Owen's photograph in Lisbeth's basement. He should have recalled that image when he saw the same one in the *Swannhaven Dispatch* article about him being lost in the forest. That story must have been a cover for the true horror of what had happened, for the real reason the Lowells had abandoned their farm and so many of their meager possessions.

The other portraits in Lisbeth's basement flitted through Ben's mind as he tore down the hallway. The jawlines, light eyes, and dark hair of the boys in the portraits were the same as his. They were the same as Charlie's.

He flung open the front door and faced the cold world. He still had Elizabeth Swann's letters gripped in one hand. Bub was on his shoulder, screaming.

Ben thought of the ancient chain he'd found in the kitchen. He imagined it squeezing Charlie's small body tight against the charred ruin of the elder tree.

The Preservation Society meetings, the Swannhaven Trust meetings, the old-fashioned church sermons, the cattle cleanup: Ben had bought it all. Swannhaven was special. It was a community that took care of its own. It was like no other place on God's earth. He wondered just how close he'd come to getting sucked into this insanity.

Above the whirl of the wind: a gunshot. Sound moved strangely here, and the direction was impossible to determine. He heard it shudder up the mountains before it faded.

As he stood on his front steps, a shadow separated itself from the dark of the north woods. He watched as it began to move up to the Crofts. Then Ben saw another one, a few paces from the first. This one was wider around the shoulders. It was difficult to see their black outlines against the mottled banks of snow. Now there were three figures moving up the Drop. He looked to the west and saw more there, wraiths across the frozen fields.

Ben ducked back into the house, gasping in the thin air. This is not your imagination, he told himself. He peered through the window to make sure.

It was then that he stopped being quiet and began to yell. It was then that he stopped waiting and began to run.

55

Ben called for them as he ran, though he doubted that Caroline and Charlie were still in the house. The villagers had taken to the forest to look for them. That was where Ben would go, too. He knew he had to leave the Crofts before the people coming up the Drop reached him. He knew this as well as he'd ever known anything. Every part of him screamed to leave this place.

"I'm sorry I yelled," he whispered into Bub's hair. The boy's cries were klaxons in his ears. "But we need to be quiet now," he said. The boy buried his head in Ben's shoulder. His sobs were lost in layers of down.

From one of the back doors, Ben searched the Drop for shapes in the night. He saw nothing but the icy fields that lay between the Crofts and the forest. Above all of them, the mountains towered. Silver cirrus clouds streaked the black sky above their heights.

The wind's gusts burned at his face as he ran the fields. They whipped a dusting of snow along the land like white water. Ben's tracks disappeared after him as if he ceased to exist beyond the moment his trailing foot left the ground.

Ben chanced a few looks over his shoulder, but the dark house did not tell him anything. He ran as fast as he could through the deep drifts. He made for the tree line. Elizabeth Swann had written about demons in the wood, and Lisbeth had told him about the wendigo, but Ben did not believe any of that. No demons necessary where men suffice. He fell only once, and he managed to twist himself so that he didn't land on the baby. He lay there for a moment. Beyond the lattice of clouds above, stars blinked their cold light. He stood up and threw himself again into the banks of white.

His ragged breaths made his throat raw, but he kept his pace up as long as he could. When he finally had to slow down, he saw a series of footsteps ahead of him. They were impossible in the wind, but they were there. A fluke of the currents. Some of the prints were small, made with child's boots, and the ones alongside them were a bit bigger. He did not question them but followed.

Ben glanced back at the Crofts. When he turned ahead again, a huge man stood in his way.

He was dressed in bulky clothes and was draped in fur. He must have been at least half a foot taller than Ben. His face was heavily bearded with a wild tangle of hair, but his small eyes held no malice.

"JoJo," Ben said.

The man nodded. "Come."

His voice had a timbre that seemed to begin in his feet. Even in the wind, Ben could smell him.

"Where are they?" Ben asked. He did not move.

"Come," the man said again. With a thick walking staff, he pointed to the woods beyond the lake. He reached out his hands as if to take Bub, but Ben only held the baby more tightly.

"No," he told the big man.

"Hurry," the man said. He began to run toward the forest, and, after a moment, Ben followed him.

"Why did you take him?" Ben asked when he caught up. Despite his size, the man ran like a deer.

"Wasn't safe."

"Because of the villagers?" Ben asked.

JoJo nodded.

"Where are Caroline and Charlie?"

The man pointed ahead to the trees. They ran side by side now, their steps synchronized. Along the ring of woods, the trees swayed in time to their pace.

"They blame you for the fire," Ben said. "For Mark and Liam Swann dying."

"Mark was my friend." JoJo shook his head. "They wanted to hurt him. Like they want to hurt yours. I tried to help."

"So you started the fire to stop them from hurting Mark."

"They don't stop," JoJo said. "Was it wrong?" he asked, looking at him.

Ben saw in his eyes that he wanted a real answer. He could tell that JoJo had been asking himself that question for thirty years.

JoJo blinked. "What I did?"

"I don't know," Ben said. He could not say what was right and what was wrong when you found yourself in a place where the only choices left were bad ones.

"Did you set the fire in our shed? Did you leave the deer's head?" Ben asked.

"Was not safe for them. I didn't want it to happen again," JoJo said. "If I scared you, if I scared the boy, you would leave. But you didn't."

Ben fell again and landed heavily on his side, sliding a few feet before coming to a stop. Bub wailed in his ear. The ground was as even as a pane of glass. JoJo offered his hand and Ben accepted. When he pushed himself up, he saw that they were on the frozen surface of the lake.

"Thank you," Ben said. That was what this valley had become to him: A place where the kindest hands belonged to kidnappers. A place where he ran from friends because they had murder in their eyes.

"Careful," JoJo told him.

The ice creaked underneath them.

"I'm sorry," JoJo said.

Ben looked and saw that the big man's eyes were full of tears. "For what?"

"The dog. He didn't know I was helping. But they couldn't find me before I helped you." He pointed to Bub. "When he got sick, I didn't know how to make him better."

Ben couldn't think of what to say. There were no words for this.

They crossed to the far side of the lake. Ben followed JoJo to a thicket of spindly pines not far from where Charlie had built his blind.

"Dad!" Charlie was crouched on the ground behind the trunk of a wizened tree. Caroline sat behind him with her hands on his shoulders. They ran to him, and Ben was so relieved to see them that he nearly lifted them all off the ground with his embrace.

"Thank God you got away from them," Ben said. He buried his face in Caroline's hair.

"Why are they after Charlie?" Caroline asked. She and Charlie both looked half frozen.

"They're crazy." Ben shook his head. "The whole village. We need to get out of here, but we can't get to the cars. Bub can't stay in the cold for much longer, and I don't know how many of them there are."

"We heard a gunshot," Caroline said.

"I think it was some kind of signal." Ben turned back to the fields and saw three dark shapes moving across the Drop. The shapes were running. The one in front loped through the drifts with a lupine grace.

"If we stay away from the drive, we might be able to get to the county road and meet up with Ted," Ben said. He turned back to the Crofts to watch the three shadows making their steady way toward them.

"They're coming," JoJo said. He pointed to the frozen field.

As Ben watched them, the joy he'd felt when he first laid eyes on Caroline and Charlie turned cold. The men hunting them knew where they were, and Ben knew that his family would never be able to outrun them.

Ben put a palm on Charlie's head. Even through the boy's winter hat, Ben could feel the thick thatch of his hair. He savored the texture of it in his hand.

Lisbeth had been right about one thing. You had to keep up the light. And Ben now knew what had to be done. He had promised to be better, and now was his chance.

"Take Mom to the cemetery," Ben told Charlie. "Can you find your way in the dark?"

Charlie looked at Ben carefully before nodding.

"Aren't you coming with us?" Caroline asked. "Ben, we have to get out of here."

"I'm going to talk to them," Ben said.

"Talk to—are you kidding?" Caroline said. "You said it yourself: They're *crazy.*"

"I'll just tell them that I'm looking for you, too," Ben said. "It was true enough two minutes ago. While I help them look, I'll separate from them and get to the car. Wait for me outside the bookstore in Exton."

"*Ben.*" Caroline's eyes were wide with horror.

Ben clutched her arms and leaned his forehead against hers.

"You have to get our sons out of here," he said. "Charlie will show you the way. He'll take you and Bub over to the cemetery, then down the Drop as close to the mountain as you can get." Ben turned to Charlie. "Walk down to the county road, but stay inside the tree line so no one can see you." He gave Caroline his cell phone. "Call Ted. He can't be that far now. Make sure he doesn't go to the Crofts."

"They're not going to hurt you?" she asked.

"It's not me that they want," Ben said. He turned to Charlie and met his son's gaze. Though it was dark, Ben could see the silver rims of his irises.

"You have to be careful, okay?" Caroline said. She hugged him with Bub between them. She was crying, but Ben made himself smile. Ben kissed Bub on the head and he suddenly felt light-headed. *This is how we say goodbye.*

Bub's mittens had come off, and Caroline worked to put them back on his tiny hands as Charlie moved closer to Ben.

"Need to hurry," JoJo said. His voice was like thunder beyond the horizon.

Charlie hugged Ben's leg, his face pressing again his hip. Ben turned to watch the men's progress up the Drop. They were close now, just on the other side of the lake.

"We can't let them see you," Ben said. He knelt in the snow to be as close to Charlie as he could. He tried to memorize the shape of the boy in his arms. So many things to say to him, but there was only time for two. "Take care of them. Now, *run.*"

Charlie and Caroline were both crying when they turned away from Ben.

He watched as they disappeared between the trees, until he could see no trace of them through the dark wood. As Ben pushed himself up from the ground, his hand brushed against a wedge of rock that sat just under the snow's surface. It was better than nothing. He slid it into the deep pocket of his coat, then fixed his eyes again on the men who hunted him.

"These men will hurt you," he told JoJo. The big man stood behind him, blending with the trees and shadows. "You should go, too."

JoJo shook his head. "They hurt my friends," the big man said.

Ben waited a few minutes, until the men reached the edge of the lake; then he stepped out onto the shore and waved. He recognized the chief's silhouette in the lead. He watched as the chief hesitated a moment, then sped the group's progress toward him. Ben began to walk across the frozen lake. As he stepped onto the ice, he felt a strange lightness come over him. It was a vertiginous feeling to realize that all your choices have been made. The wind had weak-ened, and the night was quiet except for the rattling from the trees and the crunch of his footfalls. Beside him, JoJo was as silent as a ghost.

"Hey, guys," Ben said, raising his voice into a shout. He wondered if they'd even give him a chance to explain the mountain man beside him. "Did you just come from the house? Are Caroline and Charlie back yet? I can't find them."

Now that they were so close, Ben could see that Deputy Simms and Walter Harp were with the chief. Ben had seen the chief only a few hours ago, but that time had transformed him. The bones of his face were sharp in the moonlight. His rangy body was poised for violence. Ben had prepared himself for hostility; still, he shivered under the man's look.

The chief seemed to contemplate Ben's question, then he carefully picked his way along the ice to JoJo. He moved with an otherworldly economy. He appeared to sniff the air, never breaking eye contact with the big man. JoJo stood utterly still as the chief looked him over, and Ben could not read the lawman's expression. Then the chief smiled, pulled his gun out of its holster, and shot JoJo. The sound was deafening.

Ben threw himself down and slid a few feet on the ice. When he looked up, the chief still had his gun trained on JoJo. Ben had not seen the big man go down, but he'd felt him fall.

"Shoulda done that thirty years ago," the chief said. His voice was low and rough and sounded as if it came from deep inside his chest.

"And woulda, too, if he hadn't hid in the woods like a scared girl," Simms said. He spat at JoJo's still form, then looked nervously at the chief.

"Talked with Lisbeth, Ben," the chief said. He did not point the gun at him, but he did not holster it, either. "She said she tried again to explain matters to you but had no more luck than before. Where's Charlie?"

"I don't know where he is," Ben said. "I'm looking for him, too."

"Gotta be either brave or stupid to lie to a man with a gun," Simms said. Ben put his hands above his head but did not stand up from the ice.

"You got nowhere to go, Ben. It's a hard thing that has to be done, but he wouldn't ask it of us if we couldn't do it," the chief said. "We cannot question his plan. Your people, Swann and Lowell alike, knew that as gospel. How can you say any different?"

"Listen, we can still just leave this place. No harm done," Ben said. He thought of his family trying to make their way through the forest. He would give them all the time he could.

"Our village is dying, Ben. You've seen it yourself. The herds are sick, the banks are closing in, the people want to leave, they want to undo everything that we—that *your family*—have given so much to preserve. We would not be in such a bad spot if this one hadn't gotten in the way last time." He gestured to JoJo's prone form. "We have existed by the grace of God since that terrible winter, but we have been on borrowed time for too long. Charlie is God-sent for us to prove ourselves worthy one more time."

"The only reason we're here is because you told us that the Crofts was for sale once you found out my grandmother was a Lowell."

"And your great-grandmother a Swann. God be praised. But it was not chance, Ben. Nothing in this darkening world is chance. You're one of us. Do you accept that?"

Ben allowed a moment to pass, then nodded. "I can accept it. But it's the blood that matters, right? So take mine."

The chief squinted at him.

"You need blood," Ben said. "Swann blood. And I have more of it than Charlie does, so take it. It's yours." The last thing he had to give. "Just leave my family alone."

"That's not how it works, Ben," the chief said. "Losing this life is no sacrifice. Don't you see that the dead are free? They do not mourn; they do not suffer. We here know well that it's a harder thing to live than to die. I still hope you get to learn that."

Ben exhaled into the cold air and rolled onto his back. He'd tried.

It was almost over now. He looked up at the stars. He hoped he'd bought Charlie enough time. The price had been high, but it had been paid gladly. "You have to know I won't help you hurt him."

"Think on it, Ben. Think of Bub, if not yourself. We can't let the Swanns go now that they've finally returned. God would not forgive that. The baby boy is young enough that any one of us could raise him as our own. But blood matters, Ben. And a boy should be with his own father."

Ben saw there would be no end to the horrors here. The villagers had invested too much in their madness. Even they had no choice now but to see it through.

"We tried with you, Ben. Lord knows it," the chief sighed. He pointed his gun at Ben.

"Chief—"

"You've chosen wrong, Ben. But maybe the Lord will forgive you." Then he pulled the trigger.

56

Charlie brushed the snow off his face and shivered. The Drop was steeper here, and it was hard to find the right footing through the deep drifts. Both Mom and he had fallen more than once. Bub's cries had quieted into whimpers. The baby was sick and very tired, and Charlie was afraid for him. He knew they could not go on like this for much longer, but it was the only thing they could do. There was no one left to save them.

His eyes welled with tears, but he did not want Mom to see him cry.

And he told himself it was still possible that Dad could get away from the men. Dad knew his words as well as JoJo knew the forest. If anyone could do it, then he could. Compared to the strange things in Dad's stories, it was not hard to imagine a man talking to three other men on a cold night to convince them they were all friends. The world was filled with things far more amazing than this.

A gunshot broke his thoughts and made his heart jump in his chest. Mom looked at him, eyes wide.

"Another signal," Charlie said. His voice cracked in his mouth. "We need to be careful."

Mom nodded and turned forward again, searching the forest ahead for movement.

Charlie felt hollowed out, and it was a moment before the tears came. This time he let them flow. He tried to stay focused and not think about the gunshot, but he couldn't help it. *At least there had only been one,* he thought, and felt ashamed of himself.

He tripped again but was able to catch himself this time. He tried to pay attention to the forest. He knew they couldn't help Dad and JoJo up by the lake. They had to get to the road to find Uncle Ted. Dad and JoJo had gone out into the open to meet the men so that Mom, Bub, and he could get away. If they turned back now, it would have been for nothing.

Mom had called Uncle Ted after they left Dad and JoJo by the lake. He was close, and she'd told him to meet them by the road. But the road was long, and the Drop was wide, and Charlie was very cold.

"Is that it?" Mom asked him. She pointed ahead.

There was a band of open white beyond the trees. Though Charlie knew that the road hugged the mountains this far south, he still did not think they had gone far enough. When they got through the trees, they saw that it wasn't the county road but the access road to the state preserve. They had reached the southern edge of their land.

The access road would take them to the county road, and it had a gentle slope and thin snow cover. Walking it would be easier than hiking through the forest. But Charlie was very tired.

"Maybe Uncle Ted can find us here," he said.

Mom tucked Bub into the crook of her arm and made the call.

She was talking to Uncle Ted, and Charlie was thinking about the heat in his uncle's car, when the second gunshot rang down the mountain. It was softer than the one before it. Much of its roar had been lost to the snow and forest that separated them. Mom had not heard it, but Charlie had.

His legs gave out and he sat down heavily in the snow while Mom finished talking to Uncle Ted.

"Ted thinks he saw the turnoff for it when he was looking for a place to pull over," Mom told him once she shut the phone. "If it's the right road, he'll be here in a couple minutes."

Charlie nodded. He could not stop his hands from shaking. He could not swallow the lump that had swollen in his throat.

"You're cold, honey," Caroline said. She sat next to him in the snow and hugged him. She rubbed his back to warm him. "Uncle Ted will be here soon, then we'll head to the bookstore to wait for Dad. Then we'll go back to the city. Won't it be nice to be back there?"

Charlie buried his head in his mother's side. He thought of the gunshots. He thought about Dad, alone in the cold and the dark.

Headlights painted the frosted trees, and Charlie shielded his eyes from the glare. The car stopped just ahead of them, and Charlie squinted to see who it was. For a moment Charlie thought it was Dad, and he jumped to his feet. But it was Uncle Ted. His face had the same angles as Dad's. He had the same dark hair and light eyes. He looked just like Dad. So did Charlie.

Mom moved to the car, but Charlie did not. He stood on the side of the road, trembling in the cold.

"Wait," he said, and Mom turned back to him. He wanted to say so many things to her, but he couldn't just then. "Wait."

He ran back through the trees before she could stop him.

57

You never hear the shot that kills you.

When Ben was a teenager, he'd gone through a noir phase. Raymond Chandler, Ross Macdonald, Dashiell Hammett: He couldn't get enough of them. He loved their ambience. How they could immediately conjure a place that was utterly foreign to a suburban teenager like himself.

He also loved the bon mots that peppered them. It had always appealed to him, how just a few well-chosen words could make a page sing. *To say goodbye is to die a little. The past was filling the room like a tide of whispers. He felt like someone had taken the lid off life and let him see the works.*

Ben would sometimes creep up behind Ted to whisper in his ear, "You never hear the shot that kills you." It was a great line because it could mean so many things.

It was strange that these were the first words to come into Ben's mind when he fell back into himself, but there they were.

He'd been shot. Ben knew this because he felt wetness under his coat. He didn't know if he'd lost consciousness or if his mind had just wandered. He didn't think he'd been on the ice for long, because he heard Simms and Harp talking to each other about where to look for his family.

When Ben opened his eyes, the chief was leaning over him. He had his gloves off, and his fingers glistened in crimson. His lips glistened, too. His mouth was stretched into something like a smile.

Ben felt the wetness spread across his chest. He thought it would be warm, but it was cold, and he did not think that was good. He expected pain but felt only heaviness. But when he tried lifting his head, it was not as hard to do as he thought it would be. He looked down at his chest and saw the blackness of his blood and the scruff of white where the insides of his coat had been blown away. There wasn't as much blood as he'd expected, but he figured there was more under his coat.

Then he realized that the wetness he'd felt wasn't all blood. The bullet had gone through him and into the ice. It had chipped a hole through the lake's frozen surface. When he shifted his legs, he heard the ice underneath him creak.

Walter Harp saw him moving and nudged Simms.

"Let the cold finish him," Simms said.

The chief turned his glassy-eyed stare away from Ben. "Hafta make it look enough like an accident that the FBI won't think anything of it," he said. "Bad luck that they're here on account of the baby going missing. An animal attack, maybe. Something messy like that could slow down the ID." He walked over to the others, then he turned back to Ben. He again made that face that looked like a smile.

"Not a crier, though," Simms said. "Didn't expect that from him."

Ben rested his head. His ear was pressed against the ice, but it did not hurt. He could hear the beat of his heart against the frozen lake and hear the bending of the ice underneath it.

He forced himself to sit up. There was a black smear against the ice he'd been lying on. He took the rock out of his pocket and hit it against the hole the bullet had made.

"Trying to swim himself out now," Simms said.

Walter Harp laughed. "Must be half a foot of ice, if it's an inch."

Ben timed the impact of the stone to the beat of his heart and the movement of the trees and the rhythm of the wind. He put everything he had into striking the ice. The rock was well suited for this. Perhaps Lisbeth had been right about this, too. Maybe there really was an answer provided for every problem.

When he slammed the stone down a third time, the crack split a little farther in both directions. The men from the village stopped grinning.

"Enough of that," the chief said. He walked toward Ben to take the stone from him, but a massive black weight crushed him down onto the frozen lake. JoJo howled as he mashed the chief's head into the ice. To Ben's ears, it sounded like the wind.

Simms and Harp pulled at JoJo to get him off the chief, but he was too big and it was hard for them to keep their footing on the ice. They tumbled over each other as they grappled with him. The chief threw his head back and sank his teeth into JoJo's neck.

Ben continued to slam the stone into the ice. The crack widened and spread. Soon the sound of breaking ice was as loud as the cries of the men who fought in front of him. Soon the crack had taken on a life of its own and Ben stopped hammering at it. The piece of ice he lay on became dislodged. He flattened himself against it.

He watched the men tumble as he lay there. Deputy Simms tried and failed to regain his footing after his boot broke through into the freezing water. His head made a wet sound as it connected with the lake's frozen surface, then his body slowly slid into the dark maw beneath the ice.

A geyser of blood exploded from JoJo's neck where the chief had found his carotid artery. But JoJo did not stop mashing the other man's head into the ice. Harp was on top of JoJo, trying hopelessly to wrest the big man from the chief. Their combined weight was too much for the lake's fractured surface. They plunged through the skin of ice with enough force to send a surge of water into the air. For a moment, there was nothing but ice shifting, where a second before there had been four men. Dark arcs of blood stark against the broken surface were the only evidence of any of them having been there.

A gloved hand burst from between two sheets of floating ice, but then it was yanked under again. If Ben closed his eyes, he could imagine JoJo, with his hair and fur pelts floating, pulling the villagers down to the lake's cold bottom.

Then it was quiet except for the noise from the trees. The world began to slow.

Ben rolled onto his back so that he could see the stars. The sky was beautiful. He could see the jeweled haze of the Milky Way so clearly up here, far from the city. He should have spent more nights appreciating it. His chest began to hurt. He started to feel very small in front of a universe that was so unimaginably vast. Up against the full sight of it, he dwindled and diminished, until at last there was nothing left.

58

You think: This is it.

The end of not just a page or a chapter but of your entire book.

This isn't the way you thought it would go. But, unlike a novel, a life has no useful sheaf of unturned pages with which to estimate its remaining length. Instead, you amble onward cluelessly until the words of your world run out.

It's a shame, because the narrative doesn't conclude with you. Charlie's tale continues, and Bub's, and Caroline's, too. You hate to leave a story only half read, and, besides, you've become invested in these characters.

A boy like Charlie could grow up to be almost anything or anyone. But he's had setbacks, too. What if other people can't keep him safe, the way you've tried to? If you've learned one thing from this life, it's that it has so many twists that just about anything could happen to him. Without your help, who knows what kind of man he'll become.

And Bub, well, you didn't get to know him at all, did you? Will he like to read? Is he athletic? Does he have a sweet tooth? You have no idea. In a year, he won't even remember you. You'll be a story to him.

Of course, what you really don't want to think about is how this could all be academic. It matters only if you've bought them enough time to get away in the first place. Even now, Caroline and Ted could be lying gutted in the snow, with Charlie chained fast to a tree.

A surge of agony crashes over you, but it's not from the gunshot. You thought you were done with this. The pain, the worry, the questions. You thought the tethers of this world had finally uncoiled from you. But not yet.

The world remains insistent. Like the sound in your ears and the rapping on your shoulder. Someone is crying, you realize. When you open your eyes, you see a figure kneeling next to you. He's very small against the drifts of snow and the edifice of the trees. He's pulling on your arm, as if you're an uncooperative plaything.

You tell him that he shouldn't be out in the cold.

The boy makes a choking sound. His face is blotchy with tears, but he looks less upset than he did.

He stoops to wrap your arm around his neck. The idea of standing seems impossible to contemplate, but he is intent on it. You don't want to disappoint him any more than you already have.

———

Standing is maybe the worst thing you've ever had to do. But the pain wakes you up. You remember more of yourself.

The fields around you are empty in the moonlight, and the ice underneath you has resettled itself. You follow Charlie back into the woods. The drifts slow him, but slow is the only speed you can go.

You remember that you have to be careful. That there are other people in the forest. Though they look for you, they are not your friends. You hear them call to one another through the noise of the trees creaking above you. They are close.

Charlie knows another way, deeper into the trees, but the way is difficult. He falls into a drift and for a moment is lost. When you pull him out, he blinks like a newborn. You make him get up onto your shoulders, even though it hurts terribly. You fall. You stand. You run. You fall. Each time it's as if you're freshly ripped open, but Charlie helps you up. You're too weak to stand, and he's too short to walk. Alone, neither of you would make it. But neither of you is alone.

The villagers who hunt you shout through the woods, and the forest in its strange way answers. Sound is different here, and in their tracking they become lost as the trees lure them deeper and deeper. Farther from you, and closer to the frozen heart of the mountains. This is a piece of fortune that feels overdue.

It's troubling how the rows of trees only give way to more trees. But finally you see headlights ahead. You lower Charlie to the ground, and through the forest's pillars you see your brother. He runs for you, and your wife is just behind him. Ted wraps his arm around you as he leads you to the car. Caroline takes your other side. When you look at her, something in your chest takes flight. You realize that she is crying and so are you.

———

They ease you into the backseat. Charlie sits up front, and Caroline squeezes next to you with Bub on her lap. She unzips your coat, puts her hands on your face, and tells you that you are going to be okay. You have no choice but to believe her. She knows you better than anyone.

The car takes off in a rush of snow and light. There is talk of hospitals and highways and state police.

Caroline gives Ted directions as she presses your wound. As the blood from your chest slows, your worries begin to mount. You remember that all your money has been flushed into a house in a village rife with lunatics from another age. You realize that everything you've worked toward has been lost. *A home that you can be proud of. A life where you and your family can live in every comfort. Can you see it?* For the first time, you can't.

For a moment, it's almost as if you've learned nothing.

The ranks of ice-glazed trees march by in their uncounted armies. Wind buffets the car from every side. But the warmth from the vents is true, and you feel your fingers begin to thaw.

You see the familiar lines of your brother's profile as he checks on you through the rearview mirror, and you feel your wife's unyielding grip on your chest. Bub has a tiny fist clamped to your sleeve, and Charlie's steel-blue eyes do not even for a moment waver from your own, and you realize that you've been imagining the wrong kind of future for as long as you can remember.

You understand that you don't need a dream of some distant place or time when all the pieces of a perfect life have seamlessly aligned.

A man doesn't need everything. He just needs the things he can't live without.

Can you see it?

You can see it because they're all around you. They've been here this whole time.

ACKNOWLEDGMENTS

I'm enormously grateful to my editor, Mark Tavani, for his keen insights, thoughtful edits, and all-round wise counsel.

In addition to being a crucial source of advice, my agent, Elisabeth Weed, has been a champion nonpareil as well as an inexhaustible source of enthusiasm.

A special thanks to Jane Fleming Fransson, Charlotte Hamilton, Sarah Landis, and Alessandra Lusardi for wading through many, many drafts. Your (usually gentle, occasionally painful, always necessary) edits made this happen.

I'm deeply grateful for the guidance of Kendra Harpster, Jenny Meyer, Dana Murphy, Betsy Wilson, Pam Dorman, and the excellent Jennifer Hershey.

Gigantic thanks to Patricia Gilhooly, William Duffy, Kevin Duffy, Mary-Kate Duffy, Bridget Raines, Aaron Raines, Ann Marie Ricks, Theresa Maul, Robert Maul, Susan Halldorson, Hillary Lancaster-Ungerer, Michael Ungerer, and Cameron White-Ford.

I'm also very appreciative of the extraordinary team at Ballantine, especially Gina Centrello, Libby McGuire, Kim Hovey, Susan Corcoran, Mike Rotondo, Dana Blanchette, Vincent La Scala, and Kathy Lord.

Read on for a sneak peek at the
next chilling novel from Brendan Duffy:

THE STORM KING

Available February 2018 from Ballantine Books

THE BOY WHO FELL

I

For Nate, Saturdays in the spring mean baseball.

His teammates think playing the outfield is ignominious, but he likes it. There's a meditative appeal to a morning spent watching for hard-struck balls as they spin and slow at the height of their parabolas.

He's not the most attentive of fielders, but Nate does all right at the plate. He's third on Greystone Lake's junior varsity team in RBIs, and when he takes warm-up swings the shouts from the bleachers are authentic.

His mother, father, and brother are among those cheering this last Saturday in April. It's just a scrimmage against North Hampstead, so Mom's attendance is unusual. She goes to the real games, but most weekends find her up with the sun and working in her vegetable garden. Nate's little brother, Gabe, would play in the grass as Mom fussed over her plants. Neither of them are in the garden today, because Mom strained her back, and her seedlings can survive a few days without weeding. Gabe doesn't mind, because he likes baseball. For some time, he's been counting the days until he graduates from T-ball. Dad doesn't make it to all of Nate's games, either, but this is the kind of day that makes every cell in your body sing, and he can read the *Times* during lulls in the action as easily as he could at their kitchen table.

Nate's team wins thanks to a triple he hits in the ninth inning. Though the matchup isn't an important one, there are whoops and smiles all around. His coach gives Nate the game ball, and Nate feels proud that his family was there to watch him play well and win.

Mom calls him her baseball hero. What type of pie would her baseball hero like for dessert tonight? she wants to know. There's an organic market at the Wharf, and she'll make any kind he wants. She asks to see Nate's game ball, and that makes him feel proud, too.

His team plays on one of the high school's fields, near the center of Greystone Lake, and it's just a few minutes' drive from there to the Wharf in Dad's old black Passat. The Wharf itself is only a few minutes from the McHales' home on Great Heron Drive. The town along the shore is not a large one.

It's early in the year for tourists, but there's still a good crowd at the market. Visitors browse for honey, jams, and baked goods while the locals from the Lake and nearby towns buy produce trucked from afar and fish fresh from their home waters. The sky being bell clear and the breeze warm, Dad suggests they picnic in the headlands. This isn't something they do often, but it's an intoxicating day. The lake glitters in the sun, and from that height the town will look like a jewel set into the crown of mountains.

They buy baguettes, cured meats, cheeses, and sun-brewed iced teas. Gabe wheedles himself a bottle of artisanal root beer. Vendors sell cherries from California and strawberries from Arizona, but Nate is drawn to the first of the season's peaches from Florida. He touches them as carefully as he would an infant's head. Mom buys a basket of the fruit.

The Passat's trunk is full of baseball equipment and a pile of uncorrected papers from Dad's AP U.S. history class, so Dad places the bags of food in the back with Nate and Gabe while Mom rides up front with the peaches on her lap. Nate's game ball is still where she left it on her seat. To avoid sitting on it, she gently places the grass-stained ball in the basket with the peaches.

This is important.

Nate realizes later that it had all been important.

The headlands rise along Greystone Lake's western shore. Hiking paths are carved throughout the protected woodlands, with parking lots marking the major trailheads. Among the nooks of interest that dot the headlands, Nate's parents favor a particular meadow. In the deep of the old-growth forest, an open space slopes toward the water and offers an unmatched view of the lake and town.

To reach it, they drive beyond the great houses of the Strand, where the boulevard branches from the shore to the headlands. The road there climbs the hills in switchbacks above the lake; it's closed during the winter months when its blind turns are too treacherous to be passable.

But this Saturday in April, winter is a distant memory. The wind carries ripe forest smells into the car, and waterfowl patrol the shore below them.

Nate is watching one such flock when the Passat swerves and he's knocked hard against the window glass. He looks up to see a green Jeep with flashing lights looming beyond the windshield. His mother gasps, and the basket of peaches overturns in her lap. There's another car now, a shiny SUV straddling the center line like an elephant walking a tightrope. Dad accelerates to get the Passat out of its path. A curve is just ahead.

Nate sees Dad stomp the brakes, but their speed does not change. He hears Mom scream his father's name as she bends to pull at something at his feet. The peaches, Nate realizes. *No,* he thinks a moment later. *The baseball.* Dad cannot slow the car because it's wedged under the brake. Mom tries to pull it away, but it will not budge while Dad presses all of his strength into the pedal.

Gabe reaches across the space between them to grab Nate's hand. In the flurry of the moment, this surprises Nate as much as the knock against the window, because Gabe made it very clear on his last birthday, his sixth, that he expected everyone to stop treating him like a baby. Nate looks at his brother and sees that his mouth is wide open but no sound is coming from it.

He wants to tell Gabe not to worry, but then they're through the guardrail. The bright sky that had filled the windshield darkens into the empty slate of the lake. No more than a few seconds have passed since Nate had his head rapped against the glass, but that life is already over. He realizes this when Mom turns to look at him.

He often tries to recall the look in her eyes. What does a mother try to convey to her child when they have moments to live? Fear or regret? Sadness or pity? When Nate summons her expression in that instant, he tries to find love. But the only thing on her face is horror. They fall too quickly for it to be anything else.

In the movies Nate has seen, events like this are shown in slow-motion. This underscores the importance of the scene. In these fraught seconds, the slightest look and gesture is given momentous gravity. Consciousness extends as it senses the imminence of its conclusion.

But these moments don't stretch for Nate. The Passat falls like the ton and a half of metal that it is. One moment they are weightless and his mother is looking at him, and then the windshield explodes and the lake takes them.

Nate comes back to himself on the rocks. There's a tortured sound around him. A raw and gasping cry like a person torn in half. It echoes across the water and up the cliffs as if it cannot find a place to rest. His chest feels as if it's crushed in the fist of a giant. To breathe is agony. He cannot feel his arm, and his baseball uniform is now more red than white. His first thought is that the lake's glittering surface was a lie, because he is cold to his marrow. There's a phantom memory of ice water locked in a vise around his throat.

His body is wracked with pain and seizing with chills. He wipes blood from his eyes and searches the stony water for his family, but they are gone.

Only then does he realize that the scream he hears is his own.

1

Nate had missed holidays and weddings and more birthdays than he could count. It took a funeral to bring him home.

A Greyhound got him to Syracuse, where he transferred to a local line that made the long haul to the North Country. Eight hours after leaving Port Authority's sticky fluorescence, he was again in the foothills of the Adirondacks.

A medical journal sat open on his lap, though he hadn't read a word for miles. Instead, he was on his phone, listening to one of his section's residents detail this morning's battles. White blood cell counts, biopsy data, and scan analyses. Numbers falling, rising, and static. Today, more skirmishes were being won than lost: the closest thing to victory anyone who fights cancer could hope for. But the failures ached.

He'd called for the path results of a bulky lymph node resection he'd performed on Nia Kapur, a mischievous nine-year-old with huge amber eyes and the best, snortiest laugh Nate had ever heard. He'd worked with Nia and her parents since the beginning of his pediatric surgical oncology fellowship. But the results from her lymph node were not good. The data his resident delivered meant that his time with the Kapurs was drawing to its end.

"Dr. McHale?"

"Sorry, Gina, spotty reception up here." He cleared his throat. "Can you give that last part to me again?"

Nate listened to what he'd missed, thanked her for the update, and wished her luck in weathering the coming storm.

Churning ever closer, a hurricane tore along the coast.

Medea.

Someone at the National Weather Service had been steadily replacing retired hurricane names with classically inspired monikers—Antigone, Brutus, Circe—giving each storm gravitas and a suggestion of animus. Nate thought the time might soon come when storms were named after forgotten gods, their energies stoked by millennia of human neglect.

The timing of the storm was terrible. But in its own way, it was also perfect.

The bus shuddered around a curve, and Nate watched as the lines between land and sky fell into familiar contours. It was September, but the window was ice under his fingertips, the luminescence of the summer mountains already fracturing into color. The wild forest began to lose ground to tidy colonials with manicured lawns and sculpted flower beds. Through the trees, he caught the first flash of light gleaming against dark water.

It had been a long trip, but Nate was finally there.

He was one of the last riders remaining on the bus, and the only one to disembark at the town green.

At first, Greystone Lake looked much as he'd left it. The town hall's neoclassical dome was still painted the red of the autumn maples. The limestone façade of the Empire Hotel still shone like a great pearl through the dogwoods that lined the green. To the north were the headlands, to the east was the Wharf, and to the south were the foothills. This was Greystone Lake. This was home. And Nate knew its every corner as if it were part of his own body.

He extended the handle of his bag and made his way down to the Wharf. It had been fourteen years since he'd walked these streets, and he had to remind himself with each step that this wasn't a dream.

The outline of each building, the arc of every curb and lamppost. Everything was familiar, but everything had changed. Nate had changed, too.

As he picked his way down Kingfisher Boulevard he understood why there were so many adages about this kind of homecoming. Each step was a new round of Spot the Difference. Fresh signage on familiar storefronts, obsolete pay phones replaced by sleek bike racks. Renovations, restorations, and new construction. Returning home after a long absence was a unique mélange of recognition and discovery.

A cluster of children, too young to be in school, were herded gently by their keepers along the edge of the town green. A gust kicked a drift of dried leaves at them, sending them into high-pitched squeals of mock terror. They were closer in age to Livvy, but right now Nia Kapur was the child at the forefront of Nate's mind. He'd have to call her parents. It was the kind of news he'd rather give in person, but it'd be days before he'd be back in the city, and little Nia might not have many days left.

He tried to think of exactly what he'd say, but they'd not yet invented the right words for this.

Nate got his first unfettered view of the lake once he neared the base of the hill. It glittered in the sunlight, though its serenity didn't fool Nate. There was a well-known saying in the little town along the shore: *The lake returns what it takes.* This applied to fishing nets as well as drowned bodies, jetsam as well as secrets.

While here, Nate planned to push this gem of lore to its limit.

In his pocket, his phone vibrated with a text message.

Meg: you home sweet home?

A host of adjectives could describe the town along the shore, but "sweet" wasn't among them. *Just got here,* Nate typed back. *You in NJ yet?*

The bus was an atrocious way to travel here, but with a Category

3 edging past the Carolinas, stranding Meg without the car hadn't been an option. Two days ago, it had looked like the hurricane would pinwheel into the Atlantic, but high pressure had kinked the jet stream from its usual course. Medea would strike inland, and when it did it would be the worst storm the Northeast had seen in years.

He'd been updating Meg regularly with the notifications pinged to him by his weather apps: wind-speed stats, pics from obliterated beach towns, the inevitable comparisons to Katrina and Sandy. When it came to such things, he had an abundance of caution that his wife rarely shared. Nate believed he'd successfully convinced Meg to take Livvy out of the city to weather Medea at her parents' home in the suburbs, but he wouldn't relax until he got confirmation that they'd arrived safely. According to Google Earth, his in-laws' house was 134 feet above sea level and two miles from any river likely to flood.

Even without Medea, this trek to the northern hinterlands was poorly timed. Meg felt she was on the brink of making partner at her law firm. Livvy had another ear infection. Things were busier than usual at the hospital. The schedule of their lives was like a chess match in three dimensions, but right now the Lake was where Nate had to be.

He could have rented a car for the trip north, but there was something in the monotony of the bus that appealed to him. The jolt of its acceleration, the lurch of its brakes, and its faithful pauses at each waypoint of its rambling route. More than a drive, taking the bus felt like a journey. A necessary transit between the world he'd made and the world that had made him. He'd worked more than he'd meant to during the ride, but Nate knew those long hours had helped him adjust to the idea of returning home. Even under the best circumstances it would be jarring to see the lake's silver skin lap the shore, hear the wash of traffic along the wet asphalt of the Strand, and smell this tree-spiced wind.

His grandmother had called him three weeks ago, as soon as they'd found the body in the headlands. This was before any official identification had been made, but Nate hadn't needed to wait for dental records or DNA.

Grams's pub, Union Points, was across a cobblestone street from the Wharf. The establishment and the tidy brick building that housed it had been in Nate's family for more than a century. Generations of McHales had manned its taps and swept its floors. Nate no longer knew where he fit into his family's legacy in this town, but he still felt a swell of warmth at the sight of the place.

Other than a plastic tarp fixed where a plate glass window should have been, the old pub looked good. Inside, its black wood surfaces had been polished, and its exposed brick walls hung with stylish photographs of the town and the lake. The place was empty except for a trio of college guys at the counter and a boat crew occupying a booth in the back. A girl with shoulder-length black hair pressed at a flat-screen register behind the bar.

The bartender had a smile on her face, but when she turned to Nate, her body went rigid. Her open expression closed like a flower on the brink of night.

"She's in the back," the bartender finally said after an uncomfortable pause. She barely looked old enough to tend the bar. "Want me to get her?"

"Sure," Nate said.

In this town there was no point in wondering how a girl this young knew him by sight.

The college guys paid no attention as Nate settled in a few stools away, but the locals in the back got quiet. Their curiosity pulled on his shoulders, a familiar weight.

He heard Grams's sure stride before she burst through the kitchen doors. He Skyped with her every Sunday but hadn't seen her in person since her last visit to the city back in July. She'd been spindle tall and steely gray for as long as he'd known her, and she looked only a little more stooped than he remembered.

"My beautiful boy," she said.

Nate bent to kiss her on the cheek and she pulled him tight.

"I'd have met you at the green," she said.

"And abandon the place to this crowd?" His gesture encompassed the empty tables and half dozen patrons. "Can't trigger a riot in my first ten minutes home. Got to pace myself."

She cuffed him on the shoulder. "Be good, you devil."

"What happened to the window?" he asked.

"Oh." She glanced at the front of the bar. The plastic sheet tensed with the breeze like an inflating lung. "That last thunderstorm. Fella keeps bringing the wrong size pane. We'll need to plank it good and tight for the hurricane. You're so thin, boy." She poked him in the ribs. "I'll bring you something."

When she disappeared into the kitchen, Nate's phone buzzed with a new message. A pic of Livvy and her china doll grin ensconced in her grandmother's lap. She and Meg had reached the New Jersey hills. They were safe.

He tucked away his phone, and the girl behind the bar slid him a pint.

"Looks like you could use that." Perhaps it was an apology for her initial reaction. "This can't be an easy place to come back to." She was pretty, with her high cheekbones, green eyes, and porcelain skin.

He nodded. Something he liked about the city was how so few of its millions knew or cared about his business. The beer gave him an excuse not to look at her.

"I'm TJ," she said. She bit one edge of her red lips, and Nate couldn't tell if the flicker in her eyes was hospitality, curiosity, or something else entirely. He didn't want to find out.

"Nice to meet you, TJ," he said. He rubbed his eyes as if he were tired, displaying the flash of his wedding band. Focusing on the static undersides of his lids, he wished for the girl to dissolve into the floorboards.

The girl remained, but Grams returned from the kitchen with a grilled cheese and a cup of tomato soup.

"Tommy know you're coming up today?" Grams asked as she

settled in next to him. TJ moved on to the college guys, who seemed happy to have her.

"I emailed him and Johnny. I think we're going to meet up later."

"He came in for lunch with the chief. The station'll tell you where he is. Anyone else you want to catch up with?"

"Maybe." There were, in fact, a good many people he intended to renew acquaintance with. "I guess I'll see people at the—you know, at the funeral."

He took a deep pull from his pint. The lager was a local microbrew. It tasted of the summer fields and youth, and in this moment these were painful things to be reminded of. The memories that kindled retracted the tendrils of his consciousness from Meg and Livvy. They pulled him away from Nia Kapur, the hospital, and everything else in his city life. But this was necessary. This was what he'd come here to do.

He sensed Grams's eyes on him.

"I know nothing good brought you here," Grams whispered. She kneaded his shoulder with a papery hand. "But it's so good to see you."

He let his forehead rest against her bony shoulder and shivered with the chill of wet skin on a summer night. She placed her hand on the thatch of his head and leaned into him like they were back to being the only people in the world.

Nate reminded himself that this was Greystone Lake. This was death and loss and secrets and lies and rage. But it was also home. For the next few days, he must make himself belong here again. This was the barest minimum of his debt.

When Nate sat up, Grams's gray eyes brimmed with tears.

"Who loves you more than anyone, boy?"

After eating, Nate left the Union to take a look at the waterfront on his way to his grandmother's house on Bonaparte Street. Grams had offered to drive him, but the pub was beginning to gather a crowd, and Nate didn't mind stretching his legs.

Despite the approaching hurricane, small craft still cut across the undulating plain of the lake. A group of swimmers broke the waves along the far shore. Nate knew the devoted tried the waters no matter the weather or season. The Daybreakers, a loose confederation of eccentrics, took their exercise by swimming a lap of the lake's southern bulge whenever it wasn't iced over. Each day, often at dawn, they let themselves be erased by the frigid water. Even after so many years, thinking about this still made Nate light-headed.

He saw that a tourist storefront had sprouted between the pub and its back parking lot. GREYSTONE LAKE emblazoned golf shirts and sun visors, locally made ceramics and woodcarvings. Nate scanned the store's wares for a plush toy he could take home to Livvy or a knickknack for Meg's parents. He told himself he was shopping, but what he was really doing was stalling.

Seeing Grams had been good. Livvy adored her great-grandmother, and Nate loved watching them together, but he'd enjoyed having Grams to himself this time. For a little while, it had felt just like the old days. But spending time with Grams was the only easy thing he had to look forward to during this homecoming. He'd need to see Tom and Johnny next. Like Nate, they'd been there from the beginning, when things began to go wrong.

The shop offered towers of postcards: images of the lake in each season, time-lapses of the sky and shore. Some depicted the colorful wares of the weekend markets and the fall forests, but there were also black-and-whites from long-gone eras. During Prohibition, some resort towns withered while others blossomed. Thanks to its proximity to the St. Lawrence, Greystone Lake had flourished as a center for smuggling across the northern border. This was the Lake's time of legend, when wealth and crime and giant personalities wrought stories equal parts myth and history.

Nate was drawn to one such postcard. A staged photo of overall-clad men astride lumber freshly mounted above the waterline. The uninitiated might take this for a snapshot of the Wharf construction, but Nate knew otherwise. The stocky man in the center of the picture, dandy as a vaudevillian in seersucker and a straw hat, was a young Morton Strong. On the back, "1919" was printed right under a description: "The construction of the Greystone Lake Entertainments Pier, popularly known as the Night Ship."

The Night Ship.

Until the development of the Wharf area in the 1950s, the Night Ship had been the center of Greystone Lake's tourism industry. In its prime it featured restaurants, shops, and game rooms. It also included a nightclub, the Night Ship, from which the pier eventually took its name. During the sixties the tourist district consolidated around the Wharf, and the Night Ship found itself isolated in the residential part of Greystone Lake. It was bankrupted, condemned, and barricaded soon after. The town had tried to tear it down, but preservationists thwarted those plans.

As a child, Nate had been glad it hadn't been demolished. It was a ruin, but a spectacular one. While its boardwalks sagged and buckled, its graceful roofs and fairyland spires did not seem of this world. It was a relic of a more optimistic age—and like everything that old, it had a story all its own.

Nate focused on the lines of Morton Strong's face.

He tried to pull meaning from the pilings that struck up from the silver water, to discern intent in the arcs of steelwork in the background. He searched this moment of the Night Ship's birth for any hint that the pier would come to shadow his life as it had.

"Look what the lake dredged up."

Nate turned to see Tom in the shop's doorway.

"Deputy."

"Doc."

Nate's oldest friend offered his hand, and Nate used it to pull him into a bear hug.

"You look good." It was strange to see Tom in a uniform, but it suited him.

Tom laughed. "Look at you in here, browsing like a weekender. You want a ride to Bonaparte Street? I'll run you up."

"Can we use the lights?" Nate had been about to buy the post-card of the Night Ship. A strange impulse. Instead, he returned it and gave the tower a spin to conceal his interest.

Tom clapped him on the shoulder. "Even let you work the siren. You solo this weekend?"

"Livvy's got this ear thing again." Nate followed his friend back onto the street. "Long drive for a sick three-year-old. Plus, there's the hurricane."

"Believe me, I know. Been filling sandbags with the Kiwanis club all morning."

"Really? Sandbags?" The lake was tempestuous, but hardly the Atlantic.

"Gosh, you've really gone full-tourist, haven't you? A four-foot storm surge will swamp the embankment. You should know that!" Tom laughed. "A bunch of places got reamed by the last hurricane, so we're going all out on prep this time."

"Got to keep the place pretty."

"Pretty's what pays the bills around here. How does it look to you?"

"The Lake? Fantastic," Nate said, and it was the truth. The town's storefronts and waterfront were exquisitely maintained, just as they'd been in their youth. The grandeur of the Lake's vistas were also extraordinary. The peaks of the headlands. The rippling forests of the foothills. The way all of this beauty was doubled by the mir-ror of the lake.

It was a storybook town, but as in any fairy tale, things were not as perfect as they first appeared.

"Lots of improvements since you were last around. Johnny opened up that place last year." Tom pointed to a tea shop down the block. Its windows were planked over in preparation for the coming onslaught, and its awning was being rolled up. "Desserts and pastries supplied by the Empire's kitchen. Oh, and Emma runs it. That's her right there. Want to say hello?"

Emma Aoki, who'd once been their classmate, was the woman closing the awning. Her head was tilted to the surge of clouds whipping in from the south. She'd always been slight, but now she looked made of paper. Nate was a block away, but in the push of the wind, he saw that her dress hung on her as if from a hanger. She frowned at the weather, and then her eyes crossed the distance between them. Something in her expression changed, but the frown remained. More than a decade gone, but she knew him at a glance.

"She looks busy," Nate said. He waved to her, and after a moment she raised her hand to match his own. "Maybe later."

They turned down a side street to where Tom's cruiser was parked.

"Actually, I'd like to catch up with everybody at some point. Do you keep in touch with them?" Nate asked.

"Mostly. Some more than others."

"And Emma? You see a lot of her?"

"Sometimes." He chucked Nate's bag into the trunk. "Oh, like, date? Nah."

Nate got into the passenger side and let the battered seat mold to his body. "She's very thin. Has she been sick?"

"We're not all your cancer patients, Doc. Not yet, anyway." The cruiser lurched onto the wide arc of the Strand, the street closest to the shore.

Tom himself seemed in good health. He looked like he kept in shape, but they'd reached the age where some men begin to fall apart. He had a touch more weight in the cheeks. A new groove in his brow. The angle between his chin and throat had begun to loosen to a curve. Nate wouldn't have called his friend's hairline receding, though he had more forehead than he used to.

"Emma's been having kind of a tough time, though," Tom said. "She's living in those apartments by the packing houses—they might be new since you left? Anyway, they had a sewage problem a week or so ago, and her place is on the ground floor."

"Shit."

"Exactly. I think she's staying with her parents."

Grams's street was named not for the French emperor but for a species of gull. If Greystone Lake were shaped like a boomerang lodged against the western shore of the lake's southern bulge, then Bonaparte Street was laced through the center of its length, with her house located halfway between the town's center and its northernmost edge. Imposing mansions built in the late 1800s glittered along the Strand, while more modest homes like hers sat farther inland. The center of town comprised the Wharf and tourist district. Fishermen, rundown work piers, and old packinghouses took up the bulk of the Lake's southern wing. The Night Ship was a dark blade struck deep into the waters close to the town's northern limit.

Clouds now shrouded the sky, and the lake trembled in the growing wind. Nate guessed this would be the last of the sun they'd see for days.

Tom pointed out some of the changes to the Lake's homes and businesses as they traveled the few blocks to Grams's place. Familiar houses had been painted in new colors. Yards had been landscaped. Fences had sprung up, and new expansions loomed just shy of property lines.

These were all signs of a prosperous town, and this was good. A living place had to change. Families come, families leave, yesterday's students become tomorrow's teachers. This was natural and right, but heading toward his grandmother's home, Nate found it wrenching. One day everything they did would be forgotten. One day everything they loved wouldn't matter to anyone.

They parked in front of Grams's little yellow house. Tom turned to him when Nate made no move to exit.

"Tommy, you know I've got to ask. I need to know what they know."

Tom cleared his throat.

"Grams said hikers found her."

Tom nodded. "During a cloudburst. Picked their way through the rocks, trying to get out of the downpour, and there she was."

"What do they know?"

"Dad's not letting me anywhere near it. But she—her body—there wasn't much left. Fourteen years, Nate."

A moment passed with nothing but the tick of the cruiser's cooling engine to mark it. Nate had already known the scant information Tom gave him, but such conversations had to begin somehow. Easy questions blaze the path for the harder ones that must follow. Nate touched the glass of his window. Cold as the lake at dawn.

"He wants to talk to you, you know," Tom said. "My dad."

Tom's father was Greystone Lake's chief of police, as he had been for twenty years.

"I've been thinking about her mother," Nate said. "Is it better to know for sure?" Since Livvy's birth, Nate wondered what he'd do if she ever disappeared. If she vanished and was never seen again. This fear was always with him. Even in his most euphoric moments, it waited like a rock under the waves. When Nate sang Livvy to sleep, he could never decide if closure was better than hope. "I keep thinking about what I'm supposed to say to her."

"Not to mention her dad."

Nate's response was a sound, the noise of an old scar torn raw.

"Grams *must* have told you."

Nate could only shake his head. The car's close air felt too thick to breathe.

"He's been out for years. Parole. I thought you knew. I'd have told you if—"

"It's fine. Doesn't matter." Nate said this as calmly as he could. He unbuckled himself and pulled at the door handle. He had to get out of the car.

He counted his breaths as Tom opened the trunk to pull out his bag.

"You don't have to talk to him." Tom's expression was the one he'd worn so often when they were younger. A veneer of geniality over panic. "No one'd expect you to. Jesus, I really thought you knew."

"It's fine," Nate said again. The breeze from the lake was brisk, and standing in it helped. "You just took me by surprise." He smiled and patted his friend on the shoulder.

Nate took his bag, and they made their way up a short stretch of slate flagstones to the front stoop. Nate pressed the handle, but the door didn't budge. He rammed his shoulder into it as if it might have warped in its frame. He'd opened this door a thousand times and never once found it locked.

"Hold up, Doc." Tom dug through his pocket and slid between Nate and the door.

"She gave you a key?"

"I'm very trustworthy. Got a badge and everything."

Tom unlocked the door, and Nate walked into the life he'd left behind.

Dried hydrangeas on a console beside a pile of unopened mail. The scent of lavender soap behind a smell of wood polish. The shuddering of the floor under his feet as the furnace thrummed.

He wandered the length of the foyer, looking around like a tourist in a museum. The colors of the place seemed to have faded. A wall he remembered as yellow was now cream, a forest green armchair toned down to olive. Though Nate was the same height he'd been when he graduated high school, everything seemed smaller. More delicate and somehow less real. As if the couch in the living room was more a concept of furniture than a place a person would actually sit.

A mosaic of photographs cluttered the far wall. At the center, an old black-and-white of his father, and the rest rippled from it. Shots of Nate's med school graduation, his wedding, Livvy with a grin as big as the world.

"She's beautiful," Tom said.

"Thanks, buddy." Tom had visited them in the city just before

Livvy's birth, but their talk of additional get-togethers never panned out. It occurred to Nate that all his best friend had seen of Livvy came from holiday cards and the occasional texted photo.

They ascended the creaking stairs to Nate's boyhood bedroom. Inside was a narrow twin bed, rows of thin pine bookcases, a dresser, and a little desk. Horror movie posters covered the walls where books did not. This was nearly a replica of the bedroom he'd had at the house on Great Heron Drive before the accident, before he'd moved in with Grams. Nate had lived here on Bonaparte Street for just over two years, but of all the years of his life, these were the ones that had left the deepest marks.

"Just like you left it, huh?" Tom said. "Good to know that some things don't—"

Nate turned to his friend. He followed Tom's gaze to a shattered window by the bed. On the faded blue plaid comforter, he saw a chalk-white ball lipped in red stitching. A baseball.

A *baseball*.

Nate's world narrowed to the three-inch sphere.

Behind him, Tom said something. Nate could hardly hear him over the thunder of his pulse crashing inside his ears. He went to the window to peer through its diamond shards.

For an instant he felt one with the window's jagged edge.

Through that window, beyond the trees, Nate caught the glow of the lake. It occurred to him that the mountains around the town looked like jaws that could slam shut at any time, the lake itself an insatiable maw. For a vertiginous moment, he recognized nothing about this place along the moody plain of deep water.

But this was Greystone Lake. This was home.

PHOTO: © PATRICIA GILHOOLY

BRENDAN DUFFY is an editor and the author of *House of Echoes* and *The Storm King*. He lives in New York.

brendanduffybooks.com
Facebook.com/BrendanDuffyAuthor
Twitter: @Brendan_Duffy